FAMILY
VALUES

HarperChoice

FAMILY VALUES

A NOVEL BY

FORREST EVERS

HarperPaperbacks
A Division of HarperCollinsPublishers

HarperPaperbacks
A Division of HarperCollins*Publishers*
10 East 53rd Street, New York, N.Y. 10022-5299

❖ 10 9 8 7 6 5 4 3 2 1

To Cora and Clarence
for everything

Drive me out of my house,
I'm comin' to yours.

—Chuwehta Collins
Los Palos Hills, CA
June 16, 1997

FAMILY VALUES

CHAPTER

1

O ut of all the dreamy and forgotten Ohlone laws of life and the universe, remember two. Remembering is a dream, they said. All dreams, they said, are real.

Remembering is a dream as real as the buzz of fluorescent lights in the halls of hospitals after midnight. As real as the squeak of nurses' white shoes coming and going, dragging shadows past a boy's open door. As real as waiting for their squeak, squeak, squeak to fade and disappear.

The boy rolled out of bed and pain stabbed his chest through a curtain of drugs. He lay on the floor, drowsy as an old man, and remembered seeing nurses' faces under those funky little white hats hovering over him, and he thought maybe they were angels. Worried angels, saying, "They broke his ribs." Saying, "Poor kid, kicked in the face like that."

When he crossed the river of linoleum to her room across the hall, the girl was hunched on her side, knees drawn up and head down. She didn't move when he stood inches from her face, her eyes open but not looking at him, not even turning away. She was too tired to move; the only thing moving in her was the wondering what he was going to do to her. Like she was curious but didn't care. She didn't care at all.

What she was feeling was dirty, used and empty as a cup nobody washed.

He knew she was awake—he'd heard her crying across the hall. He lifted up the sheet and covers, climbed into her hospital bed behind her. He lay still, not touching her. Listening to her breathe.

First thing he said was, "Way back in like the beginnin of the world there was no light. Nothin. Not even a spark."

She could relate to that.

On a hillside, early in the morning, Chuleta said, "See the light move?"

"No way. Where?"

Chuleta pointed to the hills on the slope of Mount Diablo. "Over the other side of the valley. Look above the freeway. Hold still, keep your eye on it."

Chuleta was fifteen going on twenty-five. A little skinny-ass kid in a floppy white T-shirt and baggy black jeans, looking like he had an older brother handed down his funky worn-out stuff. Pointy little face under a backwards Oakland A's baseball cap; clean white teeth; black eyes moving all the time. When he was five and six his momma used to run her hand over his fine black hair and tell him he had this Indian dream groove on his brain. Right there where a lump of hard Spanish common sense ought to be. All brain, his momma used to say, and no damn sense.

Blue Girl leaned forward and went still as a cat. Big brown eyes narrowed down to slits. A shifty breeze, warm in the cool air, served up camphor from the eucalyptus, balsam from the tall pines up the slope, and the spice of bay trees. Gonna be another nice warm Friday in May by the San Francisco Bay.

After a while Blue Girl said, "Oh yeah, I see it

creepin. Looks like they drainin the dark off of the hills. Where's my house at?"

The rising sun threw shadows from San Lucas, America's fastest-growing city, all the way across Silicon Valley. Chuleta pointed to rows of houses submerged in thin blue smog miles beyond the tall office towers. Like ghosts, he was thinking, from some other time. "Somewhere down there."

"I don't see nothin, Chuleta. They all look the same."

"Why we here. They is all the same."

"They only look the same from here, Chuleta. One of them houses is my momma and my sister's. Where I had my baby."

"Hey, two years ago."

"The hell you know? You wasn't there."

He looked down at her, smiling his half smile. "I was down for you in the hospital."

"You don't know nothin what I went through."

Silver called from the car. "Gimme the fuckin keys. I'm freezin my ass off."

Chuleta stood up, stretching, outlined against the valley. Telling her "You keep lookin back, nothin changes. Can't change nothin after it's over. Let it go, girl." He pulled her up and put his arm around her. "See, you live down in those streets, you think that's where the world's at. Like you can't look up, you gotta watch every damn car 'case they a drive-by. You come up here, you can see a long ways. Watch the sun light up the world."

"Hey, you hear me?" Silver, the oldest, almost eighteen, was standing by the Lexus, arms folded across his chest, legs crossed, head back, little Sundance Boa .25 hanging in his hand, pointing at the ground like a chrome finger.

"Lotta people hear you, you don't shut up, bro," Chuleta said in a loud whisper, blinking from the sun in his face. "And get that damn thing outta sight. Sticks out like a dick on a duck. Get your ass back in the car 'fore somebody see you. Shut the door."

Chuleta put his hand up to shade his narrow face, checking two nearby houses for signs of life. Listening for cars coming down the street. Shifting from foot to foot, like his momma was after him about something. Nothing but birds and the low roar from I-280 five miles away down there in the valley.

A window lit up on the top floor in house behind the Lexus; a fuzzy yellow square of light in the white concrete-and-glass structure poised on the side of the hill overlooking the bay. Inside, no doubt, a CEO of a new IPO, an overnight billionaire, flipping on his computer screens, checking the opening markets in New York. Chuleta said, "See that frosted glass for the bathroom way up there? Like they afraid some like hawk gonna peek in, see them havin a crap. They so afraid somebody gonna see in, they can't see out." He gave her a friendly little tap on her shoulder. "But somebody gonna see us, we don't get movin. Suckers get up early round here, hit the floor runnin."

Blue Girl, a couple of inches taller than Chuleta, put her hand on his shoulder, pulling him to her for a kiss on his cheek. "Like you," she said.

The Lexus was all honey leather and glossy walnut inside, a frosted gold egg on wheels rolling past the quiet houses of Los Palos Hills, tires hissing on the street still wet from last night's fog. Lexus appropriate for the area, Chuleta thought. Nobody look twice.

Virtually invisible, the Lexus moved in and out of shadow in the morning light. The two heads in the front seat were so low the car looked as if it were driving itself: Chuleta and Blue Girl, baseball caps on backwards, dark eyes peering over the leather-and-walnut dashboard. Whopper and Silver in the backseat, lying back in the leather, heads rolled to the side, peering out their windows like they didn't give a shit, eyes just above the windowsill. Whopper, same age as Blue Girl, sixteen, sits up all of a sudden, and goes, "Hey, man, lookit. That house got a pool, barbecue with them tables, chairs 'n' shit. You could eat out there, right by the water."

"We do this right, you have you own pool," Chuleta said. "We almost there. Keep your head down 'less you want somebody to remember your face, you copy?"

"What's this copy, shit, bro?" Silver said from the backseat.

"That's like the shit they say." Chuleta was good on this stuff. "Lotta these rich suckers talk all this computer shit, you got to talk their talk. You hear what I'm sayin? Walk their walk. Like you can't pass, you can't go."

"You copy what they say," Blue Girl said, watching a three-story mock-Tudor mansion with a wrought-iron fence and cement nymphs slide by, "walk the way they walk, you still look like some cholo from the hood."

"We gonna fix that, too," Chuleta said.

"Copy," Whopper said. Feeling that empty, early-morning feeling he always got before he had breakfast; like just a little breeze could blow him away. He leaned forward, turning up the CD from the rear-seat controls. And the four of them, heads bobbing, hands stacking, chanted along with the cool and slinky whispers of Tricky's new chill rap. Knowing every word by heart.

> I since need a reference to get residence
> a reference to your preference
> to say I'm a good neighbor, I trust
> so judging from my labor

lobotomy insures my good behavior
the constant struggle insures my insanity
as in the evenings insures the struggle for
    my family
but hungry, beware, of our appetite
distant drums brings the news of a kilter nut
the kill which I share with my passengers
and take our fill, take our fill take our fill . . .

The "hills" of Los Palos Hills are long-dead volcanoes overlooking San Francisco Bay, part of the Santa Cruz Mountains running south along the San Andreas Fault from San Francisco to Santa Cruz. Two hundred years ago vast herds of elk and antelope grazed in the marsh grasses and clouds of geese, heron, ducks, and pelicans filled the sky over the bay. The Ohlone Indians gathered acorns, fished, and hunted there for five thousand years. You can see their photographs in the San Lucas Museum: broad-faced men and women who were not one tribe but over a hundred extended families, each with a separate language and territory. The first Europeans were appalled how "poor" "they" were. Archaeologists, digging in their thirty-foot-high shell mounds, found "nothing of enduring value." Even their dwellings were temporary, built to last a season instead of a lifetime. To the Ohlones wealth was an abstract, a measure of generosity. If you gave away the deer you killed to the village, they owed you. Obligations, piled up over a lifetime, were easy to carry from the seashore to the mountains to the meadows as they moved with the seasons. Possessions were a drag. So they made nothing that endured, except their intricate system of belief and custom called culture, which lasted five thousand years. A world record in human history; five thousand years of peace, stability, and ecological balance before the

Spanish missionaries baptized them and put them to work for God and Spain but not for pay. Along with saving Indians' souls, Mission San Lucas, to pick the nearest example, ran 75,000 cattle, 82,000 sheep, and 11,000 hogs in 1823. The missions were big business for Spain and for the Holy Roman Catholic and Apostolic Church. Between 1802 and 1822 the good fathers of San Lucas baptized 7,324 Indians; 6,566 died. When Mexico freed itself from Spain the missions were turned into ranches, and the Indians were pushed aside to make way for two-thousand-acre horse farms and cattle ranches. And then, of course, there was the gold rush of '49. The gold rush brought men who cleared the land by cutting trees and shooting the Indians. They shot whole villages at a time, including the women and the children. After World War I the pastures were cut up into orchards for peaches, almonds, and apricots. Now, since Hewlett-Packard, Silicon Graphics, Oracle Systems, Sun Microsystems, and Apple Computer took off, Los Palos Hills became the Beverly Hills of Silicon Valley—a park of dream homes, gardens, pastures for the horses, and million-dollar views.

He said, whispering in her ear, "A hawk was flyin around, tryin to find his way in the black sky. Couldn't see nothin 'cause it was total darkness. And way down below, down on the ground, Coyote was stumblin around, bumpin into stuff. Coyote bang into a big redwood trunk nose first. Damn. Coyote starts goin uphill, and he figures maybe he gets up high enough, there might be a little light. Like just one ray of light be a big improvement. He keeps goin up and up, bumpin into rocks and trees and thornbushes, slippin, slidin, and scrabblin trying to get to the top. He gets all skinned up, scratched, bruised, and tired but he makes it up to the top of Mount Diablo. Same time, Hawk, thinkin he gets a little closer to the ground, maybe he might be able to see somethin, swoops down and bangs into Coyote's nose. Coyote goes Yeeepppyeeepoooooaaaww. And Hawk makes this big screechin sound 'cause he's just got smacked in the beak. So Hawk is shakin his feathers straight goin "Hey, I'm sorry I hit you, man, but I can't see nothin. Damn, you damn near scared the feathers offa me."

She shifted a little, pulling the hospital sheet tight around her, so he knew she was listening.

The children in the Lexus rolled past houses copied from the old Hollywood dreams of Ginger Rogers and Fred Astaire. Past sprawling dream ranches with Latino gardeners working the hedges, lawns, flowers, and pools. Past abstract dream cubes of glass and redwood with six-car garages and private screening rooms. And Scarlett O'Hara dream plantation repros with white fluted columns and carriage lamps. And owner-designed lumps of brick with tile roofs and locked wrought-iron gates. The dream houses were sheltered from one another by Monterey pines, eucalyptus, twenty-five-year-old redwoods grown seventy feet tall, and two-acre zoning. Los Palos Hills was what any American suburban community would be if it had more money and better weather. And the dream that money will make you safe in America.

Silver could take the houses or leave them. As they rolled by his window, Silver was studying his reflection in the tinted glass, checking his clear dark eyes, smooth, tanned white skin, movie-star, gotta-kiss-him mouth, and his slender, perfect nose. Like a fuckin bullfighter, he thought, got moves too slick for the chargin bull. All those Latino chicas do anything to get next to him. He leaned forward, bare arms on the leather of the back of the front seat, and said, "I get on TV, first thing I do, I'm gonna get me a car like this. Hey, Chuleta, when you gonna let me drive the unit?"

"Hush up, bro. You drive when you get a license."

"Hey, you ain't got no license neither. You ain't old enough."

"Don't give me that age shit. We all livin in the same age."

At the end of Black Mountain Lane, number 3057 lies at the bottom of a steep downhill drive, facing the hills. Upstairs, in the master bedroom, a wide picture window frames the pool, the steep valley, and the green mountains rising up like waves in front of the early pink-and-blue sky. Dan Messina, All-American, Stanford, 1973, was having his old dream, the one that kept coming back to him and made him happy. He was pale beneath his sleep-messed tangle of black hair. His eyes flickered, his mouth opened, as if he were about to say something. He turned his face into the pillow as the dream begins, the clock on the walnut dresser glowing 5:45.

In his dream, Dan is at a party in a seaside room, surf crashing in below, the boom and rhythm for the bass, lotta jackets over T-shirts, like heavy credit cards in the hip pockets and loose women swishing around, perfume in the air. Here in Malibu. His fingers move over the keyboard with confidence and ease. Beatles, Stones, Doors, Dylan . . . Dan can play all the golden oldies. Even jump back another generation for the real-estate brokers in the room, like Cole Porter, Hoagy Carmichael. *"Blue Moooon. You saw me standing alone."*

Dan rolls into his raspy Billy Joel, *"Still rock and roll to me."*

Back over to Tom Waits and then, yeah, Melissa Etheridge. *"I WANNA COME OVVVVER."*

In his dream, Dan knows them all. In his dream his voice has that after-midnight rasp that could have gotten him an Eagles gig, or maybe Hootie and the Blowfish now. Instead of doing computer nerd full-time. Dan feels the warm ripple of laughter at his jokes. He is so handsome in his ripped and faded shirt. Like one of the original rip your head open rockers, man, but civilized now. Like Dan is bronze under that shirt, man. Women smile at him, trying to catch his eye on the sly. The moon is out, and the stars shine, the roof rolled back at the Starshine lounge tonight as Dan shifts into a song of his own composition, everybody's favorite. And Melanie Griffith sits down on the piano bench beside him. Her hand is on his thigh. She is loose and wobbly under her low-cut silk dress, and she says, "Don't stop." Only she is not Melanie Griffith. She is Page. Even better. He'll take reality every time. *"I WANNNA COME OVVVVER."*

Goofy grin under his big nose, dreaming his dream, half-awake hearing Page stir, Dan wondered at the great cosmic miracle that someone else could find us sexy. His green, maroon, and orange internal organs, hidden and slippery under his skin, loom into his dream like overhead balloons. He sees his bruised and leaky body naked on the piano bench, sprouting hair, moles, pimples, lumps, sags, and wrinkles. And it doesn't matter. Page is there looking good and wanting him. After twenty years of marriage and knowing her almost all his life she can still take his breath away. She is there on the piano bench, wearing the long and flimsy tie-dye hippie dress she wore to the prom in high school cinched at her waist with that wide brown leather belt she stole from Dan, with the big bronze buckle with a deer head complete with antlers. And he would see her doe eyes looking up at him through the fringe of her blond hair, and feel the antlers of the damn buckle pricking him as he danced with her for the first time. And he remembered the amazing softness of her thighs dancing against him, giving him a gently swelling hard-on under the soft yellow blanket.

She looked so soft on the outside and was so strong and prickly underneath. When he was away, at a trade show or with a client in some other time zone, Dan would be looking at the menu and out of nowhere he would remember that spring picnic in Vermont twenty years ago. And he would be lying with Page on the hillside meadow by the brook, green grass and sunshine and the sound of the water burbling, the sound of happiness, she said. He would remember kissing her that sunny afternoon, her eyes urging him on. Completely forgetting he was in another city, having dinner with some shy techie with a wart on his Adam's apple and a head full of graphic coordinates.

Dan and Page had been kids together in Pleasantville, twenty-five miles north of New York City. Home of *Reader's Digest*. In the days before crack, AIDS, herpes, and semiautomatics stuck under kids' basketball jackets; in the days when the summers went on and on, and they thought the world was going to get better and better if only they could get their heads in the right place and get out of Vietnam. Dad commuted to New York City on the train, Mom stayed home, and everybody in the eighth grade knew each other from kindergarten. Dan and Page had known each other since she was ten, the new kid in school, and he was eleven. They had been married forever and slept side by side in a house in Los Palos Hills with the perfect view of the perfect hills and a mortgage as big as a mountain.

Page, hearing Dan stir and sigh in his dream,

looked at the clock creeping up on seven and started making her lists for the day, what to do.

She leaned over, giving Dan a quickie kiss on the back of his neck, and got out of bed, wearing the T-shirt she always wore to bed, and pulled on her sweatpants and sweatshirt to start the coffee before she went out for her morning run. So it was Page, the kids still sleeping and Dan in the shower, who was in the kitchen when the doorbell rang.

H e was going to prop himself up to have a look at her, see if he could see her face, but his arm and shoulder hurt too much. The broken ribs made him take shallow breaths. So he settled back on his side, propping his head on the corner of her pillow, whispering the story in her ear. "And Coyote goes 'Hey, man. Ain't your fault. I can't see nothin neither, or I wouldn't be stickin my nose in your flight path. You hear what I'm sayin?'

"Hawk takes off and he is flutterin over Coyote and they talk about how it was good they got to meet up but it would be a whole bunch better if there was light. Wouldn't be bumpin into stuff all the time. 'Yeah, beautiful,' they say. Coyote thinks for a bit, and he says, 'ain't nothin gonna happen we just complain about it.'

"Hawk says, 'Yeah, but we just a coyote and a hawk. What we gonna do?' Coyote thinks about it, tryin to figure out a way. Hawk is up above, flutterin his wings, and it is still dark. Maybe even darker. Only color in the world is black.

"Then Coyote gets an idea. Says he is goin down to the marsh and get himself a bunch of bulrushes, roll them into a ball.

"Hawk says, 'That is the dumbest thing I ever heard,' and flies off. So Coyote feels abandoned, like he is all alone. He stumbles down the mountain in the dark, bumpin his nose into trees and rocks, until he gets to the marsh and he starts pullin up these reeds. And he gets tired from pullin up all these damn reeds and his paws get sore, but he figures if it works, who is gonna care about sore paws. When he has a big pile of swamp reeds he wads them all up into a little ball. Then he wraps another reed around it and pulls it tight, so it's like solid. And he adds another one, and he keeps addin to it until it is humongous."

She stirred again under the covers, thinking, the fuck he talkin?

"Meanwhile," he said, "Hawk is gettin lonely and feelin bad 'cause he like run out on Coyote. So he flies around until he hears the sound of Coyote stompin the grasses into a big ball. Hawk is flutterin overhead and he goes, 'Hey, I'm sorry I took off on you, Coyote. You think this is gonna work, like bring light to the world, hey, I'll help you. You hear what I'm sayin?'

"'About time you come around. I ain't makin no promises here, but if this is gonna work, I gotta have help.'

"Coyote and Hawk felt around in the dark until they found each other.

"'Here you go,' Coyote says, 'you hang on to this big ball of swamp reeds I got wrapped up tight. Don't go away.' Coyote scrabbles around on the ground till he finds a couple of pieces of flint. 'You take these, too, fly up there high as you can fly. You get up there, smack them flints together so they make a spark and light up that big ball of reeds. Then you get your ass out of there, 'cause it is gonna get incandescent. Like hot, man.'

"Hawk is pretty happy about this 'cause he can fly and Coyote can't. So he takes that big ball and the flints and he takes off. And he is strainin every muscle in his body 'cause he wants to fly higher than he has ever flown before. His

*wings goin whooff whooff and Coyote down on the ground
yowlin like crazy, urgin him on."*

"The fuck you talkin?" she said.

*"It's a story," he said. "How they got light in the
world."*

*She still wasn't moving, her voice low and soft. "So the
hawk gonna light up the ball, and it's gonna be the sun,
right. Like some kid's story."*

"It's not a kid's story."

*"Oh yeah," she said into her pillow. "You think that's
how it happen? Fuckin bird lights up a grass ball?"*

"It's an Indian story. From the Alonies."

*"I heard of like, Apaches. Navajos. Nez Perce. I never
heard of no Alonies."*

"My dad is."

"What, he a full-blood?"

*"I don't know full-blood. Maybe just a drop. How much
you need? Like you drop a drop of ink in a glass of water?
Maybe it don't change much, but it changes everything."*

"But like he was alone, huh?"

*"No no. That's just the way it sounds. They lived here.
All around here, they had tribes like around San Francisco,
Oakland, San Lucas, over on the coast for like five thousand
years. Everywhere they look there was stuff to eat. They ate
acorns, mussels, clams, smoked salmon. Venison. It was like
paradise, you know what I'm sayin? They didn't wear no
clothes in the summer, and they had saunas; they go in there
every day, then they go dive in the river or the ocean and they
were clean, man."*

"Women go in the sauna?"

"It was like for the hunters, you know."

*"Yeah, I know. Like next you gonna be goin you some
kind of warrior." She turned to face him. "I don't need this
macho shit."*

— CHAPTER —

When Blue Girl saw the house spreading out at the bottom of a steep drive, looking as if it had slid halfway down a valley, she sucked in a deep breath and squeezed Chuleta. "It's just like I dreamed it, Chuleta. It's perfect."

They saw a white woman looking up from whatever she was doing to see the Lexus through the kitchen window. No doubt about it, she saw the car. Maybe not their faces through the windshield, but she definitely scoped the car. Nice-lookin woman.

Thirty fifty-seven had cedar shingles on the roof, and the walls were faded blue-jean blue, with white trim around the big windows. The wide, polished-oak front door was grooved with Churley's scratches from his morning mantra: feed me, feed me, feed me. Five years ago Dan and Page had paid $1.47 million for four bedrooms, a three-car garage, a pool, a hot tub, four tall redwoods, two acres, and a view of the Santa Cruz Mountains without another house in sight. The mountains rose up like a wild blue-green sea, the ridges of the hills looking like waves rolling in above the valley. With no other house or road in sight, they could pretend that their property line ran along the far ridge of Black Mountain, six miles away. When they bought it Dan liked to joke that "the fifty square miles came up and Page and I just fell in love with it."

Sometimes the drone of a single-engine plane burrowing through the night sky set coyotes howling their old berserk-killer song. Background music for the dream of Los Palos Hills. You know the dream, the oldest of all American dreams, going back to the first Indians. The Ohlones had come up from Southeast Asia, crossed China and the Alaskan bridge, and made their way down the Pacific coast to the nearly perfect climate of the central California coast. Coming down out of the cold and snow, their dream was to turn their backs on the rest of the world, live out on the edge, breathe deep, and face the wilderness alone.

When the doorbell rang Page was thinking who the hell owns a gold Lexus, all that ostentation, maybe Jim and Honey got a new car, and Honey can't wait to show it off. But Jeezzzuz, seven o'clock in the morning. Somebody lost maybe. Some boozer, off his normal rat run, trying to stagger home before breakfast and the commuter rush. If Dan wasn't lying in bed, he could go to the door. Save her the agro. You wanted something done around this house, you better do it yourself.

Page opened the door and saw a tall, worried, teenage black girl. Long straight hair down to her shoulders, big brown eyes slanted like a cat's eyes, a good chin, a pink tank top showing too much of her boobs, and a silly little gold chain with a gold heart, looking like it came out of a cereal box, a tiny bulge of fat over the tight stretch pants (God are the girls wearing those bicycle pants to school now?), and black Reeboks. Page thought of a cartoon she'd seen in *The*

New Yorker years ago—an elaborate bird, long tail feathers drooping, sitting on a broken fence behind a house with junk in the backyard. The caption read, "I am a bird of paradise. Needless to say I am lost." But that wasn't right. This was paradise.

Blue Girl said, "Can you help me?"

Page was saying, "Sure," when Chuleta stepped out from beside the door, holding his matte black assault weapon. Page's mouth went wide, and she took a deep breath to scream. Chuleta quietly said, "Don't make a sound, and we'll all go away happy. That's it, just relax, no problem. Last thing I want to do is blow holes in your face, you understand?"

He's so ordinary-looking, looks like a little squirrel, Page thought. Don't panic. Just a little boy. Panic never helps. Jesus what an ugly goddamn gun. OH CHRIST, ROBBY AND BAYLOR. DON'T HURT THEM, DON'T HURT THEM. Or I'll kill you, she thought.

The boy holding the gun couldn't be much older than Robby, she guessed. He looked like any other Latino kid she'd seen at that age, baseball cap on backwards, scruffy Nikes. So ordinary. Page told herself to concentrate, pick out the details, memorize his face, like the little mole just below his eye. He was thin, nervous. Kind of buck teeth. Face like a squirrel. Eyes jumping around. Oh shit, he's more scared than I am. "Then take your finger off the trigger," she said. "You don't want an accident."

There were more of them, two more at least. A tall one with a little pencil mustache, tanned white skin, narrow nose, big blue eyes. Handsome in a childish way. Probably carries a knife. Oh shit, this has got to be a dream. Close the door, they will disappear.

But they were inside the door. Inside her house, dirty feet on her clean marble floor. Page felt a scream coming up again and clamped her hand over her mouth. And even as she held herself back, she could see herself standing there, as if she were a spectator, watching herself watching them. The other one (were there four or was there a whole gang of them?), was short and wide, with a flat wide face and tiny black eyes, leaning forward as he walked. Fat from the junk they eat, she thought.

Motioning Page back into the house with his gun, Chuleta said, "Finger stays on the trigger until I trust you. Okay?"

Page nodded. Thinking—Anything you say.

Chuleta, keeping his eyes on Page, said, "Silver, you want to drive the Lexus? You go put it in the garage, out of sight." Chuleta tossed the keys to the tall good-looking boy, flicking his eyes to the girl and back to Page. "Let's go in the kitchen," he said. "You were fixin somethin." Page looked at him blankly. "In the kitchen. What's up for breakfast in paradise?"

Page didn't answer.

Chuleta said, "Hey? You awake? You got coffee, juice, eggs, bacon, and that shit, or is it granola and low-fat bagels? Hope you got somethin. I am fuckin starvin."

Chuleta waved Page back into the big kitchen with his gun. The thug-looking black boy and the tall beautiful black girl followed him. Page backed against the counter, thinking maybe there would be a way to get to the phone. Maybe later.

Whopper was taking in the details of the kitchen, neat sunny yellow cabinets, clean white counters, black-and-white floor looking like nobody ever walk on it before. A refrigerator around the size of most folks' kitchens. What kind of food, he wondered, you make in a kitchen like this? White bread? Cream potatoes? Bland white shit. The counters look like plastic but cool to the touch. Racks of spices in alphabetical order, shining pots and pans hanging over a center counter with a butcher-block top. Place is clean, man, like licked, Whopper thought. Mess of catfish on the stove, I feel at home in a kitchen like this. Maybe have a couple of chickens in the oven.

Chuleta smiled at Page, leaning his elbows on the butcher-block service island in the middle of the kitchen. "A little juice would be nice. What's your name, Sista, tell me your name. I don't want to be sayin 'Hey you' all day. Like, Hey you, I'd like a cup of coffee. See, it don't sound right."

The gun was hanging by a strap from his shoulder. Looking larger than any of them, taking over the room. At least his finger wasn't on the trigger anymore. If his finger was on the trigger, he could trip, or jerk because his coffee was too hot, and spray the room with bone-smashing bullets. There were four of them; nothing she could do about it. "My name is Page."

"Hey, like a book, right. You must be the good part. Good mornin, Page. You can call me Chuleta, means a little pork chop in Español. Okay? This here is Blue Girl, and Whopper. Whopper, Blue Girl, shake hands with the pretty lady, let her know there's no animosity here."

Blue Girl stepped forward to shake hands with Page as if she were in a receiving line. "Pleased to meet you," Blue Girl said.

Page, looking at Chuleta's gun, seeing the barrel as a large dark hole, said nothing.

"Come on, Whopper, say hello to the woman. Name is Page."

Whopper gave Page a look. She thought he looked like a gorilla, big arms sticking out from his thick body, no neck, low eyebrows, mean little beady eyes. "Hey, Page. You got anythin to eat?" Whopper said, his voice surprisingly light.

"No, no, no, Whopper." Chuleta was patient, explaining. "Your mother never teach you nothin? You say, 'May I have a cup of coffee, Page, please . . . if it is not too much trouble for you.'"

Whopper glared at Chuleta, thinking, Fuck you. Fuck You, dis me like that in front of everybody. Little fuck knows I never saw my momma. Not even a damn picture. Probably she was beautiful like this white lady. Whopper went, "Yeah, I mean, please."

Page, thinking maybe I could throw the hot coffee in his face, turns and takes down a coffee mug from her cupboard. The cupboards are glossy, shining like sunshine, but she has been thinking they really ought to replace them with something more colorful and a little more contemporary, they just scream seventies high-tech and look so dated now, but with both kids headed for college they've been trying to put every cent. . . . She takes the glass coffeepot from the coffeemaker on the counter, pours the coffee into a cup, and hands it, stretching, to Chuleta, who reaches to take it with one hand. But he doesn't take the coffee because he sees Page looking behind him.

Just behind Whopper, Page sees her daughter, Baylor, in the white terry-cloth robe she had given her for Christmas, and thinks, Oh God, it needs a wash. Barefoot, still half-asleep, an upside-down bowl of blond hair, round face, freckles, bright blue eyes close together, little thin line for a mouth, Baylor half-asleep, pauses at the refrigerator door, not really looking at the door, but her face is pointed in that direction, showing Chuleta her profile with the pug nose. Chuleta sees her out of the corner of his eye and flicks a quick look at her. He thinks, she has an unfinished face that could go either way. Pudgy now, maybe in a couple of years turn into like a bowl of cottage cheese. Maybe sixteen. But she has dimples and cheekbones under those round cheeks, and she could turn out to be a nice sweet piece in a year or two, hard to tell.

Baylor opens the refrigerator door. It made a soft everyday little pop of a sound, and for a moment Page hopes they won't hear it.

But of course they hear it, and they all turned to watch the girl, her head in the refrigerator, saying, "Hey, Mom, I thought you were gonna get some more ojay. This stuff's been in here for ages."

"Well shit, bring out the damn juice, let me sniff it for you, girl. Might be okay," Whopper said.

Baylor, still half-asleep, but waking up fast, still holding on to the open refrigerator door, looks around and sees the short, wide black kid who said bring it out, sees her mother holding the coffee cup and Chuleta holding a gun pointing at her.

Especially sees the gun. A short, fat, black barrel, smooth, looking like it was made out of graphite. Looking nasty. Looking like a hole you could fall into and fall forever. Baylor shoots a glance at her mother and starts to scream. The short fat kid has his hand over her mouth, and Baylor is tasting the salt of his palm before she can make any noise. Baylor bites down hard on his palm, and she tastes blood as the fat black kid jerks his hand away and smacks her hard on the side of her face, knocking her down to her hands and knees.

Baylor see little points of light and hears a buzzing sound inside her head. Her eyes are shut tight, so Baylor doesn't see her mother fling the cup of hot coffee at the kid who hit her, the cup sailing across the room and missing him by a mile and shattering against the refrigerator door. Baylor opens her eyes to see the fingers of cooling coffee spreading on the black-and-white floor between her hands like a shadow.

The wide black kid has his hand in his mouth, sucking on it, staring at Baylor. The Latino kid with the gun is saying, "You open your mouth, you see what happens? Every damn time you open your mouth, Whopper, we got a problem. I love you, bro, but you got to keep your mouth shut here, okay? Go upstairs, find the daddy, bring him down here. And don't you hurt him; we don't want no cuts and bruises. Just tell him we are all down here having coffee with his wife and daughter. Bring him down here, you copy?"

Whopper looks at Chuleta and back at Baylor, deep into her gaping robe. Seeing her on her hands and knees and seeing her pink nipples inside her white robe as she bends forward takes the anger out of him. He stands there looking, sucking his bleeding hand, until Chuleta shouts, "Go."

Baylor jerks her head up, pulls her robe shut, and Whopper reluctantly turns and goes through the door. After Whopper is out the door, going up the stairs, Chuleta tells Baylor, "And you keep your robe shut. Fucker ain't called Whopper 'cause he's tall, you copy that?"

Chuleta turns to Page as Baylor stands up, clutching her robe. Page has no idea tears were streaking her cheeks. She holds her hands out and walks over to her daughter to help her up. Chuleta, holding his gun pointed at Page, says, "That's right, Momma. Show the girl some love. Nobody wants to hurt nobody around here. That's right, hug her good. You were getting me some coffee. Maybe you better make some more. You like some, Blue Girl?"

Page ignores him, hugging her daughter as if she is

squeezing the tears out of both of them. She thinks he didn't shoot me when I walked across the floor, maybe he's not going to shoot me. Maybe the gun isn't loaded.

Baylor buries her face in her mother's sweatshirt and smells Tide, Bounce fabric softener, and vanilla, a bouquet that has always meant mom. Baylor thinks the sons of bitches, the goddamn sons of bitches. There has to be a way to hurt them. Has to be. They've gotta be dumb to do something this stupid. If they think there's any money in this house, they are dumb as dogshit.

Blue Girl says, "It's okay, I'll make the coffee. One of you want to show me where stuff is?"

Upstairs, in the en suite master bedroom bathroom with the ugly blue tiles on the floor, the ones they were going to change before they moved in, and the big hanging glass globes above the two marble-top sinks, Dan is having a shower in the shower stall at the end of the room and Whopper is sitting on the toilet.

Whopper is thinking that this was better than the best hotel. Like some MGM Palace in Las Vegas, maybe New York, with all this glass and mirrors.

He looks at himself in the mirror, sitting on the lid of the toilet. A hard man, a handsome dude, but don't fuck with him; he looks heavy, but he is hardbody. He thinks, little cunt downstairs got nice tits, they feel nice and warm against his chest, he ever get the chance. Maybe just talk to her, let her feel how good he feels. Talk to her nice, let her see his nice side. Let those little white fingertips just brush the Whopper.

Whopper, stirring on the toilet seat, lets go of the thought, brings his mind back to the present problem. Gotta stay focused here. His small black eyes survey the room, taking in the thick green-and-white towels hanging on chrome rails, the blue tiles on the floor.

Whopper keep his ass out of jail and above ground, Whopper gonna have a bathroom just like this except bigger, man. And have himself a nice lady like that girl Baylor in his shower. Fuckin bitch can bite. She owe me. But I can tame her. Shit, she be grateful, time I finish with her. I can see her naked in the shower, like if this was my bathroom, all the faucets, all the handles, towel racks be gold. Maybe not so many mirrors. Why anybody want to look at themselves that much? Kinda bathroom Silver'd like. Yeah, he'd like that, all mirrors.

Dan was slender like a runner who doesn't run much anymore, a little layer of fat on his stomach; ropy shoulders and arms and dangling hands that looked like they could chop wood. His dark hair was starting to retreat, giving him a widow's peak. He was thinking maybe shampoo less often, hang on to the hair he has. And his mind started in on his major project at Gopher Graphix: Fisherman. Fisherman is scheduled for spring release next year and we are way off the pace. All fucked-up. Garland and fucking Widmer making it worse.

Whopper was a blur through the shower door, but Dan was pouring shampoo over his head, working up a lather on his balls, giving his floppy cock a couple of extra slides with the slippery soap, his eyes shut. He was thinking maybe for the Danielle character he'd like to see the Graphix team try a Polhemus Ultratrac 120 space trailer with a stylus sensor input, run it over Maureen, she is about the right height, and God knows she has the shape. If ever there was a woman built for 3-D video. That, with a Cyberware range scanner, would give them a faster jump motion capture, getting the characters to move like real people. Do that with Maureen, go over the coordinates again, maybe get Fisherman back on schedule. Christ, this 3-D animation was fifteen times the work, and they'd never make it if he didn't throw more bodies at it.

The big players like Amiga and Nintendo weren't buying up the competition anymore; they were pouring every penny they had into R&D, so they weren't about to rescue Gopher with a buyout. A buyout would not be all bad. After fifteen years he had enough stock to make him wealthy, retire at forty-two. Jesus, get to know the kids instead of hearing about them from Page like the news at ten; Today Robby and Last Night Baylor . . . How much time did he and Page spend together? Cup of coffee in the morning. Supper, sometimes, at night. She had a bug up her ass about something. Jesus, don't ask. Like when was the last time they really made love like they used to? She made him feel like he should be grateful for his small ration of sexual joy. When he did all the work. He was rinsing, raising his arm up under the shower, turning around to get all the soap off.

Amiga and Nintendo had their new 64-bit stuff out there on the shelves already, and unless they could get the bugs out of Fisherman, they were six months or six years away from production. You never knew because nobody, not even Dan, knew when they could solve the screwed-up tints, with flesh tones going acid green and green going pink. It should be easy, but it wasn't, and Intel had 107 pages of data proving, they said, it wasn't their CPU's fault. Dan picked a small white-and-gold plastic bottle off the ledge and squeezed some of Page's forty-nine dollar Salon Ricard shampoo and color conditioner hair rejuvenation system on his head. Which he wasn't going to do, he thought, rubbing it in. Because the bottle was almost empty and Page would know he had been using it. Well, fuck it. Tomorrow he wouldn't do it.

God is in the digits. AmDell was already screaming because last month some doofus in accounting double-billed them $37,987. A figure he would never forget since Widmer had screamed it at him at least a dozen times. Another half-year review coming up with AmDell this afternoon; another catalogue of sins, fuck-ups, and arguments about major trivia while the world was exploding with bombs and pinheads in boots were carrying bazookas.

He should just say to hell with it. Quit. Set up a consultancy, work at home off the net and get to know the kids before they moved out. Spend time with Robby, show the kid a little support. Find out what was bugging Baylor. She had been looking at him like she'd caught him drowning pussycats. And Fisherman, Fisherman was sinking like the bottom had fallen out of the boat, he thought, letting the water stream over his head, washing away the special salon color-enriching shampoo. He turned off the water.

Opening the shower door and, reaching for his towel, he saw Whopper sitting on his toilet seat. Heavy, powerful black kid. Just sitting there on top of the lid watching, sucking on his hand.

They looked at each other for a moment, Whopper noting the grey on Dan's chest hairs, seeing Dan's cock and balls shrunk from the shower, dripping wet. Dan taking in the kid's sloppy black basketball Nikes, the laces not even tied, and baggy black shorts down to his knees and a black sweatshirt with a hood over his head. Made him look like an executioner, Dan thought for a moment.

Whopper took his hand out of his mouth, looked

at it, the neat curved row of punctures from the girl's mouth looking not too bad, he could deal with it. He could stand a whole lot more pain than that.

Whopper said, "We got your wife and daughter downstairs in the kitchen. You wanna come down with me?"

Dan was in his house, in his castle. He clenched his fist, feeling the strength in his arm, feeling his Sicilian blood rise, knowing he could knock this fat kid across the room, moving toward Whopper, saying, "Who the hell—" But he didn't finish because Whopper, bracing himself with both hands, kicked Dan in the balls.

Dan's head flooded red, the pain amazing him, rising like an ax up his spine to cleave his brain with a wedge of red pain. The pain drove every thought out the top of his head, and he went down, wet and pink from the hot shower, curled up on the blue-tile floor like a snail without a shell.

Whopper stood over him, little black eyes in a big face, looking down, sucking on his hand again. Whopper was going, "Don't fuck with me, my man. Ain't worth it. Just throw some shit on, like you got a robe? Your wife, your daughter downstairs. We'll go down, see them, have a cup of coffee, maybe have ourselves somethin to eat. Yeah, talk about what we do today. You hearin me?"

Dan looked up, his eyes watering with pain, trying to get a breath. So much pain it took a while to realize he was out of breath. His jaw was working. This is my house, he thought, hoping this wasn't happening, feeling sick with the pain.

"You don't have to say nothin," Whopper said, starting to get impatient. "Just do it."

■   ■   ■

Silver, looking over his shoulder, backs the Lexus into the big garage, slips it into Park, and leans back in the seat, head back to the headrest, listening to the motor run because it makes such a sweet sound. Like money, like major investments, big money in the bank. He loves that powerful hum, that working-for-you sound. He runs a hand along the slick honey-colored leather. Smells good, too. Smells like rich, like it's gonna last for fuckin ever. Never wear out. Never look cheap.

Silver checks out his face in the rearview mirror, and his face looks okay. Pulls on his lower lash to get a good look at his eyeball. No yellow, not bloodshot, okay. He sits back, thinking, just slip the car into D for Depart . . . nose of the car is pointing out, engine running, D for Drive-A-Fuckin-Way. Out the driveway and be on the 280 headed south for LA in five minutes. Cut over to the 5. Maybe head east to Vegas. Hey, fuck it, ride this sucker all the way to New Orleans. Engine running, could go anywhere. Like go to Hollywood, get a job, like a runner for some studio, break into films. Okay not overnight, but he could work hard, maybe take some acting-class shit, make contacts, get a bit part in a feature. Live with some amazing chick, cook for him, suck his dick by the pool. Okay, Chuleta be pissed off, I take off now, but Chuleta don't need him. Chuleta got too many homeys as it is. Could get fucked-up. See, he could be out of here, riding a fifty-five-, sixty-thousand-dollar automobile down the freeway into a new life. Coast to coast. Easy.

Silver reachs in his jacket, takes out a jay, lights up, holding the smoke, feeling good, feeling his heart slow down and the whole car get bigger. Feeling better now. Thinking, don't cut, bro. This could work.

So sweet the way Chuleta picked up this car, easy as pickin a banana off a fruit stand. And it was obvious, once Chuleta pointed it out, all the money was out here in the fuck in sub urbs, bro. That's the way he said it, like it was four words. Chuleta was like a little Columbus, discoverin the virgin land. No doubt there would be thousands of gangbangers after him, but Chuleta was the first, the pioneer. And there was so much of it, all of it within a gas tank from the hood.

"What're we fuckin around here for?" Chuleta said when they was back in the hood. "Ain't no money here in the damn street, it's out there. Sitting out there like a drive-up take-away. What we do is drive up, take it away."

Silver takes another deep hit off the jay, holds it, and feels a chill, thinking, what really happens he gets to LA, like Hollywood, say Sunset Boulevard. Okay, okay, he drives down Sunset Boulevard, big billboards, slick cars rollin up and down and he's there but he's gotta sell the car 'cause he's got like five dollars left for gas. And maybe one Big Mac if they got any ninety-nine-cent specials in LA. So he has to sell the car or he goes hungry. Lucky to find some dude give him five grand for the Lexus 'cause it's just been stolen and priority one on all the cops' computers. So as soon as you sell it, the man's got you by the balls 'cause he can turn you around anytime he likes. And how you gonna know the dude ain't some undercover asshole? Local boys, they know that shit, but Silver don't know jack shit about LA. Can't get no real job, 'cause he's got no social security number. Take some messenger shit. Plus, he sells the Lexus, he's an easy hit for Grand Theft. Gonna go up for Grand Theft, might as well take a shot at something gonna propel him along for a while. On the river of life. Something big.

Silver turns in his seat, checkin out the garage, taking in all they got in there. Sucker is bigger than a

fuckin apartment. Like a family of five could live in
here, no problem. What they got in here is skis, chain
saw, ski parkas hangin on hangers, surfboard, swimmin pool chemicals and poles. Shovels and all that
gardenin shit all lined up against the wall. Plus, the
man has a whole wood shop in here, table saw, lathe,
couple of bicycles on the wall, toolboxes. Christ, lookit
all that wine, must be a couple hundred bottles. Plus,
there is the slick Volvo, the new wagon, turbocharged,
all black leather inside. Nice little Mercedes coupe for
the lady to tool around in. They got money coming
out of their fuckin ears. What do I got? Little gold
around my neck, nice jacket, two pair of jeans, and
fuck all. Got like twenty-four dollars in the wallet.
Couldn't even buy a piece of the man's junk in his
garage. Have to suck gas out of some dude's tank to
make it to LA.

Silver checks his face in the mirror again, a quick
cut to a close-up. See, a face like that it could happen,
definitely. Got to believe a face like that make it to the
screen. Just take a little extra change, like maybe
thirty, sixty, go for a hundred grand. See, a hundred
grand he could find himself an agent, take some
lessons, buy some kick-ass clothes, rent a place right
there in Hollywood. Give his career a kick start.
Chuleta say the truth when he say the way out of the
hood is not in the hood. No point even lookin for it
there. It is up here, in the hills. Like with Chuleta,
they got family. They stick together, look out for each
other. *Todos por todos.* They could make it.

One more deep one, suck it in, and that shit really
kickin in now you crazy, crazy fucker. Feeling wired,
like steel, supple steel, feeling the hard ripples of his
stomach, warm under his shirt. Feeling the dope kick
in and getting that sense from a high overhead shot.
Like 3-fuckin-D, see himself from a height sittin in the

Lexus headed for Hollywood in the fuckin beautiful golden automobile. And feeling himself, right there at the same time, behind the wheel. He is good, very good, his body is fuckin perfect. Like run a tongue all over the surface and there is nowhere that is not tasty, hard, wired. And he is wise. Yes, wise to go inside, back in there, and take the wheel of the whole situation, steer clear of the razors and all that shit that sprays around a thousand bullets a minute, looks like a couple of coat hangers with a big barrel, and it can blow a refrigerator into bits the size of dimes. Like no way you can be too careful. Silver separates the red and green wire drooling from the empty socket in the steering column where the ignition lock was.

The engine dies.

Churley, deaf and nearsighted, seventy-four years old in dog years, raises his head in the corner of the garage, sniffing something. Definitely something. His nose up like a periscope, he gets up from the old sheepskin coat Page gave him after the moths got to it. It is not recognizable as her coat anymore, but he is happy because he can still smell her in the matted sheep fur lining. Feeling the cold from the night in his old dog bones and the ache of arthritis in his back hips, every step is an invitation to sit down. But he is a good dog. He smells something strange. And his food is waiting for him in the warm kitchen, in his dish.

Silver squeezes the handle down, hearing the click, like a bank vault opening. Probably got a whole team of Jap engineers working on the sound of that click it is so perfect, so solid, so expensive-sounding, easing the door open . . . and oh shit, across the garage floor, Homer is coming for him fast. Showing teeth. Homer, fucking pit bull beast they had running the fence at the fuckin juvie home in South San Lucas. Fuckin Homer that chewed up Rodriguez's leg, bit

Shaleen in the face so bad Shaleen is walking around with a face looks like a catcher's mitt with all the stitches.

Silver is out of the car and grabbing a shovel stacked up against the wall.

Churley smells this strange heavy smell and sees the blur moving off the wall toward him. This is Churley's garage, his place where he goes when he is tired, which is most of the time now. The old protection mode kicks in, and Churley is growling, no way anything gets past him, baring his teeth. At the same time he is also wagging his tail, thinking food, could be food here. Like I didn't volunteer for this guard dog, like pet me, pet me, feed me, feed me. Churley sees the blur swing something and starts to duck his head.

Silver feeling like a major league baseball player. Major league long-handle shovel has a good swing to it. Feel that shovel head hit that fuckin mean-ass Homer with a clang. Good follow-through. Dog is down there, on his ass, turn the shovel sideways up over the shoulder and bring it down like an ax on that mean-ass fucker's neck. For you, Shaleen. Keep that fuckin Homer fucker from coming after him again.

Churley feels nothing.

And Silver is feeling good. Like no way no animal, nobody is going to stand in his way. Not To-Day, my man. No Way. Silver leans the shovel back up against the garage wall and is on his way into the house, long strides in his baggy grey shorts and black tank top, brushing his hair back out of his blue eyes, smelling fresh coffee.

5

When Silver came into the kitchen, Chuleta had the assault gun pointed at Dan, asking him, "How you feelin? Maybe you should do yourself a favor, have some breakfast."

Dan was in his blue flannel robe with the Indian arrowheads on it. He wanted to throw up. But he couldn't do that; he was in enough disgrace in front of Page and Baylor. A spasm of pain bent him forward. He gritted his teeth and put his arm around Page. Baylor was standing behind them, looking really pissed off, like she'd like to stab Chuleta in the eye, but meanwhile she was hanging behind Mom and Dad. "Get the fuck out of here," Dan said, looking up, his voice husky. Trying to talk himself up. Be the dad. The ache between his legs felt like a bone bruise. Maybe there was permanent damage.

"I told you not to hurt him," Chuleta said to Whopper. Whopper was leaning back against the kitchen counter, testing his palm against the cool surface, leaving a dotted line of blood smears.

Whopper pushed off the counter for the refrigerator,

still checking his palm. Opening the refrigerator door, he said, "Didn't hurt him. If I hurt him, he still be suckin on blue tiles upstairs. Fucker was comin at me. I already got bit once. The fuck you expect me to do?" Whopper was moving jars and bottles around inside, taking out a plastic container and peeling back the green lid, sniffing it. "Where's the food at?" he said, snapping the lid back on and diving headfirst into the fridge. "Maybe they got some of that funky foreign cheese rich people got, and jam like got brandy in it. Maybe I'll make me a samwich. What's this?" he said, backing out and holding up a green plastic bowl sealed with cling film.

"Tuna fish," Page said. "Take it."

"Where's a spoon at?"

"In the drawer behind you."

Seeing Silver come in, Chuleta said, "Two things now. First, Silver, get the kid, bring him here. Next go get all the phones, cut the wires, bring them here, and set them up. Give me one, hooked up to all of them so I can listen in. You know what I'm sayin?"

Silver went, "Yeah, splice up a split-bridge. No problem."

"Then get all the knives, anything like a weapon, out the drawers, out of the closets, anything you find you bring in here. You got straps?" Chuleta said, turning to Dan.

Dan looked at him, not understanding.

"Straps. Burners, Dan my man. Where you got your guns?"

"If I had a gun, I'd have blown your head off," Dan said. Thinking how the hell did they get in here? Twelve thousand dollars for an alarm system, and it never even goes peep. Page must have let them in. And where the hell was Churley? Probably came up to them wagging his tail, hoping they would pet him. But that's not the point. The point is how we get them out.

"You pull a gun, you be dead," Whopper said. "You got a gun, tell me where it's at. 'Cause if you don't tell us, and we find one, Whopper is gonna be pissed off."

"And you think he ugly now," Blue Girl said under her breath. Whopper turned on his mean face to glare back at her.

"We don't have any guns." Except under my nightstand, Dan was thinking. So what if they found it. They already had guns. Maybe he could get to it. Or Page could.

Chuleta, a Napoleon taking charge, pointed a finger at Silver. "Okay, like I said, two things. Get the kid, the phones, and see if they got any knives or guns."

"That's three things, dude," Silver said, acting bored, looking out the window.

"Okay, three things. Prob'ly gonna be more, soon as I think of them."

"So what's Whopper gonna do," Silver said, not wanting to go because what it was, was going down here. "Feed his fat face?"

Whopper had the green bowl cradled in his sore hand, scooping out mounds of tuna-fish salad with a soup spoon. "I'm injured in the line of duty. Takin a break. But hey, you can't handle the kid, I'll go get him."

"They're gonna miss me at school," Baylor said.

"What you wanna go to school for? They just gonna make you memorize a lotta shit you gonna forget," Blue Girl said. "Whopper, bring me some milk for my coffee."

"Hey, you fetch for me, bitch. What you bring her for, Chuleta? She gonna dis everybody, want us all to bring her shit? Get you own damn milk."

"Hey," Blue Girl said quietly, "I'm a G same as you, same as anybody. And I am down for mine. Show me love."

Whopper, frowned, looked at the floor, put down the plastic bowl and fork on the counter, looked up, and held his arms out wide and he and Blue Girl hugged each other. Blue Girl was careful not to spill her coffee. "Down for you," Whopper said to Blue Girl, letting her go.

"Down for you, too," she said, meaning it. Meaning she would lay down her life for him.

"You bring the kid here, Okay, Whopper?" Chuleta said. "We gotta get movin. See if you can bring him down here without kickin his balls off."

Whopper leaned over the counter, scooped out another mouthful of tuna fish, sucked it in, and chewed thoughtfully. "You got lemon in here. That's a nice touch."

Blue Girl put her cup down carefully on the counter. "You finish feedin your face. I'll bring him down."

"Take Silver's gun," Chuleta said.

"He's fourteen, right? I don't need no gun."

Silver started to follow Blue Girl out of the room. She stopped, and said, "And I don't need you. He's just a boy, and I don't need another one, make it complicated."

"I need you to pick up the phones, get us set up in here, Okay?" Chuleta told Silver, making sure he didn't lose face. Blue Girl was already headed up the stairs, two steps at a time.

The second night she was curled up tight, like a ball. He stood by her bed, his bare feet on the hospital linoleum floor, feeling goose bumps on his legs, shivering. Her eyes were open and she saw him, little skinny-ass street-wise kid around thirteen maybe. She acted like she didn't see him. Like she didn't care whether he was there or not.

He went around to the other side of the bed and got in. Not saying anything yet, just lying there, feeling the warmth coming off her back. She didn't move or give any sign that she noticed he had gotten into her bed. But after a while, she said, "So what happened with the Coyote?"

"Like you said."

"You mean like the hawk lights up the big ball of swamp weed and that's the sun? That's it? No wonder they Alonies. Tellin shit like that."

"Listen. Maybe you find out something you don't know already. You know who hung the moon?"

"I'm listenin." Relaxing. Feeling lazy with the Darvon.

"Okay. Well a little later Coyote is thinkin the sun is good and all, 'cause it's warm, and they don't have to go around bumpin into stuff. And they can see the grass is green and flowers and the hummingbirds looking like they wearin Christmas foil. And they are pretty happy because it took both of them to do it. Like they are almost like brother and sister, helping each other out."

"This hawk is a female?"

"Look a lot like you. But then the sun goes away. Every damn day it goes away. And for a lot of the time, while the sun is sleepin, they got no light at all. And Coyote comes on to Hawk that is not as good as it could be.

"And Hawk goes, 'Hey bro, I did it like you said. Ain't you like never satisfied?' And Hawk goes over to this rock to sun himself. Soak up all those good rays.

"So Coyote, he goes and he hustles up another humongous ball of those swamp reeds and he brings them over to where Hawk has got his wings spread out, sunnin himself.

"'Here you go, man,' Coyote says."

"I thought you said this was a female this hawk."

"You gonna let me tell this? Okay, Coyote goes 'You the only bird can light up the sky. Now you can be the one, light up the night.'

"Hawk waits until it is night, feelin good 'cause she knows she is the only one can do this, and she takes off."

"And she lights it up and it is the moon, right?"

"You gonna miss the whole thing, you keep interruptin. See, the first time, you missed the part about the wind. When Hawk goes up for the first time, she has a hard time gettin that stuff lit up cause the wind keeps blowin the spark out. This time, same thing. But she gets up there, and she does it. Only this time the reeds burn kinda pale, with a lot of smoke. Sometimes the wind way up there is blowin hard, and there is just this little sliver of a moon. Sometimes it's not blowin so much, but it never really gets to burnin hot. So Coyote is all over blamin himself 'cause he was in a hurry and used a lot of damp reeds. And that's why coyotes, they see the moon now they sit and go HOOOwwwoooooooolllll."

She didn't say anything, just breathing in and out, asleep.

The big surprise for Blue Girl, coming into the kid's room, was the kid asleep in his bed had green hair. Kind of a tinge, but definitely green. Must be dyed 'cause it was blond at the roots. She hadn't seen no kid with no green hair before, and it made her pause. If he was her kid, she'd make him wash his hair, get the green out. As far as she was concerned it didn't even look weird. Just looked dumb.

She stood there looking at him and realized something else. Robby was lying on his back, green head rolled to the side, breathing the slow rhythm of sleep. Underneath the soft blue blanket his cock was sticking up like a long thumb. Blue Girl looked around the room—blue jeans, Reeboks, dirty socks, dirty shirts in a heap, comics and computer magazines on the grey carpet, rock posters, bookshelves on the walls. Shit, the kid had stereo, about a million CDs, computer, TV, couple of remote-controlled toy race cars. Kid had everything. She looked back at the sleeping white boy with mild distaste. Seeing his eyelids flutter, she thought he must be having some white-boy dream. Curious, wondering what a white boy's cock felt like, she sat down softly on the bed and touched his cock, her long fingers with the long purple fingernails holding him lightly through the blanket. Didn't feel like much. Felt like a blanket.

Robby groaned, deeply asleep. In his dream Robby is on a hike up in the Los Palos hills with Wanda Sandowski. They are crossing the high Alpine meadows, and the sun is warm. Wanda has the biggest honkers in school, and he knows it's her because she is just in front of him and walks with that kind of shy, hunched-over way she has like she's trying to hide her boobs. Wanda stops and turns to Robby. She has a nice warm smile, and he has never minded her braces. She is not wearing anything. He can't really see her body, but he knows she has no clothes on. She kisses him and, to his stupendous surprise, touches his cock through his chinos. He feels the warmth of the sun go though his whole body, and he kisses her back. Wanda lies down and smiles at Robby, holding out her hand in invitation. His hard-on feels like a vibrating baseball bat. She is lying down, and her hand is still touching him. "Wake up," she says.

Robby opened his eyes and saw not Wanda with the braces, but another face, a girl, with makeup, big brown eyes slanted like a cat's eyes, really beautiful. Maybe the most beautiful face he had ever seen; a sweet dark face with those warm pussycat eyes smiling at him. "Hi," she said. "You were dreaming, weren't you?"

Complete opposite of Wanda, but even better. She was beautiful, and she was sitting on his bed. Sleepy, sitting up, realizing he had a big boner, he pulled up his knees to hide it. "Hi," he said. "Who are you."

"Blue Girl. Who are you?"

"Robby."

"Good mornin, Robby," she said, smiling at him. She had on this like hot pink spandex top, like a dancer, maybe, and you could actually really see her nipples, although he was embarrassed to look. She touched his face with her hand, such a light touch. She left her hand there for a moment, and it was soft and warm. "Your momma and daddy downstairs, waitin for us. You want to come down with me?"

"What are you doing here?"

"They asked me to come get you. There's a surprise for you downstairs. You want to come down now." Not a question, a statement.

"I gotta go to the bathroom first," Robby said, stalling for time, thinking, Jesus, maybe she saw his boner. She was close to him. He could smell her perfume. Shit, he was never gonna get rid of the damn boner.

Slowly, with no hurry and no shame, smiling at him like it was the most natural thing in the world, she took her hand off of his cheek and put it right on his pecker. Right there. And left it there. All the way through the blanket and the sheet, right through the covers, he could feel the warmth of her hand.

She leaned even closer to him, her lips almost touching his ear. "You come down now."

For a moment, Robby thought he was going to pass out, it felt so good. Jesus, she was the first one to ever touch him there. Of course he did, mega times, but that didn't count. And for sure it didn't feel this good.

Blue Girl stood up. "You want me to get your robe or something."

"No, it's okay, just give me a second." He tried to think of turnips in a bowl, then of the time he sprained his ankle, something to make his hard-on go away. "Can you like, look away for a minute. I gotta get out of bed."

"Sure," Blue Girl said, turning away, knowing he would follow her like a puppy, anywhere. Like Momma Nature put that handle on men, make them easy to steer. "You take your time," she said to the wall.

Silver was in Dan and Page's bedroom, carrying an empty Nordstrom's shopping bag, thinking this would be a good carpet to go barefoot on. Like feel it between your toes. This house was so clean. The bed was unmade, the yellow blankets falling over the side, yellow-and-green sheets all messed up; but the room was perfect, sun coming in the windows, everything in place. Like a tall white cabinet with couple little statues and plates and stuff on each shelf, each shelf looking like a little stage with a cast of china stuff and little framed photographs placed just right. The big window overlooking the big swimming pool, the valley, and the mountains. And the telescope on a tripod, that was really good. This thing drag out like they were still here at night, he was going to check that out. See if he could find what was on the moon. He looked around for a wristwatch, loose jewelry. He didn't see any, but that didn't matter. If they were going to take any of that stuff, there was plenty of time. Nice TV set in the corner, look like one of the new digital twenty-seven-inch flat screens. Fuckers had taste. He could live here, no problem. Telephones on each side of the bed. What blew him away, though, was they had separate numbers. No shit, his and her telephone lines. He unplugged the phones, dropped them into the shopping bag, and went into the bathroom to check, see if they had a phone in there. He wouldn't be surprised.

As he came back into the kitchen with a shopping bag full of telephones, the kitchen phone rang. Page reached for it.

"Let it ring," Chuleta said.

"They'll call back," Page said, reaching for it again.

Chuleta put a hand on her wrist. "'Course they gonna ring back. They gonna think they got a wrong number." He turned to Silver. "Soon as it stops ringin, rig up another phone on the line so I can listen in."

Silver put his shopping bags with the telephones on the kitchen table. "There's four lines. Four separate fuckin numbers. Every one of these suckers got their own phone line. I can rig them all up with Y snaps."

Chuleta looked suspiciously at the jumble of phones and wires in the paper bags. "You know which number is which?"

Silver picked up the two bedside phones. He looked at one, sniffed it, and got a whiff of perfume, maybe body lotion. Some damn rich-lady shit. "This one's hers. Gonna take a while. I gotta run lines from their bedroom and the kids' bedrooms to the kitchen. You got any wire, like extension wire?"

Dan looked at him, thinking they were going to tie them all up. Thinking how cool these wild children were. He was dying with the pain and the shame.

"There's all that tool shit in the garage. You must have some out there," Silver said to Dan. Thinking, plus you got one dead fuckin dog out there.

Dan didn't respond. He was thinking he should have seen it coming. Stopped it. Done something. While they had the guns and controlled the phones there was nothing he could do until they were gone.

Until they were gone. Dan's dark face, with the long nose and the dark eyebrows, creased with the pain radiating from his balls and the pain he felt in his heart.

Chuleta put his face in Dan's. Chuleta didn't look angry or cocky. He didn't look anything. Little squirrel face. Kid would make a hell of a poker player. "We are all in this now. Together. You know what I'm sayin? We work together, we can all get out of this, maybe not smilin," Chuleta said, "but alive. You hear what I'm sayin?"

"What do you want?" Dan said. He felt bruised and queasy, His balls were swollen eggs, too tender to touch. He wondered again if Whopper's kick had done permanent damage.

"Same as what you want. What everybody wants. Money, honey." He gave Dan that grin he had. Like he was really full of himself. Kind of grin that really pisses you off.

"I've got about one hundred and sixty in my wallet. Page may have some more. We don't keep money in the house."

"Sounds like money to me," Blue Girl said.

"And credit cards?" Chuleta said.

"Sure, take them."

"What about you, you got credit cards, kid?" Chuleta said to Robby.

Robby kept his eyes down on the floor, and quietly said, "No."

"They don't let you have your own credit card? They still treatin you like a little kid?" Chuleta laughed. "Don't look like that, bro, I'm just fuckin with you." He came back to Dan, hand loosely on the gun hanging from his shoulder. "So, come on, be straight with me Dan, and I won't fuck you around. See, I wanted the money in your wallet, and credit cards you cancel the first time you get to a phone, the fuck I come to your house for? Risk six million years in jail? I jack you on the street, walk away, maybe somebody, maybe whole bunch of people see it happen. See me. Tell the police who they look for. Two, three hundred dollars, last me maybe a couple of days I got to do it all over again. Don't make no sense. Sooner or later, somethin trip you up. And they out there lookin 'cause they got all them new prisons they gotta fill up. Go to prison for two hundred dollars, that's too fuckin dumb."

"What do you want then?" Page said.

"What you got," Chuleta said. "We want what you got. What do you got?"

"Just what you see. You want to take a piece of furniture, the cars. Paintings, Christ, take the paintings. But I'd leave the house," Dan said, coming back to life a little, making a little joke. "The mortgage is just slightly larger than the value of the place."

"Tell you what I want. You got homeowner's, right? You covered?"

"Yeah, but there's a deductible."

"So I steal from you, you get it back less like five hundred."

"Something like that."

"So what you got is some stocks, bonds, CDs, insurance policies. I know you got insurance. So you got all this shit plus you are savin to send the kids to some swish college, right?"

Dan just looked back as if he didn't quite follow.

"So that's all rosy, plus you got your salary." Chuleta swung toward Page, the gun coming around with him. "Plus you, Momma, you got some money you got stashed dealin real estate, right?"

"There's nothing here," Page said almost under her breath.

"'Course it ain't here. It's underground like in bank vaults, mutual funds, on some fucking computer." He raised his gun barrel at Dan. "Go get it."

"I can't get it," Dan said. "Even if I could, it would take days. Settlement date for my mutual funds is five days."

"That's not my problem. You go out, go to work, just like you always do, come back with four hundred thousand in cash, and we will smile and disappear."

"That's it?" Dan was really surprised. Thinking, This is too fantastic to be happening, so maybe this isn't happening. Like being in one of our computer games. Maybe I'll wake up in a moment. "Four hundred thousand dollars? I'm worried about where I'm gonna get $4,653 to pay this month's mortgage and you want me to give you $400,000?"

"Tell the cops it's $1 million. What do you care, you got insurance. In fact, you do it right, you can come out of this with five, six hundred thousand extra, stick in your pocket. Like tax free. You know what I'm sayin?"

"Six hundred thousand dollars, extra." Page said sitting at the breakfast table with her arm around Baylor. "You are talking $1 million in cash." Baylor held her bathrobe drawn up tight around her throat, wary of the fat, nasty, stupid black kid who hit her.

"Sure, if you can get it," Chuleta said, moving away, looking out the window, checking the driveway. "Listen, you got a lot to do, and I want to get started here. But if this goes right, you're gonna come out of this with somethin to show for this."

"Go fuck yourself," Page said.

Whopper was leaning against the counter, the empty tuna-fish bowl beside him. He pushed off, slow and easy as a ship leaving the dock, moving toward

Page. Chuleta, seeing him out of the corner of his eye, raised his hand in a kind of backhand wave. Whopper kept coming and Chuleta raised his hand another half inch and Whopper stopped and went back to leaning against the white countertop.

Chuleta, not really looking at Whopper but aware of him, was saying, "See, you keep anythin you get over four hundred thou. Like a bonus. You help us out, you could come out way ahead."

"Four hundred thousand dollars," Dan said, the anger starting to revive him. He was unshaven, shaken, and in pain, wearing his old bathrobe, but he was alert, falling into his old role as the project manager at Gopher Graphix, the wise voice of experience; reasonable, the head of the family, ready to deal. "I hate to tell you kids what I have in the bank, but it's more like four thousand than four hundred thousand."

"Hey, so you got $4,000 in the bank. That's what, your checkin account? Shit, that's change, man, loose change. We are not here for change, Dan, we are here for our lives."

Chuleta took a breath, looking at Page, Dan, Robby, and Baylor one by one. "So you tell me. Your life worth $400,000 to you? Your wife's life, she worth that much? Your kids? We're the ones takin the chance here. The difference is we got nothin to lose. I ain't goin back to gangbangin, hangin out in the street, waitin for some motherfucker drive by shoot me in the head. Wait for some cop drop some blow in my pocket throw my ass in jail. I ain't goin back to the street, simple as that."

"We ain't goin back nowhere," Blue Girl said. "You better believe that is nowhere."

"That's right, my man," Whopper said. "We goin forward from here. Ain't no goin back."

"Think about it." Chuleta started pacing the kitchen. "What's $400,000 to you? A year's salary? Maybe two? Shit, you probably got four or five million you add it all up. You do this right, you won't even lose a dollar. You can claim it on insurance, deduct the loss at tax time. Keep the extra for yourself like a bonus."

Page leaned back in her chair, gaining a little of her natural confidence. "You don't even know what $400,000 is."

Chuleta whirled around at her, his voice bitter and hot. "I know exactly what $400,000 is." He casually pointed his gun toward Robby and Baylor, "You gonna send them to some fancy colleges, like $25,000 a year. Am I right, Silver?" Chuleta gave Silver a look.

Silver shrugged, and said, "Twenty five, thirty thousand. That's what they askin. Check it out."

"Okay call it twenty-five a year just to keep it simple. That's one kid for one year. Forget you got to pay for their your clothes and books and shit. And travel back and forth to like nowhere Massachusetts, Vermont. Maybe get the kid a car, insurance, medical shit, and you're spendin another twenty grand. Easy. But let's just say bare bones it's twenty-five grand a year for four years. That's 100,000 for four years. You see where I'm goin with this? Look around the room, man. I'm not askin you to spend more on us. I'm just sayin I want you to spend on us what you are gonna spend on your kids. A hundred grand apiece, we can make it out of that shithole. Okay? Nobody ever bought us nothin. So it's like you gonna send us to college. Give us the money to do what we want to do. We want to go to college, we gonna have the money to do that."

Chuleta smiled for a moment, lowering his gun, rubbing his chin. "You been to college, you do the math. Four hundred thousand dollars for us four here. Like a scholarship."

Chuleta went back to the window, smiling at that last, that "scholarship." He had just thought that up. He turned around and boosted himself up on the counter, like a boy in his mother's kitchen, legs swinging. "See, you go in to work like this a regular day. Nothin special, except you got to come home with a package. You come home with that, and we'll disappear, drop out of sight like we were never here. You come home with a million, you keep the extra six hundred thousand, claim a million-dollar loss. Hey, plus you get another six from the fuckin insurance company. I don't give a shit. See what I'm sayin? Banks close at three-thirty, four o'clock. You be back here by four-thirty, Okay?"

Chuleta jumped back down off the kitchen counter, flicking the hair hanging on his face back on top of his head. It fell back again. Feeling wired. Feeling like they almost had the money and were on their way out of there. Telling himself they hadn't got nothin yet, they had a long way to go.

Baylor looked up at Page, her round face scrunched up, her voice whiny. "Mom, I gotta go to school. I got another exam coming up in physics, and I gotta ace it. I can't miss another class."

"You *want* to take an exam in physics, girl?" Blue Girl said. "You got a serious attitude problem."

"Hush up, you might learn something, Blue Girl. You ain't goin to school today, kid," he said to Baylor. "You gonna be home sick. We're gonna be a nice normal family here at home while Daddy runs around and get the money for us," Chuleta said. "You got any toast?"

"Sure have some toast. Help yourself," Dan was muttering to himself. "Toast, huh. That's why you're in the ghetto. Big dreams, no vision."

"What vision you talkin about?"

"To tell you the truth, Chuleta, is that your name, Chuleta?" Dan pronounced the name to rhyme with beta.

"Yeah, close enough."

"To tell you the truth, Chuleta, I can't get excited about risking my life and my family for $400,000."

"Say what?"

"I was thinking more in the neighborhood of a million five."

"Each?"

"You and me. Each."

"I could see that."

"Well how about two million each? No, wait a minute, let's get real here, make it four. Or five. How does five million sound?"

"The fuck you talkin?"

"What I'm 'talking' is I don't think there is a chance in hell I can get $400,000 in cash, Chuleta. Maybe it's possible, but I have to tell you I don't think it is. Come upstairs into the study and I'll show you a stack of bills I can't pay. You can look at my bank statements. I'll show you how close to the line we are."

"The fuck you say."

"I'm saying 400,000, or $5 million, it doesn't make any difference. Name any figure you like, and if it is over 4,000, I don't have it, and I can't get it. You came to the wrong house."

Chuleta walked over to the kitchen table, pulled out a chair, and sat down across from Dan, facing him. Man to man, the gun lying on the table pointed at Dan, Chuleta's finger on the trigger. Dan looked at the open barrel of the gun, thinking of the black hole he had fallen into. Was still falling. If this was just him, he might have a chance, might do something. But the black hole of the barrel told him whatever he did it wouldn't be brave. It would be stupid because the gun was pointed at Page and Robby and Baylor.

Chuleta said, "You come home with $400,000 in cash, we all walk away. Word. You keep any left over, that's your business like maybe 50,000, maybe 500,000, up to you, for your trouble. Claim it on the insurance. But you send the cops up here like some UPS van full of SWAT?" Chuleta looked from Page to Baylor to Robby, and said, "First thing we do is kill her, then her, then him. If I even smell cops, we gonna kill 'em. All of 'em." Chuleta let that sink in.

"I prefer," Chuleta leaned forward, his face inches from Dan's, "I prefer to keep it all simple, but what the fuck, it gets out of control, it is your fault. You copy, Dan?"

Dan nodded yes, forgetting, for a moment, the pain between his legs.

"You want to come home early, you got the money, we be glad to see you. The sooner the better, long as you got the cash."

"Nobody has that much cash," Dan said, looking at Page.

─────── CHAPTER ───────

6

Dan, wearing jeans and one of his soft down-home flannel shirts, a soft red check, couldn't get his Reeboks tied. His balls ached, and he kept losing track of what he was doing. Crouched over, sitting on the end of the bed, he was trying to concentrate, get a plan going, forget the sharp ache in his crotch. Thinking that tying his shoe is not important. Thinking, Goddamn AmDell and Fisherman are not important. Not at all. Nothing is important except getting us out of this alive. He looked down at his shoe again, pulled the laces of his left shoe tight, and the lace broke. He was having trouble, he realized, because he couldn't see his laces. Because his eyes were watering. He was a grown man. Grow up, he told himself.

"Wear loafers," Page said, watching him.

He looked at her, standing in front of the dresser, in her grape velour sweatpants and faded yellow sweatshirt. God how he loved her, the high-school cheerleader from the class of '76. "Fight, team, fight!" "Go, Dan, Go!" He stood up and pulled her to him.

"You guys are going to be okay," he said softly into her ear.

"We'll have these little bastards tied up in knots when you come home," she said, loud enough for Chuleta to hear.

Chuleta was standing in the doorway, his gun hanging from his hand, pointing at the floor. "What time you usually get to work?"

"You mind leaving us alone for a minute," Dan said, still holding Page.

"Yeah, I mind. You get your shoes, get going. This is gonna be a busy day for you. You do it right, we all come out ahead. Walk away like it never happened."

"Fuck you," Dan said.

Page gave Dan a little kiss on his cheek, throwing in a feel on his butt like a coach sending him into the game, saying, "Don't worry about us, honey. We'll be fine." Page watched him walk into his closet in his socks, Reeboks in his hand. She turned to Chuleta. "You going to watch me get dressed, too."

"You can stay in what you got on."

"I can't go to work in my sweats. My clients would have a fit."

"You're not going to work. You're stayin here with the kids. You all got flu."

"I don't get sick."

"You'll be over it by tonight."

Dan came out of the closet, Reeboks tied, thinking maybe if he dived behind the bed for the nightstand, he could come up with the pistol. Thinking, that gun in the little bastard's hand would shred both of us in half a second. Dan was trying to think of something, trying to think of a reason to stay home.

"You lookin like you takin the day off, Dan," Chuleta said. "How come you don't wear no suit an' tie?"

"It's what I wear to the office. What we all wear."

"No wonder this country so fucked-up," Chuleta said, waving his gun as if he was showing Dan the way out. "Let's go."

Watching Dan's car from the kitchen window, seeing him drive down the driveway and disappear, Page started to shake. She told herself to hold still. Tried to act as if she was tending the plants she kept on the kitchen windowsill. She pulled off a dead leaf from an African violet, poured a glass of water from the tap, and watered the maidenhair fern she had already watered before the Lexus showed up. She looked up and saw her face reflected in the window, tears running down her face.

I'm not scared, she told herself. These goddamn little punks don't frighten me. She wiped her face with the back of her soft sweatshirt sleeve. She had to turn around and face them because Chuleta was asking her for another cup of coffee, and she was afraid that if she didn't turn around and do what he said, they would do something horrible to Robby and Baylor.

There was a way out of this, she thought, opening the cupboard to get down another cup. She just had to calm down and she would think of it. Her hand came out with the chipped blue-and-white china mug that she and Dan had bought at Walgreen's in Palo Alto when Dan was at Stanford. When he first started working on Doom Room. Practically the first video game. The cup was the last survivor of a dozen heavy and cheap-looking mugs. She had no idea why she kept it. But it was the one she always got down after Dan went to work and the kids went to school. The one for a last cup of coffee with the paper, checking the real-estate listings before she left for her office. Putting the mug on the counter, taking the carafe from the cof- feemaker, Page thought of the other people, neighbors, people she hardly knew; people all over Los Palos, having coffee and reading their papers as if today was just another beautiful northern California day. She wanted to kill the little son of a bitch. But there were four of them. If she could just relax, she would think of something. She looked over at Churley's empty dish on the floor. Time to feed him. Where the hell was the damn dog when she needed him?

D an was staring at the phone in his car, inside the cocoon of his Volvo sixteen feet away from plowing into the back of a Porsche on Interstate 280 as they roared over the Stanford Linear Accelerator. Some internal radar made him look up and he swerved, just missing the woman. Ah, that good old Messina intuitive sense, what made him an All-American. Okay, third string All-American, but almost good enough to turn pro. Sharpened by twenty years of playing video games. As if he could hear the bullet hit the target before the gun went off. But it came at a price. He couldn't concentrate. As soon as the gun went off his mind goes pinging off in another direction. No focus. The modern video man with the attention span of a sound bite.

He lifted off the accelerator and the speedometer dropped from eighty-five to sixty-five. On the most heavily patrolled road in northern California. Maybe he should put his foot down and get stopped by the police. Tell him that there are these kids in his house with an automatic weapon pointed at Page and his children. Shit, if they heard as much as a rustle in the weeds, this Chuleta kid, maybe Silver, maybe the fat fuck who kicked him, one of them would go bananas. It could all come apart in an instant. Some slice of time so thin you could see right through it and the gun would rattle off four dozen rounds and Robby or Baylor or Page or all of them would be gone, never to come back.

What could the police do? No idea what the police would do. Try to talk to the kids maybe. Surround the house with fifty shotguns and ten sharpshooters. Whatever they did, it would overload the balance, and it would all slide into catastrophe. It already was a catastrophe.

Deep down in his bones he had a Sicilian suspicion of police. His great grandfather was Sicilian. And he got out of there, took the ferry from Sicily across the straits of Messina and walked to Naples in 1905. Worked on a freighter for no pay, just the passage and the food, stopping at Genoa, Barcelona, Liverpool, and Boston. By the time they sailed into New York harbor the nineteen-year-old kid had worked up enough nerve to jump ship. Just a kid, with Norman eyes as clear and blue as the Mediterranean Sea outside his village door. "Where you from?" they asked him on Ellis Island. "Messina," he said, because he thought if he said Sparta, they'd think he was from Greece instead of a little Sicilian fishing village just around the corner from Messina. So that was his name, Messina. At least they could pronounce Messina in America. Not like Mezzogiorno. This was America. Leave the fucking Mezzogiornos in Sicily.

Sicily is only a couple of miles off the tip of Italy but as far as the Sicilians are concerned, it is another continent. The Normans invaded Sicily in 1060, six

years before they got around to England. The Normans
were on their way to the Holy Land and you can still
see their blond hair and blue eyes over the island.
Phoenicians, Greeks, Romans, Vandals, Ostrogoths,
Arabs, Saracens, Turks, Germans, Americans, everybody invaded Sicily. A real genetic tutti-frutti.
Grandmother Smilkstein was born a Jew in Poland.
Mom's maiden name was Fagan, Irish Protestant. So
what? Go back far enough and we're all Meso-
potamian. Still, there is a wine-dark stream of the
Sicilian in the Messina blood. Omerta, the Sicilian reli-
gion of silence. Speak to the police, we cut out your
tongue. Tell the Guarda di Finanza who built those
tenements outside Palermo last year, already falling
down, smelling of sewage, we burn down your house.
Dad had migrated from New Jersey to California in his
Chevy Bel Air on Route 66. Sicily was a family story
Messinas don't tell anymore.

This was his family, too important to risk with
anybody else. It was down to him. And he was an
All-American. Okay, okay, third-team wide receiver,
but he had made the team. Christ, if anybody could
handle it, he could. He could do it. He could make it
would work. There was a chance. If he came home
with the money, the bastards would go away.
Question was, with his intuition, why didn't he sense
them coming, why didn't he get up first instead of letting Page face them alone. How did he get so slow
that he let himself get kicked in the balls. The kid
took him out like he was a fly in a level-one video
game. When did he get so old and so slow? Like
Churley. Poor old dog was probably still asleep in the
garage.

He had just thought that five minutes ago. Same
thought, same conversation keeps on going around
and around, lap three since I left the house. Bottom

line doesn't change. Those fucked-up kids have a gun pointed at Page's and the kids' foreheads. And the slightest little thing, a twig snapping, a flashlight battery going dud, could fuck it up. He could not tell the police. Former All-American kicked in nuts, runs for the cops. He had to make it right. It was his house, his family, his fault. He could do it. Had to. For Page and Robby and Baylor.

His balls ached.

Dan looked down at his cellular phone again. He could circle back, park the car down on Alta Ridge, come in through the open land, sneak up on the bastards. But he had been that route in the bathroom. One on one, and he had been gasping on the floor. There were four them with weapons against one of him. Dan pictured himself going in, and doing it, but however he played it, the video always came out with Page or Robby and Baylor wounded, maybe dying. The police would handle it better than he could, and that still wasn't good enough. Because he knew in his bones the cops would fuck it up. Turn it into another Waco. He had designed computer games where commandos blew away the bad guys with guns. Good guys just jumped up over the lasers and dodged the bazookas. Tore the bad guys' heads off. That was Head Ripper, which did great in the Far East but had never gotten near their target distribution figures in the North American markets. That was digital electrons, illusion, pixel blood. These kids with guns in his house were real, and the oldest living video game designer in Silicon Valley did not know what to do.

For one shameful moment he thought he could call up the house around four in the afternoon and say sorry, but there was another meeting and he was staying in town. Call the kids' bluff. Leave the little bastards holding the bag because if he didn't come home, they wouldn't get any money. Page and the kids could handle it.

He was already feeling shame that he had let this happen, and the shame opened up into a mine shaft of guilt that he could even think of being such a coward. Look, he told himself, he was just trying to consider all the options. Walking away was not one of them. He couldn't walk, he couldn't call the police. He was going to have to play their game. And he was a player. Former All-American. Remember that.

Except this was not a game. Maybe those kids wanted to kill somebody. Maybe that was the real reason they were there. To kill. Kill them all whatever he did. If he came back with the money, how did he know they wouldn't shoot all of them so there weren't any witnesses? So they could get away. He pictured Page and Baylor and Robby smashed to pieces and lying in blood on the kitchen floor. Oh Jesus. Was this my fault? he wondered, feeling the tears threatening to start again. Was this for something I did? Or the just the random bazooka of America just swinging around, coming to a stop pointed at me. And Page and Baylor and Robby.

Outside the car window, the Santa Cruz Mountains were flooded with sun, still green in the early-summer air. The long lake down below, running parallel to the six-lane interstate, a blue and sparkling leak along the San Andreas Fault. Red-shouldered hawks, peregrine falcons, condors, ospreys, buzzards, and bald eagles soared and dived through the blue sky above the lake. Just above the water there was a gliding white flutter of seagulls. Mist hung in the hollows, making the hillsides look like a Chinese watercolor. This was California state land, a green belt of wild hills and valleys stretching from San Francisco to San Jose. A coastal range of micro weather systems, rich with ancient oaks, Alpine meadows, redwoods, lakes and streams, mountain lions, bobcats, coyotes, screech owls, black-tailed deer, yellow-legged frogs, pygmy nuthatches, and blue-bellied lizards.

Dan didn't see any of it. Hunched over the steering wheel, eyes on the concrete, he went through his numbers again. Less than four thousand in his checking account, which was less than nothing because the month's mortgage payment was due next Monday. A brokerage account with around $500,000 in stocks and bonds, his nest egg left over from Doom Room. Plus that dumb CD he had for the kids' education if they made it to college. He had his biweekly salary check coming next Tuesday for around $8,500. Too late. He had his big nut, $1,353,000 in his retirement fund which maybe he could get out with a ten percent penalty plus income tax. But that was all in stocks and bonds, and it would take his broker at least a week to get it out. He had $15,000 in AmDell stock he had bought to show solidarity with their client. And he held options on 25,000 shares of Gopher stock at $19 a share. Which should be worth a bunch because Gopher was selling at sixty-three last time he looked. But he hadn't exercised the option, so he didn't have the stock, so he couldn't sell it. Even if he could, the settlement check wouldn't be cut for three, maybe five, working days. Add it all together and it was more than enough. But he couldn't put his hands on it. And even if he could, it wouldn't be cash. It would be checks, paper that would take days to clear. Maybe his broker could lend him some money. Maybe the Shadow. Maybe, please God, somebody.

Stop whining, for Christ's sake. Get it all. Every

damn dollar you can. If it was more than enough, so be it. But don't stop to count it, just get it.

A sharp honk in his left ear woke Dan up to the reality of the interstate. He had wandered out of his lane and had cut off a woman in a Taurus. She had a face like rhubarb pie, heavy red cheeks, big glasses shaped like hearts, making a gesture like, "Why me?"

Dan left her face in the rearview mirror, looked at the road ahead again, and forgot her. Page's Mercedes was a little sweetie, but it had ninety thousand miles, so maybe they could get around $19,000 if they could find a buyer. The Volvo only had 8,500 miles on it and it was worth maybe $35,000, but Gopher owned the lease, so there was no way he could sell it with no papers. A blue-and-grey van loomed in front of him, the back door dented and rusted, a name—Pepita— scratched in the paint, growing large. Shit, he thought, slow down. Think. He couldn't think. He leaned over the phone console and punched the numbers.

"How are you doing?" he said, just to hear Page's voice.

"Lousy," she said. "I want to go to work. I want these little shits out of our house."

"Is he listening?"

"Right next to me with the phone in his ear. And that horrible gun pointed at me."

"Listen, Chuleta, this is going to be okay. No reason, you have no reason to point that gun at her." Dan's voice was low, confidential, friendly. Act like you're talking to your best friend, he told himself. "Listen, if it goes off, you can't undo it, you know? Listen," he said, thinking, don't repeat yourself. Sounds like you are scared. Don't act scared because he'll pick up on that. Be confident. "Listen," he said again, "I know you are just a kid, but if the gun goes off, you are really screwed. Are you there? Do you hear me? If you hurt any of them, any of them, you won't get any money. And you will have to kill me, because I will come and kill you. Do you hear me?" Shit, not what he meant to say. The phone was quiet except for the usual cell-phone static. "Does he hear me Page?"

"He's nodding his head, yes."

"Is he still pointing the gun?"

"Yeah. Okay. Don't worry about it. We'll be okay."

Dan tried to put a smile in his voice. Confidence was an effort. "Did you have a gun when you were a kid?"

"Nobody had a gun in Pleasantville."

"I mean a toy one. Like a cap pistol."

Page laughed, relaxing a little. "My aunt sent me a cap pistol with a holster for my sixteenth birthday. I couldn't believe it. I don't know if she thought I was a boy or was ahead of her time."

"Well this isn't a cap pistol."

"I know, Dan, Jesus. Believe me I know."

"I just don't want you to take any chances. How are the kids?"

"Robby's okay, I guess. I haven't really talked to him. Baylor is really upset."

"Can I talk to her?"

"He's shaking his head, no."

"Tell her I'm sorry, and I love her. And I want her there when I get back."

"What are you going to do?"

"Go to the bank. See my broker. See what I can get out of the Shadow. Nick usually has a bunch of cash for his musicians. Sit tight, I'll be home soon."

"Soon. Soon as you can. I'm glad you called."

"Me too. You want to fool around later?"

"I want to be able to take a deep breath."

When Page put the phone down, Chuleta lowered

his gun. "It's okay," he said, "I won't point the gun at you if I don't have to. Okay?"

"No, it's not okay," Page told him. "Nothing is okay."

Robby was keeping his eye on Blue Girl. He couldn't help it. He told himself it was because if he kept looking at her, he didn't have to think about this mess. The one good thing, the only good thing, was when Blue Girl stood under the light over the sink he could see her nipples underneath the pink spandex. And Blue Girl was standing under the light, smiling at him like she knew he could see her nipples. He had seen Mom's and Baylor's boobs plenty of times, so it shouldn't have been any big deal, but it was. They were big nipples, wide, looked dark. No question she was a cock-teaser, just using him. She was probably just trying to please the Chuleta kid with the gun. Maybe he was holding her captive, too. Maybe he could rescue her, and she'd be grateful . . . Oh shit, fuck, Jesus these assholes are holding a gun on them and he's trying to figure out a way to get her to touch him again, like some pervert. If he could talk to her maybe, without Mom hearing.

Chuleta was saying "We gonna pair up, okay? Listen up. Blue Girl, you take the girl. You be her best friend, be with her when she gets dressed. She goes to the toilet, you go in with her. She is always in your sight and in your reach, okay?"

Blue Girl nodded and moved across the room to stand next to Baylor, who moved a side step away.

Robby kept his eyes on Blue Girl. The light was perfect.

"You ain't gonna catch nothin from me, girl," Blue Girl said to Baylor. "I'm not gonna hurt you."

"I can't believe you are this stupid," Baylor said. "You do everything he says?"

"I don't," Blue Girl said. "But if you got any sense, you will."

Chuleta went on. "Silver, you look after Momma, here. Don't let her out of her sight. Whopper, you look after the kid. Just like Blue Girl and Baylor, keep him where you can reach him."

"How come you give me the kid?" Whopper said, thinking he could use a little time with the girl. Watch her change her clothes, like, maybe get to see her put on her brassiere, that would be useful. "Who you gonna watch?"

"Everybody. You. I spend half my time, watchin you." Chuleta turned to Baylor. "Do you understand that if anybody runs—like you take off when Blue Girl's not lookin—I find you gone, I kill your mother, and I kill your brother. You understand what I'm sayin?

"You're saying you are a homicidal maniac," Baylor said.

Chuleta lowered his gun and walked across the tile floors to stand in front of Baylor. "I never killed anybody. And I don't want to. And to tell you the truth, I don't know if I could. I really don't know. I might just shoot your brother in the stomach or something. You want to find out, you run away."

Baylor realized she was as tall as he was. She could smell his breath, like fish, maybe. She looked back at him, like toe-to-toe, saying, "I'm not going anyplace. Neither are you."

"Just do what he says," Page said. "Both of you."

Chuleta went back across the room to lean against the counter again, gun pointing at the floor, black eyes bright, moving all the time. "Right. Listen to your momma. You can move around the house, do what you gotta do. You want to make a phone call, you ask me, and you make it here in the kitchen. You stay in your robe, that's fine. Somebody like FedEx come to the door, we want them to think we all one fine happy family except you home with the flu. You hear what I'm sayin?"

Chuleta looked at Whopper, taking in the Whopper's long baggy black shorts, his dirty, hooded sweatshirt and his black hi-top Nikes with no socks. "Whopper, you look a mess, you know that? Anybody see you in this house, they know you a fish out of water. Go up to the kid's room, maybe he's got some stuff fit you. Put on some clothes make you look like you at home here. Same with you, Blue Girl. Go look in Peaches' closet, see if she got something look white on you."

Thirty miles south of San Francisco, Gopher Graphix International Corporate Headquarters are in Mountain View, in a grassy and pleasant tree-shaded industrial park on the filled-in marshland alongside San Francisco Bay. Gopher is down the winding four-lane avenue from Sun Micro, almost directly across from Virtual Space. The Gopher building looks like Candyland; a four-story glass-and-steel architectural showpiece of grape and raspberry sherbet poles, red-and-white-striped-candy support beams, a fountain spraying three stories up inside the building, and several acres of semi-transparent lime green glass. From certain angles, you could see reflections of San Francisco Bay and the color-ful sails of the sailboats in the bright green glass. The building was "the graphic statement of a company that knows how to play the game and win because it makes the rules," Chief Executive Officer and Chairman Garland Grant Jr. had said when he tossed the com-pany keys to all the employees from one of the bal-conies overlooking the reception desk.

The keys were a company joke. They were blank

because there were no locks on the doors, no guards patrolling the campus grounds. The building was always open owing to the bizarre hours of the techies and the constantly increasing pressure from the competition. Pencil necks were always in the building, working, eating, goofing off, making presentations, and banging their foreheads against the walls, trying to think up new games to play, technical solutions for, say, making the river of blood flowing down the city street reflect the sunshine.

Dan came into the parking lot too fast, the back end of the Volvo skidded, and he almost hit a funky old VW van as his car swung wide, sliding across the parking lot. Braking hard, tires squeeling, Dan nosed into an empty space. He was out of his car and running for the front door, as Les Freeman, world's oldest living assistant video art director, leaned out of his faded raspberry-and-lime VW van with the big peace symbols on the side that Dan had just missed. "Come back and fight like a man," Les called after him with his usual good nature. But Dan was through the front doors.

"Hiya, Cowboy," Rebecca said, as he came charging into his corner office.

Rebecca was in her cubicle with one remaining slice of banana bread and a paper cup of coffee on her desk in front of her. She wore a long, flowing, beige jacket and baggy trousers, scarves and full blouse; an outfit designed to conceal a body that rarely saw daylight. Rebecca felt it was important to be at her desk when the Shadow came in at 7:30 A.M., score a point with the Shadow.

"Have a nice day," she said as Dan ignored her, plunging into his office. She had a pretty, soft face with a muffin of short brown curly hair on top. She wore rings on every finger and had dimples on the backs of her hands where her knuckles hid.

Dan came out again. "What can we cancel?" Thinking—Who should I call first—Thinking—Maybe it makes more sense to raise the cash from a lot of places, spread it out, instead of going for one big hit. One big hit, though and he was home. Go for it all, he remembered. Get everything.

Rebecca was saying, "For openers, there's a meeting with the Fisherman graphic team starting like now. They're waiting for you in the conference room, and I don't think you want to skip that because you called the meeting. Or maybe you don't remember saying you had a new idea for Maureen with a stylus. So we're all real curious about that one, especially Maureen. The Shadow has some producer"—Rebecca checked her screen—"Walt Berenson in his office at eleven, hopes you'll join them." Dan remembered the bright floppy-looking overweight kid who had produced *Starwalker* and *Nightshade Memories*. Normally he'd get a kick out of seeing Berenson's story boards, see the weird special effects Berenson would be asking them to bid on.

"Can't. What else?"

"The Shadow says he wants you to go with him over to AmDell this afternoon. He says Widmer's beating up on him, and he'd like you to take a few hits. You'll be there anyway because you're scheduled for lunch with Widmer, then Deltner wants to go over Fisherman's budget with you, says you are about to have your plug pulled. That's for as long as your guess is as good as mine, but Deltner and the Shadow want you in on the AmDell budget review this afternoon at six at AmDell and that could go like late—nine? ten? You tell me."

"I'm out of all of it. Tell them I'm sick."

"You tell them," Rebecca said, taking a thoughtful sip of coffee. "You're the game player." But Dan was past her, going into his office. "And I'm not your fucking secretary."

Dan sat at his desk, making mental lists and categories. The Fisherman team would be pissed off and frustrated. Maureen would be especially pissed. She'd think because he wanted her body for Fisherman, he didn't appreciate her brain. Which was true. Her big droopy boobs and slender waist gave her heroic, cartoon proportions, perfect for the Danielle character. And he vaguely lusted after her from a distance, perking up when she came into his office and glad when she left. She was brilliant at shaking the bugs out of software. But apart from that methodical task she had the brains of a squid. He'd love to see the producer, Berenson, that would have been fun. Fun, Jesus what a small stale word. Like "fun" with Widmer, with his wonderful racist tales of weekends with The Militia. Ha, ha, ha. They'd fight about compensation, what AmDell would pay for Gopher's services. And they'd fight about Fisherman because the AmDell dealers were saying Fisherman's launch had been delayed so often they were calling it Messiah.

On a normal sunny spring day it would be the usual mix of tedium, play, and torture. But not today. Today a day of meetings, anxiety, and corporate trauma seemed as remote as Easter Island. The clutter of Gopher Graphix was floating away from Dan like broken planks bobbing off over the horizon after the ship has gone down.

"Cancel me out of all of it," he called out to Rebecca.

"You can't," she shouted over her shoulder.

"I know I can't. Do it anyway."

Rebecca got up and stood in his office door, smiling as if this was a joke. "You know how you can tell an extrovert computer nerd?" Dan didn't look up. "When you say hello, an extrovert nerd looks at your shoes instead of his shoes." Dan was staring at the walls, past her as if she were invisible. She tried again. "The Shadow finds you bailing out of the budget review this afternoon, he will have your ass, Dan. You know Widmer will go batshit if you aren't there."

His eyes came off the wall to see her in his doorway. "Widmer will go batshit whether I am there or not. He is batshit."

"Yeah, but you'll handle him. If you're not there, the Shadow has to deal with Widmer's tantrums. Big difference."

"Just get me out of it. I'm tied up. As a favor?"

"Maybe. But you do this, and I'll never get my chance to sexually harass you because you will be vapor in the cosmos." Dan was not noticing her, thinking if he had just been a little quicker coming out of the shower . . . "The Shadow is having another cash-flow problem, and he needs a problem with Widmer like he needs another infected tooth. Why don't you give the Shadow a ring, test the water, see how he feels about you bailing out on him today?"

He waved her away, thinking if he had kicked the kid in the face while he was sitting there on the toilet instead of trying to hit him, he might have had a chance. His problem was he was fighting fair.

"They're in there," Baylor said, pulling back the sliding door to her closet. The skirts and dresses were neatly arranged, the hangers equidistant from one another; whites, pale yellows, dusty pinks, light reds, powder blues, and tans. The shoes were lined up on the pale blue carpet in two perfect rows. Blue Girl started to leaf through the pinks, thinking, Maybe there's a nice pair of trousers here. Baylor said, "Maybe you should take a shower first."

"That's a shitty thing to say," Blue Girl said. "I had a shower this morning."

"You want me to be nice to you? Go fuck yourself." Baylor was watching, arms folded, her face showing freckles and an imitation smile.

"You don't have to be nice. But you don't have to be nasty neither. I didn't hurt you."

"You just rob me and hold a gun to my head. But hey, go ahead, steal my clothes. Get that stinky perfume you wear all over everything."

· "It ain't cheap."

"It just smells that way. You gonna try anything on?"

"What would make you the least upset?"

"This old blue summer dress. I always thought it sucked."

"I see what you mean. I'll try it on if it'll make you happy."

"It's not gonna make me happy."

"You gonna go to college, huh. What you gonna study, manners?"

"Just get out of my room, out of my life. Give me a call. I'll be nice to you on the phone. You think your friend is going to kill us?"

"He might, you fuck with him." Blue Girl let that sink in. Like this girl had a lot to learn.

Baylor said, "Try the pink one. No, the one next to that one. Yeah. That could be a color on you. Kinda tarty."

"Hey, maybe a little heat would do you some good, girl. Look at all this tight-ass beige shit. Ain't you got no color? You got nothin hot? You oughta loosen up girl."

"If I'd known you were coming, I'd have got something a little more to your taste. Something cheap and nasty. You know people can see your stupid boobs through that tube top? It's not good for you to go around with no bra on."

"What the hell you know about how a girl's supposed to look? You can't even walk." Blue Girl did a clunky stride across the bedroom, mocking Baylor's flat-footed walk. "You got to learn to walk from the hips, give it a little push, know what I mean? You're a virgin, ain't you, girl? I can tell by the way you walk."

"And you're not. I can tell by the way you walk."

"You all high and hincty cause you got all this shit." Blue Girl did a slow wave around Baylor's bedroom to include the tennis racket, the Rollerblades, skis propped up in the corner, the queen-size bed with the down comforter and the pretty white duvet cover with pink and red roses, the computer, TV, and stereo with CD. "You didn't do nothin for this shit. They just give you all this shit, right? Like free. Like all these fuckin tight-ass little-girl clothes, they all a gift. You didn't do nothin for none of it. All you got to do is sit on your ass, and they bring you any shit you want."

"I didn't steal it. Which is what you are going to do. What would you do with all this, sell it? Buy dope?"

"I don't want none of your shit."

"Then what are you doing here?" Baylor was shouting, furious.

"Hey, calm down, girl, it's gonna be okay. Nobody's gonna hurt you. You goin to college, huh?"

"Premed." Seeing the lack of comprehension in Blue Girl's face, Baylor explained, "It's courses you take to prepare you for medical school."

"What you gonna be, a nurse?"

"An obstetrician."

"Ostra what?"

"Trician. Obstetrician. Deliver babies."

"Shit." Blue Girl went over to the window, looked out over the deep valley and the mountains rising up beyond. "Like Chuleta was sayin this morning. Whole different angle from up here. I never would have thought of that." Blue Girl came back from the window and sat down on the bed, pausing for a moment to look around the room as if there was something there, something that might hurt her. Then she looked into her lap, deciding it's okay to tell. "That's somethin I know somethin about."

"You helped deliver a baby?"

"I had one."

"What happened?"

"Came out blue. And died. Why they call me Blue Girl."

Silver sat across from Page, watching her as she looked out the kitchen window. Thinking, Page was a foxy-looking old lady. Kinda sexy in a funky way. He wondered if she smelled good like his mother did when she came to visit him in the home, bringing him presents, like the pocketknife he still had. Like all she had to do was take him home with her, and she wouldn't do it. Like she didn't have no extra bedroom with just the baby in it. Plenty of room for him. When she came to visit him she lookin hip, wearing a baseball hat, and smelled so good with the perfume. She told him it was going to get better. That she was going to take him back with her to her parents in Minnesota. Fucking Duluth. She showed him a picture of the house, and said he could have the room in the front on the top floor. Same as her room when she was a girl. He thought about that room, of all the stuff he was going to have in it, but she never came back.

Silver wondered if Page fooled around, had a little thing going with like some younger guy on the side. Like some telephone guy came to the house when everybody else was away.

Page thought Silver looked pretty enough to be a girl. Those clear blue eyes with the long lashes. His mouth was soft and pouty under that dopey little mustache that made him look like somebody selling jewelry on TV. Maybe if he shaved off that idiotic mustache, he would be a nice-looking kid. But she still wouldn't trust him. The way he looked at you as if he was watching something behind you; as if you didn't really matter that much. Maybe he is just frightened, she thought. If any of these kids kills me, it will be him. He probably has a knife hidden someplace on him; someplace sweaty. His gun is in his tight trouser pocket.

A toilet flushed upstairs. Chuleta was upstairs. Doing what? Going through their things, stealing her jewelry? Page said, "I have to go to the bathroom."

Silver said, "Hey, no problem, I'll come with you."

"You can't," she said. Thinking—I can't do it if you watch.

"Fine with me. You want to go, just let me know."

Page thought, if I kill him, no one will care. Except he must have had a mother; she would care for her son. She must have cried for him. Changed his diapers, brought him toys to play with. "I thought you were going to rig up the phones," she said.

"Hey," Chuleta said, coming into the kitchen, "you got that right, Lady Page. Set them phones up here, on the kitchen counter."

Silver looked at him like he didn't want to do anything right now. He said, "She says she's gotta go to the toilet. You want me to go with her?"

"You got no sense?" Silver was so dumb sometimes. "You can't ask a lady sit on the toilet with you watchin, bro. You got to leave a woman her dignity. You dis a lady, you don't know what they gonna do." He turned to Page, his small face looking in her eyes as if he saw someone he knew there. His face lit up with a sweet smile, like he was glad to see her.

You could forget, Page thought, that he is just a boy. Only a year or two older than Robby.

Chuleta said, "Blue Girl, she'll go with you she comes back down here. You hang on that long?"

With a minimal nod of her head, Page said yes. Thinking to herself how prudish she was. These teenagers were threatening her life and her children's lives. And these bizarre self-confident adolescents were going around her house acting as if they belonged here. As if there was nothing to worry about. As if they didn't quite realize that something horrible could erupt at any time for no reason. While she was worried that one of them would watch her while she peed. Well it wouldn't be that entertaining for the girl either. But she wasn't really that uptight about being watched on the toilet. What she hated was being watched all the time with no relief. She wanted to get away for a minute, for a rest, for a chance to think. For a chance to do something. She thought of Churley, probably sleeping out in the woodshed. The old fraud should be here, protecting them. Ripping these kids' throats out.

Dan sat at his desk staring at his computer monitor. Buster Keaton stood still as the front of a house fell on top of him. An open window left him standing as if nothing happened. It was Dan's screen saver, and even though he was looking at it, he didn't see it. He was thinking he should start with Widmer. Widmer was rich enough to have fifty thousand-dollar bills in his wallet, but it would take a battalion of marines to take it off him. He should think up some cause for Widmer, something like Guns for God. Get serious, this wasn't funny, but he needed a plan if Widmer was going to give him a dime.

Dan was looking at his watch, seeing 9:30, when the Fisherman Graphic team charged in. Slanski, the short, balding, spiky twenty-eight-year-old animation designer slammed his drawings down on Dan's cluttered desk. "What is this no meeting shit? Gael and I worked our asses off last night."

Gael, the tall art director, was holding back, leaning against the door, shaking her head, saying, "Speak for yourself, Max. I'm always happy to miss a meeting." Gael had a small smile she kept permanently lit beneath her deep-set brown eyes. Dan wondered if she was stoned.

Dan, trying to think of something, said, "My father died last night. There's a lot of arrangements." All good lies are simple. The last thing he wanted was the office knowing, somebody calling the police. He had to get out of there.

"Oh, Dan, I'm sorry." Gael's eyebrows arched concern. "We didn't know." She hugged her layout pad, smiling bravely through her grief. "Was it sudden?"

"No, no, no, lingering," he said, drawing out the word, thinking that was what he was doing, that he had to get moving. Get them out of his office. "A blessing. Now I've got a lotta . . ."

"Does that mean you sign off on the shit we did last night?"

Slanski's eyebrows twitched, sending a row of furrows up to his scalp. Dan saw a decent painter trapped in dragon killer combat video games and putting on weight. Two kids at home and no way out. Would Slanski call the cops if the kids came to his house? Dan said, "Work out a little song and dance with Rebecca. Gael, you do most of the talking and lean over Widmer to show him the layouts and he'll go for it with a low moan."

"You're a sexist oink," Gael said, smiling as if that was just fine. "I'm real sorry about your father."

"Just go," Dan said, holding the bridge of his nose like he had a headache. "Go," he shouted at them, sending them scurrying down the hall.

The Shadow looked up from his desk to see who it was, his blond curls alight from the sun over the bay, a halo around his head. Seeing it was Dan, something dim like ten watts of regret flickered in the Shadow's grey eyes. He went back to his papers, spreadsheets with six-figure numbers in columns and rows, giving Dan a chance to study the top of his head and wonder if Gael was right, if the Shadow wore a wig. Looked like a wig.

"I want you to read this," the Shadow said, holding up a thick blue report, his head down, sniffing over the numbers. "I hate to say it, but I think this fits us like a wet T-shirt." The cover said: Unscrewing the Dim Bulbs—GE Downsizes for Brighter Profits. Across the bottom, small gold letters said: Forbes Executive Report prepared for Garland Grant Junior.

Dan tried again. "I need your help, Garland."

"Is this something you can't handle yourself?" The Shadow was talking to his financial reports, not looking up. His voice had a whiny quality left over from being an ignored only child. "If you can't handle it yourself, maybe we've got the wrong guy on the problem." The Shadow looked up, his face a cherub with a sweet smile and bags under his eyes. "Every time somebody comes in here they've got a monkey on their back, and they try to put it on my back. I've got enough on my back. I don't want your problems." Junior lifted a page of his spreadsheet, peering under the paper as if there could be a spider hiding in there.

Now that Dad was gone, Junior still wore tailored pin-striped British suits with the large shoulder pads, a replica of Senior's proper British banker's suit in every way, except for color. Today's suit was lime green. It made him look like the drummer of a rock band dressed up for his mother's wedding.

Dan sat down in a square of blond-and-fawn upholstery and let Junior's executive report drop quietly on the carpet. Through the green tinge of the window he watched the gulls, white points of light, floating over the dark blue bay. Just above the near shore, a line of pelicans, gangsters in rubber masks, cruised low over the water. There was no time, but you couldn't rush Junior; the man would just retreat farther, like a snail back into his shell. Complete opposite of Page. Page's natural instinct was attack, never retreat. She could overreact, threaten that little squirrel. He could get pissed off, pull the trigger. That skinny good-looking white kid, he had a gun bulging in his tight trousers like he was hot to use it. And Baylor could never keep her mouth shut. Shit, anything could happen. The one who kicked him in the balls, looked like Mike Tyson's little brother, he was acting like he wanted to molest Baylor. Christ, what was stopping him? He had to do this fast, get back there before some horror happened. He didn't have time to sit here, waiting for Garland. But he knew he had to wait for the Shadow to come out of hiding. Out into the land of the living, Rebecca would say.

He had to cleanse the mind of anxiety. Concentrate on the deep blue carpet, heavy, gold, and champagne curved upholstered eighties-modern sofa and chairs. Fresh replicas of Garland's father's office ten years ago, when the company was called G G Graphics. Get it? Go Go? Today's hip is tomorrow's kitsch.

Dan looked at the blond cabinet that opened to

reveal a mirrored cocktail bar and wondered if he should go over and pour himself a brimming glass of gin while he waited for Garland to come out of his shell. It was ten o'clock in the morning. Garland, who drank only designer spring water, would be horrified. How, Dan wondered, do you ask a man for four hundred thousand dollars? Or one? If he told Garland some teenage kids held a gun to Page's head, would he listen? Would the Shadow call his friend the police chief in San Lucas and turn Dan's house into a war zone?

A bronze foghorn rested on top of the old cocktail cabinet, engraved with Garland Grant Sr.'s contribution to graphic marketing: "Keep it simple, keep it sweet, keep repeating." The people in the agency called Junior's office, with some cruelty, Grant's tomb.

Garland Grant Jr.'s pale schoolboy face rose up again from his papers, bushy blond eyebrows lifted in anticipation, lips pursed, mildly pissed off. "You said this was important."

"I need four hundred thousand dollars in cash this afternoon, Garland," Dan said, thinking, oh shit, he should have led up to it. Asked Garland about his boyfriend, his wife, his kids. Confided in him. He should have been a little more circumspect. Less impatient.

Garland Grant Jr. took off his half-frame reading glasses, folded them on his desk, and looked up, his pale face looking younger than his thirty-nine years. And weary, like this was what everybody asked him. "Don't we all," he said.

"You don't understand," Dan said. "I have to have it. For my family. You won't even miss it, and you'll get it back. On any terms you say."

"You know, I'm glad you came in, Dan. I've been meaning to sit down with you. Um, talk about things. Have a little chat. How do you think you're doing here, vis-à-vis your goals?"

"I need the money this afternoon, Garland," Dan said. "Cash. Has to be cash."

"Dan, I've always—"

"Look, I know it's not easy, but you can have my house, my car. I'll pledge anything, sign anything. You'll be saving lives. My life, Page's life. The kids."

"If you are through interrupting." Garland closed his eyes and leaned back, giving Dan the benefit of his wisdom. "One thing I've always believed, Dan, is that you can't buy your way into success." Garland treated Dan to his quickie imitation of a smile. It came and went, leaving his face untouched. Grey eyes peering out, afraid. "But sometimes, Dan, you can listen your way in. You want to borrow nearly a half a million dollars, and I say 'don't we all.' And you go on as if you didn't hear me. Well, uhm, let's uhm, try again. I wish a half a million was all I needed. Do you want to see the figures for our next ten-day forecast?"

Dan shook his head, no. He didn't want to hear any of this.

"We are looking at a $3.5 million shortfall, Dan. Our stock dropped another two and three-eighths this morning—thirty-four percent in three weeks."

Garland leaned forward, his eyes pleading, the whine in his voice pushed aside by real fear. "This is a family business, Dan. Everybody here, from me on down, is part of the Gopher family. We sink or we swim together, and, uhm, the market is flushing our little bowl." He bent over his spreadsheets, lowering his eyebrows, talking to his desk. Man to Man. "Cash flow, it's all cash flow. It's all outgo. Nothing is coming in." Garland looked back up at Dan, pleading now. "Nothing. That's why we've got to twist AmDell's arm. Get them to pay their damn bills. We don't have any new product out there. Your Fisherman project is

three months late and $1,547,000 over budget."
Garland's voice was back to full whine, his face showing migraine pain. "Fisherman is starting to smell like
a dead loss. We are going to have to pick up the pace,
and we are going to have to go through some serious
downsizing. Are you listening? Your team is what,
around two dozen people?"

"Twenty-eight," Dan said.

There was a pause as Garland got up and went
over to the window to stand by the drapes and stare
out at the bay, his little paunch profiled. His hand
rested on a bookcase packed with modern business-
management books. "I want you to lose half of them
by Friday, and I'll tell you how to do it." He turned to
face Dan, his back to the window, keeping his distance
across the sky-blue carpet. "Ask them one by one how
they are improving this company. If they can't tell
you, get rid of them. Let's start with you."

Garland walked back across the room, to come up
to Dan's face like a prosecutor. Garland had missed a
few black bristles on his cheeks shaving. "What are
you doing for me around here apart from asking for
absolutely impossible sums of money before you have
even sat down to work?"

Garland turned around and went back to his
chair, trailing his long fingers along the glass top of his
desk. He sat down and looked up at Dan, his hands
making a soft steeple under his chin.

"Thanks for your help, Garland." Act like you
don't care. Don't need it. You really want something,
walk away from it.

Garland leaned forward on his elbows, genuinely
curious. "What do you want it for?"

"For my family."

"What do you mean your family?"

Dan pictured Garland picking up the phone,

calling his friend the San Lucas police chief, SWAT teams running toward his house. Gunshots. "I can't tell you."

"Oh fuck," he said, sinking back in the soft leather of his chair, "get out." Dan turned to go, and Garland called after him, "Listen, you gonna sit in on Berenson's presentation this morning? He's got some graphic effect like the earth swallowing up Meg Ryan. Should be a lot of fun."

"I can't make it."

"Too bad. I'll see you this afternoon for AmDell's budget review."

Dan stopped in the doorway of Garland's office and turned around. "No you won't."

Garland's voice went soft, caressing. "What do you mean, you won't? You have to. This is balls to the wall day, Danny. If you are not there, they are gonna go for my throat, and I won't know what to tell them. They'll be attacking me for some damn detail, something I never heard of before. It's what they always do to keep from paying us. You understand, we are hanging by a thread. They don't pay us, we have to start firing people. I don't care if you are going to your funeral; you have got to be there."

"Then loan me the 400,000," Dan said, coming back to Garland's desk.

"You have a drug problem?" Garland said, leaning away from Dan like he had bad breath. "Actually, forget that. I don't give a shit what your problem is. We are sinking, and if you are not at that meeting, you won't be in trouble, you'll be out on your ass, facing a lawsuit for gross incompetence." Garland flashed his cherub smile again. "Okay?"

"How about 200,000, then, Garland? Pay you back tomorrow." Dan had no idea when he could pay the money back. He didn't care. Or not care. He couldn't think that far ahead. Take what you can get and keep moving. Whatever it takes.

"Jesus, you are a lousy listener, Dan. I don't have two cents. I've got creditors crawling up my ass looking for loose change."

Dan turned to go. "Always an inspiration talking to you, Garland," he said, thinking—walk away.

"But you'll be there this afternoon."

"You are still not hearing me, Garland. If you don't lend me the money, I can't be there." Dan was headed out the door again.

"Wait a minute." Garland was up out of his chair again, coming across the soft blue carpet in soft green canvas shoes. "Listen."

Dan stopped. "I've got a lot to do."

"Ah, what about $50,000."

"What do you mean?"

"I mean 50,000. I'll loan you 50,000. Get the cash to your office by lunchtime. I can take it out of your salary. Just be there."

"Garland, $50,000 isn't going to help. I need 400,000 in cash this afternoon." Dan started to go again. "I can't tell you why, but we are talking about my family's lives."

Garland put a hand on his shoulder. "Okay, 100,000, but don't jerk me around. That's 100,000 more than I can afford. I've got to borrow it myself, so I'll have to add the interest."

"In cash?"

"You want unmarked bills? Just a joke. Just be there this afternoon, goddamn it." Garland's arm followed his hand around Dan's shoulder. "Listen, I have a family, you've met Daphne, I know it can be tough sometimes." Garland gave Dan a hug for emphasis. "But if we don't get a transfusion from AmDell, our little happy Gopher family of"—Garland swept his free

arm out to include the Gopher main building and the
entire Gopher campus complex of office buildings scattered across fifteen acres—"4,557 computer geeks will
be out on the street. Talk about littering."

8

Whopper opened one drawer of Robby's built-in dresser, a nest of underpants and balled-up socks. Mostly white sweat socks. Mostly *single* white sweat socks. He slammed it shut, opened another. Blue jeans. Whopper pulled out a pair and held it up against his waist. The legs were long enough, but the waist was like a girl's, way too small. "What you got, looks white?"

Robby watched unhappily. Worried that Whopper might have seen his stash of *Club* magazines stuffed under the socks. Hating watching somebody going through his stuff. Especially Whopper. The guy was so numb. "You mean like a white shirt?" he said, thinking how satisfying it would be to kick Whopper in the nuts.

"No, fool. I mean somethin makes me look like I live here. In this house. Like you got somethin maybe too big for you? Somethin I can wear?"

"There's a lot of baggy stuff in that drawer," Robby said, pointing.

Whopper opened the drawer and pulled out a

pair of baggy black shorts. "Shit, man, that's like what I'm wearin."

"Then what do you need to change for?"

Whopper gave Robby his killer look and went over to the closet. He ruffled through the shirts and jackets hanging on hangers like a shopper in a men's store. "So what's your sister like?" he said, pulling out a black sports jacket with silver threads woven in the fabric, wishing he was watching her, the sister, what's her name. Baylor. Helping Baylor get dressed. Those nice little pink titties.

"She's a pain in the ass. Blue Girl's really nice. What's she like?"

"She's like a worse pain in the ass."

"She can't be worse. Baylor picks her nose when she thinks nobody's looking." Whopper was holding the jacket up to the light coming in the window as if he were checking it out for stains.

"Hey, take the jacket. Be my guest. I only wore it once to a dopey wedding."

Whopper wedged himself into the jacket and looked at himself in the mirror; the jacket was stretched tight across the shoulders and his arms stuck out straight, with the sleeves ending halfway down his forearms. No way was it going to button. "Pick her nose, huh?" Whopper looked at himself again, wishing there was some way he could wear the jacket. It had a kind of suburban class, real conservative, like the kind of clothes he was going to buy for himself when he got the money. But again, he would go gold with the threads and buttons. *Gotta have gold buttons.* "I bet you pick your nose, whack off to those dirty magazines I saw in your dresser drawer."

"Fuck you," Robby said.

Whopper looked at Robby in the mirror, turned, and backhanded the boy across the side of the head with the ease and speed of a tennis player, the blow making a wet smacking sound, knocking Robby hard against the wall, leaving a red welt on his cheek. Blood leaked from Robby's nose. To his shame, Robby felt tears start down his cheeks. Shit, he thought. Shit, shit, shit.

"Don't you dis Whopper, hear?" Whopper turned away to look in the closet again. "Ain't you got nothin fits? Go in the bathroom, wipe your fuckin nose."

Four phones were lined up on the edge of the kitchen counter. Silver was explaining, "Okay, the first one is the girl's phone, second one belongs to the boy, third one is hers"—he nodded toward Page—"and the one on the end belongs to the daddy."

"Mark them," Chuleta said, waving his gun across the phones.

"Hey it's easy to remember. The first one . . ."

"Easy for you 'cause you set them up. You don't want the girl all upset answerin Daddy's phone. Get a Magic Marker, write the names on them."

"Yeah, okay. The other phone over there on the kitchen table is yours. You can listen in to any phone, and yours is the only one that can call out 'cause I set them up with a D4 buffer loop. So yours is like the command phone. You want me to paint it red?"

"Paint it gold, 'cause that's what's gonna come out of it."

"If I can't call out, how can I make my calls?" Page asked from the end of the kitchen table. "People are expecting me to call them."

"Then they'll call you," Chuleta said. "You tell them you've been on the toilet all mornin. The fuck is this?" he said, big smile moving across his small face.

Whopper stood in the kitchen doorway: white

tennis sneakers, powerful Hersey-brown bowlegs
sticking out of white shorts, his arms bulging out of a
white-on-white tennis shirt. He moved into the room
with his head down, studying the black-and-white
diamond pattern of the kitchen floor, saying, "All the
kid's shit is too small. I can't get none of it on. So I
tried the man's suit, like I was some kind of executive,
I could be that. Only the pants was too long, draggin
on the floor. This the only stuff I find that fit."

Page couldn't stifle a snort. "Dan's tennis outfit,"
she said, her hand flying up to her face to keep from
laughing.

"Perfect," Chuleta said.

Whopper looked up and nailed Chuleta with his
eyes. "The fuck I got to look like a fuckin monkey
for?"

"Hey don't ask him, ask your momma, Whopper."
Blue Girl was standing in the doorway behind
Whopper, wearing a pale yellow summer dress and
sandals. She walked past him, her dress swishing,
smiling at Chuleta. Stopping in the middle of the
kitchen, she twirled around, making the skirt fly out.

Whopper put his hand on her shoulder, stopping
her. "Hey, bitch," he said quietly. "We get out of here,
I'm gonna cut you, serve you up. Teach you respect
for a man's momma."

"Whopper," she said, honey and grit in her voice,
"we all G's here. Got to help each other, stay focused,
know what I'm sayin?"

Chuleta, moving toward Whopper with the barrel
of his gun pointed at Whopper's stomach, said, "You
right, Blue Girl looks sweet enough to eat." He gave
her his big smile, his little squirrel face making her
frown drop a notch. "Meantime, you be nice to her.
Meantime means now." He gave the gun barrel a little
jerk for emphasis, and Whopper took his hand off Blue

Girl's shoulder. Chuleta lowered the barrel and came up to Whopper, putting his arm around Whopper's shoulders, talking as if Whopper was his little brother. "See what it is, is costumes. What you wear and where you are is who you are in America. Like you a playboy now. On your way to spend the afternoon at your tennis club. It's like that location, location, location shit, you know what I'm sayin?" Whopper's forehead was still wrinkled, eyes looking doubtful. "We been wearin the wrong shit, hangin out the wrong places. You want to change your life, the place to start is what you wear. And where you wear it."

Whopper, head down, said to the floor, "Back in the hood this stuff look like shit."

"Well, bro, you put your old homey clothes back on, go on back to the hood, take a bullet backside of your head, come out the front of your face. See how good you look then."

The phone rang, and Chuleta jumped. "Shit, which one is it? I thought you was gonna mark them."

"Hey that was like a second ago. Gimme a second, bro." The phone rang again.

"Fuck, listen." Chuleta put his head down on the second phone as there was another ring. "This one," he said, pointing to the third phone. "Call's for you." Page looked back at him, shaking her head. "Hey, what's the matter? You got flu. You feel terrible. You're sorry, but you can't go out and see nobody, you just want to stay home. You'll feel better tomorrow. Come on."

The phone rang again.

"You're in real estate, right? Shit, you can tell a good story. You don't want nobody comin round here. Keep it simple." Another ring. He held up the phone in one hand, his other casually pointing the gun at Page.

"I can't talk if you point that at me," she said. It rang again.

"Oh, yeah, sorry. Here, take the damn thing." Chuleta handed Page the white instrument that had been her kitchen phone for years and let the barrel of his gun point down at the floor.

Her eyes on Chuleta, Page picked up the phone, and said, "Hi," with a rasp in her voice. "No, no, fine, Lucille. Yeah, look, I'm really sorry, but I've got this wretched flu, I might as well be chained to the toilet."

She looked away from his narrow face, the hair falling over his bright black eyes, to her kitchen window; the little violet was finally about to bloom again. Outside it was a bright warm spring morning. She didn't even get her run. Sometimes Churley came with her. Where was he? "No, listen Lucille. I can't get in today. I know, I know. Look in my files under 1272 Hamilton, there's a contract in there. Just copy what you need. Could you cover for me today? Call that woman at 850 Kidder, tell her we we will bring the food for the open house on Tuesday, just get that damn mangy dog out and get somebody to clean the kitchen. In as nice a way as only you know how. Would you? That's wonderful. If she'd spent the money to stage it, it would have sold weeks ago. No, I've had this before, nothing to worry about. No, really if you could field the calls, and call Pacific Title, that would be a lifesaver. Oh, Hopper. That Eichler on Hopper was ratified last night? Yeah, finally. So call Pacific Title, make sure they have everything they need. Do what you have to do, I'd be really grateful. I just don't want to talk to anybody today—Omigod." Page stood up, looking past Chuleta and Whopper. "Omigod, I've got to run, and you don't want to know why. Good-bye." She hung up and ran across the room, pushing past Chuleta and Whopper, stopping

just short of her son. She looked up at him, wanting to
hug him and not doing it because she knew he would
hate that in front of everybody. "Robby, sweetheart,
what did they do to you?"

Robby looked away, out the kitchen window to
the driveway. "Hey, it was nothing. Don't worry about
it." Thinking, Jesus don't make him look like a wimp
in front of Blue Girl, with his damn mother fussing
over him. He could take it, and he would get the
sucker back, but damn, Blue Girl looked amazing in
Baylor's dress. He gave her a confident smile. Kinda
smile maybe Keanu Reeves would give her after he
came out of the smoking elevator shaft with a gash on
his scalp and not caring.

Page said, "There's blood on your lip. He hit you."

"It wasn't anything."

"You son of a bitch," Page yelled, going for Whopper.
Whopper took a step back and gave her an easy chop
to her side, sending Page skidding awkwardly across
the kitchen floor, half-catching herself and crashing
headfirst against the barstools under the kitchen
counter. "I'm not a son of a bitch. I'm my momma's
boy, just like he is," Whopper said. "I didn't hurt
him."

"Chill, homey," Blue Girl said. "She's a lady, like a
momma worried 'bout her boy. You don't have to be
hittin everybody." Blue Girl turned her back on him
and knelt, holding out her hand to help Page up from
the floor.

Page was on her hands and knees, feeling dizzy. A
needle of pain spread out to hundred of needles stuck
inside her forehead. Blue Girl was waiting patiently,
bending over Page, her hand outstretched.

Page ignored Blue Girl's hand and started to get
up, saying, "That dress doesn't belong to you. Take it
off and put it back where you found it."

Blue Girl stood up and looked down at Page still on her hands and knees on the floor. "You ain't got no class at all," she said.

Page sat on the living-room sofa, looking out through the large window at the end of the house, making a mental checklist, alone for a change to her great relief. She didn't know where Silver was, somewhere. Fiddling with the phones, it didn't matter; as long as he wasn't watching her she felt as if she had been let out of a cage. She liked looking out onto the field of tall dry grass that fell into a deep valley and into the woods, the grass under the first few trees like a park. On the other side of the valley dark clouds rose over the top of the ridge, fog from the ocean. Their black shadows slid across the ridges and canyons of the mountains. The clock radio on the white wicker end table read 10:17.

Page made a mental list. Baylor was in the game room, watching some dumb guys-running, things-blowing-up movie on TV with Blue Girl. Chuleta, with that horrible gun, was upstairs again. She could hear him moving around in the bedroom with that Whopper creature and Robby. Going through Dan's things to see if there was something that made that boy look less like a bad joke. Dan was at work or with the police, she had no idea. How could he possibly raise any money? They were just scraping by, not saving anywhere near enough for Baylor and Robby's college education. Dan had made all that fuss about a security system, and these hoodlums had just waltzed right in. Well, she had opened the door for them. Churley was probably still asleep out there.

Security was an idea she had never really understood. Men liked to talk about security; they like to lean back in their chairs like they were cowboys with

their boots on, and talk about security as if it were
something you could make, like a fence. There was no
security in nature. Out there on the mountain there
were deer and cougars and bobcats and coyotes and
hawks, squirrels, mice, hummingbirds, little slippery
newts alongside the creeks. Not a single one of those
creatures was secure. Not one.

She remembered walking along Ohlone Creek last
summer. If the trees didn't hide the creek at the bottom of the valley, she could see the spot from here.
She had come down from the sunny ridge on a
switchback path and was headed back for the road,
enjoying the coolness of the air after the hot sun, the
deep shade and the sunlight coming through in long
shafts of yellow light. The clear water burbled, and if
you looked carefully, you could see trout suspended
above the pebbles, killing time, and clouds rippling on
the surface of the water. She was startled to see a deer
lying still on the wet bank alongside the water. Too
still; it was a moment before she realized it was just
the deer's head. The eyes were open and bright, deep
liquid brown, the gentle startled look of deer eyes.
Below the neck all of the flesh had been stripped off
the rib cage, the ribs standing out against the leaves
and grass of the stream bank with little flecks of red
meat still clinging to the bone as if the deer had been
scraped with a knife. She thought it was probably the
work of some berserk hunter and hurried back to the
road, looking over her shoulder, feeling the electric
zing of near panic until she was standing out in an
open field in the sun again. When she told Dan about
it, he said that it was a mountain lion. That the big cats
cut up their prey and bury a piece at a time nearby; a
leg, say, or a shoulder to feed on later. And that the
mountain lion had probably been a few yards away,
watching her.

Now wild children were inside her home because she had invited them in. So why couldn't she think? They were children, really; almost the same age as her kids. Which was worse. This was her house, her space and castle, the place she had worked so hard for, the showplace for her real-estate business. The home for her family. The house where she ate and slept and made love. There had to be a way to get them out. She turned in her seat to see if someone was in the room, or standing in the doorway, watching her. No one.

Robby seemed okay, and the lump on her forehead had stopped stinging. So no one was hurt yet, but that could change in an instant. She turned back to look out the window. Two hawks were circling over the first high ridge, riding a current. They could see the ocean from up there and the whiskers on a bobcat, she thought. She watched the dark birds circle in a blue sky, feeling that her house was a cage now. And she couldn't get out because she couldn't leave the children behind.

There was a slight pressure and a warmth on the back of her hand. Page looked down and saw a hand resting on hers. She yelped and jumped up out of the couch, facing him. He must have crept up from behind, the little sneak.

Silver was holding his hands up in front of him, like hey, quiet down, no offense, no danger. "I didn't mean to scare you," he said.

"Well you did."

"I just wanted to see if you were OK. I mean you took a hit in the head back there, and I thought, if you wanted somethin, like a glass of water or a beer or somethin, I could get it for you."

"A glass of water," Page said, anxious to get rid of him if only for a minute or two. She stood up and watched him go. Why, she wondered, do I think he is the weakest? Because he tries to be nice? Why does he look so creepy? It'd be nice to think I could shoot him with that gun he carries in his pocket, but there's no point thinking like that. If there was a way I could set him against the others, make him get rid of them . . .

He was back too soon. What did he do, run?

When Silver handed her a glass of water Page put it down on the glass end table without taking a sip. "What's your mother like," she said, with just a hint of a smile, as if she was interested in him.

"I got some pictures of her, and she was real pretty, like she maybe coulda been a model like an actress or somethin if she hadn't had kids." Thinking, his mother was a lyin bitch.

"Was?"

"Yeah, she like died when I was thirteen." He remembered the kid, one of the seniors, telling him at the home he was in then. He could feel the cold coming in from the window, see the sunlight making a pattern on the floor like bars. The guy telling him the social worker wanted to see him. And he asked the guy what for. And the guy said your mother died. He wanted to kill the guy, but the news hit him so hard he felt like he was underwater, sinking, no arms, no legs, no nothing. His mother told him she was coming to see him before Christmas. Another lie. She always lied.

"Who brought you up, then?" Page said, sitting down again, looking up at Silver.

"My aunt for a while, then she moved out and we stayed in the house until they threw us out because there wasn't nobody pay the rent."

"So you what, went to live in a foster home?"

"I was in foster homes before that. They were like a preview of what it would be like to be in a prison, you know what I mean?"

Page gave him her short professional smile and nod as if she understood.

He shook his head. "No you don't know what I mean. I mean like this is another planet here. The last foster home I was in had dirty green tiles like an old lavatory in the halls and smelled like piss. There was always all this noise, somebody always yellin. It was like you were doin time because all you wanted to do was get out, and they wouldn't let you without a whole bunch of bullshit like credit points for good behavior. Which was just a way to shut you up because you couldn't do nothin without losin credit points."

"Sit down." Page patted the cushion next to her and gave him a nice smile. He sat down carefully, not leaning back. "Where do you live now?"

"Well, you know, I don't want to tell you too much, but I guess it don't hurt to say for a while there I lived with the gang. We had our own house, you know. Like we owned it."

Page thinking, these children own a house? They couldn't spell escrow let alone come up with the down payment. "How do you own a house?"

"One of the kids, Boxer, was dealin a shitload, and the dealer got short of cash, gave it to him. Got lawyers fix up the deed and shit. Boxer got shot in the face, but it don't matter 'cause as long as the taxes get paid, nobody gives a shit. Anyway I ain't never goin back there again. Every damn day some gangbangers drivin by shootin. You be kickin it there, on the porch, or maybe you just walk out the front door, you have to be lookin both ways, watch every car, be on the point twenty-four seven." He looked back and forth, like a spectator at a tennis match. "'Cause soon as you let go, kick back, that's when one of them snake you. One of your best friends in the world gets shot in the head, in the neck, in the stomach, you lose your best friend, and that's when you get deep into it."

"You think this is the way to get out?"

"Hey, I'm open to suggestions." He looked at her, hands up, like don't shoot, waiting for an answer. "So what do you think I'm gonna do? Go to college like your kids? Listen, I was in George Washington High School, and I got good grades." Page lifted an eyebrow. "Nobody was helpin me, and nobody gave a shit. I was doin it all myself, and I got good grades. And I called up the State College in San Lucas, see if they send me an application. You know what they tell me? They tell me it don't make no difference what grades I get 'cause the high school is so shitty no college in the world is gonna take me. Can you believe that shit?"

"Who told you?"

"What I said. Some bitch in the office at San Lucas State. I called them up, they said, like fuck off. We don't want nobody from Washington. I mean I can see that 'cause sometimes you just copy shit out of a book and they give you an A. See what I'm sayin? The only job I can get is like McDonald's out in the suburbs 'cause nobody who lives out there will work for that kind of money. Can't get one in downtown because your like Burger King, 7-Eleven, Jack in the Box, they only want to hire adults now, and there's ten of them for every job."

"Come on. If my kids can get a job, you can."

"Hey, I had a job with the phone company 'cause they hirin inner-city kids. Some federal program. Government was payin the phone company to hire us, they pay us minimum wage, pocket the difference for what they call administration. Anyway, you know, it was simple stuff, but I learn fast, know what I'm sayin? And I liked that shit. Lasted like five weeks, then they fired me and all the other kids. One mornin we show up for work and the gates locked. We hang around for a while and a guy comes out and says piss off. Like somebody cut the fundin. Listen you got some ideas, share them with me, sister, I'm happy to hear them. Hey, I know I could be out there on the street sellin concrete candy-like crack makin a hundred, two a night. Like my friend Keno, he's puttin away five hundred a week. But I don't want to live like that. Some dude always pullin a knife or a gun on you. Slugs comin around all the time wantin a cut, throw your ass in jail you don't give them what they want. So you tell me. See what I'm sayin?"

"No, I don't see. I hear of a lot of excuses, but do you have a plan? I mean, have you any idea what you are going to do with our money? Oh, I know, you're going to put it into schools."

"Hey, come on. Don't jerk me around. Yeah, I got a plan. And it starts with gettin way the fuck away from this place." Silver put his arm on the back of the sofa, behind Page. "I got a lotta plans." He leaned close to Page, long thin nose, the black hairs on his upper lip shining, wide and soft lower lip stretching into a smile, perfect white teeth behind the smile, not much older than Robby, maybe seventeen, eighteen at the most, Page guessed. He said, "You know. you got a really nice body on you."

Page stood up quickly, shaking. "You have a lot to learn."

Silver leaned back, sinking into the comfortable cushions, smiling up at Page. "You could teach me," he said.

The next night she was waiting for him, holding up the sheet for him to get into bed with her. Seeing he was a little skinny kid limping and acting like he was sore all over. He climbed in and she rolled over, turning her back to him as if she could accept him, but she couldn't face him. "What's your name?" he said.

She thought for a moment and decided to tell him her real one. "Alice," she said. "What's yours?"

"Chuleta."

"Huh-uh. Nobody called Chew-later."

"Means little chop in Español. Like pork chop."

"Jeeesuuus," she said, still turned away from him. Smiling for the first time in weeks. "Nobody called Pork Chop neither. Little Pork Chop. Shit, that's worse."

"Yeah, well, my dad said my name was really Chu wheh ta."

"Chew way to what? Shit, that's bad as pork chop. What's that s'posed to mean?"

"Means coyote in Alonie."

That got her, and she sat up in bed, her stitches giving her a sharp sting between her legs, reminding her she was supposed to lie flat. Looking down at his little face, she said, "You the coyote?"

"That's right," he said, age thirteen. "I hang the moon."

"You don't hang no moon," she said, grinning. Glad to see him. "You already tole me Hawk, she the one be hangin the moon." She gave him her high-ass hincty look, make him smile. "She hang the sun, too."

———— CHAPTER ————

The game room was on the uphill side of the house with doors leading to the living room, the laundry room, the deck, and the kids' bedrooms. It was a big room, paneled in oak, with rows of books, a pinball machine, a pool table, and a built-in wide-screen TV and sound system. Baylor sat on the chamois-leather sofa with her legs drawn up, wearing a sweatshirt, blue jeans, and sneakers. Blue Girl sat on the Persian rug, in Baylor's yellow summer dress, arms around her knees, leaning against the sofa at Baylor's feet. They were watching *Family Feud*, the fogbound fifty-two-inch SuperWideScreen TV flickering pale light in their faces.

"You wonder why they do it," Baylor said.

A woman with bags under her eyes made a prune of her mouth, straining, trying, for eleven points, to name something that married couples share that they wouldn't share with anybody else.

"My hood the answer be needles," Blue Girl said.

"Why they do what?" Baylor said without looking away from the screen.

"Go on TV and make fools of themselves."

"We already fools, girl. Shit, I'd do it. Lookit that woman, she's gonna win ten thousand dollars."

"You'd do anything for money, wouldn't you?" Baylor said, still staring at the screen.

"You ain't got no money, what else you gonna do? You bet your ass nobody is gonna ask me to be on no game show. See the only way you can get some money is to have some. You ain't got none, you can't get none. Like Chuleta says, you gotta break out or you stay in."

"You could work."

"Sure, that five dollars an hour pile up so fast you can almost pay the rent long as you don't eat and don't buy no clothes. Jesus," she said, turning from the screen to the doorway, "what happened to you?"

Whopper was coming in the room, a little bounce to his step, wearing the rainbow colors of a warm-up suit. "Thought I'd remove the dangers of you ladies goin crazy over the sight of bare Whopper flesh. It's what you wear going to and from the tennis court." Whopper grinned, pleased with himself. Then he frowned, pointing to the TV. "What's this shit?"

"Called *Family Feud*. I thought you was supposed to be watchin Robby, fool."

"He here. The Robby be just a little shy round you, Blue Girl. Come on out, my man."

"Shit, you the one oughta be shy, Whopper. You got plenty to be shy about." She called out, "Robby?"

"I'm not shy," Robby said to the polished oak floor, coming around the corner from the living room.

Blue Girl patted the turquoise-and-gold Persian rug. "Come on sit down next to Blue Girl."

"Yeah, right, well, okay," Robby said, moving over to the other end of the sofa and falling down on the floor in a big way, not looking at her. Like it was no big deal, sitting practically in her lap. Smelling her perfume.

Whopper sat down on the sofa next to Baylor's feet, watching her from the corner of his eye, then gave his attention to the screen. "What you watchin this shit for? Lotta good cookin shows on in the mornin. Who's got the remote?"

"Cooking show?" Baylor scrunched up her face.

"Yeah. What's wrong with that? I bet you couldn't boil a damn egg. Come on, change the channel, maybe they got a movie on. Gimme the remote." On the screen, the ex-husbands were trying to guess the three things wives never tell their husbands.

"Don't give it to him," Blue Girl said. "He'll just surf around, drive you crazy."

"'Cause I got a lively mind. 'Sides, how you know there ain't nothin good on? Like maybe one of them cable channels they got a rerun of *Reservoir Dogs*. Member that, cop is tied to a chair and the guy just got out of jail slices off the cop's ear?"

"Yeah, right," Robby said. "Then that guy gets blown away by the undercover cop so the gangster's kid comes in and shoots the cop in the face. Cool."

Coming into his branch of First Citizen's/Ameribank in Mountain View, Dan thought they ought to be serving Big Macs; the place had bright lights, a low ceiling, bright red carpet, dying palms in pots, and yesterday's air. The tellers waited behind the counter with the same weary look as the kids trapped behind the counter at McDonald's. Dan went to a teller with her head down, counting twenties. The engraved name plate on her counter said Elena Parisi. Her hair was curled and teased high for maximum effect, her lips moved as she counted, and a little gold cross dangled between her impressive breasts. Pictures of her two- and three-year-olds were on the side of the cubicle. Elena said hi how are you this morning and Dan said less than perfect. He said he'd like to withdraw his CD, and she said she would have to have authorization to do that. Ms. Brockow, third desk, two rows back, will see him, Elena said, pointing.

There was a low chair alongside Ms. Brockow's desk. Dan had to half turn and look up to talk to her like a schoolboy at the side of his teacher's desk. She held up a hand indicating just a minute. He waited.

Her desk was fragrant with furniture wax and piled with work to be done. Ms. Brockow was a platinum blond with blond eyebrows and a long Scandinavian face with plenty of bright red lipstick, long legs and a long neck. She had a red tailored suit showing a lot of padding at the shoulder, a low-cut yellow satin blouse with green parrots, and a serious hairdo, hanging down straight and long at the back, with a low wave at the front, signifying that she dealt with more serious financial concerns than the country singers behind the teller's counter.

She got Dan's name and account numbers, listened to him ask for his money, and looked at her computer screen as if it smelled bad. She tapped a pile of papers with her pencil as if she was waiting for Dan to go away. She punched some more buttons, frowned at the screen again, and looked up. "I'm sorry, Mr. Messina, it's against bank policy. And even if I could, we just don't keep that much cash on hand here."

"Suppose I went to your main office in San Lucas?"

"Well, I expect they would have the funds, but they would still need five working days to process your withdrawal of your CD. Subject to substantial penalties as I mentioned."

"It's my money."

"Of course it's your money. If you like, I can show you the terms of the agreement you signed when bought your 365-day certificate of deposit. Or tell you what, would you like talk to Mr. Hong? He's our branch manager."

Dan, thinking of Page at home in her sweat suit, said, "I'll talk to anybody. Bring him out of his cage."

"Oh, he's not here, Mr. Messina." She gave Dan a smile, forgiving him his naïveté. "Mr. Hong manages all our Peninsula branches. He's in the main office. I'll ring him for you if you like."

Dan nodded, and Ms. Brockow punching the numbers in her phone, said, "Hi, Dick, I have a customer for you," and handed the phone to Dan.

As he took the phone Dan thought he should call Page. Her face loomed in his mind, looking wistful, hopeful, frightened. Focus, he told himself, focus. "Look, I need your help. I've been a customer here for ten years, and I have a sudden and severe financial emergency. I need to cash in my CDs and withdraw all of my savings and checking accounts. Can you do that for me?"

A pause.

"No, dammit today. I need the money today."

Another pause.

"No, I'm not going to take a deep breath for a couple of days. Tomorrow is too late, let alone next week. Let me talk to the president. Of the bank, goddamn it. São Paulo?" There was another pause. "What's he doing in São Paulo? Never mind. I am talking about my children's life, for God's sake."

There was another pause, and Dan put the phone down.

"He always says no," Ms. Brockow said. "Dick's a real prick." She smiled wistfully at her joke. "I mean,

I'd love to help you, I really would, but he'd fire my ass right out of here."

"Thanks for letting me talk to him."

"I was just trying to help. I mean there's always a chance."

"You think so? Look, just sign this check so I can take the money out of my checking account."

"I'm sorry, but without sufficient prior written notice we can only let you withdraw $500 in cash at any one time from our Premier Lo-Ball Moneysaver checking account."

"I'll come back. Cash 500, go out the door and come back, okay?"

"In any twenty-four-hour period."

"Suppose I asked for a banker's check for the combined balance in my savings and checking account."

She checked his printout again and wrote the numbers down. "That's $3,748 combined checking and savings including the $1.87 interest we credited to your account on the twenty-third. Yes, we could do that. The service fee would be $17.50, so actually the total would come to $3,720.50. Would that be all right?" She smiled the smile of a woman who has found the answer.

"No way you can cash my CD?"

"Not today, no. Not without five working days' notice, minimum. And of course the substantial penalty for early withdrawal. I wish I could, Mr. Messina, but no, I'm sorry, no way. Just go stand in line over there, tell the cashier what you want, and I'll sign a banker's check."

"Where do you keep the cash?"

"I beg your pardon?"

"Just a thought."

The cashier cut Dan a check, he went back to Ms. Brockow's desk, got her signature, and cashed it. A hand tapped him on the shoulder. Mrs. Brockow said, "The Dan Messina? Doom Room man?"

Dan nodded, eager to get moving.

"Could I have your autograph? My son was crazy over your game. He said it's what really got him going on computers. He's in medical school now," she said, as Dan signed the back of a blank deposit slip. "I know he'll love to have it." As he went out the door, she called after him, "If I could help, I would."

Meritage Discount Brokers was half a mile away in the Town and Country Mall. Senior Investment Marketing Consultants Sam and Ambrose ran the franchise behind the desks and phones.

Ambrose, the one with the skull-cut fuzz on his cranium and the gaunt and wary look of a wolf on ice, was talking numbers on the phone, saying, ". . . a million six, a million six five." He looked like a skinhead in a pin-striped suit, gripping the phone with both hands, saying, "Yeah, well the trick with derivative hedges is balance. You go short now, you are going to capsize belly up if the market gets stormy. You want to talk microcap variables for ballast?"

Dan went for Sam because Sam was "his" broker.

Sam, a mild round face with round gold-rimmed glasses, wore an expensive, freshly pressed, lime green, raspberry red, and grapefruit yellow lumberjack shirt and blue jeans. Not as woodsy as Dan's rumpled red flannel lumberjack shirt, Dan thought. Not as sincere. More San Francisco than Silicon Valley. Sam's face, polished as an apple, beamed good fortune and gladness. Even with his bald spot, he looked around the same age as Ambrose; twenty-four, twenty-five. Maybe younger.

"Hiya, uh, Dan, right? It is Dan, isn't it? How are

you keeping, Dan? Good to see you." Sam turned his attention to one of the four monitors on his desk. "The market is drifting today, no real energy, kinda bouncing back and forth, shore to shore with not a lot of water in between. I'm keeping my ears open for the roaring in the distance, could be we're in for a real Niagara if you know what I mean. If you are planning to do anything, I'd say sell. Let me pull up your account. What's your last name again, Dan?"

Dan put his hands on Sam's desk and leaned over, thinking that the kid couldn't be much out of high school. "Messina," he said.

Dan tried to picture Robby in a job like this, cheerful as a balloon, full of corporate policy helium. But the picture wouldn't focus. Robby couldn't do this job for ten minutes. He was too bright and too goofy for a job like this. Robby could be what, a stunt pilot? Except his mind wandered. One day, Dan thought, he would have an answer for Robby. It would come to him, about ten minutes after the kid took off for Ethiopia or got a degree in particle physics. Dan felt a stab in his gut as he pictured his fourteen-year-old son, brave and confused and frightened. Those kids were so much tougher than Robby, and they had guns. They could kill him, shoot him. In the head. Dan sucked in air.

"You okay, Dan?"

"If I sell all of it," Dan said ignoring him, "how soon can I have the cash?

"You want to sell all of it?" Sam looked up from his screen. "Gee, I don't know. Looks to me, we're talking, off the top of my head," he bent over his calculator, tapping the numbers quickly, "Four ninety, maybe five here. If I were you, I'd hang on to the Chrysler until this electric vehicle thing shakes out. I mean, I know it looks like a long shot, but the upside is like double your money, and downside the stock hangs where it is."

"All of it, goddamn it. Sell all of it. How soon, Sam?"

"Hey, relax. Three working days, corporate. Five working days, private. We're looking at a week from today."

"How much of it could you advance me now?"

"None."

"Fuck!" Dan slammed his hand down on the desk, making Sam jump in his chair.

For a moment the smile was gone from the stockbroker's eager, round face, then it came back. "Hey, look, don't get mad, Dan. I'm sorry, man, but we get that question fifty times a day, and the answer is engraved in the stone of my mind. Listen, if you need a pile of cash, what's your feeling about a margin loan?"

"I don't have any feeling about it. What's a margin?"

"Your margin loans got kind of a bad rep because a lot of traders use the money to buy long thinking the market's going up. Market goes down, and they get whacked. Fact is margins are a leading indicator of maybe a crash is coming because right before '29 and '87 you had a record number of punters going margin in the euphoria of a rising market. Another fact is, margins are gonna catch on real soon because the rates are pegged to the broker call rate, which is way lower than your car and mortgage. Another good thing about your margin loan is as long as you pay the interest, you can pay them back anytime you feel like it. And if that isn't enough for you, uh, Dan, and if you have an account with us over a hundred thou, which you do, there's no fee. Which means you can borrow—"

"My problem isn't getting the money, it's getting it

today in cash," Dan interrupted. "When can I have the money?"

"Hey, this afternoon, no problem. You fill out some forms, give me a couple of hours to set it up, then all I have to do is write you a check. The law says I can let you have"—Sam punched numbers on his keyboard, peering into his screen—"Fifty percent on your stocks, that would be"—he punched more keys on his keyboard his keys flying like supermarket checkout clerk—"in round numbers that would be 178,000, plus . . . Plus you can borrow seventy-five percent on your corporate bonds, for uh, wait a sec, 68,000, eighty-five percent on your municipals, for, coming right up, 42,000 and ninety-five percent on your treasuries but you don't have any treasuries. So that would be, uh, 288,000 at, and I have to tell you this is the preferred rate for the heavy hitters with loans above the 200,000 mark, at 4.8 percent."

Dan thought 288,000 plus 100,000 from Garland plus his 3,000 from his checking account would be 391,000. Almost there. Except all he had in his pocket so far was 3,720 from his checking account. Maybe Garland would come through, but he couldn't count on it. Garland could change his mind or forget. Garland was great about forgetting things he didn't want to do. He wouldn't trust Garland to pick up the mail. "Fine, do that. Can you do it in cash?"

"Oh no no no. We never touch the stuff. If you need cash, I could do a wire transfer, and maybe your bank could give you cash. But you better arrange it with them and make sure they have it. They don't like to have the stuff lying around 'cause they can't make any money on it."

"Can I use your phone?"

Back at First Citizen's/Ameribank Susan Brockow spread her hands wide on her well-waxed desk, leaned back in her soft leather chair, and said into her headset, "Sure. I think. It depends on the float, and if it's a drop-off day from the Fed. Look, normally I'd say no way. But after you left, I checked, and we do hold your mortgage. As soon as we confirm reception of the wire transfer we can issue cash within five working days. There will be a .5 percent service fee for a cash payout. Please, Mr. Messina, I don't make the rules. We have to charge . . ." There was a pause. "As I explained to you, Mr. Messina, we don't carry a large cash float. Perhaps you could arrange something with our core office in San Lucas." She leaned forward, brushing an imaginary strand of platinum hair away from her broad face, the smile gone, a touch of worry in the crease between her eyebrows. "I'll call them for you if you like. I mean, normally we'd need more notice. But I would like to help. I don't think my son would have made it to college if your Doom Room hadn't turned him on to computers. Does it have to be cash, Mr. Messina?"

10

There was a tapping in Dan's study. Tap tap. Tappity tap tap.

Dan's study was at the front of the house, with sliding glass doors leading to a small deck and a view of the hills sloping down to the bay. Books and papers lay on the green carpet and cluttered the shelves on the walls. There was a long wide desk in the corner facing the interior wall, with a twenty-one-inch monitor looming over a computer keyboard. A small kid tapped the keyboard. They had a computer at the school library, and this one wasn't much different. Type in a word. Point and shoot. Chuleta scrolled through the files, clicking on them one by one until he found the one with Dan's financial records. Chuleta double-clicked on the icon, and all of Dan's accounts—stocks, bonds, mutual funds, and his CD— were there with deposits, withdrawals, and balances. Dead simple. A child could do it.

Was doing it.

He clicked on Dan's checking account. Not a lot, three thousand and change. But shit, look at that, there was a deposit of $8,354 every two weeks from Gopher Graphix Inc. Chuleta multiplied twenty-six times eighty-four in his head. Like 220,000 a year. Sucker was hauling it in. He clicked on Dan's CD account. Oh shit, sucker's only got like fifty grand in there. Looked like he was gonna have to get into all that tricky stocks and bonds shit. Looked like the whole fuckin thing was gonna be hard for the man, but that was not his problem. Chuleta leaned back in Dan's chair, stretching his arms, luxuriating in the money to come. There was a sound, like tires, brakes. A door slam. He was up, quick-stepping across the room to the window. A UPS truck was coming down the drive. Chuleta scooped up his gun, ran out into the hall and down the stairs.

Silver heard him coming and sprang up off the couch, turning, tossing his hair back, pulling his little chrome-plated .25 caliber Boa out of his pocket. Ready. Behind him, Page was edging back away from the couch.

Chuleta was holding his finger up to his lips, sssshhh. "Where's Blue Girl, Whopper, and their kids?"

Silver whispered back, "Be watchin some shit on TV. What's up?"

"Tell them shut up, leave the TV on, stay where they are. Watch them."

Page took a couple of steps back, toward the sliding glass doors leading out onto the deck, thinking if somebody comes to the front door, draws their attention, she could, if she could get the kids' attention without the gangsters seeing her . . . But she can't. The kids are watching TV. And she can't leave the kids, can't even think about it. She sighed, and Chuleta turned to see her by the glass doors, her hand on the door handle. He lifted his gun so the barrel was pointed at her stomach from the other side of the room. "What you backin away like that for? They're not comin in the back, they comin the front. Come walk to me now. Talk to me, Page. Tell me where you goin?"

The gun fascinated and horrified Page, that small black hole of total darkness growing larger, step by step, as she walked across the carpet, drawn to the gun. The hole grew huge as she came closer, big enough to stick her head into. That can't be right, she thought, and looked up at Chuleta's face, and realized with a shock that he was sweating.

The doorbell rang, and Page wondered in a distant way, watching him turn toward the front door, if he was going to shoot her. Of course not. Not with a delivery at the door. It would make noise. "You are not going to shoot me," she heard herself say.

"Not before you answer the door," Chuleta said, thinking that the timing would be about right, from the time Dan left. Plenty of time for the slugs to get their shit together, get some SWAT dude dressed as a UPS deliveryman, fill the whole fucking truck up with SWAT for backup.

What got him started, wired on this whole thing, was another UPS truck making another delivery. It was vague, but the details started to fill in. What it was like a couple, maybe three, months ago. He kept trying to put it out of his mind. Chuleta remembered being on the front porch at Ernestine's, thinking, Maybe when Ernestine come home maybe he and Blue Girl could crash in her sister's room for a couple of days 'cause her sister wasn't comin home no more. And there was some guy in the UPS brown uniform standing on the doorstep of the house next door. Couldn't see his face. And out of nowhere it was a drive-by.

Maybe some ten-year-old kid, they give him the

gun, or maybe they just didn't give a shit. They were Craps in blue rags, red Buick convertible, and they pulled off a burst of assault weapon, AK, UZI, some shit like that, and they took the guy's head off and chopped off the legs of the little girl answered the door. Mother standing behind her took two in the chest, screaming just once, then making gurgling sounds, pumping blood all over the place. The little girl screaming, dying. Looked like the UPS guy had a red, pink, and grey mess the top of his neck, head wasn't anyplace. Pieces of him up against the house. It was such a fucking mess.

UPS stopped coming to the hood after that, but every time he saw one of their trucks he was spooked. He felt that fear again, saw the blood. Trying to be cool, to hang on, he thought that if the truck was full of SWAT, there was nothing he could do. You got to play the cards they lay on the table in front of you. Even more, the cards you deal yourself. Play it. Gotta die sometime.

The doorbell rang again, a chiming electronic bong-bong that had them both staring at the door.

Thinking, they don't have drive-bys here, no street to drive by. If they are SWAT, they won't shoot her. Saying, "Answer it. You home with flu, remember."

"I remember," Page said, taking a deep breath and walking past Chuleta, down the three steps, into the entranceway. The doorbell bonged again, making her jump. She grabbed the knob and pulled the door partway open, sensing Chuleta moving close behind her. The UPS was a white woman, maybe eighteen or nineteen, brownish mop of hair, gold-rimmed glasses, kind of pudgy, sort of shapeless, but it is hard to tell under those dumb brown uniforms.

In the background Page could hear applause on

the TV. She thought, that's what this is, a performance. She told the woman, "Don't come near me, I've got the flu."

"Don't worry," the UPS woman said, handing Page an electronic pad to sign. "You're 3057, Messina, right?"

"All day," Page said signing.

The woman handed Page a brown parcel. "Nice place you got here."

"Come back soon," Page said.

Inside, peering through the narrow window next to the front door, they watched the UPS truck turn around and head out the driveway. Chuleta took the package and read the label. "How you know it's not a bomb?"

"I don't. You open it."

He gave the package back to her. "Says, 'Crew.' For Robby."

Robby was in the game room sitting happily on the Persian carpet next to Blue Girl, propped up against the sofa, watching the big TV. Blue Girl smelled so good. He kept stealing glances at her boobs, but the light wasn't right. Then his mom came in, walking like on tiptoe, and looked at him hard, like she was seeing milk on his lip or something. She handed him a brown package. "For you, sweetheart," she said.

Robby put it on the floor like it wasn't anything special and went back to watching the dumb game show.

"You just gonna leave it there on the floor like that?" Blue Girl asked him. She leaned close to him. It was tough to know the cool thing to do with Blue Girl watching.

"Yeah, I guess I could open it if you want me to,"

he said, acting above all the kid stuff. Like, you know, worldly.

Blue Girl gave him a little friendly poke in the ribs with her long finger, saying, "Hey, you get a package every day, or what? Come on, it's like Christmas. Open it. Let's see what you got."

He ripped it open. Inside, wrapped in blue tissue paper, there was a dumb white shirt—button-down collar, for Christ sake. And, oh shit, chinos. Chino pants. Straight leg. Pleats. He wouldn't wear them in a closet. They'd laugh him out of school.

"Don't you like them?" his mom said. "Hold them up, let's see how big they are." He was thinking if she would just go away. She was such an embarrassment. How can you be cool with your mother standing around telling you what to do?

He stood up and held up the shirt. It was about fifty sizes too large. What the hell was she thinking of? "You can grow into it," she said. Which was terrible to say in front of Blue Girl. Okay, he wasn't as tall as Blue Girl, but he was like almost above average for his class.

"Hey, what you holdin, dude?" Silver was standing behind the couch, coming around to the front, holding out his hand. "You don't want it, let me have a look at it. Throw them trousers, too." He caught them on the toss, let them drop on the carpet, and started unbuttoning his shirt.

"The fuck you doin, bro?" Whopper said, his head moving slow and steady like a tank turret from the TV to Silver.

Silver had his shirt off and was taking his trousers down. His legs pale white, long and smooth, shiny black hairs coiling around the drooping sack of his purple satin Jockey shorts. "Didn't I tell you, Whopper," he said, pulling on the chinos, slipping his arm into the new white shirt. "I can play anybody. Few minutes ago," he said, nodding toward Page, "I had the lady over there thinkin I was like attracted to her. Made her get all uptight. So hey, I can play a rich suburban white kid, too. Just gimme the costume." He pulled on the pants, zipped them up. The pants and shirt smelled new, had creases from being folded in a box. "What do you think?" He held out his hands for approval.

"Find some nice shiny shoes," Chuleta said, looking at him with a sideways grin, "nice belt, and you be home. And, Blue Girl, get your stuff put on this white girl. That way somebody come here, they think she's the one don't belong here."

"So what you gonna wear, Chuleta," Silver said, tilting his head back, trying on a new attitude—what it's like to feel rich. "Looks like you stole them rags offa some bigger dude."

Whopper, heavy arms outstretched along the back of the suede leather couch, looked Chuleta up and down, frowning like a man about to sell him a suit, measuring the boy with his eyes. "Yeah, maybe you find yourself some stretchy outfit, Chuleta, fit your personality. Like blue tights, cape, red boots 'n' all that Superman shit."

Chuleta was thinking, Be a good idea, dress up a little. He was still spooked from the UPS van. Suppose the driver got a look at him. Could happen. If he looked like somebody who lived here, and she saw him, she wouldn't think about it. Just take it as natural.

"Only stuff that'd fit you," Blue Girl said, "be Robby's." She put her hand lightly on Robby's knee, flooding his whole leg with warmth. Robby prayed for no hard-on. Blue Girl said, "You got a whole closet fulla nice white clothes. Look good on Chuleta." She ruffled the boy's green hair, making him feel weird.

Like he was liking her attention, but it was like he was her pet. And how come it always had to be his stuff they were after?

"Yeah," Whopper said, stretching, putting his hands behind his head, his arms making his head look small. "There's a nice jacket up there, silver threads. Way too small for Whopper, maybe about right for a little poke chop like you."

The phone rang from the kitchen. Nobody moved. It rang again. There was another pause, and Chuleta jerked his gun into Page's face, touching her forehead with the barrel, holding it there against her forehead. Then he was waving it at Baylor, whirling around, poking Robby in the stomach with the barrel, screaming, "Answer the fuckin phone. Who is it? Who is callin you? Get movin, or I'll shoot your fuckin faces off."

Page, horrified, backed out of the doorway and ran for the kitchen, Robby and Baylor scrabbling after her. Whopper leaned forward on the couch, levering himself up, standing in front of Chuleta. Taller, wider than Chuleta. "The fuck you doin man? It just the fuckin phone."

Chuleta raised his gun to Whopper's face, the barrel an inch from his forehead.

Whopper pushed the barrel aside, saying, "Don't you give me this shit, homey. Get in there, get those folks relaxed 'less you want them screamin for help on the damn phone." Whopper went past him, leaving Chuleta staring at the empty TV screen.

The phone rang again. Silver said, "Shit," turned and ran into the kitchen. "Come on, Chuleta," Blue Girl said, getting up. "Maybe it's for you. Somebody want to give you a free gift, sign you up for MCI."

In the kitchen Page and her kids were standing in a line, looking at the phones. The phone rang again, and Silver was saying, "That's your phone, Baylor, you answer it." She picked it up, and he told her, "You're sick, remember? You got flu."

"Yeah, hi," Baylor said. "Oh yeah, no. No, I'm sick, Brad. No don't. I look disgusting. Don't. I mean it's flu, and I don't want you to get it. No, it's okay, I don't want anything. I'm in the bathroom mostly. Both ends if you really want to know. Well what do you think? No, dammit, don't be so damn stupid. I said don't. No. Well screw you, too."

Chuleta came into the kitchen, his face pale, looking as if he had been sick. He saw Baylor on the phone, gave her a little nod like good, yes, you're doing fine.

"Look, I gotta go. To the toilet, dummy. I'll be okay tomorrow. Come on, Brad. Stop that. Goodbye." She hung up the phone.

"You gotta boyfriend, huh?" Chuleta said, sitting down at the kitchen table. "Look, I'm sorry. I guess I was like spooked with that UPS thing. I thought maybe they was gonna be like cops with assault guns. Like maybe I was gonna die. I really don't want to hurt any of you."

"Then get out," Baylor said.

"Yeah," Whopper said, leaning in the doorway, "go ahead, Chuleta. You get your skinny little ass on outta here. We'll handle this."

"Two more words, and you are goin to fuck it up, so shut it up." Chuleta said. "Who's that?" Outside the kitchen window two men were getting out of a beat-up pickup truck.

Page went to the window, not seeing anything. When Chuleta pointed that weapon at her forehead she saw his face tighten, saw how frightened he was, and she thought, I am going to die in front of my children, make a horrible mess. Page couldn't bear the thought of letting them down so badly.

Bizarre, she thought. It wasn't the thought of death that had scared her. She realized she wasn't especially afraid of dying. Getting old, watching her face turn into a wrinkled, bloated thing, would be grim. But she could face that. She could face death, but she did not want to die in front of the children. She wanted to keep her dignity. Not look feeble or stupid. The bright round spot where the barrel of his gun had touched her forehead still glowed. If he had shot her, sending a bullet through that spot to tunnel and expand in her brain, taking away the back of her skull, it wasn't the dying that worried her, it was the mess. What worried her was it would have been unbearable for the children to see something as ugly and violent as that. It would be a horror of a mess and would scar them, seeing that. Besides, she wasn't through with them yet. They weren't grown-up; they were her babies. Not that she had been any use to them that day. She was dumb enough to let these criminals into the house. It was her fault.

Still looking out the window, she realized she was watching a man in a straw cowboy hat, faded flannel shirt, dirty jeans, and beat-up work shoes, getting his tools out of the truck. "It's Gustalvo," she said. "The gardener."

"Yeah, right," Chuleta said. "I know it's Gustalvo. But it's Thursday. The fuck is he doin here Thursday? He comes here Wednesday, right? Silver, get your ass over here. You see anybody else on that truck? Maybe you should go outside, circle around the back of that truck, see if there's anybody hidin in the back."

"Say what? Get my new chinos dirty? Hey, don't look at me like that; lighten up, Chuleta. I'm makin a joke. He sees me, he's gonna recognize me, and that's not funny, bro. I got a face people like to remember, and I worked for the man two, three years ago. Just like you, only he didn't fire my ass. I quit."

Chuleta, up on his toes, ignoring him, peering out the window. "What's he doin here today? Man's supposed to come yesterday."

Page leaned forward, her arms on the counter, letting her forehead touch the cool surface of the window. Feeling the glass cool the bright spot in the middle of her forehead; feeling unspeakably tired. "Maybe he switched dates with the Stevensons. Maybe there's something special he had to do yesterday, like go to a funeral. Or his kids were sick." She lifted her head. "How do you know he comes here on Wednesday?" Page stood and looked at his back as he watched the gardeners. "How do you know? You were here, weren't you? You worked for him. You little sneak."

"They got their clippers out," Chuleta said. "They gonna do bushes and hedges." He stood there watching. "See that. That's the kind of work I got available to me. Make four, five dollars an hour. No medical. No retirement, no meals, no vacation, no nothin. You'd like me to do that, wouldn't you? You wouldn't do shit for that money. But that's what you want me to do. Trim and rake and pick up shit for you. With my brain. You go," Chuleta said, switching to a high, sweet, lazy voice, picking up on Page's speech: "I want my roses in front clipped and there's a leak in my sprinkler system and would you be sure you get all the leaves off the front walk, you missed some last time. And sweep all the way around the pool.

"Yeah, I was here, and you never once asked me how I was, never asked me inside the house, out of the hot sun, never offered me a drink of water. You never even saw me. I was here once a week for sixteen weeks, and you never saw me. So now I got a gun, and I am in your house, you see me loud and clear, right?"

Chuleta walked over to Page, his nose almost touching her nose. "You see me now, right?" His voice was low, almost a whisper. "Look carefully. After tonight you won't see me again. But you won't forget me neither." He went back to the window.

The hell they doin here today? Chuleta said to himself, watching Gustalvo open the door to the pickup, reach in, pull out a pair of leather gloves and put the gloves on with the slow care of a surgeon. If Gustalvo sees him inside the house, he was gonna want to know what was goin down. The downside of crime. Soon as you do crime, anybody out there, like even Gustalvo, can fuck you up big-time.

CHAPTER

11

Dan going north on 101, the San Lucas to San Francisco concrete connector tube, flat, straight, and solid traffic, not a living green thing in sight unless you counted tooth decay or whatever the green stuff was that grew in the cracks. Head down, speaking into his car phone, keeping one eye on three lanes of traffic, sixty-five miles per hour bumper-to-bumper as he wove in and out of lanes, trying to gain a little time. He was saying, "Yeah, well no, Nick. No. I'm not so great. I need a big favor. No, nothing to do with tennis, this is real serious, and I need a huge amount of your help. No, no, Nick, I don't want to tell you about it on the phone. Can I come see you? I mean do you have a session going or something, because the sooner the better. No, no, nothing to do with a sound track. I need a ton of money. Cash. Can you lay your hands on a bunch of cash? I'll tell you when I get there."

He clicked off, punched autodial 1. Page answered on the fourth ring, just after he'd given up, thinking something horrible had happened. He said, "Thank God."

She said, "You okay? Where are you?

"Going over to Nick's studio. Is he listening?"

"Yeah, practically in my lap. He's got that Silver creature assigned to me, following me around everywhere. He's here, too, watching."

"So you can't talk all that freely."

"Well, they already know I'm scared. We're all scared. We had a UPS delivery, and they acted like it was black helicopters. I mean yeah, they're listening."

"But you're okay?"

"When are you coming home?"

"As soon as I can. This is hard. Even the banks don't have cash. I'm working on it, and it's going to be okay, but it's going to take a while."

"I'm really frightened, Dan. They keep pointing their guns at me and the kids."

"Remember that picnic we had?" He braked hard to avoid a dirty half-ton pickup loaded with rakes, shovels, and tree branches. Foot hard on the accelerator again, cutting in behind a yellow Datsun, looking for an opening.

Page was saying, "Which? When? What are you talking about?" Her voice went sharp, irritated. As if he hadn't been paying attention.

"When we were in college. Remember, up in that vineyard off of Skyline. You remember, Clos Coyote Vineyard? It was a spring day, probably April, and very warm, but the ground was still cold, and I bought a bottle of wine and the grass was soft and green. And we had a blanket alongside the stream and the sun was hot and we were kissing and I felt your breast."

Page laughed. "You were so daring. You put your hand on my sweater. And I wanted you to make love to me, and you were such a fink you wouldn't do anything."

"Yeah, well, we all make mistakes. But it's a day to think about. I mean, it was twenty years ago, but it always makes me happy when I think about it. Do you remember the sound of that creek? And the smell of the grass? There were all those little white flowers . . ."

"Lily of the valley."

"Right those. And those little purple ones that looked like bunches of grapes."

"You were sniffing the flowers? And you could have been making love to me."

"Hey, it's a good day to think about."

"And the day Baylor was born. Remember that morning? Remember you held my hand all the way through. When I looked down, and her head was coming out, you were holding my hand. Jesus, Dan, I wish you were here now."

"I'll be there as soon as I can."

"No hanging around in strip joints." An old joke. He'd always teased Page she could have made it big time as a stripper.

"I'll come home and rip your pants off."

"Just come home. Get rid of these assholes."

"Chuleta."

"Yeah, man."

"You're listening in."

"Yeah, man. I gotta."

"Anything happens to her, I will find you. I will find you and kill you. You hear me?"

"I heard threats all my life, man. Like every fuckin day. But don't worry. You come home with the money, nothin is gonna happen."

"I'll be there. Love you, Page."

"Love you. Hurry up."

■   ■   ■

Ear Candy Studios was twenty minutes from Mountain View, and Dan was there in fifteen, hitting the off-ramp at seventy-five. He slid to a stop in front of the old familiar grey industrial block building with the big pink ear on the front door. Opening the door was like entering an airlock, the whole building insulated for sound. They could be playing a ten-thousand-watt demo of a 747 jetliner plowing into Sunset Boulevard backed by a band like Neutron Bomb, and you wouldn't hear a peep outside that door. Although, of course, the building wasn't designed to keep noise from leaking out; it was designed to keep the noise outside from leaking in.

Sheila, the frail little blond receptionist with the nose ring, watched Dan out of the corner of an eye outlined with black mascara and iridescent purple eye shadow. Seeing it was Dan charging in, bounding toward her, she went back to her magazine. Whatever it was he wanted, she knew there were way more important things going on in the recording studio. Like he was lucky to be at Ear Candy, where The Who laid down their first American track, and Pink Floyd remixed "The Wall" when they were on their first tour of the US and Canada, and hey, Pearl Jam had a session just last week and Tori Amos was coming in this afternoon to lay down a backing track for John Lee Hooker. And her favorite, Surface to Air, was over-dubbing their new disc almost ready for release, next week. They were gonna call it *Fresh Air*, but she liked their original working title, the one they were going with in all their sessions, *In the Clear*.

Where, Dan wondered, coming to a stop, breathing hard, did Nick find these baby-faced predators.

Sheila said, "Hiya," looking idly past him at the

closing fan of light from the door. "Looks like they're gaining on you." She tossed her long blond hair with black roots, went back to her ZOT magazine, and said, "He's in A, doing a remix. Some new doofus at EMI thinks bubblegum rap is gonna go ballistic."

Going through the control room door in studio A, Dan was hit by a wall of screaming: a boy's voice rapping, boosted past the breaking point over the honk and squeal of saxophones and heavy brass. Electric guitar vibro. Feedback screech laid on top:

> *Got no time to learn,*
> *Got too much to burn.*
> *Daddy never grew up,*
> *He just gave up.*
> *So don't tell me slow up,*
> *Gotta run, gotta run wild,*
> *Got no time to be a child.*
> *Got NO TIME*
> *TO BE A CHILD*

Nick's balding head, puffs of curly red hair coming out from behind his ears like smoke, was bent over a vast console of levers and winking lights set in glossy blond wood. In the recording studio in front of him, on the other side of a triple plate-glass window, rows of folding chairs sat empty behind music stands. Microphones hung from a ceiling of upside-down empty boxes. Two recording engineers on either side of him were at the console, sliding the levers up and down, bringing up one scream, bringing another down. The air was still, heavy with the fragrance of old cheeseburgers, curled-up pizzas, cigarettes, and an undertone of yesterday's grass.

Nick turned his head around, saw it was Dan, and

went back to shut down the console, sliding the track levels down to zero and flipping switches off. "Take a break, kids, okay."

His assistants, high-school refugees, gave Dan a knowing nod on the way out, like "Hey, dude, how you doing, you're cool, we're hip to where you are coming from" condensed into a quick, knowing tilt of the head. They walked with the halting, stilted walk of inner-city gangstas.

"So, asshole," Nick said, as the noise was still ringing in Dan's ears, "isn't it amazing man? Forty-eight-track digital; virtual mixing, instant access, plug-in environment; this is the future of sound right here, Dan. You got all these guys in the industry still hanging with analog saying that's where you get the fat warm sounds, and I have to tell you they are blowing smoke. You try two locked-up analogs, throw one of them out of phase, and you'll hear flanging all over 'cause you got time slop in the tape travel and swimming voltages to the motors. All that shit you have to go back and fix. I'm still big on ana-log for that big bass, like this afternoon with John Lee we're recording with the old Studer twenty-four-track in C, mixing to half-inch analog get a little more air in it; and . . ."

Nick took a deep breath, catching himself, coming down from the high of the music, "Oh, man, you scared the shit out of me."

"I need a favor from you," Dan said. "A big favor."

Nick checked out his Top-Siders, blue jeans, polo shirt, the same outfit he wore when Dan had first met him at Stanford. "Hey, I still get a royalty check every month for that sound track I did for you on Doom Room. Okay, it's down to just a few bucks now, but I owe you everything, Dan. Like you're my brother. So whatever it is . . ." Nick braced himself against the console, looking like he was expecting a high wave. His face was heavier, years of all-night sessions had grooved deep lines around his eyes, and freckles had pushed the red hair off the top of his head. But he still looked like Santa's little brother, the way he'd looked when Dan had met him in the Tressider Student Union café at Stanford. You could still see the cherub kid from Julliard who played Mozart in the Stamford String Quartet and heavy metal at McNasty's in the city. Nick was saying, "Whatever, I can handle it. Hey, bro, if I can handle bubblegum rap, I can handle anything, right?"

Nick nodded toward the speakers hanging from the ceiling. "CPU. Name of the group is CPU. You know, like central processing unit?"

"I got it."

"Yeah, well remember them because they are going to be very, very big. The leader is this fifteen-year-old white kid from Hillsdale with a $5 million contract to do two albums before the end of the year. Takes him about twenty minutes to write a rap, then the grown-ups spend five weeks putting it together. Is that deep shit or what?"

"That's just marketing, Nick. Deep shit is what I am in. Except it's worse than that."

"You run over somebody?" Nick's baby face bunched up, ready for the pain.

"Some kids, fifteen, I don't know, maybe sixteen years old, are in my house with assault weapons pointed at Page and the kids."

"Holy shit, what are you doing here? You talk to the police?"

"Would you?"

"Sure, they deal with shit like this. It's what they are trained for."

"The kids say what they want is $400,000 cash and

they'll go away. Think about it for a minute. What's going to work, a bunch of cash or a bunch of cops?"

"Oh shit, man, I'm sorry. I mean I don't know. Listen, you think maybe there's a way we could sneak in, surprise them?"

Dan looked at him.

Nick started pacing, then stopped, "Yeah, right. You gonna go in, you'd be better off with cops. I'd probably shoot myself." Nick grimaced, scratching his scalp. "How much cash you got?"

"I think I can get around 280,000 from my broker. And Garland says he thinks he can get me another 100,000 from Gopher. I'm working on it."

"I got around eleven grand in my company account."

"That's it, eleven grand?"

"Hey, man, last week I had 55,000 for the session talent for Fake Space, but that's gone. The only reason I got eleven in now, is I'm gonna do a little rewire in B, and the dude that does it will only take cash. I mean I could raise $250,000 in cash, but it would take a few days, maybe a week. Let me think. Shit. I've got a couple of, maybe five, grand in my checking account; shit, take that, too. I just wish we had some time."

"There's no time."

"Listen, I'll call the bank. Take the eleven whatever's in there, and I'll write you a check on my checking. I put three, four million a year through them. They'll cash it. Shit, if I had more, you could have it. I just like never see cash anymore. Only guys I know do cash now are little girls selling Girl Scout cookies and drug dealers. And even the dealers run for the nearest American Express soon as their pockets fill up."

■   ■   ■

Heading back for Gopher Graphix, the traffic along 101 was bumper-to-bumper stop-and-go. You can't be down, Dan was thinking. You can't afford to be down. Think like a game, like strategy. Ways to blow their heads off. Except this was not a game. There was no video and no rules, and he couldn't turn it off. Three lanes each way, and the traffic north roared toward San Francisco at a steady sixty-five to seventy. While southbound was a slow-rolling parking lot, a concrete chute past the industrial wasteland that rings the mud flats of the San Francisco South Bay.

On the way back to 101 from Nick's bank he saw a sign—American Way Loans—and pulled into their parking lot, thinking it was worth a shot. American Way Loans was plywood paneling, cheap furniture, cigarette burns in the carpet. The man with the basset-hound face, with a grease stain on his yellow tie and the nicotine stains on his teeth, was happy to lend him as much as he needed at 23.789%, as long as he had collateral. So sure, fine, the house fit that bill. They could have up to $15,000 cash in five to ten days, no problem. If the bastard had told him that up front, he wouldn't have wasted a half hour. But he had to cut through the glad-to-meet-you-tell-me-about-yourself crap, and even then the "account executive" was programmed to go one step at a time. Like, "I want you to feel right at home," he told Dan when Dan said he needed cash. Jesus, home.

He called Mrs. Brockow, and she said there was nothing as she had explained that she could do, but he should call Andruw Finally in San Lucas. "Pronounced Fah-Nally," she said.

Finally, the hard currency transfers manager at the First Citizen's/Ameribank Core Banking Center in downtown San Lucas, said their Federal Reserve cash delivery wasn't until next Tuesday. But he thought he might be able to get the cash together because they did, after all, hold the mortgage on his house. And they were expecting cash receipts from some shopping mall. However, since Dan was a customer of the satellite bank in Mountain View and not a depositor at the core bank in San Lucas, Finally said there was just no way they could accommodate him. "Why don't you have a word with one of our executives at your personal banking center, Mr. Messina. In Mountain View."

"I did, and Mrs. Brockow said to call you. "

"Ah, Mrs. Brockow, yesss." There was a pause.

"Yes what?"

"Oh, sorry. I mean I'm sorry, Mr. Messina, but you have to go through Mrs. Brockow. If you don't go through Mrs. Brockow, I'm afraid there's nothing I can do for you."

He punched Mrs. Brockow's phone numbers on the car phone.

"I'm really very sorry Mr. Messina, but . . ."

"Helen," he broke in. "Do you mind if I call you Helen?"

"Sure, Mr. Messina." She sounded uncertain. "If you like."

"Helen, you said your son is in medical school."

"One year to go, thank God."

"Thirty thousand dollars."

"I'm afraid as I explained . . ."

"Not for me, for you. Wouldn't $30,000 cover a year's tuition?"

"Well, yes, but . . ."

"Helen, I have $288,000 from my broker that I will wire wherever I need to if you can persuade Finally at the San Lucas Central Office to get me 288,000 in cash this afternoon . . ."

"I'd love to but . . ."

"If I get that money, I'll give you 30,000. Give it to

you." Thinking, 30,000 more or less, it really doesn't matter.

"Andruw Finally is a real stickler for . . ."

"Thirty thousand, and you don't have to do anything illegal. I'll even give it to you in cash if you want. When and where you want."

"I don't . . ."

"Tell him you'll split it with him. Tell him anything you like."

"You'll have to have a wire transfer . . ."

"That's all taken care of."

"Cash?"

"Cash. I'll take it off the top. You can have it tomorrow." If he was still around tomorrow. If, if, if.

"I'd prefer you wire it to my American Express account."

"Just give me the number, and I will do it. As soon as I have my cash."

"What's your car phone number? I'll have Andruw call you."

Mrs. Brockow put down her phone. She sat for a moment and stretched her long legs under her polished oak desk. Then she reached under her desk and brought up her handbag, a woven wicker basket with brass buckles and fawn-leather trim. She took out her mirror and a comb and studied her face. One side, then the other. She combed a stray strand of bright blond hair that had fallen out of place. She put the comb back into her purse and took out a lipstick cup and brush and carefully touched up her bright red lipstick. She put the lipstick cup and brush and her mirror back into her bag and put her bag back in its usual hiding place under her desk. Then she punched Finally's number on the internal phone.

"Andy," she said.

Even if he hadn't been hoping she'd call, he would have recognized the way she said, "Andy."

He said, "I thought you were never going to call me."

"Well I am. Calling you." She paused and he waited. "You remember all those years ago we used to talk about South America. And how we were going go to all those places nobody goes?"

"Lose ourselves for a month," he said.

"Belem, Vera Cruz, Florianopolis," she said.

"Valparaiso," he said.

Five minutes and a half a mile later, when Andruw Finally called Dan, he said they would never normally do this, but they were always glad to go the extra mile for a significant First Citizen's/Ameribank customer. Unfortunately he would have to charge a one-point fee, but given the need to put aside other important projects to assemble this substantial sum in cash by three-thirty, it was really the very least they could charge. He was sure Mrs. Brockow would be happy to explain it to him. It would fit in one large attaché case; had he considered how he wanted to carry the cash out of the bank?

No, Dan hadn't considered how he was going to carry it. An attaché case would be great, he said, thinking it was going to be okay. Okay, he was stuck in traffic. Cars and trucks going nowhere, but it was going to work. Okay, it was almost noon, and all he had was the 3,720 he had taken out of his bank account. Plus 16,247 from Nick's accounts. But, add to that the promise of 100,000 from Garland. So, around 120,000 plus the 288,000 he was going to get from the bank when the wire went through added up to . . . Jesus, 408,000 and something. He was going to make it. Yes.

High white clouds, like a child's innocent cartoons, floated overhead in the deep blue California sky. "Pluffy," Baylor used to call them when she was a little girl. And he thought of the day when Baylor was five and they bundled her up and took her over the hills to the beach at Pescadero, leaving Baby Robin Leckonby Messina with a baby-sitter. Walking alongside the great rolling breakers coming in from Okinawa, Page led the way in her pink-and-blue windbreaker with Baylor just behind, stomping through the warm sand on her short little legs, struggling to keep up. Suddenly she was shouting, pointing at the waves. Dolphins, just the other side of the breakers. Their smooth black muscular backs were rising out of the sea and rolling back in again with the fluid ease of balanced power. Walking down the beach that magical day, out of the corner of their eyes they saw a little brown flurry of legs and tail. Pointy little face, soft brown fur jumping up when they came over to inspect. Page picked him up and a quick red rag of a tongue licked her face, so she put the dog down. Baylor dived for the dog, and he easily sidestepped the child, barking, jumping from side to side. A good game.

Dan said they were the kind of family that attracted strays and bent to pick up the puppy. The dog was so excited he nipped Dan on the back of his hand. "Churlish little mutt," he said, pretending to be pretentious, pass off the pain with a joke. Sucking his hand. And little Baylor, down on all fours in the wet sand, was saying "Churley," and the puppy came to her for hugs, little tail wagging happily. They asked the rangers, notified the police, but nobody reported him missing, so Churley was theirs. Damn dog wouldn't chase a sparrow from their door. Probably run up to a cougar and lick him on the face. Where the hell was he this morning? At least he could have barked. But he was so deaf he probably never heard them. Dumb dog was probably still asleep. When Churley started scratching the front door in their new house in Los Palos Hills, Dan thought he'd have to have the door replaced. And Page said, "Oh leave the scratches. As a welcome for strays."

And look what had shown up. His mind was numb with these fucking kids. He felt the rage rise and grow red—the bastard kicking him in the balls. It was still painful to drive, the ache was low-level now but still there. Maybe he should go to the police. He pictured the pleasure of seeing those kids in cuffs, bloody, heads down being led into a police car. Going away for life. This was kidnapping, and they would go to prison for the rest of their lives. The punishment didn't seem right. It wasn't enough.

Gradually, with the slow roll of a wave coming in to shore, Dan realized he was going to hit the car in front. Amazing how time slows down when the world spins out of control. The traffic was creep creep, stop and go, so he wasn't going fast. Maybe five, maybe ten miles an hour. His foot was lifting off the gas in mid-arc on the way to the brake, much too late, when he heard a headlight shatter, then the heavy metal crunch of his grill and front fenders folding up. The crump zone, he thought as he was flung forward. His seat belt dug a stripe of pain across his right shoulder. And that was all. To his complete surprise, the same face was looking back at him in the rearview mirror. The crash was over, and he wasn't hurt, hands and feet all there, movable. The car had stopped.

He had hit the back of a beat-up old Honda. A Civic. They were stopped in the center lane. A blond head poked out of the Honda. Yelling. He couldn't hear her above the wild honk of cars behind. People were shouting behind him. She pointed to the side of the freeway. Her car moved forward, across one lane and off onto the shoulder. Dan followed.

She was pretty, maybe twenty-five, thin with long runner's legs in a short wispy little blue-and-white summer dress, standing knock-kneed, bent forward and staring at the back of her car. She looked up and saw him coming. "Why does everybody have to run into my car?" It was hard to hear above the traffic, and she had to shout. Just below the rear window of the Honda a bumper sticker said, *Wouldn't it be great if schools had all the money they need and the Pentagon had to give a bake sale to buy a bomber*. "Whatever were you thinking?" she said. Not angry, curious. Wanting to know.

Dan thought of the gang in his house, and said, "I'm sorry. I know it was my fault." Thinking, he couldn't stop here, he had to keep moving. The back of the Honda was crumped like an old beer can. "What's the damage?"

"Damn," she said. "I'm already late. I don't know. It's sort of hard to tell. Are you okay?"

Dan said sure. "You?"

"I'm all right. Just kinda pissed off. Damn," she said, touching the broken taillight with the tip of her finger. "It's been hit so many times parking in San Francisco, I'm not real sure what's the old stuff and what's yours. I don't think the taillight was broken before."

Dan looked at the front of his Volvo. Smashed grill, bent bumper, one headlight, both fog lights out. The hood buckled. At least two thousand damage. Maybe four. Good thing Gopher had insurance, but Garland would give him a lot of shit over it. "Look," Dan said, pulling out his wallet. "I've gotta go. Do you think $500 would cover it?"

"Hey, that's way too much. Maybe it's just the taillight."

"Four hundred."

"Oh wow, that's still too much, but that'd be great." He gave her the money, and she smiled. Pretty brown eyes. "You sure you're okay?" she said. Dan was already back in the Volvo, relieved that it would start. "Have a nice day," she called out to him as he eased the car with the broken nose back into the crawling traffic. In his rearview mirror, she was standing there, looking at him disappear in the river of rolling metal, giving him a wave.

He waved his arm out the window. Thinking, with the four hundred gone he still had over $400,000 if everything worked.

Back in his office he skipped his e-mail and listened to a dozen voice messages. Garland saying where are you? Seibert from accounting wanting a revised budget for Fisherman; Rebecca reminding him he was down for lunch with Widmer in Widmer's office. Nothing from home. Maybe he should call. And say what? That he had nothing? That he couldn't get the money? Lie, say that he had? He picked up a large brown envelope with his name on it.

As he opened it, Garland was coming into his office, sweet smile luminous in his ruined angel face, saying, "I'd have put confidential on it, but then you know somebody would have opened it."

The money was in hundreds. Surprising how small a $100,000 stack of hundred-dollar bills is. Not wanting to talk to Garland, Dan started counting it, getting to 2,000 and realizing it wasn't anywhere near $100,000. It wasn't even 10,000. Dan kept counting to the end, 7,500. He counted it again, Garland watching, counting along with him. "What the hell is this, Garland?"

"It's your money, on your desk, just like you asked. You have no idea how hard it is to get ahold of cash these days. People don't even know what you're talking about. You practically have to draw them a picture of the stuff."

"You said, a hundred thousand."

"I know what I said. I said I would do the best I can. I had a meeting with our friends at Silicon Graphics in my office, and there was just no way I could get to the bank. So I'm giving you the 7,500 we had in our cash on hand, and you are yelling at me. You can't always get what you want," he said with the intonation of the old lyric, "but if you try sometime . . ."

"Grant, I don't need 7,500. I need 400,000, you fucking idiot. This is useless." Dan threw the money against the wall of his office, hitting a virtual-landscape printout and fluttering down onto the couch. Dan looked at the scattered hundred-dollar bills on his couch, his face red, his hands shaking. "Useless," he said.

"Working here, at Gopher," Grant said, going over to the couch and gathering up the bills, "is not a right, it is a privilege. I am not your employee, I am your employer. And the deal we had was that I would gather up as much money I could in virtually two hours' time, and you would show up this afternoon for our AmDell review. I have kept my end of the bargain," he said, carefully putting the stack of bills on Dan's desk. "And I expect you to keep yours."

"You could have gotten twenty times, a hundred times that much. And it's a loan, for Christ's sake. For a day. Or, okay, a week. You'd have got it back. No way I can go to your fucking AmDell meeting now. I have to find, Jesus, somehow, another 100,000 this afternoon. Because you didn't get it." Dan was aware that he was losing it. Christ, lost it. But it didn't help. He longed to hit Garland in the middle of his pudgy, self-satisfied face.

Garland, his creaseless lime green pin-striped suit looking brand-new, his white shirt fresh out of the box, looked around Dan's office. And Dan saw it with sudden, stunning clarity through the Shadow's eyes. Ten years ago the black sofa was a slick architectural combination of wood, leather, chrome, and coarse fabric. Now it looked old, soiled, and starting to fray. The once-plush red carpet sported coffee, cigarette, and wine stains from a decade of meetings and office parties. The carpet was worn down to the fiber in front of the door and in front of Dan's desk. Dan's Italian drawing desk was a confusion of papers, memos, drawings, and yesterday's sandwich paper. And the blurbs of color from Mandelbrot sets he had framed seventeen years ago when Doom Room first took off were faded now, looking as dated as bell-bottom trousers.

Grant said, "Fine," and held out his hand. "You go do whatever it is you want to do, Dan. Whatever that may be, I wish you the very best of luck. You are fired, Dan. Right now, as of now. And I want you out of this office and out of this building now. By all means, do whatever you want to do. Just don't do it here and don't expect me to pay you for it."

Grant was walking away, not turning around, past Cheryl, Tom, Philippa, Vivienne, and Arno, their heads sticking up out of the tops of their grey steel and frosted-glass cubicles. Cheryl and Vivienne were looking back at Dan, pity and wonder shining in their dark eyes. Witnesses to the execution.

Dan shouted, "You bastard. You prick."

Grant stopped, turned, and came back, coming right up to him, face-to-face. There was that patch of black whiskers that Grant had missed shaving on his cheek and a yellow rim of tartar along his lower front teeth.

Grant, relaxed and enjoying himself, spoke just loud enough for the gathering crowd to hear. "Maybe you're right, Dan. Maybe I owe you a bit more in the way of explanation."

Dan tried to interrupt, holding his hand up, saying "wait," thinking there is a way around this, but Grant was not going to be interrupted.

"So let me explain," Grant was saying. "You are out-of-date, past it, and it is as simple as that. You have got the Fisherman project so tangled up in dead-end technical minutiae I think the kindest thing to do is kill it, don't you? Forget it and start over. I've got half a dozen superbright kids just out of graduate school, any one of whom would kill their mother to take a fresh look at Fisherman, pick up the pieces, and go at it twenty-four hours a day, break their heart over it seven days a week for as long as it takes. Christ, I could put five of them on it for a fifth of what I'm paying you. And I'm still not sure it's worth it. So don't think I'm being petulant or overreacting. I've been thinking of firing you for a long time, Dan. A long time. You have a certain celebrity value. Kind of a kick having one of the pioneers of Silicon Valley around. But this is a growing company, not a museum, and I can't afford to keep you as an exhibit." He started to go, and stopped. "It's just a business decision, Dan. We'll give you a month's pay for every year you've been here. How's that sound?"

"I need $400,000 because a teenage gang is in my house. They are holding assault guns to Page's head. To the kids' heads."

"See, that's your problem, Dan. The old imagination has just faded away. I mean that's the sort of thing we stopped putting into our game scenarios five years ago. Now if you'd come up with something remotely fresh, I might be in a position to help."

"It is the truth."

"Just be out before noon, would you?"

Garland was out the door and down the hall. Bright lime green going past the techies' heads rising out of their cubicles like gophers in a field, turning to look at Dan. Dan was saying, "It's the truth."

CHAPTER

12

Seeing the boy with his head in the refrigerator, small butt in chinos, white shirt tucked in, Page automatically said, "Robby. Robby. Out of there. You'll spoil your lunch," knowing she'd be ignored.

The boy backed out, holding a can of Diet Coke, and Page couldn't help it—she yelped. Chuleta, in Robby's white shirt, chinos, and loafers looked like a prep-school boy home on Sunday for the day. Shoes shined, new leather belt. And Chuleta felt it. Could feel like a young man with a future, money out there for him all the way. Money in the bank to pay for his clothes, a car, nice vacations. Pay for college, then maybe be a lawyer, doctor, some big-time guy, have a lot of people working for him, like maybe run like a corporation. Limo come pick him up in the morning. Felt good.

"Hey," Chuleta said. "Come on, lighten up, Page. I didn't mean to frighten you." Page sat down in a kitchen chair and started to cry.

Chuleta, looking around the room, not knowing what to do, a grown woman crying. He yelled out,

"Hey, Silver. The fuck are you, man? You supposed to be watchin this lady." He went over to Page and knelt at her feet. Putting his hand on her knee. Page twisted away. "Relax," he said. "We ain't got a lot longer here. It's gonna be fine. Nobody get hurt. Nobody fuck up your house. Come on, don't cry. What's for lunch?"

Silver swanked through the doorway, wearing the white button-down oxford shirt and brand-new chinos Page had bought for Robby to grow into. Chuleta stood up, "The fuck you been man? You supposed to never leave her alone."

"Whatta you think? I was havin a crap. I can't make her watch me havin a crap. You the one said leave the woman her dignity. What kinda dignity she gonna have watchin me shit? What was you sayin about lunch? I'd like me a couple cheeseburgers. Bacon an' all that tomato lettuce pickle shit. Maybe a chocolate malt."

"Yeah, right," Whopper said, coming in, a blaze of color in Dan's warm-up suit, looking like Buddha on his way to the tennis court, heavy on his feet, pushing Robby in front of him. "Say what we order a pizza, get them to deliver. Put it on the lady's bill." Whopper went into his white voice. "Hello, Domino's? Send up a two-foot primavera special with double cheese, quadruple pepperoni, and a deuce of Colt sixers if you would be so kind. We're having a luncheon party with our lovely local neighborhood street gang, and we thought it would be amusing to have a pizzah."

Chuleta said, "Hush up, Whopper." To Page he said, "See, we all dressed like we live here, now we gonna act like we always been here. Act like it's a normal day, okay. Like what you got planned for lunch?"

Page shook her head.

Chuleta put his hand under Page's chin and lifted her face gently. "It's okay, nobody's gonna hurt you.

You the momma. Come on, what else we got to do? We all sit down have lunch together. You got somethin planned?"

"Don't touch me."

Chuleta took his hand away. "I'm just tryin to find out you got somethin for lunch."

"We don't have lunch here. We're all out at noon." He kept looking at her as if he didn't get it. "Working, at school. Oh, I'm sorry, you wouldn't know anything about work or school, would you."

"What about Saturday, Sunday? And don't tell me you all out for supper. You gotta have some food in there."

"There was some tuna fish. He ate it."

Whopper headed over to the refrigerator, saying, "Hey, don't worry 'bout it. Let the Whopper whip somethin up. Find some leftover stuff, stick it in the reactor. What else you got in here." Whopper stuck his head in the Amana, rummaging through the shelves. "Probably a lotta bland shit, turkey breast, white bread, mayonnaise, shit like what white folks eat." He stood up. "Pretty damn weak, you ask me. Hey, Blue Girl, come in here." He looked at Page. "You got any tomatoes, like in cans? Stuff like garlic, onions, maybe some anchovies? Maybe a box of pasta. Blue Girl," he shouted out again, "bring that other bitch in here. Let's get cookin." He was opening cabinets, looking through shelves, and came up with a prize, a long blue box of Italian pasta, "Do a spaghetti like Mario does. What's he call it, Putanesca." Blue Girl was in the doorway, coming in, so he asked her, "Hey, Blue Girl, you know what Putanesca is in Italian?"

"Yeah, Fat Boy, means you gotta pay for it."

"It means whore's pasta," Baylor said behind Blue Girl.

Blue Girl, opening a cabinet, looked back at the

white girl, seeing the round face with freckles, the short, almost boyish, hair, the plain jane no-makeup look in Blue Girl's pink tube top and way too tight stretch pants, acting as if she knew everything when she didn't know shit. "What I said, little girl. You got any olive oil round here? You know, like virgin?"

Baylor gave her a look and was going to tell her what an asshole she was, but she thought it's just not worth it. She thought let's just get through this, saying, "Mom, we got those good tomatoes yesterday from Webb Ranch. And there's fresh basil in the garden."

Whopper smiled his big Whopper smile at Baylor. Liking how she was tough but could go with the flow. Liking her better and better. Plus those little pink titties. "Perfect," he said.

Whopper cut the ripe red skins with a big chopping knife, the juice flowing out onto the cutting board, sections of bleeding tomatoes rolling off in quarters, then in eighths. "See, Robby, my man, your tomato is like corn, gotta be as fresh like just off the vine, so you go for the ones still got a stalk on them, keeps them thinkin they still alive. And you don't want to put them in the fridge 'cause the flavor gonna roll over and die in around twenty minutes." He looked up and saw Baylor watching them, eyeing the big sharp knife. "You got that olive oil, girl?" he said. "And garlic. Hey, Robby, maybe you like to learn how to make some garlic bread."

"All we have for bread is a loaf of that Santa Cruz seven-grain Mom always gets."

"That be fine. Watch the Whopper now, see how you slice a garlic." Whopper held the peeled clove of garlic like a pearl between his thick black fingers and his thumb, slicing parallel slices down the length of the clove leaving a hinge to hold the slices together at the bottom. Turning the clove he sliced the thin leaves again at right angles. He put the clove down on the chopping board and began to chop with the big wide chopping knife, his hand moving almost too fast to see, perfect little garlic squares piling up on the board by the tips of his fingers.

Baylor said it before she could stop herself because he was so irritating. "Do they call you Whopper," she said, "because you have a big dick?"

Whopper stopped chopping, looking up at the girl. "So what?"

"Then I guess I'll just call you Dickhead."

Whopper chuckled. "Yeah, an' I'll call you Pretty Tits. See how you like that."

"Hey, bro," Silver called out from the dining room, where he was putting out glasses of water. "When we gonna eat?"

"Soon as Pretty Tits gets the water boiling."

Baylor, blushing, furious, slid off the stool and got a big stainless-steel pot out of the cupboard under the sink.

"Put some salt in it, Pretty Tits," Whopper said. "Pasta gonna taste flat you don't put some salt in the water.

"Dickhead," she said, feeling helpless. Looking at the big knife lying on the cutting board.

Whopper poured the dark green olive oil into a white porcelain bowl. Then he stirred in the bleeding red tomato pieces, torn dark green basil leaves, scraped the white dots of garlic off the cutting board into the green oil, covered the bowl with a dish, and put it in the refrigerator.

"Aren't you going to cook it?" Page said.

"Gonna chill it. See, you cook the pasta, and when it's done, right after you drain it, and it's boilin hot, you mix in the olive oil, tomatoes, basil, and stuff cold from the fridge and the heat from the pasta make the flavors *ex*-plode."

"I thought you said that putting tomatoes in the refrigerator kills the flavor," Robby said.

"Yeah, mystery ain't it? My theory goes the oil keeps the flavor in 'cause the flavor can't swim through the oil, like no place to go."

Robby, looking Whopper in the eye, picked up the chopping knife. "It's not a mystery. You just don't know what you are talking about."

Whopper went cold, looked at the boy for a beat. "Why don't you chop some garlic like I showed you, make us some garlic bread for lunch."

Page watched Whopper turn his back on the boy and go to counter in the corner and pick up a shallow blue bowl decorated with green and yellow vine leaves; the Greek bowl they got that summer before Robby was born. They bought it in one of those junky ceramic shops in Piraeus waiting for ferryboat to take them to Lindos. The bowl held that summer on the blue sea along with Page's onion and garlic. They had made love every day in Lindos after lunch in the cool room with the open window overlooking the transparent blue sea, and if Robby had been born a girl, they would have called her Linda.

Robby, holding the knife, judging the distance to Whopper's broad back, looked at his mother, thinking he could stab Whopper, if he could just force himself to move. Page, seeing her son, so amazingly brave, just a baby compared to the big man, thought for a flicker of time it could be worth it, and flicked her eyes over to Chuleta. Chuleta was watching Robby and raising his gun.

"Robby," she said, forcing herself to smile, keeping her eye on Chuleta, "you want some help chopping?" knowing that would be enough to stop her son from trying to stab Whopper and almost certainly getting himself killed. Knowing he would say no, he'd chop the garlic himself. Knowing that he couldn't stab Whopper unless she gave him some sign that it was okay. She looked at her small son, holding the chopping knife, her brave protector grudgingly bending over the chopping board and starting to chop chop chop. His green hair needed a good brushing, and her heart flooded with love.

CHAPTER
13

Dan, walking out of the front door of Gopher, feeling the heat of the sun rising up in waves from the sticky black parking lot, stopped to look at his home for the past twelve years. Maybe for the last time. It had a kind of perky, hip, and playful look, like a high-tech toy, some structure showing through the glass, bright sherbet colors splashed on the walls. Dan guessed the building would look out-of-date in two years. But that was the price of being on the edge. Now it took five minutes for the new cutting edge to cut you in half. Yeah, famous for fifteen minutes was a great thought, but now it was more like five. Well, he had had his run, and maybe there wasn't going to be another one. Dan turned toward his car, moving slowly, as if he were underwater. Hot, weightless, floating but still above ground, as if he had no arms and legs and the slightest breeze would carry him away like a leaf. From a distance he could feel the anger rising in him like the heat from the pavement. Garland could have given him the money. It would have been so easy for him. Banks loved doing favors for Garland.

He had Garland's 7,500, but of course it wasn't Garland's. It was his. Garland would simply take it out of his paycheck. But none of that mattered. It was so little money it might as well be nothing. He didn't have nearly enough, and he was drifting backward. Garland's parking place was headed by a small sign painted with Garland Grant CEO in fresh blue, green, red, and yellow paint. Dan's name at the head of his space had faded to chalky pastels, as if when he drove away they would disappear. Dan looked at the Volvo, its fish-mouth crumped like the car had been sucking on a lemon. At least he still had the car.

Until they took it back. And they would take it all back. No more salary, no more profit sharing, no more stock options and expense accounts. No more free health care, executive checkups, life insurance, and membership at the Los Palos Country Club. No more sales conferences in Lanai. No more expense-account dinners in San Francisco, business lunches, all-night sessions, no free coffee and Danish in the morning, gossip and Shadow stories. No more paid two-month sabbatical every five years. And no more fresh-faced eager young hotshots challenging his every idea, his every move, keeping him on his toes. He would have to be careful with his money, try to keep from going stale, find a job, find, God help him, a hobby. Something he could pretend to be interested in. He felt light as a balloon, floating as if everything inside had been sucked out of him, and now he was just above the surface of the earth with the power cut off, drifting.

It meant something being a pioneer. It meant he made thousands instead of millions like the guys who came in later. Doom Room was big before the money was big. He sold it to Widmer at AmDell before anybody except Widmer knew how big games and computers were going to be. Anyway it was finished now. Doom Room had gone from Version 1.0 to 5.4, and the royalties had bought his house. Widmer and AmDell made millions from Doom Room, while Dan made a few hundred thousand. Even that was finished now.

If Garland gave him a month's salary for every year he had been at Gopher (which was doubtful, Garland would try to wriggle out of paying him anything), that would be a year's salary to carry them for a while. But not forever. And damn, damn. Fisherman was dead, just another game that nobody would play. He had given two years of his life to Fisherman, and the bastard was going to kill it. Two whole years for nothing. Three-dimensional motion off the net was going to be as big as stereo was in the sixties. Look what stereo did for pop music. Three-dimensional motion was going to create whole industries they hadn't even thought of yet. Of course there were problems. There were always problems. But they could have been there first. He couldn't even take Fisherman to another company because it was mired in several million digits on the Gopher LAN.

So he had no big success in the last five—*shit, seven years*— where he could say he was there for version 1.0. He could tell HP or Sun what didn't work for Fisherman, but they were writing it in RISC, writing for their own chips. And Grant would call them up and lie. Slander him. Maybe if he was in Japan, he would be declared a National Treasure. But this was the valley of the electrons, where last month's new zinger hardware was today's junk. Where yesterday's heroes are not cast in bronze and put on pedestals. They are cast down the toilet and flushed into the wide bowl of the San Francisco Bay.

He got in the car, turned the key. The engine rattled, and there was a scraping sound, metal to metal, but it started. He moved out of the lot, down Rengsdorf toward 101. Question was, where was he headed? He was supposed to have lunch with Widmer. Now that he was fired, at least there was one real benefit. He didn't have to have lunch with Widmer.

Then he thought why not? Why the hell not? The bank didn't want to see him before three-thirty. What else did he have to do. Okay, Widmer was a boring shit. But he was a thousand times richer than Garland. *So screw Garland.* Widmer probably spent more than $400,000 watering AmDell's corporate lawn. He had the money; the only question was how to prise his hands off it. Dan pointed the folded nose of the Volvo south, onto the on-ramp of 101, to AmDell and lunch as it was miscalled. You didn't really have lunch with Widmer—you watched him have lunch.

Along with Wozniak, Jobs, Packard, and Andy Grove, Howard Widmer is one of the giants of Silicon Valley. Among the few who care about the origins of video games, Dan is a legend. But Howard throws a shadow from Silicon Valley to Wall Street to Osaka. When he was seventeen, working out of the back of his dad's newspaper and cigar store in Waldo, Texas, Howard realized that computers were born to play spreadsheets. And anybody with any cents (Howard's joke) needs a spreadsheet.

Bent over a first-generation, secondhand Apple computer, perched on piles of *Field & Stream*, *AMMO!*, and *Gent* magazines, Howard wrote the first spreadsheet program with a graphic interface and sold it in Apple's footsteps, paying Apple salesmen and -women extra on the side to hawk his software to their business customers. The feedback from the salesmen gave

Howard the courage to drop out of East Texas Tech and hitchhike to Cupertino, California. He camped out in Apple's world headquarters, a one-story building then, until he got in to see Jobs. Steve Jobs bundled his next program, Tabby (after the Apple engineers cleaned out the bugs and glitches), with their Macs.

Tabby was a monster success, and Howard's new AmDell International Computer Software was listed on NASDAQ for $2.19 a share. It now sold, having split seven times, for $137 a share. With twenty-seven offices around the world, and worldwide headquarters in Sunnyvale, Widmer's personal wealth was rumored to be somewhere above $3.7 billion. Last spring, *Fortune* put Howard on the cover, driving his red Ford pickup truck. Which he bought to drive to his local militia meetings.

As a rule, Widmer preferred being chauffeured in an armored limo. "When you are as rich as I am," he once told Dan, "every asshole in the world wants to get their mitts on your money." Howard wasn't just suspicious, he was deeply afraid. He lived in a modest ranch house on a fifty-acre spread in Woodside next to John Sculley's estate when John was running Apple. Last year, after years of being married to his office, Widmer married Margaret Sneath, a mild young woman from AmDell's market research department. Which changed his life. Widmer had been famous for working seventy-two hours nonstop and showing up at a board meeting looking fresh as a cactus. Now he went home every night. His hobbies, as revealed in the official AmDell biography (*HOWARD SAYS!* $32.95 from AmDell Press), were guns and shooting.

Howard was having lunch, as he almost always did, at his desk twenty-seven stories up, on the top of AmDell tower. He was going a little bald on top, with

156   FORREST EVERS

a short ponytail pulled tight with a rubber band. His face, however, commanded your attention. Flat as a dinner plate, too big for his body, perched on a stalk of a neck featuring a large Adam's apple that went up and down like an elevator as Widmer downloaded a swallow of Big Mac. Howard's face looked as if he had been standing in a raw East Texas wind—blotches of red on pasty white cheeks sporting bits of dried and flaking skin. With his eyes set close together and magnified by large round glasses and his little beak of a nose, Howard looked like an owl. His voice was high and scratchy as a barbed-wire fence. If you happened to bump into Widmer at the checkout counter at Robert's grocery in Woodside, you might think he was an aging hippie. A first-generation Dead head, maybe fifty-five, maybe even sixty. But looks, as we all know, can be deceiving.

The forty-three-year-old billionaire was twitching between bites of his Big Mac, as if random sparks of excess energy were popping off him. Dan was sitting on a white silk sofa, wondering when Widmer would get to the point and tell him why he wanted Dan here.

Widmer always had ideas, most of them off-the-wall, impractical, impossible, or dumb. But Widmer didn't mind. It was one of his more endearing features; like a child, if an idea didn't work, he just went on to the next one. Widmer said he "liked to keep in touch with the Video Graphic goofballs." Watching him talk, seeing his ideas bounce freely off the walls, Dan had the feeling he was watching a precocious child waving a loaded gun. You never knew with Widmer if he was going to put his arm around you or blow your head off.

Widmer put down his Big Mac and put his feet up on the desk, cowboy boots crossed, as if they both had all the time in the world. "Most people said that's a hell of thing to do on your first date, but I knew she'd like it," Howard was saying in his high nasal whine. "First time I took Maggie out we shot beer cans behind the barn. Let me tell you, shooting is sexy as hell. You want to get a lady riled up, put a gun in her hand and let her pop off a few rounds."

Dan, avoiding Widmer's narrowed stare, let his eyes wander to the cot behind Widmer's desk; the legendary cot Widmer used to sleep on when he was building AmDell. Years of confinement in his office staring into computer screens and the faces of his managers had given Howard a unique understanding of the world of computers and computer marketing. On the other hand, his view of the outside world was as distorted as a goldfish looking out of a fishbowl. He knew there were other points of view; he just didn't want to hear them. So Howard still loved to tell the lawyers and MBAs out of Harvard and Stanford who ran AmDell these days what to do. But with Maggie home for supper, the cot was no longer in service. Dan idly wondered if old Pieface and shy Maggie with the popping eyes reclined, sexually intertwined, and waved their bare feet in the air on the cot in their courting days. On the narrow Widmer spreadsheet.

"We ought to teach gunsmanship in school," Widmer was saying. "If we had shooting ranges in every public school, made it part of the core curriculum, teach the kids to use guns properly, maybe even throw in a little gun history, kids today'd be more relaxed. Have more respect for discipline." Widmer counted the blessings on his fingers. "Be a lot safer. If they were all armed, you wouldn't have these drive-by shootings 'cause your drive-by shooter would know he's gonna get blasted before he gets to the end of the block. That's the kind of discipline these ghetto kids respect. Nothing more important than persistence and discipline. And if all the kids have guns, all you have to do if a kid screws up is take his gun away. Like taking away his dick. He knows he's gonna be vulnerable. Believe me, Dan, nobody, including kids, wants to be walking around without a dick."

"You mean boys and girls. Both. Take away their dicks."

Widmer, elbows on his desk, took another small bite of his Big Mac no cheese and, chewing thoughtfully, placed the munched bun back on his plate alongside the scoop of low-fat cottage cheese. His eyes registering irritation that, once again, Dan had missed the point. As he chewed, Widmer's eyebrows inched together, a thought gathering in a knot behind.

Dan watched the man, thinking if elegance really is denial, then Widmer ought to be the most elegant man on earth. He denied himself almost everything. But it would take heavy graphic morphing to see Widmer as elegant. His rumpled leather biker's jacket hung heavily on the back of his chair like a wrinkled black ghost rising up from Howard's twitching body. His yellow and brown short-sleeve shirt was a Kmart drip-dry, six to the box for $28.99.

Weird to have so much money and enjoy it so little. Widmer's rainbow of joy had one band, gold. Give Widmer a Big Mac, a plate of fries, and the roar of another half billion dollars surging down his pipeline, and he was happy. Dan waited for Widmer's thought to float to the surface. Lunch with Widmer, CEO and holder of 68.5 percent of AmDell, consisted of two things. Waiting and listening. You were welcome to eat on your own time, not on his.

Widmer finished chewing, put his hands behind his head, and leaned back with his eyes closed, sunning himself in the warmth of his own thought. "I've been thinking about money," he said. "You got a dollar bill?"

Widmer's wide mouth snapped open like a pickerel anticipating a minnow, and he leaned forward, hand out.

Dan looked in his bulging wallet. The smallest was a ten.

Widmer took it, stretching it between his hands. "Okay, a ten. Doesn't matter. This stuff," he said, "is out-of-date. It's clumsy, and it's slow. It is easy to lose and easy to steal. And it's unstable. Any asshole in the White House can devalue it anytime he wants to make a billion for himself on the international markets. When the government in Washington is finally sucked dry by the International Money Changers of Zion, like they did to Germany after World War I, you might as well tear it up."

Widmer ripped the bill in half. Then in half again and dropped the pieces on his desk.

Dan looked at him, hoping this was some dumb parlor trick.

"You want that back, don't you, Dan?"

"Howard, it is not a question of ten dollars. I need $400,000. In cash."

"I'll bet you do. Listen, let me give you a piece of advice. Forget the green stuff. I'm talking about E-Cash, Dan, Cyber-Cash. We're close. Very close. We've got the systems and the backup. We've got the hardware, and we've got the software. Only thing holding us back is encryption to keep the hackers out of our pockets. We're this close," he said, holding his thumb and forefinger an inch apart.

"E-Cash?"

"Come on, come on." Widmer was waving his hands with impatience, getting out of his chair, pacing, his black jeans too big for him. "Didn't you see the cover story in *Business Week* last month. Called E-cash the biggest revolution in money since the coin. Christ, sometimes I think you graphics guys have your heads up your asses, and you think the world is pink. Come on, Dan, wake up, I need you here. I want you to give this a look. I want you to get your top guns to put together a graphic interface for our little card here and give it a name. Make it look friendly, accessible, important. We're putting together a formal presentation for your guys later this week, but I don't want you to wait for that. I don't want you to wait ten seconds on this."

"This?"

Widmer stopped pacing, his crusty apple-pie face intense, his hands on his desk, locked in. "Okay, look at it this way. Think of pocketing a penny for every check written in America. Americans write forty-five billion checks a day. At a penny a shot that's forty-five million dollars a day in this country alone, seven days a week. So you better have big pockets." Widmer smacked his hands, and cried out, "Heee-haahhh. The banks charter jets just to fly the damn checks around. By this time next year, E-cash will be flowing around the world at the speed of light, and the mints of the world will come grinding to a halt. A little luck we'll see forty-five million dollars a day coming in the front door. You with me?"

Dan wasn't with him. It didn't matter how much it was if it wasn't here today. "What I need, Howard, is cash right now. Today. I'm serious, Howard, if I could just have, say, $200,000 in cash this afternoon, I'll pay you back tomorrow." No way could he could pay him back tomorrow. Didn't matter.

Widmer paused for a moment, then went on like he hadn't heard him. "Okay, you've got First Virtual, Cybercash, companies like that already out there hauling in cash on the Internet. But they are after the big transfers. Corporate stuff. We're after the little

ones, the everyday individual bills, supermarket shopping, video rentals. A penny a shot, that could be a
nice piece."

"Or even $100,000," Dan said.

Widmer nodded, like he heard him this time.
Then went on as if he didn't. "You want to shop on
the TV mall, pay your gas bill, stuff like that, you
won't have to write a check or keep track of your
credit-card purchases because we'll do that for you.
Isn't that great, just amazingly great?" Widmer held
his arms out wide like he was hearing the applause.
"Okay, it costs a penny a shot, but you won't even
have to buy a damn stamp, so Mr. and Mrs. Consumer
are way ahead even after we take our penny. See, we
get this running every son of a bitch in America with
bills to pay and food to buy will come out of the
woods to throw money in our trough. You with me?"

Dan gave him a noncommittal nod, thinking—
There has got to be a way to get his attention. Widmer put
his arm around Dan and started walking him around
the room, talking quietly into his ear. This was the
confidential stuff. "That's why Gates wanted to buy
Intuit, get his hands on their E-cash software. Thank
God the Department of Justice stopped them at the
altar. Only smart thing they've done in twenty years."
Widmer smiled, remembering, his round face looking
like have a nice day. In an instant the happy face was
gone, his arm was off Dan's shoulder, and he was
heading back for his desk, growling out his words.
"But that's not gonna stop Gates and Microsoft breathing down our neck. Not with sixteen and a half billion
a year out there. They are busier than a cat coverin up
shit in a litter box, trying to make up the two maybe
three months' lead we've got on them."

Widmer banged on his desk, gave Dan the old
Widmer pie-face grin, strode around his desk, and put

his arm around Dan's shoulder again. He hugged Dan as if he could squeeze another ten dollars out of him. "You're family, Dan, so I'm gonna let you in on one of the family secrets. Gates is out there gaining on us. Microsoft is working with Visa on a system for securing credit-card transactions over the Internet. But like I say, we've got the jump on them. We've got the software and the hardware in place." Widmer let go and walked back to his desk to sit down. He leaned back, put his feet back up on his desk, the corporate raider, planning his next strike. "So AmDell's got a little window of opportunity here and it is going to be open just a crack for about ten minutes, and if we can squeeze our asses through before they turn on the lights, we are going to have more money than God."

"Who's going to regulate it?" Dan said, thinking, Humor him. He'll never give you anything if he thinks you are against him. So keep him talking. Seem interested.

"Regulate it?" Widmer snorted. "You sound like one of those assholes in Washington. Greatest regulator there is gonna regulate it. The market."

"Not the federal government?"

Howard leaned forward, bony elbows on the desk. "Look, if you make your own money and you got the software to back it up, what the hell you need a government for? Fuck the government; they'll just piss it away on a lot of bureaucrats and pregnant teenage drug addicts with their hands out."

"Howard, I have got to have . . ."

Widmer cut him off, waving his hand at him, a proud parent with a new child. "Let me show you."

Widmer took a bright red-and-gold plastic card out of his drip-dry shirt pocket and handed it to Dan. The card looked like a credit card, slightly thicker and rimmed with gold scrollwork, *AmCASH* printed in green and gold across the front. Widmer was up out of his chair again, out from behind his desk and staring at his creation with his arm around Dan's shoulder again, gripping him hard. "Okay, advantages. One, convenience. Two, speed. And three, accuracy. Plus you never have to write a check or balance a checkbook. And it's a hell of a lot cheaper than what a bank charges you."

"What's the downside?"

"Downside is you gotta have a computer with a modem and a PCMCIA slot like the notebooks have these days. Stuff the AmCASH card into that, and you are all set. Everybody with any money has a computer at home, right? If they don't have any money, we don't want to waste our time talking to them."

"Could you, for example," Dan said, "transfer $100,000 in cash into my account this afternoon?"

"Sure. Your computer calls our computer. Our computer swaps pleasantries with your computer, we transfer, say two dollars, or what the hell, you want a hundred thousand, your numbers add up you can have a hundred thousand this afternoon. Christ, if you qualify, you can have twenty million. On your card."

"You mean there's no cash?"

"Jesus, did you listen to a word I said? Of course there's no cash. That's the point. Plus we tag it so you have to spend it in certain ways. Like you can buy AmDell software, any one of the AmDell family of products, but not Microsoft. Plus maybe we give you special discounts if you use our money instead of the US Treasury stuff. And the more people we fold into the network, like AT&T, Visa, GM, Paine Webber, and our friends at Intel with discounts, incentives, all that good freebie stuff, the faster it's gonna grow. Think of AmCASH, Dan, as the money of the Internet."

There was a little ringing sound, and Widmer picked up his phone, and said, "Goddammit, can't I even have my own lunch? What?"

A breath of silence, and Widmer said, "No, no, dammit. That's not even close. Shit. I'll be right there. No, no, tell them to wait for me." Widmer put his phone down, pushed back his chair, stood up, ran his hand over his scalp. For a moment Dan thought Widmer might cry. It wouldn't be the first time. "You'd think," he whined, "with the money I pay these guys, that they could get through a day without shitting in their own sandbox. I hate having to do everything. Where the hell do you get good people who can do what you say without pissing down their leg. I'm not finished with you yet. I'll be back in five minutes."

Dan watched him go and looked out the wall of glass at the bay. The water was deep blue, ruffled with whitecaps and seven miles across. A flotilla of sailboats were having a race. Sails puffed as tight and slick as balloons, mellow yellow, apple green, grapefruit pink, and cherry red, bright as tropical birds, slid across the water. For a moment he envied them, free in the cool breeze, shuffling across the bright blue bay as if time were standing still and the sun would always shine. But time was slipping away from him. There was no telling when Widmer would be back or even if. He could wait for two hours for the man and still be here, staring out the window.

Dan went over to Widmer's desk and picked up the AmCASH card. The red-and-green design looked cheap and dated. They could use the fresh-fruit colors of the sailboats, make it kind of freaky, fun for the video gamers, make it look sweet like AmCASH is good for you with no waiting and no regrets. Dan wondered if there was a way to squeeze real money out of the thing, if the chip was active and you could plug into the software and wire a transfer to his bank account. It was just a dummy. Dan put it in his pocket.

Widmer's black leather jacket hung on the back of the great man's black leather office chair, studs glinting in the dull light. Dan went over to the office door, closed it, and walked back to the jacket and felt through its pockets. He found a worn and scratched brown leather wallet in the inside breast pocket. Dan leafed through a Mileage First Platinum Visa credit card, a platinum American Express card, $187 in cash, a driver's license, an AmDell security card, and a Bank of America bank card. A membership card in the Felton Militia with a photograph of Howard's face looking like it was taken for a high-school yearbook. Dan was looking at the picture, wondering if Widmer had looked like an owl at birth, when he heard the door opening.

Widmer's secretary was in the doorway, saying, "Excuse me." Her broad Korean face smooth and pleasant, a thousand corporate secrets safe behind her mild gaze.

Dan had Widmer's wallet cupped in his hand, feeling like it was the size of a meat loaf. He dropped his hand below the back of the chair so the wallet was probably out of sight, but he couldn't be sure.

"Excuse me, Mr. Messina, I didn't mean to disturb you. You want any coffee or anything? You know he could be a while."

Dan gave her his serious professional businessman of today look, deeply concerned with the rise and fall of corporate bombs. "No, no, uh, Briony, I'm fine. I won't wait long."

"Would you like the door shut?"

"Please, if you don't mind. He's given me a lot to think about."

"Just shout if you change your mind." She shut

the door. If she had seen him holding Widmer's wallet, she hadn't shown the slightest flicker.

Dan opened the wallet again, took out Widmer's bank card, driver's license, and American Express card. American Express, the bank of choice of drug dealers, Nick had said, because unlike banks they didn't have to report transactions over ten grand. Should be easy pickings as long as they didn't ask to look at Widmer's face on his driver's license. That could be good for twenty, maybe thirty thousand. The tricky part would be getting his access code for the Bank America card. It could be his date of birth, a part of his phone number, a part of his address, part of his license. All of which he now had. But the ATM only gave you three shots before they ate the card. Widmer may have been a social illiterate, but he had a genius for numbers. So it was unlikely he would have anything as simple as 1111. Or would he like the Zen simplicity of primal initial digits? Or the nullity of 0000?

It took a while for Dan to notice the ache he'd almost forgotten spreading up from his groin and into his stomach. He was committing a crime. Okay, just a little crime so far, but you can't steal a man's wallet, his credit cards, and driver's license without knowing that you have invaded his privacy, betrayed his trust, and stolen something more than his money. It's like looking in a man's bedroom window at night. Would he feel better, he wondered, if he raised the level of theft into thousands, moved up the ladder from petty larceny to grand? It's not really a crime, he told himself, if you do it for your family.

The last time he stole he had been nine. He broke into one of the round blue cardboard Hadassah coin collection boxes his grandmother had left on the kitchen table. He was trying to shake out quarters, and the box broke, the coins rolling all over the kitchen floor. He was on his hands and knees reaching for a quarter that had rolled under the stove when his mother came in. The feeling from almost thirty years ago was bad boy. Shame.

Well that was then. Now he felt what most thieves feel about their victims. Which was, Fuck him. Widmer didn't need it, and he did. For his family. It could be hours, maybe days, before Widmer uses his bank card. I have to get the money. Have to. And of course I'll pay him back. The American Express card was virtually a sure thing. If only he looked like an owl. Widmer's face had been on the covers of *Fortune*, *Forbes*, and *Business Week*. Any clerk behind the counter would see he didn't look anything like Howard. Excuse me, I'd like a $100,000 cash advance on my American Express. Sure, Mr. Ha Ha Widmer. Just stare into the video camera there while I have our security guards club you into the ground.

The door was opening again, and Dan jammed the wallet into his back pocket.

"What the hell is the door closed for? It gets stuffy in here." Widmer looking around and wrinkling his little beak like something smelled bad. "You look like shit, Dan. Sorry I had to leave you. They keep saying the way to run a corporation is delegate, and the bastards won't let you delegate a damn dime."

Widmer strode across the room, grabbed the wreckage of his Big Mac, took a cold soggy bite, and looked around his desk. "Where the hell is that AmCASH card?"

"I've got it. I thought you wanted me to take it."

"Right. So where are you on this? Do you think you could get your team started on a designing a graphic interface, tie it in with a graphic design for an online site?"

Dan nodded sure, no problem.

"I told you, Howard. I have to find $100,000 for my family. This afternoon."

"Yeah, you told me. Usually when somebody asks me for money, they tell me why."

"It's for my family. A gang is holding Page and the kids hostage."

"Jesus," Widmer said, shaking his head. He thought for a moment, then pounded his desk. "Hey let's go in. I got stuff that'll blow the heads off their necks from three hundred yards. Surround them; we've got some good smoke. Smoke 'em out."

"Howard, they have guns to Page's head, and the kids' heads. You can't blow your way in. Lend me the money, and I'll get it back to you tomorrow. Any interest you like."

"Dan, I'd like to help you, and if you want to use my security guys here, be my guest. You want me to get Phillips up here, just say so, because, believe me, Phillips and his guys are trained in this stuff, and they are the best. But I'm not giving my money to a bunch of junkie kids with Uzis. Goddamn, you know if I could help you I would," Widmer's face wrinkled up at the thought, skin flaking off. "Anyway, even if I could get the money in cash, and I can't, you have to know, giving them money never solves anything. They just ask for more and more until you haven't got any more. Then they shoot you."

14

S ee," Chuleta said, rolling his shoulders in his spotless white button-down shirt, feeling good, sitting down at the head of the polished marble dining-room table, "just like a real family dinner. The way American families s'posed to eat. Like together."

"You s'posed to wait for the women so they be sittin down first before you sit your skinny little ass down," Blue Girl said. She was standing behind her chair in Baylor's little yellow summer dress, looking across the table at Baylor. Baylor was wearing Blue Girl's pink spandex tube top and stretchy nylon bicycle pants that ended just above her knee with the flesh bulging out like white toothpaste out of a black tube. Baylor looked tough, like a girl who would ask you for a dollar on the street and say "fuck you" when you gave it to her.

"Maybe you should do something with your makeup, girl," Blue Girl said. "Like give yourself a little color in the face."

Baylor acted like she hadn't heard Blue Girl. "I'm not hungry," she said to Chuleta.

"Then don't eat nothin. Just sit down."

Page was at the other end of the table in a Pearl Jam T-shirt and faded jeans she'd changed into while Blue Girl was in the bedroom with her, standing guard. The girl had the courtesy to look away, but Page hated the invasion of her privacy, hated a stranger seeing her in her underwear.

Silver, dressed like Chuleta in Robby's fresh white button-down shirt and ironed chinos, was fidgety like he always was before he ate, looking like a nervous preppy. "Come on, sit down," Chuleta said, patting the chair next to him. "What else we got to do?"

"Get a whiff of this, muthafuckers." Whopper was coming through the door holding a big steaming bowl of pasta, Robby trailing behind in his wake. "You gonna love this."

Page patted the chair next to her, telling Robby, "Come sit here next to me. Have some lunch."

Robby, in Silver's baggy grey shorts and black nylon tank top, looked like he had shrunk. Everything was way too big and serious ugly. Like he had on his own Nike High-Top Air Max IIs, so that was okay. But the rest of this stuff really sucked. It was way too big. And it smelled funny, like some dumb perfume or aftershave, that was supposed to make the girls roll over. Last month he splashed on some Egoist his Dad had in a fancy bottle on his dresser. Wore it to school, see if it worked.

It worked. Guys he didn't know came up to him and said he smelled like an asshole. And the girls wouldn't let him alone, asking him if it was Chanel or was it dogshit.

Chuleta and Silver were wearing his stuff, which was not too bad, he could live with that. Because the stuff they had on was that preppy crap that Mom kept trying to get him to wear. No shit, they could keep it.

But Jesus, he looked stupid in Silver's clothes. Blue Girl probably laughing her ass off at him. Listen, he was growing. Couple of years, he was gonna tear these assholes' heads off. The knife was still in the kitchen. If Chuleta hadn't seen him, pointed that damn gun at him, he'd have planted that sucker in Whopper's back. Fuck him. Fuck all of them. Especially Blue Girl. In every way.

Blue Girl was sitting down, knees together, looking kind of weird in Baylor's dress. Looking like she was Baylor with big tits, long legs, slanty eyes, and heavy tan. But she sure wasn't his sister. No way.

Blue Girl patted the chair next to her, the one between her and Mom, saying, "Yeah, come on now, Robby, sit here," in that sexy voice of hers, "next to me." And Robby's cock gave him a little twinge in the gut. Robby went over to sit down next to her like it didn't make any difference to him. He was cool. He gave Mom a nod, like he was all over sitting there for her. Nothing to do with Blue Girl.

Whopper set the hot bowl on the table, Baylor sliding a napkin underneath it just in time so it didn't mark the polished marble. "Just like home," he said happily. "No Daddy." Whopper sat down heavily next to Baylor. "Well, you just gonna stare at it, girl, or are you gonna eat my good food?"

"It's not your food. You stole it," Baylor said.

"Where's your daddy?" Robby asked Whopper, forgetting about Blue Girl for a moment.

"In jail. Up at Soledad."

"Where you are going," Page said quietly.

"Exactly," Chuleta said. "They are building a whole bunch of new cells just for us. Maximum security."

Baylor picked up her fork, pointing it at Chuleta. "Good. I hope they lock you up for life."

"So we better enjoy it while we can, right?" Chuleta said.

Whopper picked up the bowl of pasta, steam and the fragrance of garlic, olive oil, and tomatoes rising up and wandering around the room. "Hey look, if nobody gonna eat, I guess I'll just help myself." He dug in with a big spoon, ladling the slippery pasta onto his plate. "You want some, girl?" he said to Baylor.

"A little maybe."

"Anybody else," he said, tilting the bowl and showing it around the table.

"Whatta you gotta make a big show for? Shut your mouth, pass the food, bro," Silver said, reaching for the bowl, ladling the pasta and sauce on his plate, losing a few strands off the edge of the bowl onto his place mat. He picked them up with his fingers, holding up the strands one by one, letting them slide into his wide-open mouth, his face turned up like a baby bird's.

"You got any beer, maybe some wine?" Chuleta said to Page. "I'm not saying I don't appreciate your Diet Coke here, but this pasta smells too good to wash down with this fizzy shit."

Page, thinking she would really like a drink. Maybe it wasn't the smartest thing in the world, but a glass of wine would dull the saw-toothed irritation of being watched. Of having these bastards in her house. Pointing their guns at her family. She pushed her chair back, glad to get up and get away. "I'll get some."

Silver was behind her going into the kitchen, saying, "I'll help."

The chef's knife lay on the cutting board where Robby had left it. Page could take the knife off the table and stab Silver in the neck before he could react. She could do it. But Chuleta had the gun propped against the dining-room table next to him. And there was Whopper and that horrible girl. Whatever she did there were too many of them. Still, she might do it except they had the kids in the next room. Whatever she did, they had the kids.

Reaching into the fridge for a six-pack of Red Stripe, she thought, is this what it was like being a Jew in Germany in World War II? Where you were trapped because whatever you did to resist, the consequences were certain and horrific. You spoke up, and they shot your children in the face. Is that why there was so little resistance? Because they still had hope? She had hope that they might get out of this. But Chuleta, Silver, Whopper, any one of them could easily kill her and her children. She and the kids knew too much about them.

She handed the six-pack to Silver and reached under the counter where they kept the wine, coming up with two bottles of Clos Du Bois Cabernet. The everyday eight bucks a bottle cheap stuff. She wasn't drinking for pleasure; she was drinking for effect. "Why don't you take the beer in," she said to Silver, "while I open these."

To her surprise Silver went. She was alone in the kitchen, the knife was still there on the counter, and she could . . . could what? Could do nothing. Poison them maybe. Page pulled open a drawer and took out a corkscrew.

Page came into the dining room with two bottles of wine in one hand and three glasses held by their stems like a crystal bouquet in the other. "Anybody else want some wine?"

Later, Whopper was on his third plateful, twirling the long strands of spaghetti with a fork ground into a big spoon and hauling the dripping red mass to a mouth the size of a meat locker.

Page filled up her glass again and took another

deep swallow, feeling the wine warm her, relax her. She never had wine in the middle of the day. Maybe she should ease up, relax, have a little wine with lunch from now on. Help her slow down, be more natural with her clients. She put down her glass, and said to Blue Girl, "So what do you do? You don't work, you don't go to school. What do you do, drive around and shoot people?"

"Yeah, right," Blue Girl said. "We be kickin, jackin, an stackin. Then we like gangbang. Like we find rich white mothers with rich white teenage kids, blow their heads off."

"Yeah," Silver said, with a laugh. "What we here for. Hey, Chuleta, this is a good gig, man. Maybe we should stay here a few days, enjoy the good life. Party with the girls here."

Page looked at Chuleta, eye to eye the length of the table. "Don't you know you are headed for a dead end?"

"'Course we know. Except we ain't headed for it, we in it. That's why we here. You know a better way, hey, let me know. We'll check it out."

"You could go to school."

"Yeah? You send your kids to that shithole? Hey, it ain't far from here. You send your kids to George Washington?"

Page shook her head no.

"'Course not. Place is wack, fallin apart, stinks. Dirty-ass kids doin drugs in the hall. Teachers on tenure, they don't give a shit, just puttin in time till they get pension. Shit, half the kids in high school can't even read an' shit. They just come in, sit on their ass, go home. Come on, don't just be shakin your head, tell me. You send your kids there? And next you gonna say," Chuleta said, shifting into his mocking white-folks voice, "you can always work if you want to work. Let me give you the news from the street, bitch. Set your ass straight. There is no jobs down there. Not for no cholo with no high-school education. 'Less you want to sell concrete candy to the school kids. Make five, ten dollars an hour, that's it. 'Cause you can score from any little eight year old kid in the park. How you gonna compete with that? And even if you could make ten dollars dealin, you might as well spend it now, live high, 'cause you be dead or in jail in six months. Or you could always be one of them sorry-ass mother-fuckers robbin old ladies on check day. That is another career option. You check it out. Then you can give me the word how I'm s'posed to live my life."

Page took another long sip and said, "Go fuck . . ."

"Hey, Whopper," Blue Girl said, "this pasta shit is good. What you put in the sauce, make it so good?"

"Ketchup," Whopper said, "make everything taste good." He grinned and made a face, his smile wide and mindless, his cheeks bunched up, and his brown eyes round.

"Dickhead," Robby said into his bowl.

Whopper pushed his plate back, lowering his big head, his eyes small again, glittering. "The fuck you dis me for, boy? Cook you a good lunch, better than that shit you probably get. You know I can knock your face upside your head I feel like it. The fuck you got green hair for? You think it makes you look tough. Makes you look like shit. What you got green hair for?"

"Swimming," Robby said almost under his breath, his head down.

"Swimmin?"

"Robby was on the swimming team," Baylor said. "The chlorine turned his hair green."

"Was?" Blue Girl asked.

Robby looked up at her. "I quit."

"'Cause your hair was green?" she asked him gently.

"Because he was too slow," his sister said. "He kept coming in last."

"Shut up, Baylor. Only sport you do is screw that dorky Brad. You couldn't even be a cheerleader."

Page looked at her daughter, her mouth open.

"Hey, bro," Whopper said, "maybe you just wasn't tryin hard enough. Maybe a little extra workout with the weights, like Whopper do, pump you up, put you out front."

"Can you swim?" the boy said.

"No."

"Then don't tell me what to do."

"Okay, my man. You tell me," Whopper said, "what you want to be."

"Big enough to kick your ass," Robby said.

But Whopper didn't pay him no mind, already off the kid, feeling pain from another direction. The news that Baylor was not a virgin was sinking in, and it hurt him to think about it. He didn't have a choice here.

Had to think about it. The thought was that she was pristine, nobody ever touch those pink titties. That thought was over. Forget all the stuff he was going to show her. She be humping her boyfriend, how special was she? Just like every other bitch. Shit, fuck her and forget her. Give her a good stretch. Leave her wanting more. Fuck her, fucking some weak little white dick. She had a lot to learn.

He looked at her, her little white-girl pink nipples outlined in Blue Girl's pink spandex. He never liked them tube tops, didn't like the way they flatten Baylor's little-girl titties out flat. Whopper checked out her round white face, freckles, nothin little nose, short blond hair. Stumpy teeth. Wasn't no way pretty. Little white tummy pooching out over Blue Girl's black bicycle shorts. All that taboo white-girl shit down there. He get a little jack together, he have plenty of women. Good sisters know what and how, do it the way he like it. Not be cryin makin a big fuss about nothin. What the hell he want some dumb little white bitch for? She gets her kicks seein how easy it is for her lead the men around. Just because he saw her titties. Those little pink nipples. He wondered if she tasted different.

Silver holding his glass of wine, like he imagined a man would hold his glass of wine in a two-hundred-dollar restaurant, like say he drove up in a 'Vette, coming from his TV show, tipping the parking valet couple of maybe tens, sly little pussy on his arm all clingy and swish in her silk panties you can see from time to time 'cause her dress so short. Looking through his wineglass, checkin out the old lady at the head of the table, pouring down the wine like she's gonna get bombed. She's still lookin good, got those nice eyes, and that is some body for a woman old enough to be his mother. She get a little loose, he might just have to check that out. Chuleta said keep an eye on her. She get sleepy, he might have to keep real close, take her back for a little afternoon siesta, check out how it feel with mature nice lady pussy. Probably know stuff he never even thought about.

Goddamn Robby, Baylor was thinking. Telling Mom that she had made love with Brad. She was going to deny it, but now it was too late. Robby just jumped her with it, took her by surprise. And she couldn't lie to Mom. She was going to tell her. It wasn't anything to get excited about. She wasn't pregnant. Wasn't

going to get pregnant. Which was the only thing Mom
was really worried about. It was okay, but Brad was
definitely not it. But now she looked as if she had
been sneaking around, and that was the last thing it
was. God, it was broad daylight, on her sleeping bag,
so they wouldn't mess up the covers on her bed. She
wanted to know what it was like, and now she did.
Sort of. Brad looked like turkey neck and gizzards
when he took his underpants off. Next time it
wouldn't hurt, so it was bound to be better, but it
might be a while. Definitely not with Brad. He was so
dumb. She'd had to talk him through the whole thing,
and he just didn't want to listen. Teeth for God's sake.
That's what made her yell, and naturally Robby heard
them and came sneaking into her room. The little
sneak. Telling Mom like he kept threatening to do.
God, if only Brad wasn't so stupid. And now he was
following her around school like he was some stupid
puppy dog with his tongue hanging out. Like the heat
she was getting off this Whopper monstrosity. He's all
over giving her little winks and grins, like he wants to
be let out of his cage. Talk about dumb, he made Brad
seem like a rocket scientist, and the way he was looking at her was seriously scary. Maybe it was just these
horrible stinky Blue Girl clothes. At first she thought it
might be like a kick, put on something really trashy,
see what she looked like as a slut. But they were too
small. Made her bulge all over. And God she hated the
smell of Blue Girl's perfume. It was like bubble gum.
But the big thing was she better talk to Mom. Like tell
her not to worry. Maybe tell her that it was okay, Brad
wore a condom. Maybe not. She didn't want to get
into the details. Like washing the sleeping bag six
times and there was still the bloodstain if you knew
where to look. Thing that really bothered her about
Whopper, though, which she never would have

expected, was that he smelled good. Like fresh bread and butter only better. Like sexy in a funny way.

Blue Girl didn't like the taste of wine, and beer made her fart, so she was sticking with water. She was amazed how bad Baylor looked in her clothes. You definitely don't wanna wear no tube top; you don't have the tits for it. And no makeup make her look all washed-out, like somebody come along and erased her face. But she's gettin hers, some goofball got off on that lumpy vanilla pudding. All high-and-mighty like she don't leave no stink in the bathroom. Blue Girl pictured Baylor making it with some boy, and it made her laugh, Miss Piggy's feet sticking up in the air.

"What are you laughing at," Robby said, glad to get the subject off him.

"Your sister. I hate to say it, 'cause they is my clothes, but she look like she ain't gonna give it away no more. She look like she thinkin of turning pro."

"Pro what?" the boy said.

"Pro-fessional, my man," she said, giving Robby a little knowing wink. She felt bad about feeling Robby's cock. He looked at her now with a kind of trust and need, and it made her feel responsible for him. Which was a mistake, definitely. They were going to get out of this clean. This shit was for real, and, whatever happened, you didn't want to feel for them.

"You can have your stupid clothes back," Baylor said. "It's probably time for you to go back to work."

"Hey, kick it, bitches. We just a family having a nice lunch in a nice house," Chuleta said. "We be gone soon, never see each other again. But we still got like a few hours together. So we all chill, okay. Make it easy on ourselves, hear what I'm sayin?"

Chuleta thinking if he could just keep the lid on it,

keep the love high, it might work. A hundred thousand apiece. Equal shares for *quatro Todos. Todos por todos*. Okay, they always shared everything, so why was this different? The Craps and the Slobs, they dissed his little group 'cause it was so small. But small meant fast reaction time, easy to control. Easy to keep the level of love up there. He was down for them, and they were down for him. *Todos* because they took everybody in, long as they had the heart. *Uno por Todos*. Black, white, Chicano, didn't matter; kid had soul, good heart, color don't mean shit. *Todos por Todos*. Like the Folks, they take everybody, every color, too. But Folks have all that hierarchy shit. *Todos*, we take anything and everything and give it to *Todos*, equal split.

See, they try and keep us under a lid. So we can't see nothin. Think we can't see you don't have to be in prison to be in jail. We ain't goin to no prison, and we sure as shit not gonna stay in that jail they call the ghetto. We gonna blow the lid off, mothafucka, let the light in. *Todos* means everything, and that's what we gonna get. Everything.

He looked up to see Page watching him over the rim of her glass. See, her attitude is fuck 'em. Like she was sayin to me when Blue Girl cut her off. She thinks I didn't hear that "fuck you." What I heard all my life. Ain't nobody gives a fuck about us. She thinks I don't know what she thinks. She's no different. Thinks the same as everybody. She thinks, Hey, they hungry, got rats in the baby's room, no job, no heat, no hope, fuck 'em. They think we'll go away. Someplace else. You got that right, Momma. You drive me out of my house, I'm comin to yours.

CHAPTER
15

Dan standing in front of the ATM, waiting for the woman in front of him. She had the $350 hairdo, cute white, pink, and blue tennis outfit, new bright white Reeboks, and five or ten thousand dollars of gold necklace, diamond tennis bracelet, and gold earrings. If he stole the jewelry off twenty Los Palos tennis ladies, he would have enough. If a fence gave him a hundred percent. But fences gave more like ten, didn't they? So he'd have to find a hundred Los Palos tennis ladies. Then find a fence. He wouldn't know a fence if the guy was standing on his foot.

The woman fiddled with the machine, hesitated, not sure what to do next, nervous that he was standing behind her, worried that he was going to pick up her PIN. Which Dan was trying to do. Because he had no confidence at all that he could access Widmer's account. The woman had a nice trim butt and an even tan, and she had left the motor running on her Mercedes coupe with the polished wheels and the flawless gold paint. Bound to have plenty in her account just to feed the Mercedes. Spring tune-up—

$2,874. Thank you very much, *und auf wiedersehen* says your friendly local Mercedes dealer. With the sun behind him Dan could not read the screen over her shoulder. Also, she was so hunched over the keyboard he couldn't see what numbers she was punching. She acted like she knew he was trying to pick up her numbers. Nothing more obvious, he thought, than a rookie crook.

"Nice day," he said, thinking he should say something, help her relax.

The machine whirred, counting its cash, and a lid lifted. The woman took her money, stuffed it in her $375 fawn leather and green canvas perfectly darling little purse, and turned her taut, zero-smile face to Dan, no doubt committing his face to memory for a later description to the police. She had an older face, pretty in a taut and worried way, the skin pulled back to her ears, her blue eyes fading, faint bags beneath her eyes under the makeup, a light blond fuzz over her lip. She made a sound of irritation, moving around Dan, got in her car, and drove away, leaving behind a rapidly vanishing scent of Joy.

Well, Dan thought, you did want to steal her money.

Downtown Los Palos looked like a movie set, like a careful imitation of a real town. Wide streets, trees, cars parked along the curb, stores with nobody in them, a scattering of pedestrians dragging small shadows behind them from the early-afternoon blaze. Nobody was watching him. All he had to do was come up with the right number. His own ATM gave him three chances to get his PIN right. If you didn't come up with the right four digits in three tries, it ate your card. So three strikes out of a possible zillion and he was out. Random selection was not going to cut it.

Dan slipped Widmer's card in the slot, and the machine's green TV screen flashed, "Welcome to the

First Citizen's/Ameribank Family of Financial Services" on the screen. After enough time to read the Declaration of Independence the screen asked, "How may we help you?" "Do you require" etc. He punched withdrawal from checking, and the machine asked him for his personal identification number.

Driving down from AmDell with Widmer's wallet feeling like a brick in his back pocket, Dan had considered the possibilities and decided the more remote and esoteric his guess, the more likely he was to miss. The square root of the longitude of Dimebox, Texas, Widmer's hometown, multiplied by the latitude could be a possibility. As could the postal code of Widmer's mother, who was alive and well and living in Sapulpa, Oklahoma. But Widmer, like most of the movers and shakers in the industry, believed in KISS—the keep it simple, stupid, theory. So the more obvious the number, the more likely it was to click. Widmer's license said his zip was 94062. One too many digits. Leave off one. The first or the last.

Leave off the 9—everybody has a 9 in front. Dan punched in 4062. There was a pause, and the machine flashed, "ERROR. PIN NUMBER NOT VALID."

Second try, out of three. Widmer was born in 1951. That could work. Dan punched the board— 1952. Damn. Punched it again—1951. There was another pause and the machine flashed, "ERROR. PIN NUMBER NOT VALID."

One more shot. Less obvious, but more fitting to an ego of Howard's stature. The first and last letters of Howard's first and last name, HdWr. Like hardware. On the telephone keyboard that would be 4397. He punched in the numbers and waited. After the pause the screen said, "Please enter withdrawal amount."

YES. OH YES. Dan knew the glittering joy of the criminal. The payoff. Easy money. And the only question was how much did he want. He wanted $200,000 but the machine was not going to give him that. This much he knew. Even $20,000, which would mean going to the well ten times, was way too much. He punched in 2000. There was a pause as Dan waited for the satisfying little whirring sound of hundred-dollar bills being counted. The screen flashed, "Sorry. Withdrawal limit $200. Enter withdrawal amount."

Fuck. Oh fuck. I am truly fucked. He knew there had to be a limit. Obviously. His own ATM card was limited to $200. He knew that. Fuck Fuck Fuck. Fuck. That would mean a thousand withdrawals. Theoretically it was possible. He had, at most three hours. Maybe four. Four would mean two hundred withdrawals an hour, which would work out to around one every fifteen seconds not counting drive time between ATMs. And they wouldn't let him make a thousand withdrawals. There would be some safeguard programmed in. Dan punched in 200, and the machine whirred and gave him Widmer's money. The machine display read, "Would you like another transaction?" You bet your ass I'd like another transaction. He went through the process again, timing himself. Another $200 in one minute and twenty-eight seconds. OH FUCK. It was taking forever. He hit the machine again for another 200, and this time he was a little quicker, one minute and nineteen seconds. Six hundred dollars. Well he would just have to keep at it. He tried again and the little green screen said, "For your safety and protection. Limit three withdrawals any 24-hour period." Then, "Would you like another transaction?"

"Fuck you."

"Thank you for choosing the First Citizen's/ Ameribank Family of Financial Services."

Fuck you. Fuck Fuck Fucked. A little slip rolled out of the machine. Widmer's balance was $6,437.

And he knew what he had known all along but never stopped to notice. Widmer's money wasn't in his checking account. Not this one anyway. Nobody keeps serious money in checking accounts. Not even billionaires. It would be in real estate, trust funds, gold and silver contracts, stocks, bonds, CDs, mutual funds, and collectibles. It would be in banks in the Bahamas, the Cayman Islands and Switzerland and in blind corporations in Liechtenstein. It would be in the care of professional financial managers, and it would be forever unavailable to Dan Messina, who had stolen Widmer's wallet, cash, credit cards, and fraudulently accessed his checking account for a grand total of $787. Useless. Probably a felony in the state of California. Punishable by six to ten years in prison. Fuck. Fucked.

They were cutting back on her Darvon, meaning less warm gold light in the afternoon and more pain. She was also aware of the beige walls, the curtain drawn around the woman in the bed next to hers, the nurses coming and going, and time slowing right down to a stop when she heard him cry out across the hall. When he came into her bed that night, she asked him, "What was you cryin about?"

He said, "I wasn't cryin."

"Yeah, well I heard you doin somethin. Sounded like you was cryin."

"One of the bones in my arm wasn't healin right. They had to break it again."

"Shit."

"I wasn't cryin. I just yelled when they did it."

"Yeah 'cause you one of them tough Alonies, right?"

He looked back at her, not saying anything. Not knowing what he was.

"Like your arm? You got an Alonie arm. That's why they keep breakin it?"

"It's not like that. It's like part of you is from Africa? Know what I mean?"

"No, I don't know. I thought about it and maybe I am missin somethin, but I don't know about that at all. Like I s'posed to feel all those roots and shit, but my family is from Oklahoma. I'm talkin way back, like my great-grandmother, and my grandmother. So I don't know about runnin round some jungle with a skimpy little apron no top on. Where's your daddy? What happen to him he don't come visit you? I want to see what a Alonie look like."

"I'm not supposed to talk about him."

She waited.

"'Cause he's dead. He said you shouldn't even think about people if they are dead. He said when they are gone you just forget them. Get rid of all their stuff."

She waited again, knowing he wanted to tell her more.

"I don't know what he was deliverin. Some UPS parcel." He couldn't help it, he started to cry again, not making any noise, but the tears running down his cheeks. She put her arm around him, but he shook her off. He was the man, right?

She wanted to say something to comfort him, or at least change the subject, so she said, "You ever think of going back, seein if maybe you could find out where the Alonies used to live?"

"The Alonies was just a name," he said, "that was made up later. They wasn't really a tribe like with a big chief or somethin. They was just a lot of little like villages. Movin around, but keepin inside their turf."

"So you know where your, like village was at? You ever go there, see if they left any stuff lyin around?"

"Yeah," he said, "I know where they used to live. It was a tribe called Wahwehtha."

"So where's them Wah Wahs at?"

"Up them hills. Like right behind your head. You know where Los Palos Hills is at? "

CHAPTER

16

Womens do the dishes," Whopper said.

"What is that, Dickhead's Law?" Baylor said, pushing her chair back. "Women in the kitchen while the men go out and shoot? Get a life."

Page swirled the wine in her glass. Such a pretty color. So deep and clear. She drank it and realized the bottle was empty. God, she'd drunk the whole thing except for the glass Silver still had. She was so tired of all of this. Why hadn't Baylor told her? Did she make him use a condom? Was she okay? Was this a regular thing, a mistake? Did she really love the boy?

Well, Page hadn't told her mother all those years ago in Pleasantville when she was a teenager and she . . . God, what would you call it? Not making love. More like learning how to drive; kinda fun, a little scary, like a trial run. About as sexy as an armpit. What was his name, the boy she went with? The struggle on her parents' bed to get her bra undone. Phil, Phil Carnowski, her first boyfriend. Teaching high-school math in Oregon, last she heard. Phil was sweet and pretty, in a boyish way, with those long black curls. But Brad? Brad was a dodo. Any one of these little bastards was smarter than ol' Brad. If they would just go away. But it was stupid to think like that. To wish, that's what it was, wishful thinking. The point was, what can I do? Not just make it better, fix it. Kill them. Sneak her kids out. There was an idea.

Silver lit up a joint, inhaled deeply, and passed it to Blue Girl, feeling that old deep, relaxing, and oh-so-satisfying feeling flood through him. Yeah, good ol' grass, make the world green and gold. Price of grass so high, now it was a luxury item. Forty dollars an eight. Eight eights make that $320 an ounce, which was why all the little kids doin crack? Simple economics. But this was going good, could only get better. Looking over at Page out of the corner of his eye. The lady looked like she had a nice little buzz on, all the wine she was throwin down. And on over to Whopper. Whopper looking down, like he's letting the little white girl make him feel bad. So Silver goes, "Hey, good eats, my man. Don't worry your pretty head about dishes. We all do 'em. Together. Just like, a family, you know?" Silver pushed his chair back and stood up. "Hey, get up and get love, homey."

Whopper stood up, waiting for him as Silver walked around the end of the table, trailing his finger along the back of Page's neck as he walked past. He put his arms out and reached around Whopper, hugging the big teenager, saying, "Get love."

Whopper hugging him back hard, saying, "Yeah, brother, get love."

Page, seeing the two boys embrace and Chuleta and Blue Girl lazily smiling at each other, sensing her chance, caught Robby and Baylor's attention with her eyes, raising a finger for attention and silence. "Whatever it takes," she said. And drew a line with her finger across her throat.

"What it is," Whopper said happily. But Baylor and Robby knew what their mother meant.

A few minutes later the phone rang, and Page looked to Chuleta for his okay. He gave her a nod, feeling good. Feeling like the man in control.

Page, on the phone, said, "Oh, God, Dan, it's good to hear your voice. When are you coming home?"

"I'm working on it. How are you?"

"Kinda fuzzy. I had almost a whole bottle of wine for lunch, and I want to take a nap."

"What's going on there? What's that noise?"

"The kids are doing the lunch dishes. It's quite a crew. They all cleared the table, Silver is at the sink, rinsing the dishes, Baylor's putting stuff away, and Robby and Blue Girl are stacking the dishwasher. You'd think they did this every day. Did you know Baylor is having sex with Brad?"

"Brad?"

"Her boyfriend."

"I know who he is. He's a dork. Why him?"

"I don't know. I mean that's not the question. The question is, what should we do about it? Or what can we do about it?"

"Jesus, Brad. The kid is a human vibrator."

"Dan!"

"Well it's done. I mean they've done it. It's not the end of the world. Long as she's not pregnant. Is she?"

"I don't know, I haven't talked to her. Maybe we should both talk to her. Robby knew about it."

"We should get the kids away for a while. Take a vacation. Club Med or something."

"I just want to make it to the end of today. When are you coming home?"

"I don't know, should be around four thirty. Nick

helped, he had some cash. And I've got a big chunk to pick up from the bank in San Lucas at three-thirty, but I'm still way short."

"Where are you going now?"

"South on 101, just passing San Antonio. I've got an hour to kill, and I thought I'd try some more ATMs down in that Sunnyvale shopping center. I've got to pick up the cash at the San Lucas Ameribank at three-thirty."

"You remember Marly, has that nasal twang?"

"Marly?"

"From the office."

"Oh yeah, right. Tall woman, long skirt, narrow shoulders, big boobs, and a long face. Cheeks sucked in like she's sucking on a straw."

Page laughed, covering her mouth. "God I'd hate to hear you describe me. Anyway Marly had a client who borrowed money from a character down in San Lucas to make the down payment. Like a loan shark? She said he worked out of a gas station."

Chuleta said, "Duck."

"What was that? Is that you, Chuleta?" Dan was amazed at how angry he was. At the speed the anger was there, like a rush. He took a deep breath, trying to control it. "Are you listening in?"

"Right. Hangin on your every word, my man. Keepin track of the news. Dude's name is Duck. Duck's the one works out the back of a gas station."

"I'm sorry, Dan, I should have told you," Page said, thinking to herself that she had been looking right at Chuleta, seeing him pick up the phone when she answered. Was she starting to take him for granted? "I thought you knew he always . . ."

"What's the story, man?" Chuleta said, sounding cheerful. "You short?"

"I can't make it to four hundred thousand. My

boss promised me a hundred thousand, and he didn't come through. If you could wait a couple of days, I could send you . . ."

"I don't want to hear about it. Not my problem. You hear what I'm sayin? You want a tip, before you see Duck you gonna see Emmo when you go to the garage. He's like the doorman," Chuleta said, ending like he was asking a question, making sure Dan was following him. "You see Emmo, you lay a few bills on him or you gonna be half the day out on the street tryin to get in. Here, talk to the woman."

Dan said, "If this loan shark came up with a down payment for a house . . ."

"I don't think it was the whole down payment. It was a one-bedroom condo in the Redwoods, so I don't think it was a lot of money."

"Yeah, but it was something. You have an address?"

"I always have the address." There was a shuffling sound on the phone as Page went through the fat address book she kept by the phone. "Here it is, Alman's Garage, corner of Leonardo and San Gomez. I thought if a client was really horrible and desperate for a down payment, I might steer them to a loan shark."

"You sound sleepy; don't go to sleep."

"I won't. But I might put my head down for a while. Nobody ever tells you how boring it is to be a hostage."

"Love you, Page."

"Love you, too. Hurry up."

Dan in the car, driving carefully, keeping an eye out, thinking the *favelas* of California, unlike their sister slums in São Paulo, Calcutta, and Belfast, are pleasant-looking streets of one- and two-family houses, front yards, tricycles on the sidewalks, and mature shade trees. Birds squabbling up in the branches and splotch-bombing battered Continentals, sagging Sevilles, Thunderbirds, and rusted Cadillacs listing into the curb. The cars look like a museum display; vinyl peeling off their roofs, paint scratched and faded, front seat offering up the innards of upholstery, milky fog creeping up the opera windows, drooling dark fluids. The cars snag your eye, and you look a second time to notice the grass is scraggly and trampled in most front yards. And that some of the houses have broken windows and abandoned floors upstairs. Here and there charcoaled siding marks a house that scarred some children's lives before the fire was put out. And that the hard barrel of a big black boy watching you with wary eyes isn't just standing in the front door, he's standing guard.

Dan, thinking that if you know where to look, you could probably see the black stains of blood on somebody's front-porch steps from a drive-by. And the plants wilting and dying from pouring beer, the gang-banger's ritual of mourning for last night's dead. Thinking maybe he should keep a lookout for the aimless clutter of teenagers on the porch and front yard of a house, marking a gang's headquarters, and the double- and triple-parked cars in front of another with a new steel door to mark your local crack house. There would be cash in there, but you would need an assault platoon to get your hands on a dime. Like trying to take a teeth off a shark. Not seeing triple-parked cars anyway.

But really, at first glance, a surprise to see how pleasant, normal, and familiar the ghetto of today looks. It looks as if only last week or last year it was Annette Funicello's hometown, with Doogie Howser, M.D., Martha Stewart, Bill Cosby, lemonade and neighbors on the front porch. And of course it was.

Dan drove down Maple, feeling the hairs on the back of his neck telling him he was more watched than watching, seeing the sagging roof of one house with three black kids on the porch, heads turning slowly as he drove by. And in another, the glint of something moving behind the front window. Maple Avenue crossed Leonardo and he swung left on Leonardo, looking up to the corner of Leonardo and San Gomez, seeing the sign swinging on a frame, Alman's Auto Repair.

Alman's had a row of cars parked nose into the fence, an island of abandoned gas pumps and an oil-stained blue-and-yellow sun-faded banner strung up over the bays: Change, Filter, and Lube, $29.99. A dented and milky blue Buick Regal with bald tires was up on the lift inside. A mechanic, his face black under the shadow of the car, was standing underneath, his hands reaching up into the car's secret parts. With the $288,000 from his margin loan, and the $27,500 he'd collected from his accounts, the ATMs, Garland, and Nick, he was still $85,000 short. A hell of a place to look for $85,000.

Walking in the garage office door, Dan pictured Emmo, the man he was supposed to see, as a short, stocky grease monkey, bald top of his head finger painted with grease, imagined Emmo rocking in a green plastic office armchair with stuffing coming out behind his head, maybe leaning on a grey desk layered with grit, grime, and receipts. Pictured greasy fingers of one hand holding a phone, Emmo's other thick and dirty hand muting the mouthpiece. Pictured Emmo looking at him with a look of heavy irritation. Like he knew Dan was going to lie.

The look of heavy irritation, that was true. But in no way was Emmo a middle-aged mechanic. Emmo was a child. Maybe eleven maybe twelve. Eurasian, a light tea-and-cream skin, a delicate face, neatly combed hair, and a clean short-sleeve shirt, sharply pressed. Emmo was sitting behind the desk. Like a security guard. Which is what he was. There was no knowing if he had an Uzi behind the desk, but Dan thought it was possible. Thinking a child who should be in school, learning to read and write, was probably pointing an automatic weapon at him, ready to squeeze off a few rounds, shred the sucker; like Dan had interrupted his favorite video game.

"Duck?" Dan asked.

"What Duck? Who the fuck are you?"

"Howard Widmer."

"You didn't call?"

"If you want me to call . . ."

The child waved his arms, erasing the thought. "No, no, no. You don't call. Never call. I was wondering you were the asshole called this morning." Emmo left it in the air, like a question.

They went around it for a while, Emmo saying he didn't really didn't want to know who Dan was. And Dan saying he didn't want to talk to Emmo, he wanted to talk to the Duck. In the end Dan gave Emmo a twenty-dollar bill, and Emmo waited for another twenty before he nodded to the room at the back of the garage marked Men.

The room was a shed stuck on the back of the garage, with the only door punched through the garage wall. Just room for Quan Duc Pho, his desk, a PC, and one applicant. Duc gave Dan a short professional nod, like he would be with Dan in a minute. An air conditioner groaned in the wall. San Lucas was getting hot, and the room was small, with the plywood floor painted brown, and the freshly painted cream ceiling a few inches over Dan's head. Low-overhead operation, Dan thought. Duc, thin as a chopstick, taking up minimal space, looking nineteen, his face as smooth as silk, wearing a fawn chamois-leather jacket and a yellow silk shirt. The new younger, faster, smaller, minimal loan shark. Serious time spent on the perfect mustache and the perfectly combed black hair. Looking too small for the black, pigskin-leather executive swivel chair with the high back for that look of authority and the black satin finish, five-wheel base, and the tilt-back lever on the side.

Duc got through doing what he was doing, leaned back in his chair, studying Dan, said, "What's your mess?"

"It isn't a mess."

"Yeah it is." Duc said, looking sick of it already. He laid his long thin immaculate fingers across his cheek, the appraiser, sizing up Dan like he was a used Camaro. "Always is a mess. Everybody comes in here has a mess. They think I lend them some money, the mess is going to go away. And I know the money is just going to drag the mess out a little longer. Maybe even make it bigger. I see them come through my door rehearsing how they going to be making their pitch, and I know what shit they going to tell me."

"So what am I going to tell you?"

"You gonna tell me how you got fucked. Who fucked you. How you going to fuck them back, so they are not going to fuck you anymore."

Dan thought for a moment, and said, "That's about right."

Duc had a high forehead, a long narrow face, and the deep brown eyes of a dog who will take what he can get. He went back to staring into a computer screen Dan couldn't see, tapping keys. When Dan thought that Duc had forgotten about him, Duc looked up, his hand motioning to a folding chair. "Make yourself at home." he said. Outside a police siren started up and headed off in another direction, fading.

Dan sat.

Duc said, "How much?"

Dan said, "I need 85,000."

Duc winced like something nasty happened on his PC screen. "Let me see your license."

Dan handed him Widmer's license.

Duc looked at it and handed it back, going, "Very funny. Maybe it sounded good in the bar, Howard Widmer going to his local lender for pocket change. Nice joke, good for a good yuck." Duc leaned forward, his sad eyes locked on Dan's, his arms an A for his chin, his long thin fingers wrapped together for a chin rest.

"Let me impress on you something maybe you don't know. This is not the place to fuck around. You say you want 85,000, you give me a copy of Howard Widmer's license like you think this is some game."

"It's not a copy."

"So what? You want to sell it?" Duc looked genuinely surprised. "I don't want it. I'd like ten minutes with Widmer, maybe give him some investment ideas. But what the fuck I want his license for? You some kind of junkie? You want to sell your TV, your spare tire? You look straight, but selling a driver's license, a junkie would dream that up. You a junkie, you do yourself a major favor, get your ass out of here while you still have two eyes."

Dan looked hard at the man, thinking of the kids with guns pointed at them, Whopper kicking him in the balls. "I'm not a junkie, I just want to borrow some money."

"Okay, it's not a joke. I can understand that. But you have to understand something else. People don't come here for serious money. They come here for a hundred, maybe two hundred, dollars, five, a couple, maybe ten thousand at the most. They come here to make rent, maybe make a couple of payments so they don't lose the car. Only reason they come here because"—Duc looked around the room, waving his arms, demonstrating the desperation of his clientele—"because no place else they can get it. No place. They can't get it from a friend, and they can't get it from the storefront check cashers. They don't know what inside a bank looks like, and they sure as shit know they ain't gonna inherit it. So they come to me because nobody else is gonna give them shit, and I get 5.5 percent a week. They never pay it back, fine with me, as long as I get my 5.5 a week.

"Used to be," Duc said, his eyes narrowing down, "used to be, I did my own collection work." Duc let the look go, relaxing, leaning back, hands behind his head, telling the story of what it was like in the old days. "You know, you want to persuade some old lady you got to be paid this week, you break the door down into her apartment, thinking all you have to do is maybe hit her once or twice, impress her. Only now she sees you in her doorway, and she pulls out her kid's assault weapon. You know what I mean? Nasty work. But it doesn't matter 'cause it's all changed. Now you got so many kids ten, twelve, juvies for fifty, a hundred, dollars, they'll do whatever you want to whoever you want them to do it to; ladies, kids, dogs, cops, they don't give a shit. And nobody's gonna touch them. So tell me. You still serious about this eighty-five thousand dollars? That a hard figure?"

"Absolutely."

"I need something like a driver's license." Dan gave him his license. Duc went back and forth from Dan to the license, matching the photo with Dan's face. "Shit, Los Palos Hills, you must be in deep shit to come here. What you need 85,000 for?"

"This is like asking a bank."

"The banks have the law on their side. I don't, so I have to be more careful. So?"

"I need it."

"Not good enough."

"Because a gang of kids is holding my family hostage, and I have to pay them off."

"What gang? Maybe I know them."

"I don't know, they didn't tell me. The leader's called Chuleta. Then there's Blue Girl, Silver, and Whopper."

"Just four of them? Maybe be cheaper for you I get some of my kids together we root them out. You know where they got your family?"

"In my house."

Duc tapped his lips with his finger. "Black Mountain Lane. Say we go up there . . ."

"They've got automatic weapons, and if they even smell you, they'll shoot my wife and kids. Don't even think about it."

"Okay. Come back a couple of days, I'll see what I can do."

"You don't understand. I've got to have the money now, this afternoon." Dan could feel his frustration coming out again, turning to rage. This little shit here acting like he was doing him a favor. He couldn't wait until tomorrow morning. "This afternoon," he shouted.

"Shhhhh. Keep your voice down." Duc was waving his hands in front of his face. "I hear you, believe me. But there's a couple of obstacles here. First, I got to check it out. Got to check you out. You run and maybe fly away to like Portugal or Bangkok with my money. Could be tough to find you without costing me a lot of money. What can you give me for collateral, your house?"

"Yeah, sure, my house. That's worth over a million and a half now, maybe more."

"Okay, but we got to draw up the papers, do a title search."

Dan, his mind going off in a spiral, thinking, there is nothing—no tomorrow, no house, nothing if this doesn't work. "I'll give you ten percent for a week."

"I was going to ask for that. But you have to appreciate, I don't keep cash here. It's too dangerous."

"Where then? Where is it?"

"It's in the banks, where else you gonna keep it? Look, you keep those kids happy. Don't take much; feed 'em, bring 'em some dope, let them use the pool, watch TV, you got cable? Great. Come back in a couple of days. Maybe we can do some business, okay?"

CHAPTER
17

May brings a Sicilian sun to Los Palos Hills and no wind. The evenings are cooled by the onshore breezes from the Pacific, where the Alaskan current carries whales, killer sharks, and the icy waters of the Arctic. During the day lizards skitter for cover, cicadas buzz and tick in the trees, and the redwood planks on the sundeck shrivel and crack. The house had been cool from the night before, but now the sun floated up to shimmer in the clear blue sky. The temperature was 86° Fahrenheit and climbing.

Whopper, leaning on his big arms on the chopping block in the middle of the kitchen watching his crew busy with the dishes was saying, "See, we all get along. Lotta places they be fightin, kickin, and screamin an' shit."

Baylor, standing on a kitchen chair, stretching to put the colander away in the cabinet over the stove, looked back down at him with a look of pity for his terminal dumbness. Her rump sticking out in Blue Girl's black bicycle stretch pants. She shoved the colander in, flipped the cabinet door shut. Looking down at Whopper, she said, "You put your gun down, Fats, you'll see how well we get along. You could be in for a big surprise."

"Chill down, girl," Silver said, smiling to himself, knowing the effect he had on women, rinsing a plate, handing it to Robby. "It's not like it's perfect. But considerin the situation, we're gettin along pretty tight. Right?" He looked around the room for approval. Zero approval. "Hey, maybe couple of weeks we'll send you a postcard."

"Yeah," Robby said, wiping the counter. "Where you going?"

"Somethin to think about, ain't it," Chuleta said, coming in the room and sitting by the phones. "Whole life, you stuck in one place, then you get a chance to go anywhere you want. Where you head for, girl?"

"I don't want to go anyplace. I like it here," Robby said.

"I was askin your sister."

"Los Palos is just south of the thirty-eighth parallel," Baylor said, "so if you went in a straight line you could go to Seoul, Athens, Lisbon, Teheran, Tokyo. Maybe the south coast of Sicily."

"I like that. You come lookin for us, just draw a straight line. Yeah, look for us in Sicily. All them crazy Wops an' shit. We show them fuckers how to be bad." Chuleta looked down at sweat spots on his white button-down shirt. "Probably be cooler there than it is here today."

"So where would you go, Blue Girl?" Robby said, putting the sponge down on the sink, thinking of Blue Girl getting in a car with him behind the wheel. The man in charge. Just taking off.

"Lotta places, I'd like to go," Blue Girl said. "First one is swimmin."

"You can't go swimmin in the ocean," Robby said.

"The temperature is around fifty degrees Fahrenheit, freeze your nuts off."

"I meant in the pool, dummo," Blue Girl said. "Any reason we shouldn't have a little dip? It's in the back; nobody can see it."

"Hey, man, that's a great idea. C'mon," Whopper said, "let's take our clothes off, jump in the pool."

"They can't see you, Whopper," Blue Girl said, "but you go back there, they gonna hear you. Neighbors gonna think somebody let a whale loose."

"S'pose we go two at a time," Silver said. "Be real quiet. You go first, Chuleta, check it out."

"I don't wanna swim."

"Yeah you do. Come on with me," Blue Girl said. "Cool your damn head." She sauntered over to Chuleta, little sashay in her hips, and put her hand on the back of his neck. "See, you all hot. Need to feel that cold water running all over you."

"You wanna go, take the kid. Just keep it quiet. Keep it short."

In his room, Robby said, "You gonna watch me or what?"

Blue Girl said, "No, my man. I promise, no peekin. You gonna wear your special swimmin suit?"

"What special suit?"

"One you wear when you racin. I bet you look like a juicy peach in that."

Robby, blushing, feeling the heat in his face, turned away, saying, "Yeah, okay. If you want."

So while Blue Girl looked out the window at the ridges of mountains beyond the blue pool, Robby, as pink and bony as a calf, telling himself, for Christ's sake don't get a boner, took off Silver's baggy grey shorts and black nylon tank top, and, getting his foot caught on the leg hole, hopping on one foot, pulled on his racing trunks, the blue-and-gold-striped nylon suit with the little eagle embroidered just below the waistband—the Eagles, the Los Palos High School Junior Varsity Swimming Team. "Fly high, Eagles, high, for the gold in the sky," the Los Palos High School song went until the dope dealers in the lavatory picked it up for their theme song. This year the song went, "Soar, Eagles, soar, you will always reach for more." Naturally the dope dealers thought that one was even better, changing soar to score.

The trunks were tight, like he had put on a couple, maybe five, pounds since quitting the team, but they were okay. Thank God for no boner. Robby tossed his head, flinging the green hair out of his eyes, "Okay, you can turn around," he said. "I had to shave my legs for swimming."

"I can see they comin back, them little blond stubbles."

"You want to wear one of Baylor's suits?"

"They too big. I just go swimmin in my panties, if that's okay with you," she said, pulling Baylor's yellow summer dress over her head and laying it carefully on the bed. "Well?" she said, standing about a foot away.

Robby could smell her. Smell her honey-sweet perfume, maybe it was shampoo, the smell of underarm deodorant and hot girl, like soap and a kind of sweaty smell. No point trying to see her nipples through the cloth now. No angling so the light was right. Her nipples were huge in front of him, and he looked at the little bumps around the aureoles, the pink color against her dark skin. Looked down at her white satin panties with a curl of black hair coming out of the side, the soft mound underneath. Robby felt a warm rush and big tingle. Shit, shit, shit. Huge boner. Humongous. He thought maybe a towel, but he would have to walk across the room, shit, back across the room to get it. So forget that. Nothing he could do about it.

So he ran through the door, stopping to throw, "Come on," over his shoulder, running downstairs and out the big glass sliding doors for the cool water in the pool to hide the worst hard-on he had ever had in his life. Blue Girl bouncing happily down the steps after him.

Page, still in the kitchen, wiping the counter out of habit, didn't want to go swimming; she wanted to put her head down, close her eyes, forget about this horror in her house for a moment. The wine had left her feeling a little numb, thinking she couldn't watch the kids. It had not been that long, seemed like just over a year since she had been standing over Robby in his playpen, wheeling Baylor in her stroller. Robby was always happy to stay where he was. Baylor was always pulling to get away, twisting her little hand free from her mother's tight grasp in the supermarket, charging down the aisles to go explore on her own. Baylor, the tough, calculating one, knowing what she wanted and going after it. Getting it whatever it took to get it. Robby, the softy, letting somebody else make the decisions. He could have been a swimmer. He had the talent, and he loved water. She had to keep the toilet seats down when he was three or she would come into the bathroom and find him happily splashing the water in the bowl. He just didn't care about winning. It didn't interest him. She heard him splash into the pool outside and thought, He's okay. He's in his element.

She felt the stillness of the house at noon. The dry heat outside. Heard the insect buzz of summer dullness and no breeze. And wondered for a moment about the deal on 1272 Hamilton. If they were going to countercounter. Come anywhere near the asking. They were techies. The deal would drag on for weeks while they went back and forth, picking nits and squeezing every last dime. But you never knew. Whatever you thought was going to happen in a sale almost never did.

She looked at her daughter, at Baylor's round freckled face, cool cobalt blue eyes, eyes to die for, her blond head bent over a computer catalogue, marking the prices, and Page felt an ache. For what? For the brave, tough little girl that she was? For the way she reminded Page of herself when she was a girl? Except Page had hidden her grit and ferocity under a pretty face and a nice girlie smile. Baylor didn't bother with that. And more power to the kid for dumping the camouflage. Baylor always said what she thought. Or was it, yes, this Brad thing. That was the ache, the loss. Not a little girl anymore. Not so much hers anymore either. She was sure Baylor wasn't pregnant. She was far too smart and self-sufficient, and Page would have known, sensed it. But Baylor deserved better than Brad. Somebody as strong and tough as she was. She could push Brad around like a hockey puck, and she'd get tired of that in a hurry. Lord, look at the way she pushed this Whopper character around. Baylor could look after herself. Dan would be home soon. These awful kids would go away. It would be okay to lie down. Just for a few minutes.

"If you kids will excuse me," Page said, a little more thickly than she meant to, "I'm going to lie down for a moment."

Chuleta, his gun on the counter in front of him, yawning, stretching, thinking he could use a little snooze himself, said, "Keep her in sight, Silver. Let her sleep, but don't let her close no doors on you."

Silver smiled, getting up to follow her, nice little buzz from the dope and the wine still there, keeping him floating along in the warm happy glow, thinking, "Perfect."

Whopper couldn't believe it. Baylor was looking at him. And not just looking at him. More than that. She was giving him one of those white-girl smiles; not showing anything, tough to figure, but it could mean good. Just looking at him like that. Then she was saying, "I'd like a nap, too." Looking right at him. Like she wanted him to come with her. After all that shit she be givin him. Callin him Dickhead an' shit. Like she's drawn to him. Which he could understand, but it caught him off guard.

"Guess I better go with her," Whopper said, looking over to Chuleta for approval.

Chuleta nodded yes, glad for the chance to be alone for a few minutes. Nice buzz going from the wine and the dope, and heavy in the head, too. Like this was working, but there's more waiting to get through. Hey, the man was out there doing it. And even if he didn't come up with every last penny, twenty dollars would be twenty dollars more than what they had in their pockets this morning. Tough to be strong all the time, and he was thinking he wouldn't mind a little rest himself as long as all these folks had somebody watching them all the time. Which they did. Blue Girl on Robby, the little green-hair kid following her around like he was her puppy. Whopper on Baylor, nobody was gonna get around him. Silver on the old lady, everybody on somebody. Just maybe close his eyes for a moment. As long as nobody saw. Didn't want to be signing weakness. Last time he slept was, couldn't remember, two days ago at least. His brain running ninety-five miles an hour thinking what could go wrong, going over it, working out all the possible things that could happen. Even the sea draws back for another wave, he thought, closing his eyes for an instant. Jerking his head up, hearing the girl.

"Just don't come too close to me," Baylor said with another of her little sweetie smiles, like her mother as a girl, sugar on a steel cookie. Like butter wouldn't melt in her mouth, but it would smoke on the tip of her tongue. Baylor went out the kitchen, throwing Whopper another look over her shoulder. Whopper lumbered along behind her like a bear following the buzz of a honeybee. Chuleta let his eyes close, just for a moment.

The First Citizen's/Ameribank Tower in San Lucas soars fifty-seven gleaming stories over Silicon Valley. Designed by Piers and Knowlton of Seattle, the tower wears its skeleton outside, a bronze cage around a chrome-and-glass box. Dan drove the clattering Volvo down the Second Street ramp and into the underground parking lot, circling deeper into the ground down to Level EE before finding an empty parking space. He rode up the elevator to emerge into a much enlarged version of his local bank. Same bright red carpet, same bright lights. But the ceiling was two stories high, and the floor space was big enough to play football.

Dan walked across a half acre of red carpet to the first desk, where a bright young black woman in a dark green silk suit with a yellow Hermes silk scarf at her throat sat behind a New Accounts sign. She

looked so perfect, so polished, her eyes as round and
innocent as a deer. Dan, seeing the slightest hesitation
in her smile, realized the day had taken its toll on
him. He had sweat-stained crescents under his arms,
and his blue jeans and old Nikes looking tired, worn-
out, and out of place. She smiled at him and
motioned him to sit down. "I'm here to see Andy
Finally," Dan explained. She looked at him. "To pick
up some cash."

Doubt clouded her face as if he was speaking
another language. Then the penny dropped. "Oh,
Andruw," she said. "Andruw Fi-nally," she said,
accenting the second syllable. "Hard currency transfers. I'm sorry, I'm afraid I slow right down to a crawl
at closing time. If you don't mind a tip, don't call him
Andy." She picked up the phone and within moments
a bright young man in a dark blue blazer, blue button-
down shirt, and gold Rolex was leading Dan past the
rows of bankers at their desks. They paused while
Dan's escort punched code on a key pad mounted on
the wall to open the thick glass doors into the inner
sanctums of the bank. Then there was a chime, and
they walked single file through the doors, over the
heavy red carpet, down an airless hall, and into a private office with a desk, an oval table and four chairs,
and a telephone. Mr. Finally will be with you in a
moment, uh, Mr. uh . . ."

"Messina," Dan said, looking around the room. No
cash.

"Your currency," a rich baritone said behind him,
"is here." Dan turned around, and Andruw Finally
was striding into the room, past Dan, to take his place
at the head of the table. A dark, creased, spaniel face,
with the sheen of cologne, long black hair slicked
back, large Adam's apple, blue suspenders over a blue
shirt, and pinstriped trousers. Just over five feet, Dan

guessed. His voice making up in depth, resonance, and bass what he lacked in height. He was carrying a large Samsonite attaché case, which he carefully placed on the table.

"Please do sit down, Mr. Messina. Just a few of the usual boring formalities, and you can be on your way." Dan sat down. "We had quite a time assembling your parcel, Mr. Messina," he said in his Oil of Olay voice, soothing after the harsh day, confident. "Normally we would insist on at least a three-day notice. The Fed has just upped their reserve requirement, so we have to take a couple of extra steps to justify our request for more funds without a concomitant increase in our reserves. This is not a loan, of course, but we are required to report all transactions over ten thousand dollars. All this is tedious and not, from our point of view, profitable. But your banker was very persuasive. Without her on your side, Mr. Messina, I don't think we could have done it."

"Mr. Finally." The man in the blue blazer tried to interrupt.

"Just a moment, Simon," Finally said, raising two fingers of his right hand from the table to hush the underling. "Your $288,000 is not a particularly large sum for us, per se, Mr. Messina. Each of our ATMs carries around fifty thousand dollars, and as we service some thirty-five ATMs out of this branch as well as several hundred more for our one-hundred twenty-five satellite operations around the Bay, you can well imagine we see quite a bit of cash around here. But we don't like to see it standing still. My job is to turn the river into the rapids." He sat up as tall as possible and leaned forward to unlock the case. Dan got up and walked around the desk to look over Finally's shoulder. Inside the case, green-and-grey hundred-dollar bills, wrapped in packets with a yellow band with a handwritten "$10,000" and signed with initials in black ink, lay wall to wall.

"Hundred-dollar bills all right?" Finally asked as he withdrew a hundred-dollar bill from one of the packets and held it up to the light, admiring it. Dan nodded unseen behind the banker. "Good. So rarely do people appreciate cash, but there is no substitute, is there, Mr. Messina? So much more interesting than electrons on a computer screen. I sometimes envy those times when they wore green eyeshades and did everything by cash. It has a lovely feel," he said, handing the bill to Dan and taking another out of the attaché case.

"Uh, excuse me." Simon tried to get Finally's attention again.

Finally shot him a quick glance and went on. "And look how much information each and every one carries. Of course there is this fine portrait of Benjamin Franklin. But there is so much more. Here on the face we have the seal and the letter of the Federal Reserve Bank that issued the note. See, this one is from San Francisco. Hasn't strayed very far, has it? And here's the serial number, the year the note was designed, printing plate identification numbers, and the seal of the Department of the Treasury. Like a pedigree. Most of these, I am happy to say, are of the older style." He put the bill back in the stack and took one from another stack. "The new hundreds, with their larger portraits and numbers may be easier to read from a distance, but who would want to keep their distance from a hundred-dollar bill? I'm afraid these new ones are not nearly as elegant, don't you agree? Lost all their delicacy and sense of proportion. And this trick of seeing Mr. Franklin's portrait on the other side," he said, as he held the bill up to the light, demonstrating the watermark of Ben Franklin's portrait through the bill, "is just a trick. Like so much else these days, too obvious and too much. The whole country has been suckered by size. Bigger, in my experience, is rarely better."

He turned to take the hundred-dollar bill out of Dan's hand and slipped the two bills, one by one, into their mother packet. "But as I say," he went on sadly, "cash is something of an antique now, and we seldom have much to dip into. However, fortunately for you we did take in cash receipts from the Mall of the Americas this morning, so there was a little more of what we used to call the green stuff in-house. We've charged you $225 for the attaché case and a one-percent, $28,000, handling fee. Which, considering we had to turn the bank upside down and shake its pockets to get this together so quickly, is a bargain. But I'm getting ahead of myself. I've got a few papers for you to sign,"

"Mr. Finally."

"What is it, Simon?"

"We still haven't gotten Mr. Messina's wire yet."

"Oh really." He lifted his hands apologetically, "I guess I better check."

"You don't have it?" Dan said, standing up.

"I wouldn't worry," Finally said, motioning Dan to sit down again. "These wire transfers can be deflected for an hour or so in rush-hour traffic. We move a lot of money around this time, so I'll just see where your little packet has landed." He punched numbers on the phone in front of him. "Miriam, any news on that Messina incoming wire." There was a pause. "Yes, that's right, 288,000." Andruw smiled his narrow banker's smile at Dan, who was pacing up and down the small room. "I see. You want to check again, Miriam, just to be sure?"

There was a longer pause.

Dan sat down again next to Andruw Finally.

Realizing how small the banker was, the tips of the man's polished black wing tip shoes barely touched the floor, Dan thought maybe there was a way to take the case, hit Simon in the face with it, and run. But the glass doors out of the inner sanctums of the bank were two inches thick and required a pass code. There were armed guards on the bank floor. He would have to take the elevator down to his car. Maybe there was a way they could lend it to him.

Finally said into the phone, "You're sure. I see. No, never mind. Have a nice weekend, Miriam." He placed the phone carefully back on its cradle. "Well that is too bad. Not a sign of it." Looking concerned, as if he had learned that Dan had an infectious disease, he pushed his phone across the table. "Would you like to give your broker a ring? See if there is a problem? I hate to see you come all the way in here for nothing. Turn on the speaker, if you would please. Last button on the left."

It took a long, embarrassing time to get the number for Meritage Discount Brokers. He had to repeat the name several times to the information operator, wincing inwardly every time he said "discount." After five tries, he got an answer. "Is Sam there? The broker."

The speakerphone said, "I'm sorry, but Mister Otteson is with a client now. May I have him get back to you?"

Dan's impulse was to yell, but yelling was not going to help. "Tell Mr. Otteson that he has fucked up a $288,000 transfer, and I hold him personally responsible. My name is Messina."

"I'll give him the message."

"Tell him NOW." He didn't mean to shout, it just came out. Andruw gave him a twitch of a grimace in sympathy for having to deal with the Discount world. They waited in silence. Then Sam was on the phone.

"Hey, Dan, I've been trying to reach you all day."

"Why isn't my money here?" Dan said quietly.

"I checked with our head office because we need approval for a transaction of this size, and our head of Sales, Western Division, Jack LaPorte, pointed out something that could really save you from a hefty tax bite. So I thought I better check with you before I did anything."

"You mean you haven't even sent it?"

"See, if we just lend you the money, you can't deduct the interest from your taxable income. But, on the other hand, if you sell that amount of securities, like 288,000 then borrow the money on the rest to buy back the shares you sold then, you can deduct the interest from your taxable income. You know what I am saying here?"

Dan held the phone cupped in front of his face, leaning into it. "I don't care about taxes. Just send the money."

"I'm just trying to save you a nice chunk of change here, Mr. Messina. Okay, we double-end commissions on the trades, but I can give you a great volume discount."

"Send it, goddammit, just send it."

"Hey, hey, I'm sorry. Jack LaPorte's a Senior VP. He said I had to check with you first, Mr. Messina. Before I did anything. Had to."

"Send it."

"Okay, okay, first thing Monday morning."

"NOW Goddammit."

"Hey, calm down. I can't send it now. No way, Mr. Messina. The market's closed hours ago, and our computers shut down for trading and transactions for our end-of-week resolution. They're adding up all the West Coast numbers for the week. If I owned the company, no way I could do anything for you before Monday morning."

Dan looked up to see Andruw Finally lowering the lid of the attaché case, closing it, and snapping the locks shut.

Robby, in midair, flat out, eyes closed, head ducked down between his outstretched arms, legs straight and slightly apart, toes pointed, savored the last flying instant in the warm air before the cold impact of the water and the release from earth. Blue Girl, running out of the house onto the patio around the pool, saw him enter the water with the liquid ease of a wild thing, slipping in like a knife, making almost no splash. Following him with her eyes, seeing him undulate in a wave beneath the surface, cruising the length of the pool, flipping underwater, slick as a seal, finally coming up and breaking the surface with a burst of energy and stroking hand over hand to the other end, turning again, pushing off the side of the pool, and gliding out into the middle. Treading water easily, tossing his green hair out of his eyes with a flick of his head, sending a rainbow of spray over him, Robby said, "Come on, it won't bite you."

Blue Girl stuck a foot in the water. "Hey, that's cold, boy. How you stand that cold?"

"It feels good. Come on."

Blue Girl walked around the edge of the pool, pausing to look at the high grass field sloping down into the deep valley just beyond the edge of the pool. "You own all this?"

"Naw. It's state and county land. Dad likes to say we own up to the last mountain ridge, but our property line stops about a hundred yards down the hill. You just gonna stand around, or are you coming in?"

"I'm comin. I just got to stay in the shallow end

'cause I can't swim. 'Less you teach me. You teach me
to swim like that?"

Robby said, "Sure."

Page went through the living room to the guest bedroom. Sometimes, on those rare quiet Sunday after-
noons when she wasn't showing houses or holding
an open house, she took a nap on the bed by the
window. She liked the room because it was quiet,
with blue-and-green wallpaper and sliding glass
doors leading out to the deck. There were twin beds,
a mirror over a dresser, and a bathroom alongside
the closet. And outside, below the deck if you
wanted to go outside to see it, the clear water of the
swimming pool and the deep valley with the mountains rising up behind. One day she'd redecorate it,
but now she liked the impersonal feeling of the
room. As impersonal as a hotel room, with none of
the emotional furniture of their bedroom. Perfect for
a nap. She could stretch out on top of the down
comforter on the bed next to the glass door without
having to make the bed again when she got up. Just
give the comforter a tug and, presto, all made up.
She heard a footstep behind her and didn't turn
around. She knew the Silver kid was following her
and felt a stab of irritation. Like having a stone in
your shoe and ignoring it because you are too busy
to stop and get it out. Nothing she could do about
him now. She would get them through this with as
little hassle as possible until Dan came home with
the wretched money. She would think more clearly
when she had a little nap. Just a short one. Then she
could get to work on getting the nasty little shits out
of here. She kicked off her sneakers, lay down on
the bed, doubled up the pillow, rolled onto her side

with her knees drawn up, and closed her eyes. Silver moved quietly into the room and closed the door.

Baylor held her bedroom door open for Whopper. He stopped in the hall, frowning at her. "Come on," Baylor said. "I won't bite you."

Whopper went by her, into her bedroom. Like the boy's room, it was crammed with stuff. Only this was girl's stuff. Pictures of rock stars on a bulletin board over her desk. And the bed definitely got his attention. Queensize, plenty of room for all kinds of stuff. Frilly pillows on the white duvet with pink and red roses. Whopper looked back at Baylor, half-expecting her to slam the door in his face, trick him, lock him in the room.

Baylor came into the room, pulling the door shut behind her. She twisted the lock. "I don't want anybody disturbing us," she told him, coming up to him and putting a hand on his chest. "Have you always been real strong?"

"What you playin at?"

"I want to see how strong you are. Take your shirt off."

"What you playin at girl?" Uneasy, thinking of those little pink titties. What they would look like she take her top off.

Baylor started unbuttoning Whopper's white button-down shirt.

Baylor's hands were shaking. Trying to act cool, like she was used to this, but she couldn't control her shaking hands, and she was having trouble with the buttons.

Whopper said, "Hey, let go. I can do that." He undid his shirt buttons, having trouble himself, his hands not too steady, ripping off the last two.

"I bet there's a lot you can do," Baylor said. She

dragged the tip of her finger under his chin, teasing him. "I want to see the Whopper do tricks."

"What kind of tricks you talkin?"

She was unzipping his tennis shorts now, almost touching him, and he could feel the Whopper start to rise. "Come on now, step out of your pants."

Whopper, balanced on one foot, then the other, pulled off his tennis shorts, looking down and seeing the bulge in his undershorts. "What you want now?" he asked, thinking this girl really wild, those pink titties be out in the open pretty soon.

"I want to see the real Whopper. I bet it isn't big at all. I bet it's just a little one?"

Jesus, she's too much. And there was a problem. The problem was that he would be a lot more comfortable if the lights were out. Get to know each other, like a little hugging and kissing. Before they got to the serious stuff. The trouble was she was right. The Whopper wasn't all that big. Chuleta gave him that name, make him stop worrying about how big it was. Which he used to do. Used to worry about it all the time. Chuleta said it wasn't the size of your dick, it's the size of a man's heart. And he had a Whopper, right?

Now it was like a game they all played. Like it was like some kind of softball bat. So it would be a whole lot better if they could begin in the dark. Kind of work up to it. Once they got started it wouldn't matter. But if she wanted to see it, he could handle it. Okay, it wasn't called Whopper for the size. It was for the effect. He pulled his shorts down, feeling clumsy and stupid, but what the hell, a man wanted to get down to it with a woman, sooner or later he was gonna to have to expose himself. The Whopper was around half-mast. Kinda wobbly. All she had to do was touch it, and it would be right up there. But she didn't touch it.

Baylor gave him a wink and pushed him hard on the chest, sending Whopper back onto her bed. He was about to jump back up at her, pull her down with him, and she said, "Make yourself comfortable, Mr. Whopper," like over her shoulder, going into the bathroom. "I'll be right back."

Whopper heard the bathroom door click as Baylor turned the lock. He lay back, hearing the water run, thinking she is in there doing her women's things. The stuff womens do before they make love to a man. Maybe putting on a nice nightie. Something pink or peach. Peach would look nice on her. Maybe putting on a diaphragm. He'd be happy to do that little thing for her. Yeah, get to see her clam. That be good. He'd ask her about that because he sure didn't want to get her pregnant. She wasn't no virgin, which had its good side 'cause then she wouldn't be cryin and bleedin and blamin him. Bad news was she could be HIV positive, and he didn't have no rubber with him. He was sure Silver have one, 'cause Silver always be braggin about how he had to be ready all the time, so many womens comin on to him. Which was bullshit, but Silver did carry rubbers around with him. But the Whopper was not about to jump off the bed and go runnin 'round the house bareass, with his dick hangin out, lookin for Silver.

Hey, what if she come back out of the bathroom all ready to love him to death, and he be gone? That be like an insult after she be all over him. The chances her being HIV positive must be low, 'cause from what she said it sounded like she only did it once with one guy. Not like that Sally C, that last girl was nice to him. She had all the dicks been stuck in her sticking out of her she look like a porcupine. But maybe this Pretty Tits, she just make it sound that way for her momma. And how you know where her boyfriend been stickin his dick? Shit, she was takin a while. Maybe puttin on perfume, some special creams like all that nice sweet-smellin white-lady shit. He felt the Whopper with his fingertips. Felt good now. Like a rock.

In his dream, Chuleta was coming out of the mud hut a couple of years ago, like when he was fourteen, his mother still sleeping inside, the other low mud huts gathered around, the sunlight just leaking through the live oaks. The air is cool on his naked body, fluttering the hawk feathers tied to his arms. He sniffs the air for bear, taking in the warm-earth scent of the oaks and the flowers in the shoulder-high grass meadow behind the village. He senses he is the first one up in the village, no fires going except a thin trail of smoke coming out of the sweat house just downstream on the creek. The world is shimmering with power, and he can feel especially the power of his ally, the coyote. The wily, tricky, lecherous, powerful coyote, who came to him in his dream last night and told him this would be his day when he would join the men. He holds his polished and double-curved bow wrapped in cougar skin. It is four feet long, almost as long as he is, the inside painted with a zigzag design. Broad strips of deer tendons are glued to the outside like the bark of a tree, giving the bow a supple power. He spent weeks making the bow from a branch of wood that came from a tree in the far mountains. His father traded two deerskins for this wood he has shaped with an obsidian knife and polished with marrow. So he owes his father the skins of his first two deer. This will be the day he will follow his father into the sweat house with the men for the first time. To begin the two days of purification, chastity, fasting, and praying to prepare himself to hunt the deer. One by one women emerge from their low huts. They see him, but their eyes are down, and they will not look at him. And he realizes, even though he doesn't know why, that his father is

*dead. That his life has been taken by a grizzly bear. He will
throw all of his father's possessions on his funeral pyre and
never speak or think of him again. Fucking Coyote has fucking tricked him.*

Silver crouching down next to Page's bed, on the window side, checking her out. The lady had her eyes
closed, and up close her face was kinda rumpled in
sleep. Like she was on her side and her face sorta fell
down to the sheet. Whole lot more wrinkles than he
noticed before. Couple of lines running up from her
upper lip. Little brown mole down by the corner of
her mouth. Little hairs around the chin he hadn't
noticed. She smelled nice though. Kinda like vanilla
ice cream with a musky whiff of perfume behind it.
Following her down the hall, she was a touch wide in
the butt, but he liked that. Plus she had a nice way of
moving. Kinda loose. No doubt about it, he liked her.
Hoped this thing worked out for her with no downside. She would get the money back on the insurance,
everybody go away happy. His momma was nice-
looking like this Page lady. Sexy, nice tits, and stuff.
Page's hair was falling across her face, and Silver
reached over to her, brushed it back with his hand.

The instant Page felt a hand on her face she
grabbed it. Silver's face was inches from hers. That
nasty little mustache, short and shiny black hairs
above his white teeth, close up and huge. A hand
clamped over her mouth before the scream could
come out.

No warning, no warm-up, her wild fury was filling the room, too big to stay inside her. She let it go,
and it was huge, rage coming out in her flailing arms
and knees, trying to hit him, knee him, kick him, bite
him, scratch him. Kill him.

Holy shit. She was thrashing around like she was scared he was going to rape her or somethin. Silver only had the one hand free 'cause he had to keep one clamped tight on her mouth, keep her from screamin. He definitely did not want her screamin. Screamin would make all kinds of problems. Chuleta for one thing. He would be really pissed. A scream could bring the neighbors over askin questions. If he grabbed one part of her, another part was kicking him, punching. He got on top of her to hold her down, using the weight of his body to pin her. He grabbed an arm by the wrist and forced it behind her and pulled up until she stopped kicking and hitting. She was moving around underneath him, squirming, and it was getting to him. Her eyes were staring into his eyes. "You be quiet, I'll let you go," he whispered. He kept her arm bent tight and lifted his hand off her mouth, ready to clamp back down hard if she screamed or anything.

She didn't scream. But he didn't let go of her arm. She was squirming around now just a little, and it was definitely getting to him. She was soft and warm underneath him, and like maybe she was getting off on this. Like he'd heard of that. Of these women who led these quiet, you know, like normal lives out here in the rich houses. Like they went shopping and took the kids to school and did all that suburban-lady shit, but they were really bored out of their skulls and hungry for some good hard fuckin. He reached down and got his free hand on her tit.

Page bucked hard, trying to break loose. He was so damn heavy, and her arm was killing her. It felt like the ligaments in her elbow might be tearing. She tried to knee him, but he was just too heavy. She pulled his hand off her breast, and they stared at each other, breathing hard now. Outside she heard splashing in the pool. Robby.

"Let go of me," she said.

He didn't move, just looked down at her like he didn't hear her. Oh Jesus, he was getting an erection, she could feel it against her stomach. She was panicking, and that was dangerous. Relax, calm down. You need to be in control here. She had to do something.

"Let go of my arm. I won't scream." He just lay there on top of her, pushing his disgusting cock against her. "I can't make love to you with a broken arm," she said through her teeth.

He let go, looking down at her, feeling tender. Wondering how he was going to get her stuff off. Like, he had done it a lot of ways and a lot of times, but this was a new thing. Like in a rich house. And this was the lady's house, and she was like a lot older. So what do you do? Do you sorta sneak up on it, like act casual and sort of slide her T-shirt off, unhook her bra, act casual while you're talkin about somethin else, like her kids? Or was he s'posed to go right at it, like just pull her blue jeans off? He couldn't remember if her blue jeans had a zipper or buttons. Sometimes women's jeans had the zipper on the side. Maybe he better let her do it. What would be really good would be if she undressed him, like take her time about it. Make him feel good, like touch him a little here and there.

Page felt him hesitating. "You don't know how to do it, do you?" she said.

"What are you talkin? I am the best. An innovator. Some of the sisters in the hood, they do anything for me. Anything I want."

"You think it's sexy to be rough," Page said, still breathing hard. Getting her breath. "It's not. It's not sexy at all. It's a turn-off. See," she said, "you should be gentle, touch a woman softly." She touched his cheek lightly with her firebird red fingernails, slowly stroking his skin. "Please, you're too heavy."

He rolled off her and lay on his side. Looking into her eyes.

"Let me show you something," she said, stroking his cheek.

"Hey, if it turns you on, it turns me on," he said.

Page dug her fingernails into his skin above his eyebrow and pulled down hard, getting her back into it, scratching four ragged and deep parallel grooves in his forehead, down his eyelid, and into his cheek. Silver screamed, and Page was off the bed, heading for the door. Going for it.

The water was cool and delicious, with that clean chlorine smell. A shifty breeze skittered across the surface, making it sparkle with pieces of the reflected sun. Robby exploded out of the water behind Blue Girl, showering her. Blue Girl smiled, her lower half on a slant and wriggling wildly underwater. Her top half dripping, turned to him. "Hey, you like a fish, like some kinda dolphin or somethin."

Some of the water had spattered on her boobs, large wet spots the dark sweet color of her skin. She was amazing, totally amazing. She was going to kill him. "You want to learn to swim?"

"You want to teach me? Show me what I gotta do?"

"Sure. No problem. It's easy."

"I don't want to get my hair wet."

"Don't be stupid. You gotta get your hair wet, or you can't swim. See, you got to put your face in the water." He started demonstrating, taking in a breath with his face to the side and blowing the air out in the water, turning his head in time to his demonstration strokes.

"I ain't stupid. I can't put my face in the water."

He stopped. "Why not?"

"I'm scared."

"Scared of what?"

"I don't know what. Nothin. What difference do it make?"

"It's gotta be something. You can't be scared of nothin. Look!" He stuck his face in the water again. His face came up red and streaming, his light green hair plastered on top of his head like seaweed.

"I ain't scared of nothin. I'm scared of puttin my face in the water. What was you scared of, make you quit the team?" She moved toward him, peering into his face.

"Nothin."

"You just said you can't be scared of nothin." She slapped the water to splash him. Maybe tease him a little.

Robby saw the water fracture into shards, tiny white and glittering against the blue sky. Some of the spray caught Robby in an open eye and it hurt. Damn it hurt. Water ran down his cheeks.

"Jesus, you cryin?" She peered at his face closely to see if he was hurt. "You ain't nothin but a baby, are you? Come on, baby. I ain't gonna hurt no baby." She put her hand to his cheek, like a mother soothing her child.

Robby pushed her hand away from his face, squinting and blinking in the bright light. Same old shit. Everywhere it was the same old shit. Treating him like a kid, like shit. Fuck her. Fuck all of them. Fuck them. "Come on, do you want to learn to swim?"

"Yeah, I guess so. Long as I don't have to get my face wet."

He turned around, furious and happy at the same time. Fuck them all. Glad she couldn't see his face. Going for authority, like the way Coach would say it, he said, "Put your hands on my shoulders."

"What you gonna do?"

"Teach you to swim."

"I tole you I don't wanna get my face wet."

"You won't get your face wet. Put your hands on my shoulders."

Robby felt her black hands, long purple finger-nails, cool from the water, on his freckled white shoulders and started to walk toward the deep end.

"What's up?" she said into his ear, pulled along. "What you doin?"

"Teaching you to swim, if you'll shut up." Steeling himself.

When the water was too deep to stand he began pumping his legs like a bicycle rider and sweeping his arms out wide, towing the girl out to the deep blue end of the pool.

"What in hell you doin?"

"Relax, okay? Hang on."

Blue Girl slipped her arms around Robby's neck, her head pressed tight against his. No way was she gonna let this kid know how scared she was. She hung on her with her legs trailing behind, kicking a little. It would be good to learn to swim. She could go to lakes, to the ocean, maybe swim in some country-club pool when she got some money. Shit, like Chuleta said, get her own pool.

When they were over the drain Robby pushed her arms over his head, slid straight down, and was underneath her in a stroke. Blue Girl tried to grab him, still thinking this was part of the lesson, but he was diving down too far beneath her. She wasn't sure what to do and started kicking and splashing with her hands. The sky above her was blue like the water, and she realized the sky was a precious sight. And that she was running out of air. Blue Girl told herself, chill girl, be cool. But she was out of breath and sinking. She sucked in a deep breath and got water, tried to spit it out. Too late. She felt his hand around her ankle. He was pulling her down. Blue Girl tried to scream, but she was coughing, gurgling, going under.

Robby, gliding up through the water behind her, came up for air. And saw Blue Girl pushing off the bottom, coming up underneath him. Robby got a foot on her head, pushing her down. When he saw her touch bottom again, not moving much, he swam powerfully for the ladder, hauling himself out in one slick move he had practiced a thousand times, the way he was going to get out of the water if he ever won a race. Vaulting clear of the chrome ladder, Robby heard Blue Girl come to the surface behind him, coughing and struggling, making weak splashes in the water.

Robby picked up the long aluminum pole they used to skim the bugs and leaves off the surface of the water. Bringing it high overhead he swung down hard, feeling the long pole whip, hearing it make a whistle in the air, and feeling the sting of vibration as it struck Blue Girl across the top of her head and bounced off. The hollow bonging sound of the pole striking her skull vibrated in the boy's ears.

Blue Girl went still and started to sink again, tendrils of blood leaking out of her hair in the blue water.

Robby turned and ran across the pool deck and jumped down onto the steep dirt slope, running away from the house, down into the field of high dry grass; bounding in a clumsy, boyish imitation of a deer; coyote bush, thistles, and rocks spiking his shins and slicing his bare feet. There was a road a half mile away. Houses down there where he could get to the phone. Not hearing anything behind him. Not looking back.

■   ■   ■

Chuleta heard Blue Girl cough and splash in his sleep.
Now in his dream he was beside her bed. She was sick.
Burning hot. He was putting a damp cloth on her forehead, thinking this was what the doctors used to do in
the old movies in late-night TV, but it never did any
good, and I don't know what real doctors do now.
Silver's scream cut right through all that. He grabbed his
gun and was running almost before he opened his eyes.

Baylor, leaving the water running in the basin, let
herself out of the bathroom she shared with Robby,
locking the bathroom door behind her. She quick-
stepped across Robby's room, the soft carpet making
her steps silent, to Robby's door, and she was out in
the hall, just above the stairs. No sound coming from
her room. She pictured Whopper on her bed, waiting
for her, and was almost sick with fear. Pictured his
cock sticking straight out. Kind of shiny. He wasn't as
big as Brad down there, but it was definitely just as
ugly. Like a threat. She swallowed and kept moving.
He wouldn't wait for long. A minute. Maybe as long
as two. Then he would come after her, and a locked
door would not slow him down. So she could count
on maybe sixty seconds. After that it was up for grabs.
If she could get Chuleta's gun, that would do it. He
looked like he was about to pass out when she left
the kitchen with Whopper trotting along behind her.
Coming down the steps, she heard Silver scream from
the guest room and then Chuleta push his chair back
in the kitchen. Was Mom with Silver? Maybe she got
to him. She couldn't hear Chuleta's footsteps, but she
knew she had no time. If he caught her on the stairs,
Whopper locked in the bedroom, she was in deep shit
with both of them. She moved quickly down the
stairs, scanning the room. It was so quiet, familiar, the

bland ivory sofa with the watery blue-green throw cushions, the glass-top coffee table, the cream-and-blue carpet that had always been there, ever since they had moved in. The glass paperweight had always been on the coffee table ever since she could remember. It was in their house in Mountain View before they moved to Los Palos Hills and in their house in Redwood City before that—a heavy crystal globe with a planet inside, oceans and whole continents inside the clear glass. A glass swirl of a tornado rose from one miniature glass sea, and strange objects like starfish floated in the glass sky. When she was a child in Redwood City she used to stare into the paperweight and pretend she was the wise and savage princess of the big continent surrounded by blue-green glass seas. And that soft brown squiggly people who lived on Glorb made musical sounds when they were happy making her bed, picking up her room, bringing her gummy bears, and pretty much doing everything she said although sometimes she gave them holidays.

Baylor, hearing Chuleta crossing the kitchen, picked up the paperweight and slid as silently as she could to the side of the kitchen door. Chuleta, running low, holding his gun in one hand like a marine, shouted, "Whopper," as he came through the door. Baylor slammed him in the face with the clear glass paperweight.

Silver, his eyes tearing and bloody, lunged off the bed for Page, missing her, diving facefirst onto the carpet, smearing blood.

Page couldn't get the door open. The lock was stiff, stuck, then it turned as Silver, coming up off the floor, grabbed her arm and pulled her back and threw her sprawling on the bed. Page got to her hands and knees on the bed, facing him, ready to move, waiting for him to make his move. Silver didn't move. He couldn't move. He looked at Page through his blood-fogged eye and his good one, and she looked like his mother. He couldn't hit her. He couldn't do anything to her. Page crept, on hands and knees, to the end of the bed, stood up, and walked past him.

The door was open, and Page was running down the hall, going for the front door.

Whopper, lying back on the bed, starting to feel uneasy, wondering why the water kept running, heard Chuleta call his name and powered off the bed. He pulled on the bedroom door but it wouldn't open, so he unlocked it, charged out into the upstairs hall, and pounded down the stairs, heavy and hard. He saw Chuleta on his knees, holding his face with one hand and his gun with the other. Baylor, hearing Whopper, whirled and saw Whopper naked, thighs pumping, coming down the stairs. She threw the glass paperweight, smeared with blood, at the charging Whopper, aiming for his crotch. But it slipped, went high, hit Whopper in the chest, and bounced through the railings. A small glass planet, out of orbit, rolled to a stop on a sea of blue-and-cream carpet.

Whopper stopped at the bottom of the stairs, rubbing a blue-and-purple bruise spreading on his chest. Baylor was breathing hard, as if she had been running. But she couldn't move; he was too close, his black eyes glaring into hers. Whopper hit her in the jaw, knocking her back over Chuleta and into the living-room wall. Baylor struggled to get up, and Whopper said, "Stay there, bitch."

Chuleta, groggy, on all fours, started getting up. Whopper held out his hand to him and pulled him up. "Where's Silver and Blue Girl?" Chuleta said, wiping his face with the back of his arm, blinking. His fine nose was fat and swelling, blood coming out of both nostrils. He saw Page coming toward him. "What the fuck you doin?" he shouted to her. "What the fuck you do with Silver?"

"Baylor," Page cried out. Page ran into the sunny living room, breathing hard, running to her daughter, crouching over her, holding her. "Are you okay, sweetie?"

Baylor looked up at the naked Whopper and started to cry. "I wish I'd killed you," she said.

"Blue Girl," Chuleta yelled. "Where the fuck is Blue Girl?"

Robby, running hard down the steep slope, stuck his bare foot in a gopher hole and launched himself headfirst into the hot, dry grass. Facedown in the dirt and the grass, the thought that had been there, pushed way down, came roaring out. What if I killed her? Like she drowns or I broke her skull? What if I murdered her? What if they find her? What if the police find out? And he remembered Chuleta saying that if any of them ran away, he would shoot the others. This wasn't fair. This was too hard. He started sobbing, pushed himself back, turned, and ran back up the steep hill, jogging at first through the cactus bush and thistles, rocks and stones, his lungs feeling full of dust, his legs and feet aching and heavy. Then pushing himself to the limit, running.

Coming up the bank he saw her in the water, floating on the surface, faceup. Looking dead, but how could you tell? Shit, he was only gone, what? Felt like two hours, must have been around a minute. He had gone how far, a hundred yards maybe, running that would be two hundred yards, less than sixty seconds. He was taking off from the pool deck in the air and hitting the water, still calculating.

"Muthafucka," Blue Girl screamed. "Don't you fuckin come near me, you little muthafucka." Robby dived down, feeling the cool water stinging the cuts on his shins and feet. Feeling the ache in his ankle from the gopher hole. Feeling the blood and itching wash away. He hadn't killed her. He had just fucked up. He came up in the shallow end. Drifting slowly at the far end of the pool, she eye-balled him, a sideways wide-eyed look. "I can't swim, but I can float." Then she looked up. "Jesus Christ," she said. "Put some clothes on, nigger. You fright'nin me."

Whopper was naked at the edge of the pool, crouching over her, holding out a hand to help her out of the pool. The Whopper out there hanging loose, feeling the sun.

"Little prick tried to drown me," she said, taking his hand.

"See, I knew the kid was okay," Whopper said. He hauled Blue Girl out one-handed so she was standing, shivering in the bright sun and the heat, hugging herself.

"You better put that thing away, 'fore you do yourself an injury, boy," Blue Girl said. Their old joke, laughing through chattering teeth. "And you, you little fuck," she said to Robby. Robby was hauling himself out of the pool. "You are gonna get it."

CHAPTER
18

Dan was thinking his problem was concentration. The broken nose of the Volvo inhaled the waving concrete surface lines of Interstate 280, the tires thumping in rhythm to the horizontal tar strips. Tha-bump, tha-bump, tha-bump. If he had focused on my family's safety, maybe, made the place more secure, like had one of those TV cameras over the front door, Page would have seen the bastards. But shit, that's extreme. Unrealistic anyway. What he should have focused on was money. He could have, should have, made millions. If he hadn't spent half his life goofing off, going after some idea because it looked like fun. Or taking on impossible projects like Fisherman because nobody else could do it. His stupid ego telling him he could handle it. Shit, he could have done it. He could have, but he hadn't taken the time. He hadn't camped out in his office over the weekends the way he used to. You can't ask your team to sweat blood and break their hearts spending their lives in the office if you don't do it yourself.

When he woke up this morning the big problem

was what? Hard to remember. Widmer. And Fisherman. Now his problem with Widmer would be to keep him from pressing charges. And that was around number nineteen on the list. Amazing the number of pickups and campers on the roads now. Like that stupid Suburban in front, he thought, swerving to miss rear-ending it. Watching it shrink rapidly in the rearview mirror, he calculated six thousand pounds of four-wheel drive solid axle truck to drive one suburban woman five miles to get a carton of milk and some dish soap. But she liked the country image. Liked the old rural lumpy ride and the feeling she was going down to the depot to pick up a couple a dozen two-by-fours, stake out a woodshed for the back forty, check on the price of hay. A half acre of outdated fossil-fuel technology for the little lady's pipe dream. The farther we get from life on the farm, the more we hang on to the dream.

Who was he to talk, with his lumberjack shirt? With his house in the woods.

Concentrate. If he'd made real money, they'd be behind gates and armed guards. Swap good old Churley for some serious chew-your-face-off Rottweilers. Another kind of prison. But he would have had the money to buy them off. Assuming the little shits got past his private storm troopers, his Schwarzenegger replicas happy to rip arms off kids like that with their bare teeth. So even if those kids had gotten past his Private Commando Militia, he could have laid his hands on the money. Dipped his hand in Page's jewelry box, come up with a rock the size of a cue ball, tossed it to the kids, and said, "There's your five million, now go away."

Oh fuck, there he went, making up a game and running back and forth, running everywhere except at the problem. The problem was that he had feral and heavily armed children in his home holding his family hostage and demanding four hundred thousand dollars in cash. Compounding the problem he had how much? There was $16,247 from Nick, plus $3,720 from his bank account, plus $600 from the ATM, plus $187 from Widmer's wallet, and, yes the very generous $7,500 loan from Garland, the prick. So that was around $30,000—no, more like $28,000 plus the hundred and some dollars from his wallet. Minus the four hundred he'd given to the schoolteacher for bashing into her Honda. She'd said, "Have a nice day."

Jesus.

So say $28,000, give or take a few. Like five or six percent of what they said they needed to go away. He didn't have the rest, and he wasn't going to get it. Missing the problem. The problem wasn't that he couldn't get the cash. The problem was they were still there. Jesus, he hadn't felt this trapped since when. Since that time when Page was just out of college and going to Mexico on the train. And he had gone to see her off, must have been twenty years ago. Page sitting primly, one leg crossed over the other in one of those old Pullman cars, silver and green on the outside, brown and blue inside. Page had a sleeper, the kind the bed pulled down from overhead. And she was sitting there, just twenty-one, in her little pink summer dress with the short skirt and her legs crossed, engaged to some stockbroker starting out in stockbroking because he had broken up with her months before. And he had found out about her trip, got the travel agent to tell him the train, the coach, the seat, and she is sitting there with her matching red-leather luggage neatly stowed on the racks overhead, hands in her lap talking politely to Anne Barnes. *Shit, Anne Barnes.* Anne Barnes was her buddy from college, face like it was carved out of a pumpkin and talked like she was on speed.

Nonstop about he couldn't remember. Decorating her closet. Some private joke she shared with Page.

And he is sitting there, nodding politely, horny as a bull, Page smiling, acting like she has all the time in the world and he is not going to see her again for six months. Maybe never. So she was sitting there, barely noticing he was in the same compartment and he was dying to make up and kiss the girl he had known since they were ten and eleven, and the silly ex-roommate sat there gabbling away like she has a vibrator in her butt until the conductor shouts all aboard and Anne Barnes finally gets off the train.

It's hot in the train, but they don't notice or care: the instant the roommate is out the door they lunge for each other, kissing hard, wildly groping. The train starts moving, pulling out of the station, and he thinks, in the back of his mind, pushing his pants down, it's okay, he'll get out at the next station, like maybe Fresno. And they make love like rabbits, like they will never see each other again. Which could be true. Unzipping, reaching inside but leaving their clothes mostly on because the conductor could be coming any second. Page leans back against her seat, legs in the air, and Dan on his knees, trousers in a bundle, leans into her. The thumping of the train's wheels urges them on, Page holding her hand over her mouth to keep from screaming. The buildings picking up speed outside. Would the thump of car wheels on the tar strips on a concrete road have the same aphrodisiac effect? Almost no concrete roads anymore, difficult research. But worth doing.

The conductor knocks on their door as Dan was stuffing his shirt back into his pants, still kissing, just zipping up, big wet patch on his fly. And the conductor asks for his ticket, and Dan said, "Just a short one, getting off the next stop."

And the conductor said, "Next stop's Los Angeles. Los Angeles will be $227.50. First-Class Super Express Nonstop to LA."

He remembered how small the train compartment became with no way out. Twenty-four dollars in his wallet. Stuck on a train for five hours heading in the wrong direction. Thinking, We won't have a damn thing to talk about. Turned out fine. Nonstop bonking and talking and bonking Oakland to LA. The only way to fly. When he got off the train he promised for the fiftieth time he'd pay her back and asked her to marry him. She said she wasn't sure about marrying him, she'd have to think about that. But she'd be happy to fuck him again. That's what she said, "fuck," with that sweet little smile she had. She looked like a little Bambi, but she was tough.

Concentrate. Those kids, they don't want to kill us. At least they don't act like it. Maybe they'll do it anyway. Could be an accident. They get scared, and the gun goes off. Even if they didn't mean for it to happen. A hair-trigger accident waiting to happen.

It would make sense for them to kill us. All of us. Like those serial killers keep popping up in the news. Family of five killed in Nebraska farmhouse. So nobody can recognize them. So they don't have to worry. Little Robby and oh, Jesus, Baylor. Making love to that dork. Trying to act tough. She probably worked it out, and he had no idea what happened. Picked a local stud to test the water. Fuck him and forget him. To understand kids now all you have to do is turn everything upside down from when you were a kid. Makes perfect sense upside down. Kids getting the same input we do from TV, video, Internet. Kids trying to act like adults. Adults trying to act like kids.

Coming home $370,000 short is going to piss

them off. Maybe they'll just shoot him and go. Say to hell with it.

Concentrate. Will they still go away? Stay for the weekend to give him the chance to go back to the bank for the money? Start all over again tomorrow; relive this day? Say they shoot us and leave. Take the cars. That's probably the most likely way it is going to turn out. No way to know the odds. Way over my head here and sinking. The police are trained for this shit. They have resources you never hear about. Gas that knocks everybody out and they wake up an hour later, laughing. Honeyed words dreamed up by cop psychiatrists; words with sneaky power designed to make teenage terrorists throw down their guns and cry.

Cops probably have warrants for his arrest for lifting Widmer's wallet. Sneak-thief video exec lifts billionaire's wallet. It wouldn't matter, they didn't throw middle-aged white executives into jail for $187. Black kids wall to wall in there doing five to ten for selling a nickel bag of crack, but not guys like him. Except if they know he stole a wallet, it will be tough to get the cops to take him seriously.

That was not the problem. Concentrate. The problem was the kid said he would shoot Page and Robby and Baylor if he didn't come back with the money, and he believed the kid. The kid would probably feel he had to do it for the respect. These ghetto kids shoot people the way kids play video games. Bang bang bang.

He couldn't think about it. It just slid off the top of his brain. Do what you always do. Keep your head down and keep going. Steer point to point. It'll be okay. Should call Widmer and tell him I stole his wallet. He'll know it was me anyway. Might soothe him a little to know he doesn't have to replace his credit cards. Jesus,

Widmer is nineteenth on the list. Concentrate. The number one is that gun. Where the power is. If he had that gun he could handle them. Without it, he was their gopher.

Brad, driving his beat-up old green Datsun pickup out the Los Palos High student parking lot, turned right, heading up the hill on Barchester. The road was a winding, two-lane blacktop, steep and no guardrails. Not giving it a thought because he had driven up the sucker a million times. His brain going: Be okay, cutting Computer Sci b. Up there and back before Senior Civis. Maybe a little late for Civis.

If they did anything, it was fifteen minutes up the hill to Baylor's house and fifteen back, so if they did anything that would mean probably running into the next period. Meaning like deep shit, like maybe detention after school. 'Cause Miss Grunius would send his ass out of there if he like dragged his ass in ten seconds late. The old bag had a stick up her ass, the bell goes, everybody gotta be quiet in their seat. You could sleep, but you had to be in your seat. But shit, this was on a whole other level. He was cool with Compu Sci. He logged in and took off. Mr. Dingus fucking Dorkhead would never even miss him. Well, okay, he'd know, but he wouldn't care. Brad had the course waxed, and no way was the little fucker gonna degrade him for slipping out from time to time. The double D had his performance level to maintain. But this thing with Baylor was not optional. Whole other level. A man's obligation, like.

Make it with the woman you love, and it is responsibility time. Baylor was his woman now. His lady. His girl. And once you attain the unattainable, that love, the ultimate, once you attain that, you have to pay the price. You have to care for her, look out for her, protect her. Like Baylor could have their children, right? Okay, no way this time. She had a kid from the time they did it, they could call the kid Miracle. But in the future, there could be kids. He was getting a lot of stick from Harris and them, but he could blow it off; no big deal. It was what a man had to stand up to. Harris all over saying like Baylor was the last virgin. Called her Cabbage Patch. Which, okay, she sorta looked like if you didn't know her. And anyway, it was maybe an improvement over what they used to call her back in grade school. Miss Spit. 'Cause one day the kids were teasing her on the playground and Baylor got so mad she was spitting. Crying, her blue eyes all red, and spitting, she was so pissed off. So for a couple of years there she was stuck with Miss Spit. Now they were like still afraid of her but in a different way. The joke went she had a wire brush down there, shred a guy's cock if he tried it with her. Which, of course, nobody really believed, but the joke went around a lot. Well he knew her now, like in the actual Biblical sense. Like holy. What it would be like if they were married. And she was all soft and amazing. And yeah, okay, she knew what she wanted, but that was real refreshing in a woman. None of that half-assed maybe a little of this and maybe not. Girl was out front, headfirst. Real good sense of direction. Like she had the condoms and the spermicide.

Jesus, they could make that stuff smell better. But what you expect from stuff that kills all your sperms. Happy little sperms, swimmin out there, smilin, goin for it, and sploosh, big blob of poison jelly. Go aaaaaggghhh. Their little tails go limp, gag to death. Wash 'em down the toilet and they go out to sea for what, krill, those little tiny shrimp to eat. Then some tuna comes along, eats the shrimp. Tuna ends up in a

tuna fish salad sandwich. Guy that shot his load in the
first place eats the sandwich. Whatever goes around
comes around. Maybe one day he was gonna be the
father of Baylor's baby. Got to think about that stuff,
deal with it. So now is the time to be a man, standing
up, looking out for her. Better get in shape for that
now.

Besides, if Baylor was home alone, in her nightie
like, maybe they could do it again. Do it right this
time. Maybe she was like wanting him and setting this
up, like they would be in the house all alone all afternoon if he didn't go back for Civis.

Hey, like how strange being in a girl's parents'
house. Like familiar but totally different, different
smells, different rules and stuff. Almost like a foreign
country. She was never up for it since that one time,
her little dorkhead brother sticking his head in the
door, screwing the whole thing up, the little fuck.
Little pain in the ass hadn't stuck his head in there,
she really would have gotten off on it, he knew she
would of.

He didn't remember seeing Robby's little green
dorkhead at school today. Maybe they both had the
barf bug. If it happened, like she was all over glad to
see him and they did it again, the risk of getting the
bug was definitely there. But he was up for it. Hey, if
he had to barf a couple of times as payment for doing
it with Baylor again, he would be happy to pay the
price. Like if she had pleurisy, and she said, "Fuck me,
fuck me," he would do it.

Leprosy? Maybe not leprosy. Oh, Jesus, it would
be a relief to think of somethin else. Fuckin empty
computer screen in his room staring at him like it was
an accusation or something 'cause he hadn't touched
the fucker in a week. But what's the point of going online if you could get it for real. Her smell on his fingers

was so good. Not sweet but soft, kind of animal in a nice way. Anyway, unfuckingdescribable. Probably wore it out, sniffing it. He ever figured out a way to bottle that, like in a perfume, he'd be a billionaire. Maybe she was fakin this sick shit. She could be like loose with the truth when she wanted. Yeah, you never knew with Baylor. She was so damn smart.

Brad was turning down the Messinas' steep driveway, the hills a rising green backdrop to 3057, not seeing any cars parked in the drive. Not expecting any. Brad, getting out of the Datsun pickup, thinking maybe this was some test. Like she was after proof he loved her. Like if she was all over crawling with bugs and shit, would he still love her? Like if she wasn't twistin him, like she was straight on the phone and was hurlin and crappin all over the place then, okay, he could deal with that. She didn't want to do anything, he could just sit with her. Get her stuff like a Diet Pepsi with ice if she wanted it. Like sit with her on her bed, just chill maybe watch TV. Maybe hold her tits. Maybe get her to hold his cock. That would be good.

Page down on the soft carpet, comforting her daughter, kneeling over Baylor, her arm around her shoulders, saying, "You really got him. I think you broke his nose. Maybe a concussion. Good going, Baylor, good going."

Just beyond them, a small pond of blood was drying on the white carpet, seeping down, turning brown, bonding to the Scotchguard. A trail of dripped splashes led across the entrance hall into the kitchen, where the blood was smeared on the white tile floor like muddy footprints. Whopper was saying, "Gimme the gun."

Chuleta's eyes were bloodshot, the lids swollen and purple. A purple-and-yellow welt the size of a golf ball rose between his eyes. His nose was double its normal size and dripping blood, the drops blurring on the white porcelain. Chuleta had the water running, twisting the knobs to get the water warm but not hot, his head hanging. If he didn't move his head, it didn't hurt so much. The assault gun hung from his left hand, pointing at the floor.

"Come on, bro, gimme the gun, and I'll deal with the bitch."

Chuleta was trying to get the bleeding to stop. Hard to think with the heavy throb in his head. Shit, he had only closed his eyes for like a few seconds, and it all fell apart. "Go put your clothes on. The fuck you do with this gun?" The water was hot, and he cupped it in his hand, splashing his face, shards of pain shooting back into his brain.

"You know what the bitch did?"

"Yeah. What she did was she made a fool of you and she fuckin near kill me. Put your fuckin clothes on, find out the fuck Silver doin."

"Shit, you can't even see."

Chuleta squeezed his eyes shut, shook his head, making the pain worse, sending it side to side and then back to the front of his forehead in a lump of ugly, red, throbbing hurt. He stood up and faced Whopper. "I can see your ugly dick hangin out and you lookin like a plucked nigger chicken. Get your ass out of here and get your fuckin white clothes back on. And don't you touch that girl, bro. We ain't got the money yet." Whopper looked down at the floor. Remembering the money. "That's what we come here for. We didn't come to dick the women, and we sure as shit didn't come here to cap 'em. We came for the money. Somethin we can walk away with, right? So we don't want to get down to their level, you hear what I'm sayin?" He felt blood dripping on his chest and turned back to the sink, grabbing a paper towel and swabbing at his nose.

A screech made him whirl around again. Blue Girl, naked except for her panties, coming in the kitchen door from the pool, dripping and barefoot, slipped on the bloody tiles and grabbed the counter to keep from falling. "The fuck happen to you?" she said, leaning into the counter, pulling herself up, her eyes squinting like she didn't believe what she was seeing. She had goose bumps, and she was starting to shiver.

"Where's the kid?" Chuleta said.

"He out at the pool. Like cryin an shit. He don't want me lookin at him."

"You had any sense, you be shakin 'cause you know you let him out of your sight again, you really catch some shit. Look at you. What's that lump on your head?"

"He hit me," she said, "with a pole. Tried to drown me."

"Serves you right. Jesus, can't you handle some dumb little white boy? It's like eighty-five degrees, and you shakin like you got ice cubes up your ass. Well, get your cold ass out here, bitch, and you watch that kid. And get some clothes on. You want to take a warm shower, take him with you. Make his day. I don't give a fuck. But he runs away, we are in deep shit. You hear what I'm sayin?"

Blue Girl nodded yes, head down. Jesus, he could be a mean little prick when he wanted to. Her head hurt.

"Well, what the fuck you standin there for? He ain't comin to you." Chuleta's head felt like there was a red balloon inside getting bigger. Ready to pop.

■   ■   ■

Baylor, touching her face with her fingertips. The pain was low-intensity, local. Her mother was going on like what a good girl she was, and it felt good to stop thinking, stop moving, not have to do anything and feel protected, just stay there on her knees on the carpet with her mother's arm around her, kneeling alongside her. Baylor felt fuzzy. Numb all over with a kinda tingly thing in the tips of her fingers and her toes. Like her arms and legs had gone to sleep. The pain, she realized, touching her jaw, was all along the side of her jaw. Not too bad. "The son of a bitch," she said.

"Bastards," her mother said. "They are all bastards. I hope Dan comes back with a shotgun and blows their heads off."

"I mean he hit me, Mom. Here, on the face. When he came down the stairs. I guess he kinda knocked me out."

"Where, sweetheart?"

She turned her jaw to her mother kneeling beside her, holding her finger to the place where the imprint of his fist was outlining itself in pain. Her mother said, "It's red, but I don't see any bruises. Does it hurt?"

"Not as much as I'm going to hurt him."

"We've got to be careful."

They heard Chuleta shouting from the kitchen. "Yeah," Baylor said, "but we've *got* to get that gun. If we get that gun, we've got them. I almost got it before that bastard hit me. He's coming."

The naked Whopper came stomping through the kitchen door and stopped, towering over the two huddled women, who stared up at him, their faces turned up to him like birds in a nest. "Don't you fuckin move," he said. "I'll be right back."

Whopper took the steps upstairs two at a time,

and the two women got up, Page first, her arm still around her daughter, helping her up. "I think he's alone in the kitchen," Page said. "Sounds like he's running water in the sink."

They snuck across the entryway to the kitchen door. Chuleta had his back to them, bent over the sink. It looked like he was holding a paper towel to his nose because a corner of a paper towel at the side of his face was starting to turn red. A pile of bloodied paper towels littered the counter and the floor. The gun was on the counter next to him, another bloody paper towel draped across the short barrel.

"Are you okay?" Baylor said. "I'm sorry I hurt you."

Chuleta didn't look up. Last time he did that he got blood all over the front of his white shirt, and his head hurt ten times worse. "Jesus, you're sorry. You fuckin break my nose, you probably sorry you didn't kill me." He said nose like "node."

"You are making it worse."

"It is worse. Can't get any worse," he said over the running water.

"Putting warm water on it is just keeping it bleeding. And it will make the swelling worse. Just close your eyes and put your head back." She beckoned to her mother.

Chuleta shut off the water. "You a fuckin nurse?"

"I'm going to be a doctor. You need ice. Ice will help the swelling go down and help the pain."

"What I need is some Advil, Excedrin, Darvon, some shit like that. Fuckin aspirin would be a start."

"Any of the nonsteroidal anti-inflammatory drugs is going to increase the bleeding. Darvon isn't available without a prescription. It's a cocaine derivative."

There's an idea. Silver could have a whiff of coke left. Where the fuck is he?

Behind Chuleta, Page was coming through the kitchen door in slo mo. Trying hard not to make a sound. She was about ten steps from the gun.

Silver, in the guest bathroom, looking at his face in the mirror, thinking maybe it would heal without big scars. Jesus, she really clawed him. If he had big scars on his face, that was it for the movie career. Except for maybe like bit parts. The gangster who stands off to the side and does what the boss says. Or the crippled farm kid, his face almost ripped off in an accident with the hay baler, some shit like that. Jesus, it stung, and a fucking lady's fingernails were like guaranteed infection if he didn't get to the clinic; get the doctor to wash out the scratches with heavy disinfectant. Could be like fifty-six stitches in the face, new record for northern California.

Shit, he was just bein nice to her. Do the bitch a favor. See, you reach out to someone, out here where the rich people live, show love, you reach out to these people, you get your face ripped off. Like they are the lowest. Real low-grade. Moral values in the hood may not be world-class, but they were definitely way higher than here. Definitely gonna cap the bitch. Fuck Chuleta. Put a gun in her mouth. Let her suck on that.

Silver took his chrome-plated Boa out of his pocket, took aim at his ragged, bleeding face in the mirror, and pulled the trigger.

Blue Girl, barefoot, on tiptoe, hands behind her, zipping up the back of Baylor's yellow sundress, looking at her face in the mirror with that calm, no-prisoners stare that a woman gives to her own face. She turned, still looking at herself, checking the back of the dress was okay. A few wet spots from her shower, but they would dry in a sec. Robby was sitting on Baylor's bed. She knelt in front of him. "So why you try and drown me? What'd I do to you that was so bad?"

Robby said, "Nothing."

"Nothin? You gonna drown me for nothin?"

"You're gonna kill me. And Mom and Baylor?"

"I told you ten time we ain't gonna kill nobody. We ain't even gonna scratch you. So come on, you tell me. What you want to kill me for?" She put her hands on his knees. "So what I do to you?"

Robby was trying to come up with an answer, the way kids do because they are young enough to think that there are answers. Thinking she was doing it to him again, treating him like a kid, which was pissing him off again, so screw her, when they heard Silver shoot the mirror downstairs.

Chuleta heard the shot from the other end of the house, grabbed his gun, and whirled around, spreading a fine halo of blood. Page was four steps behind him. She put up her hands. "Don't shoot," she said, making herself smile, trying to make a joke of it.

He held her there with his gun, wiping his nose on his sleeve, as they heard Whopper bounding down the stairs. Whopper, charging into the room in his white tennis shorts, knocked Baylor out of the doorway and into the room, knocking the wind out of her. Baylor went to her knees, coughing, sucking in air, and starting to cry. She hated crying, didn't want to, but she couldn't help it. She would kill the son of a bitch. He kept hitting her. She would kill him some way.

"I was worried somebody shoot you, Baylor" Whopper said. "And I am thinkin shit, that is too bad because I want to shoot that bitch myself."

"We were all down we were not gonna kill anybody," Chuleta said. "So you shut your mouth."

"You don't kill her, the bitch gonna top you, sucker," Whopper said. "And if she don't, her momma gonna. Word."

Chuleta swung the barrel around to Whopper. "We cap these suckers, they gonna have fuckin FBI, every cop in every fuckin city lookin for us. We walk with the money, nobody hurt, nobody give a shit."

"Yeah, you said all that shit." Silver was in the doorway, holding a towel to his face with one hand and emphasizing his points with his gun in the other, saying, "But suckers get shot and die everyday in the hood, and nobody give a fuck. I am gonna have some fun. I am gonna shoot this lady here. Maybe shoot her in the arm first. Then maybe shoot her in the legs. See her crawl, try to get away 'fore I blow her head off the top of her neck," he said, excited, holding the gun in that cramped rapper way, like he was ducking under something, maybe fending off another blow from overhead, his elbow up and his hand down, barrel pointing at Page's arms, her legs, then her forehead. He came in close to Page, putting the gun to her forehead, his face inches from hers. "See what you did to me? I was gonna be a fuckin star."

Page looked back at him unafraid, hoping her scratches went down to the bone.

"Wash your face, bro. You gonna be okay," Chuleta said, tossing his bloody towel to Silver. "You shoot the woman, you gonna be a star behind bars. Spend the rest your life spreadin your cheeks for some gorilla with a dick like a horse, know what I'm sayin?"

Whopper put his hand on Silver's shoulder, calming him. Hoping that maybe Silver was just bluffing. He couldn't shoot the girl like that; he was just bluffing. Scare her a little. But he knows Silver, and Silver is not bluffing. Silver is talking himself into killing this woman. Thinking if Silver starts shooting, they are all gonna end up dead in some damn hole. "Everybody want to shoot somebody," Whopper said quietly, talking just to Silver. "You want to shoot somebody, you got to wait your turn. Everybody thinkin they shoot somebody, they gonna get even. Ain't no even. You up, you down, you dead, that's all. You shoot the momma here, I shoot the little pie-face here, what we got but a damn mess. But I gotta tell you one thing, bro. If you was gonna be a star, I am the Prince of fuckin Peace."

"Fuck you," Silver said, the heat going out of him. He dabbed at his bleeding face, wincing. "How bad is it, Blue Girl?"

Blue Girl, coming in the kitchen, fresh from her shower, Robby behind her, took the towel from Silver, dabbing at his cut cheek, appraising the damage. "I don't know. Too much blood to tell. A lady scratch your face, can't be the first time." She stepped back, taking in Chuleta's face, the small bruised balloon between his eyes, the swollen bridge of his nose, the blood still dripping. "Jesus, Chuleta, you better get another towel."

Chuleta was staring out the window, acting like he didn't hear her. "Who drives a pickup?" he said. "Old green faded Datsun?" He felt like he had been hit in the face with a bowling ball, and the pain and smashed feeling wasn't going away. He had heard there was a way to hit somebody on the tip of the nose with the heel of your hand, sending the nose bones back into the brain like little spears. But he hadn't been hit that way, and it couldn't have happened to him, but it felt like that, and it was a bitch dragging his mind off the pain and the thought that

maybe they had got to his brain. Slivers of bone knif-
ing into the soft folds of his mind.

Baylor was still on her hands and knees on the
kitchen floor, getting her breath back, afraid to
move. She had stopped sobbing when Silver pointed
his pistol at her mother. Of course, it was Brad in his
dumpy old pickup. He had the brainpower of a daf-
fodil, but once in a while his stupidity could really
surprise you. He must be cutting classes to come up
here. Oh shit. Maybe he could get some message to
him, but what could he understand? What could he,
like take to the police? He would probably come
charging in the door, thinking he could handle it.

Silver would have shot her mother if Whopper
hadn't stopped him, she was sure of that. She had felt
the fear freeze her, and she had watched without
moving, the taste of metal in her mouth. She couldn't
move, she couldn't say anything, and she hated herself. She could have, should have, done something.
She'd really got Chuleta. God, she hoped she broke his
fucking nose. So they had drawn the line at shooting
Mom and her, but they might shoot Brad. Especially if
he came in. And if they started . . .

Baylor thought about saying that it was Brad, but
thought no, don't tell them anything. Because if you
know something and they don't, it might help. Any
little advantage. Her jaw jumped back to the front of
her mind with its drumbeat throb.

"Fucker's coming to the door." Chuleta said in a
whisper. "Some kid. Is he a friend of yours?" he said to
Baylor. "He's actin like he's been here before. We can't
go to the door. He's been here before, he know no nig-
gers live here. Hey, Page, how 'bout you handle this?
We'll keep the little ones safe in here case you fuck up."

"It's Brad, Mom," Baylor said, getting up. "I'll handle him."

■   ■   ■

When the doorbell rang Baylor looked back into the kitchen, where Chuleta had his automatic weapon pointed at her mother. He nodded to Baylor. Baylor waited a beat and opened the door a crack, leaving it on the chain. "Holy shit," Brad said in his slow and deliberate way, "that's amazing."

Through the three-inch-wide crack Baylor was holding her hand over her jaw to hide the bruise. It gave her a thoughtful look, as if she was trying to remember something. "What?" she said, sounding pissed off.

"That's a wicked outfit, Bays, absofuckinlutely killer. Come on, open the door."

Baylor had forgotten she was wearing Blue Girl's hot pink spandex top and stretchy bicycle pants.

Baylor looked at him, and her heart went out to him. He was so eager and so dumb. He was like a dog that followed you around, tongue hanging out, wanting to be petted. Totally clueless. Well keep it that way, she told herself. "I'm going to throw up," she said.

"Well, let me in, I'll help you."

"I've got diarrhea and I'm vomiting and I don't want help with it. I especially don't want your help. I want you to go away. Go away," she said, and slammed the door.

On his foot.

Brad, wearing his Fila Superlite Decathalon Speedster sandals, choked back a scream. He pushed the pain out of his mind and peered in through the crack. Baylor's face was streaked, like she had been crying. "I love you," he said.

Baylor saw him wince and realized she had smashed his foot but "I love you" was news to her. No boy had ever said that to her before. She looked at him, pushing his face into the three-inch-wide slot between the front door and the doorframe, his eyes brimming, trying to smile. She eased up on the door. And felt a sudden unexpected affection for this clumsy, no her clumsy, clueless dork. She needed to protect him. To keep him out and get him out of there. If she let him in, it would be much worse. Chuleta had a gun to her mother's head, and there was no way to predict how Chuleta would react if she let Brad in. Or what Brad would do. Whatever he did, it would probably be stupid. She smiled at Brad. Sweetly, she hoped. Without seeing her face, she couldn't tell. But she had to get him out of there. "Love you, too," she said.

Brad's heart pounded, and he felt, yes, this really was it. The ultimate. She really loved him. They could screw all the time. One hand was on the doorframe, the other started pawing the door. He desperately wanted to say something, but he couldn't think of the words.

"But if you love me, you'll go away. For me. I'll see you tomorrow, I promise. If you go away now."

"But Baylor, I came all the way . . ."

She gave him her pathetic, pleading-orphan face, the one that hadn't worked on her mother for ten years. "Please. For me."

Brad withdrew his foot and hand. "Good-bye, Brad." She shut the door quietly. Through the windows at the side of the door she watched him hobble down the front walk, limping tragically. He turned to gaze back at the door and saw her in the window. She waved, he waved back. Behind him, the crunched nose of Dan's Volvo was easing into the drive.

Behind Baylor, Robby was saying, "You told that turkey you love him?"

"I had to, to get rid of him."

"I can see how that would work," Robby said.

Chuleta turned his attention to the driveway. Seeing the Volvo at the top of the drive, he forgot his throbbing nose and forehead for a moment. The man was back with the money, and they could get out of here. Get way the fuck out. Out of California. All the way to fuckin Miami. Stay in one of the big hotels for a few days, him and Blue Girl lie around on the beach. Silver go to Hollywood, start makin movies. Much tougher to track if they went separate ways.

Whopper was thinking Little Rock. Whopper had heard the president's old hometown had the best gang-bangin in the country. Check it out. But that stupid kid out there in the driveway, just standin by his pickup watchin the Volvo roll down the hill, was a problem. Maybe the kid saw somethin, but that didn't matter because the man already knew. Great the way Baylor got rid of him, like she had him twisted round her finger and she flick her finger and he go away. What womens do, say they loves you and get you runnin, comin and goin. That kid was not the brightest bulb on the porch. But maybe the man would tell the kid, get the police. Tell them to wait down the road.

Dan, seeing Brad in the drive, standing by the pickup truck thought, Jesus, as soon as I go out of the house the little shit comes running in to screw my daughter. Picturing them in Baylor's bed, naked, Brad on top, his scrawny backside, pimples, moving up and down, made him furious. Even though he realized, of course, with those kids inside, there wouldn't have been any screwing around. But he was still really pissed off at Brad. Baylor was his little kid. She was just a baby.

"Hi, Mr. Messina. Sir."

"What the hell are you doing here?" The kid

looked guilty as hell, head down. Rubbing his foot behind his leg. Shouldn't he be in school?

"Baylor's real sick. I was just seeing she's okay."

"You didn't go inside?"

"Oh no, sir. She wouldn't let me in."

"So long, Brad."

Brad gratefully nodded, moving to his truck, off the hook, saying, "Oh, yeah, right. Gotta go. Nice seeing you," over his shoulder.

Dan watched him start the truck, back out, and head up the drive. Thinking the advantage of stupidity. Allows you to skirt around all kinds of nastiness because you never see it. What the hell did Baylor see in him? Maybe he was good in bed.

Heading for the front door, Dan looked at his house. Seeing as always the drainpipe cocked to one side. The one he was going to fix before the rain came back in October. Thinking, there's plenty of time, then catching himself. There was no more time. And no more money except here, in the house. The money he had in the brown envelope in his hand would cover about four months' payments. They were watching him, he could feel it. Probably from the kitchen window. If he could get to that assault weapon, he could kill one of them at least. Maybe cut their legs off, wound them. Plus there was the service pistol in the nightstand. That could come in handy. But that was all bullshit. If somehow he got their assault gun or even sneaked his gun out of the nightstand, they had other guns. He'd seen one in Silver's pocket, and there were probably more. So all getting his hands on that gun or any gun meant was that there would be a gunfight, and people would get killed. Maybe them, but more likely Page and the kids.

Dan pictured his house tilting toward him, seeing the floor plan as in the grainy primary colors of video, as if it were a game with armed bandits moving from room to room. Ten points for each one you zapped. Except this was not so simple. The rules were theirs, and he had everything to lose. But he was the great game master. The man who started it all with Doom Room. If the rules were all wrong, change the rules, for Christ's sake. He grabbed the front doorknob and went in.

CHAPTER

19

D an was thinking he should be working on a
gameplan, working on an outline, like if they
could get the gang all in one room at one time,
lock the doors, when he saw the drying blood on the
carpet and felt a seasick rush of horror. "Page," he
called out, "Robby, Baylor."

"We're in the kitchen," Page said. Like he had said
honey I'm home.

Chuleta was pointing his gun at Dan when Dan
came into the kitchen, but Dan hardly noticed.
Chuleta's face was a mess. The bridge of his nose was
swollen like a sweet potato, and blood leaked out of
his nostrils in a slow drool. His eyes were bloodshot,
and tears ran down his cheeks. His shirt was splat-
tered with blood. Blue Girl had a nasty purple lump
on her forehead. Baylor's hair was a mess, but she
looked okay except for the weird bubblegum outfit.
Didn't fit at all. Fact she looked kinda slutty. Jesus,
had his daughter changed that much without his
noticing? He should have hit Brad when he had the
chance. Page looked tired, her T-shirt rumpled like

she had slept in it. She must have been through hell, but she was smiling at him, glad to see him. And Robby was dirty, his shins were scratched and he was in his blue-and-gold swim-team trunks. Silver's face was a ragged, bloody mess. Robby gave Dan a thumb's-up signal, like it's okay, Dad, and Dan felt pure joy. They were there, okay, alive. Silver had long deep scratches on his face. Only the fat kid who had kicked him in the nuts looked untouched, the wounds to his pride not showing. "You guys been having fun while I was gone?" he said happily. Maybe he was no longer the master game player, but the Messinas at home must have been playing hard-ball.

"You fuckin lucky they ain't a mess on the floor," Chuleta said. "There's kids in our hood woulda shot these suckers through the head ten times for what they did to us. You got the money?"

Dan handed him the envelope, saying, "It's every-thing I could get."

Chuleta squeezed his eyes shut; he was gonna have to do something to make this pain go away. The envelope felt light. "What are you tellin me?" he said.

"I'm telling you that is every cent I could get."

Chuleta dumped the money on the kitchen table, the bills rumpled, folded, the hundred-dollar bills standing out. Fresh green with double zeros. "Blue Girl, Silver, count it up."

Blue Girl and Silver sat down, scooping the money into piles in front of them, and bent to count-ing. Silver stopped and glared at Blue Girl. "Shut the fuck up, bitch. I can't count, you countin out loud."

"You just can't count," she said, not looking up. "Whopper, why don't you move your fat ass, get us some pencils, some paper, so we can count this shit up."

"Ain't no point," Silver said, the anger starting in

him, making him feel heat like a glow. "I done counted most of what I got, and I only got fourteen. What you up to Blue Girl."

"Two thousand, six hundred eighty-seven."

"See what I'm sayin, Chuleta? There ain't jack shit here. Fuckin prick is jackin us. This ain't no four hundred thousand. It's like a few, maybe twenty thousand, man. Shoot the son of a bitch."

"How much is it?" Chuleta asked Dan, his voice soft, reasonable.

"Around 28,000."

"Where's the rest of it?"

"That is every penny I could get. I even stole some of it."

"You jackin me, man. I looked on your computer. You got all kinds of money. You got stocks, bonds, CDs, an' shit."

"I don't have cash. Nobody has cash."

"So you didn't sell any of your shit?"

"It takes three days to settle after the sale of stocks and bonds, the banks want a week's notice before they'll cash in your CDs. You can get the money, you can get a loan, but you can't get any of it in less than three days."

"You fuck," Chuleta screamed, and, grabbing his gun by the barrel, swung it like a baseball bat at Dan's head.

Dan stepped back like a boxer, Chuleta missed and stumbled forward. Dan grabbed the gun, and Whopper charged, hitting him on his back, knocking him to the floor, Chuleta pulling the gun away from him. Something about the gun was weird, Dan thought as he went down. Whopper was on top of him, his weight crushing him, making it hard to breathe. Whopper chopped Dan on the back of his head. Dan was thinking force is not going to do it, as his forehead hit the hard tile and he was out.

When he came to a few seconds later, he saw red and thought he must be bleeding. But it wasn't blood, it was pain, flooding the front of his head in a wide ache that blocked out the voices around him. Chuleta was saying something, Whopper was saying something. Blue Girl was saying, "SHUT YOUR FACE." Gradually the pain began to recede, and he could hear them talking.

"He's got to have it stashed out there somewhere. Fuck him around a little," Silver was saying. "Make him be glad to take us to it."

"We got a gun to his wife and his kids' heads, he not gonna jerk us around," Chuleta was saying. "Maybe we could like give him a couple more days."

"Fuckin weekend. Banks shut. You stay two more days here," Whopper was saying, "they gonna fuckin kill you."

"No way can we stay here tonight," Silver said. "Too many people. See they got friends and shit, they gonna call, come round, wanna know what's up. Somebody gonna smell somethin, call the police."

"Why don't you take what you got, call it a good day's pay," Dan said, opening his eyes. Seeing Whopper standing over him, Dan got up cautiously, not wanting to move his head more than necessary or upset Whopper. The kid had hit him twice now. He was going to get that kid.

"It ain't even ten percent of what we was gonna get," Whopper said, watching Dan carefully with those little black eyes of his buried in his face.

"It is every dime I could get my hands on. Including stealing a wallet. Every dime, penny, and nickel I can get in cash. If I could get more, believe me, I would be out there getting it." He reached for his wallet in his back pocket. "Here, I'll throw in my credit cards if you like. We won't tell the cops."

"Fuckin right you won't tell nobody, 'cause we know where you live, you know what I'm sayin?" Silver said, his hand feeling his wounded face. The blood was crusting in long scabs down his cheek.

"Looks like we're stuck here. We can't go back," Chuleta said, "and twenty, what'd you say, eight grand ain't enough to go forward."

"There is one more number I can call," Dan said.

"The fuck you talkin?" Chuleta said. "You just ran through that story. Said you did everything and like robbed everybody."

"An old friend of mine I play golf with . . ." Dan was saying, giving Page his old deep bullshit smile, the one she could see right through. Page gave him the arched eyebrow trick she had learned in junior high, letting him know she was on to him. Listening closely because she knew Dan didn't play golf. ". . . at the club," Dan went on. "Charles Copely. Runs a private investment bank. They specialize in estate sales, buying and selling gold, jewelry, gemstones for clients. He wasn't in when I called. But he should be back now. If he's back, he might lend me some, I don't know, twenty, thirty thousand."

"Sheeit." Whopper said. "Man's a money man like that, he's gotta have two, three hundred thousand, easy."

"But not in cash," Dan shouted. "That's what I keep telling you. Nobody is sitting around with piles of cash. Cash is for postage stamps. People don't use it anymore. They use their fucking credit cards building up their fucking air miles." While he was shouting, Dan had lowered his hand behind the counter, pointing to Chuleta's phone by Page's elbow. Pointing and scissoring his fingers. "So. Let me call him. Maybe you're right. Maybe he has a bunch of cash in from a big sale. You never know, do you? Could be a happy ending here. We could all walk away from this." Dan twisted his face up a little. Like he was feeling Chuleta's pain but he could see his way out.

Page got the message the first time. Dan was as subtle as a horse in a swimming pool. She couldn't cut the phone, she didn't have a knife. And even if she did, she couldn't just cut it. Silver was looking at her with a scary intensity. Somebody would see her. Besides, cutting the phone would last around two seconds before Chuleta caught on that his phone was dead. But maybe that was all Dan needed. If she could unplug it, that would work. Too many people watching. She watched Dan pick up the phone and punch the numbers. Chuleta, his eye on Dan, picked up his phone to listen in. Page stood up and went over to Chuleta. He held the phone to his ear, eyeing her with suspicion. Page brought her hand to her mouth, kissed the tips of her fingers and touched Chuleta's swollen, flaming nose. He jerked back, surprised, holding the phone away from his ear. "The fuck you doin?" he said, the pain sloshing back and forth inside his skull.

Dan was saying, "Chuck, glad I caught you. No, I'm home, 3057 Black Mountain Lane. Listen, Chuck, we've got some wild kids here with assault weapons, and I wonder if you could let me have a couple hundred thousand for a few days."

It took Chuleta a moment to realize what was happening. His sharp, bloodshot eyes staring at Dan, he clamped the phone back on his ear in time to hear a woman's voice saying, "You got a crime in progress? Please, repeat that address." Chuleta swung his gun at Dan. Dan saw it coming and took it on his forearm. He just had a chance to say, "305" before Whopper hit him hard on the back of the head, sending the phone flying.

"The fuck you do that for, man? That is really

fuckin stupid." Chuleta was looking fifteen now, crying from pain and frustration. His head bent down to Dan lying on the floor. "I tole you, you call the cops, we gotta kill you?"

"Hang up the phone. Hang up the fuckin phone." Blue Girl was screaming, lunging for the phone. It was on the floor, underneath Dan, who twisted away. "Thirty fifty-seven Black Mountain" he said quietly, holding the phone out in front of him. The room froze for a beat. Dan sat up, looked around the room, got up, and hung up the phone.

Silver had his little chrome Boa out, leveled at Dan's forehead.

"You kill us, and you shoot yourselves in the head." Dan said. "You leave right now, you got at least a ten-minute head start. Look, you got the money. You didn't hurt anybody. Maybe they'll treat it as just another breaking and entering. You know, like a kid's thing." Dan felt a wave of nausea, realized he couldn't throw up, he hadn't eaten since dinner last night. He leaned back on the kitchen counter. "Maybe they won't even come after you. You shoot any of us, and you are all in jail for the rest of your lives."

Chuleta was in front of Dan, his face inches away. "The fuck you doin? Muthafucka. How come you didn't call them before?"

"Because you were going to kill us before. But you can't kill us now. You don't have time, and you'll fuck it up. And you've got the money." Dan stood up, leaning back against the kitchen counter.

"I ain't gonna fuck it up, cocksucker. It's easy." Silver started to squeeze the trigger, and Blue Girl pulled his hand down.

"You do that, you got to kill all of them," she said, whispering almost. "You ready for that? Then they gonna come find us. Fuckin kill every one of us."

Dan pushed off the kitchen counter and walked across the kitchen to Page, putting his arm around her. "You so rich you don't want $28,000? Okay, it's not 400,000, but that's not bad for one day's work. A lot better than, what you call it, jackin people in the street. Hey," he said, gaining confidence, "take it or leave it, but you better get moving. First thing the cops are gonna do when they find you, Chuleta, is crack you across the nose. Listen, just take the money. Get out."

"We ain't got shit, mothafucka," Whopper said. "And we ain't goin nowhere."

They looked at him. "Check out the window," Whopper said.

A bulbous black-and-white Los Palos police car, rack of red, white, and blue lights above the roof, one cop head behind the windshield, was slow-rolling down the drive. "You had them set up there, top of your driveway, waitin for us to drive by, right? You had us all set up, and one of thems got impatient. See," Whopper said, "I thought there was gonna be some shootin today."

"Dad?" Robby whined. Like his Dad had let him down again. Done another dumb thing.

"I didn't talk to the police," Dan said quietly. "Never. Not one word."

"Fuck you, you FUCK. You just called them up on the telephone." Silver said, his voice quavering like he was losing control.

"To get rid of you. Not to trap you. And they would never send one cop down alone. Think about it."

"The fuck he doin here then?" Chuleta said. "Shit, you call the cops in the hood, and they come around maybe next week. The fuck they get here so fast?"

"I don't know any more than you do. Let me talk to him. They couldn't have reacted that fast. Maybe he's going around for one of their damn drives, selling tickets to the Harlem Globetrotters."

The doorbell rang.

The Los Palos police station, serving Los Palos and Los Palos Hills, is a low, flat brown, wood building with a sloping shingle roof and police badges from all over Santa Clara and San Lucas County mounted on the walls inside the lobby. Behind a glass window, Donna Wu had a bank of switches and two computer screens and a keyboard for tracking incoming calls, and radio communication with the mobile units. She was a round-faced, pleasant woman, with a broad nose and pockmarks on her cheeks. She was worried about Alan, her older boy in Los Palos Junior High, because his grades stank. B's, as far as Donna was concerned, stank. Bs were just getting by. If he was going to get anywhere, he was going to have to get A's, and he wasn't doing it. She was also looking forward to playing doubles when she got off at four-thirty. Her friends called her the human backboard because she got everything back. Which was how she liked to feel about her job at the station. Nothing got by her. When she took Dan's call, she thought at first it might be a joke. But she heard fear in the man's voice. Not on top, because he was trying to sound natural. But underneath it he was really frightened. The thumps and the screaming before the phone went dead confirmed that this was no joke, and she had the first-priority button down before the caller was gone.

The only other public safety officer on duty in the station at the time was Roy George. Roy was thinking about that Janice, the woman he had stopped for going through a stoplight yesterday, 3:17 P.M. proceeding west on La Cuesta, driving a light blue late-model

Nissan Maxima. Probably a '95 or '96. A real sleeper car because it looked like a regular Jap mid-size tin shitbox but it went like fuckin stink. And she burst into tears, which usually just pisses him off, but she had these sensational hooters and this nice powder blue stretchy like jersey dress. Kind of classy. Not expensive but classy, and he can tell she is in trouble. Probably *is* trouble, but he lets her off with a warning, telling her about the kid got hit right there at that stop sign she just went through. And she gives him this big smile through her tears and says thank you, thank you. And he is saying, "Just be careful, a lot of kids out there this time of day," and she is writing down her phone number, telling him, if there is ever anything she can do for him. Bet your sweet ass there is a couple of things she can do for him. But there is a teddy bear in the backseat, and he thinks forget it, because you know you fool around with a woman with a kid, first thing you know you got oatmeal on your dick.

Trouble for sure, he was thinking. But it might be worth it. He was thinking maybe he could call her some slow afternoon, this Janice, go up to her house for an inspection when her kid is at school, when the first priority light went on, and he flipped the switch, saying "Tell me."

Donna played him a tape of the call, starting at the beginning with Dan saying, "Chuck, I'm glad . . ." At the end of the tape Donna said, "Thirty fifty-seven Black Mountain is where Luis is headed. You know we got those calls about that Volvo with the busted nose driving crazy on 280, and we traced the plate there. You think maybe it sounds like there's more going on up there than a DUI?"

The tape shook Roy. He could handle it, no problem. But it shook him because he knew it was bad. He could hear it in the guy's voice. He knew this was over

Luis's head, so the first thing he did was get Donna to patch him through to Officer Rubero. But the fucker was out of the car or something because there was no response. The trouble was there were no spare units. There was Dougherty and Artie down at the school, cruising the perimeter. They were just six miles away, so he told Donna to get their asses up there to 3057 Black Mountain, ASAP, but no sirens. "We don't know what they are going to be walking into."

Next adjacent unit, Donna said, was Ronaldson, down in South Los Palos. "Fucker is never in the car. Could take ten minutes to get him on his pager, but do it," he told Donna.

After that there was him. He didn't like leaving the station with just Donna there. Not that she couldn't handle it. The woman could handle it. But leaving just the one woman alone in the station was a risk because every once in a while some loony comes in off the street and Donna was like unprotected, with no gun. "I'll be back in half an hour," he said. "See if you can get Amato or Daly or Hashid at home. Tell the first one you can get ahold of to come in for double overtime, take the desk while I'm out."

In the car, Roy had to check the scanner. Sitting there in the fucking parking lot, he checked where Black Mountain Lane was. Fuckin Hills up there, everything hidden away. Fuckin rich assholes up there, acting like they want to be your buddy and you know they will stick your ass in a wringer you don't do it their way. Trouble with being a public servant, he thought, is you work for assholes.

Dan answered the door and there was a short, dark-skinned cop, nice-looking kid, very white teeth, acting like there was some joke. The cop said, "Good after-

noon, I'm officer Luis Rubero from the Los Palos
Police Department, and I'd like to ask you a few questions. Can I come inside?"

Dan said no.

"Okay," Rubero said, "we'll do it out here then."

Dan left the front door open. He didn't want
the kids inside to think he was trying to trick them. He
just had to get rid of this cop as fast as possible, so the
kids could get away. This cop was smiling, and Dan
hated him. Hated the easy authority this kid had over
him because the kid had a gun and a badge. Jesus all
the cop equipment the kid was carrying. The cop's
beeper went off, and the kid shut it off without looking at it. Like what he had here, with Dan, had to be
the most important thing.

The cop said, "Earlier this afternoon, were you driv-
ing a black Volvo 850GT wagon, license plate 8LG 97
GG? owned by"—Rubero looked down at a notepad—
"Gopher Leasing Corp."

Dan said, "Yeah?"

"Have you had anything to drink in the past
twenty-four hours?"

"No alcohol, no. I am very busy, Officer."

"Yeah," Rubero said like that didn't make any difference. Like they had him nailed. "We got three citizen phone calls, civilians calling the station from their
car phones saying that there was a black 850 Volvo
wagon driving like a maniac on Interstate 280 at—" He
checked his notepad again. The kid looked eighteen.
He read slowly, and awkwardly, from the pad, "At
3:47, 3:52, and/or 3:56 P.M. this afternoon?" He looked
up and smiled at Dan. "Car they described was a car
just like the one parked behind me in your driveway."
Back down to the notepad. "Black recent model Volvo
wagon, front sheet metal damage?" He looked up, really
having a good time. "Like the nose bashed in? Were

you driving a black late-model Volvo license 8LG 97 GG on Interstate 280 at those times?"

Jesus, Dan thought, three people called in. He must have been driving like a maniac. "No."

"I see. I have seen the black Volvo license 8LG 97 GG in your garage. The hood is warm, and I have noted that down. Also the tires. Noted that the automobile has recently been driven. Is there anybody else to your knowledge could have been driving that car?"

This was tough. If he said Page or Baylor, that would really complicate things. Hard to see where he was headed with this. Dan said no.

"Then I have to ask you under the rules of the state of California if you have any objection to submitting to a breathalyzer test?" Rubero had his hand in a black leather bag strapped to his belt, searching around in there.

Dan thought maybe he should take the test. But he had never taken a breathalyzer test, and suppose it took ten minutes? By that time the other cops would get here and the whole thing would be a mess. But if he didn't, then this cop was probably going to take him down to the station. Which would be worse. Tough to think clearly with a gun pointed at your back. Concentrate, he told himself. Dan thought he would ask the kid how long the test would take, but he didn't get a chance because Officer Luis Rubero's smiling face turned into a bright red exploding egg.

TV violence is like aspirin now. All those dying faces soothe us like two Tylenol. A police officer was shot today in suburban Los Palos Hills. Yesterday ten police officers were shot in Karachi and another in Tegucigalpa, for Christ's sake. A woman was shot in Ohio. A man, a boy, and a girl were all shot. Today.

Tomorrow there will be more. Firebombs will bloom
in the crowded markets of the Middle East, and
women will weep for their mangled children. Look,
here is mine, she seems to say, holding up her bleeding baby. Soldiers are grey-faced and bleeding to death
in Chechnya. We'll be right back after these messages.
A little shock of recognition, of the death that waits for
us, fingers rapping impatiently on the checkout
counter. Then the mind cools, untouched. And for a
moment we forget the shitty letter from the bank, the
credit cards collecting 17.85 percent, the rings in the
kids' ears, and the life leaking out of the marriage. For
a moment the pain fades as the electrons morph from
the tanks lined up in the distant city street to the
funky new thirty-second spot for Burger King.

Up close, violence is a different story. Up close,
violence is wide-screen wake-up horror.

Blue Girl was looking right at the cop. And later
she would tell you she didn't see a thing. Which was
true. She wasn't there. She was screaming and didn't
hear herself. Screaming to shut out the gun next to
her. Blue Girl was back in the old safe place, same
place she went to when she was raped. Her mind
switched to autopilot and zipped her to the Oklahoma
barn where her mother's grandmother always went,
to the last safe place any of the Delatraub women
knew. To that barn where she went when she was
scared and the air was soft as summer and smooth as
time. It was dark and warm in there, and the sun
came in long steaks through the cracks in the weath-
ered grey siding. The mice had names, Blue Girl's
mother told her, like Long Face, and Skitters and Sly;
Sly tryin to get on the good side of Long Face, and
Skitters always beating him to the corn. Her mother
told her the stories from the ten-acre dirt farm her
great-great-grandfather and great-great-grandmother

got in the Oklahoma land rush of 1912, and lost to the dust storms of 1932.

They had a 1925 Model T with a flat bed. The tires were bald and patched before they started. They set out for California in the evening; Blue Girl's mother's mother when she was a tiny girl and her parents. Because the evening was cooler and the dirt track road to Sapulpa, Oklahoma City, and beyond wasn't choked with raggedy old cars and pickups, all of them heading for LA. The Model T never made it to Sapulpa. But Blue Girl's memory wasn't of any of this, it was of the family barn with golden hay up in the loft and two cows in their stalls where they gave warm milk in the morning. And the skeleton of the Conestoga wagon resting by the stalls. Blue Girl's safe place, as safe as Minnie Mouse in Mickeyland. The place Blue Girl knew from the stories her mother told her when she was a little girl having trouble getting to sleep because there was so much noise going on out there on the street. So safe and quiet in the old barn, where she always went screaming when the guns went off.

Up close, haloed by the spray of blood fanning out from behind his head, the young man's face pocked with three large red burned and bleeding holes, and his eyes amazed for a slice of time and dulling, he fell backward. To leak on the ground. Up close, violence is inconceivable, and for a moment in the silence of your shock you think this is not true. There will be a replay to show the mistake. A brief pause while we rewind to the time when it was all okay.

Later Dan could hear the rush of air from the bullets going past his ear, and the blare of the gun behind him. But at the time he didn't feel or hear anything as Officer Rubero fell backward, his braincase largely voided of brain. His black-crepe rubber-soled shoes twitching. The body voiding its inner reek of fluids. Dan was coming to, back to the moment, looking dumbly at the blood on his hands and the blood spread in a dull red pond on the concrete walk. Just looking at it, not really connecting until the thought comes that there is a woman screaming behind him.

Blue Girl was screaming from inside the house. Dan heard her from a distance; his next thought was the kids.

Dan stepped back, stumbling over the front step, and was back in the house. Facing Silver, who was holding his little chrome pistol in the crouched way that city kids hold guns now, arm up, palm down, barrel pointed at Dan's forehead.

But the barrel was moving down. Chuleta had his hand on Silver's hand, pulling it down, saying, "It's over now. It's over." His broken nose made it sound pinched, like he had a cold, "It's ober."

"He saw me. He was goin for his gun, bro. Word on that, brother," Silver was saying.

Blue Girl had stopped screaming, and was saying, "The fuck you do? The fuck you do?" Whopper, at the same time, moving out the door, crouched over, like in the combat zone under the chopper, saying, "We got to get the fuck out of here." Stopping. "Who got the keys?"

Dan didn't care what they did or said, he was coming through the door into the house, going for Page and the kids. Page was shooing the kids away, back into the living room, maybe out the back. Dan, running for them, not really thinking but acting out of the old Dad instinct, shielding their bodies with his.

Roy with his foot down, mashed to the floor. The damn Impala cruiser, they pay $2,889 extra for the pursuit-package option, and the thing is squealing like a stuck pig every time you try and hustle it around a corner. Nothing but corners but all uphill, so you can lean the thing into the hill. Voyager wanders out of a side road; some mom probably coming back from her day job, shopping bouncing around the back. She sees the white-and-black Los Palos police cruiser in her rearview mirror and slows right down to the legal limit. Twenty-five miles an hour. Overhead, a single white cloud in the dark blue late-afternoon sky has more speed. Roy gives the siren a whop, flashes on his lights, and the van wobbles and pulls over into a driveway. Foot mashed down again, he roars past her, then has to brake hard for the sharp turn on the twisting uphill blacktop. After twenty years you have a sense. Like the way the guy sounded on the phone. The guy was a nut. Nuts were droppin out of the trees. Maybe it was that comet Hale Bopp. Like those Heaven's Gate goofball clowns in San

Diego couple of months ago. Fuckin kooks make a mess and leave it for the cops to clean up. Anything could be happening out there, and fuckin Luis was too fuckin dumb to ask for backup, treating it like a nice peaceful typical Los Palos DUI. Like some ashamed red-faced computer exec in jeans and two-hundred dollar loafers, no socks, a little bombed after an office party, nose of the BMW in the neighbors' bushes.

Luis is just a dumb kid. Came from a force in Greco, Wyoming. One chief, three Indians to cruise a town of 415 souls. Biggest risk in Greco was getting a fat ass from sitting in the cruiser all week, Luis said. Coming up to the cross street, Fontana Road, Black Mountain Lane on the other side. Big construction on the right. Guy must have fifteen guys working on his house, digging a pool, scraping off a hill, laying out a little garden paradise it would cost him five-hundred dollars a month to water. The big-money guys came and went; make $150 million in a computer start-up, lose 200 on the next. Moving up or down and out. Jesus, he and Shirley live out here, they'd spend half their lives busing the kids back and forth.

Driving past the elaborate gardens of the house on the corner of Fontana and Black Mountain, the feeling was getting worse. Could be mistaken. It wouldn't be the first time. The old military paranoia, trying to imagine the worst fuckin thing that could happen and planning for it. So when it happened you were set. Coming around the corner over the top of the hill, easing off the gas, letting the car coast, quiet, Roy saw the sign at the cul-de-sac, 3057.

Nothing happening.

Nothing that he could see. He felt like shit. Creeping over the rim of the drive, seeing Rubero's cruiser, door open, parked in the driveway, he felt a jolt of adrenaline, smelling the pines, and the hot tar of the drive, and smelling something else. Smelling something wrong.

Whopper heard the cruiser coming and ducked back in the house. The first cruiser was blocking the Lexus hidden in the garage. Now another one had its nose sticking in the top of the driveway like a dog sticking his nose down a gopher hole. No way could they drive past that sucker. Behind him, Blue Girl had gone quiet, and Silver was saying, "They were gonna go out the back door," pointing his gun at the man and his family. "We let them go, they gonna kill us, you know what I'm sayin?"

"We ain't playin that game, bro," Whopper said. "Put the damn gun back in your pocket 'fore it goes off again. We fucked enough."

"Get the money, Blue Girl," Chuleta said. "We got to move."

"We got to kick these fuckers," Silver said, pointing his gun at Baylor, then Robby. "They saw us."

"They saw you. You the one shot the dude. And you ain't got enough bullets left," Chuleta said, turning his back and heading into the kitchen. "'Less you wanna line them up front to back. Think about it."

"I don't need no gun," Silver said.

The cruiser was going beep beep beep because the door was open. Roy was sitting sideways behind the wheel, feet on the ground, shaking like he was cold. Shit, shaking like a damn Katharine fucking Hepburn. Couldn't stop it. He held one hand with the other, to punch the numbers on the caller. He knew the fucker was psycho. Could feel it. But Jesus, poor stupid fuckin Luis. That wasn't Luis down there, it was a mess. The worst. Jesus, the prick was probably watching him from a window. Fucker was inside the house, probably had his finger on the trigger, Roy in his sights when he came down the drive and stopped when he saw Luis. Maybe watching Roy in his scope, crosshairs on his forehead.

"Roy, what's goin on?" Donna was on the caller.

"Donna," he said, staring down the drive, seeing the Los Palos cruiser and what was left of the top of Luis's head on the walkway about twenty feet beyond. Fuckin gallon of blood out there drying. "Donna, who'd you get?"

"Dougherty and Artie are on their way. Should be with you any minute. I told them no sirens, keep quiet. And Hashid said he's just finishing a couple of things. He'll come in soon as he showers and changes, okay"

"No way is it okay. Luis is down. Gunshot. We got a real one here. I don't know what's in there, but I want Higgins, Macklyn, and Abrith up here now. I want backup from every unit you can get ahold of in Redwood, San Lucas and, and . . ."—the name of the next town he was thinking, the name he knew as well as he knew any name, but couldn't think of, wiping sweat from his face—"Hill fuckin View. Call Hillview first, get some units up here. And I want that CDCF up here as fast as they can get their asses in motion. When Hashid gets in I want him to run a NatSys Profile on this guy Messina, see if he belongs to militia groups, religious cults, sects. Go down all the kook lists. Get Hashid, give him a hand if he needs it, get him to call the banks, find out who his employer is, if he's got one. Call them up, see if they got any news on this Messina. I don't know what the hell we got up here, but we are going to handle it." A surge came up from his stomach, making Roy feel like the driveway was heaving up and falling back. Roy leaned forward out of the car and let go, throwing up on the sun-softened macadam and his dusty, scuffed, tightly tied black crepe-soled shoes.

Inside the car, Donna was saying over the radio, "Uh, what C D C F?"

Tears running down the front of his face, tasting salt, throat raw from throwing up, Roy sat up again, and said, "Right in fucking front of you. Jesus Donna, I took it off the fax and pinned it up on your bulletin board. That FedOp bulletin from the CNCCO, Congressional National Crime Control Office. Civil Disorder Control force. Get their asses up here. The forms are right there, A, B, and fucking C on down. Tell them"—he sucked in a big breath—"you got all the paperwork and we got a bunch of armed fucking crazies holed up in this house. Tell them you got all the paperwork done, that's all they care about. And call Junker in San Francisco, see if he can send a SWAT team." Thinking he had to call Junie, Luis's wife, and tell her. Oh Jesus H. Christ. His buddy Luis, gone. Wasted. A fuckin waste.

"What happened Roy?"

The shaking was almost gone now, and Roy George looked around him, at the tall, dark, and scraggly Monterey pines circling the cul-de-sac with their scent of pine resin making it all seem all right, the sky behind starting to go pink and orange in the west. As if this was too pretty a place for the mess of violence. The sun moving on to another part of the world with a flourish of red streaks in the sky.

Could be the bastard was creeping through the bushes with an automatic weapon in his hands, coming up behind him now. Could be there were several of them. Don't dive in headfirst if you don't know where the rocks are, Luis used to say. Christ, this Messina guy could be anyplace now, aiming at him.

Roy leaned back into the car and spoke directly into the little mike mounted next to the radio. "Luis is shot dead. I don't know. Look, hold off on the SWAT till we see what we got. See if you can find phone numbers for Rubero's family.

"You want me to call them?"

Roy wiped his big goldfish face with the back of his sleeve. Another wipe for the no-lip line of his mouth. Gasping for air like a fish, looking down the driveway at the scene so quiet it was unreal. Luis's cruiser with the door open and the lights going round, the Volvo wagon with the bashed nose backed up to the garage behind it. The house quiet, looking as if it were just a facade, like there was nothing behind it except the steep drop down into the valley and the mountains behind rising up like the waves.

Why did he get into this, he thought. To be on the front line. To be there when something happened and to be quick enough and smart enough to stop it. The linebacker of society. Like what was the guy took over from Caruso, the Latino guy, Smits in that asshole TV show NYPD Blue. See, be there. Take control. Like when he was starting linebacker in Masilon High, a fucking sophomore, college scouts already sniffing around, before he broke his shinbone. He was going to puke again.

Take control. A day is not a personal challenge, a day is a thousand personal challenges. Meet every one head-on. Butt heads with reality. Roy had to lean out to puke again, but it wasn't so bad this time. He straightened up, and said, "I'll do it when I come in. First I am going to personally nail this prick to his front door. By his prick."

Roy punched the "end" button then "send" three times, impatient. He looked to see if he had missed his uniform with the barf. Brushing his shirt just in case.

Inside the house Dan was pulling back the sliding door to the back deck, thinking he could get the family outside, when the phone rang. Chuleta, whirling his gun around to point at Page, said, "Answer it." Chuleta looked back at Dan. "Come on, answer it."

Dan went into the kitchen, leading a procession of Page, Baylor, Robby, Chuleta, and Silver, filing into the room as he picked up the phone.

On the phone Roy was sounding folksy, casual. Like he was at home with his feet up on the coffee table and there was a TV in the background with the Niners, with another victory wrapped up, cruising through an easy fourth quarter. "How you feelin, buddy?" he said to Dan. "How can we put a little shine in your day?"

"We're okay," Dan said. "We'd be better if you could get us out of here."

"No problem. That's what we're here for, Danny. Whattayou need?"

CHAPTER

21

Whopper crouched by Robby's window, looking at the mass of lights punctuating the night at the top of the driveway. Overhead, helicopter blades washed down the roar and kerosene stink of a jet turbine. Whopper said, "Shit."

Robby, wearing Silver's clothes, peering into his TV screen, said, "Don't say that." Silver's baggy shorts drooping below the boy's knees, Silver's tank top looking half-full on him.

"The fuck you say. They keep bringing more shit out there, they got a helicopter overhead, the fuck I'm s'posed to say? Same fuckers won't spend five dollars put a child in school happy to spend a half a million put his ass in jail. Shit."

On Robby's screen a little girl in a pink dress dissolved into a monster red spider with claws and spike teeth. Robby punched buttons on the Sega Saturn control module, adding the boom of bombs and flamethrowers to the sound of the helicopter outside. "It's all you've been saying for half an hour. Shit. Shit. Shit. Maybe you should just shut up. It's not going to get any better. Like you keep saying 'copy' all the time. Sounds stupid."

"'Copy' is what computer people say. Like mens who's workin with computers."

"Doesn't have anything to do with computers. Just sounds stupid."

"That's not what Chuleta says." Whopper got up, careful not to let his head show in the window, and moved carefully across the room, still looking out the window. "Anyway, you too right it ain't gonna get no better, gonna get a shitload worse. What you got there?"

"It's this twenty-four-meg game called Evermore. You got to break through the spider's rib cage, beat on its heart."

"Mothafucka looks nasty."

"This one is pussy. I mean the gameplay and the graphics are okay, but they got a new Ultra 64 just came out makes this look like kid stuff. But hey, you want to fry some bodies," Robby said, slipping out the CD disc and pushing in another, "check out this action. It's like a successor to Slime Ella, which is like the maybe fifteenth-generation descendant of my dad's game.

On the screen a slimy iridescent dragon oozed out of the ground. A cartoon kid with a laser gun blew holes in its guts, turned its heads into fireballs. Three more dragons oozed out of the ground and slid forward.

"It's part of the Sewage Suite. Slime Warp 2. They got nine different kind of slimy monsters and like fifteen texture-mapped environments and their motion capture's pretty smooth. But the neat thing is you get like ten weapons to choose from, including chemicals."

The kid on screen threw a cloud of dust at the

nearest ooze with eyes, and the creature screamed and twisted in agony.

"Cool, huh?" Robby looked up over his shoulder at Whopper. "But if you really want to mow down dudes, like blow off a lot of heads," Robby said, inserting another disc, "this is really great." On the screen a small tank was shooting into a crowd of people on a city street, making arms, legs, and heads fly through the air, and blood flow down the gutters into the drain. "You can disembowel, decapitate, and dismember," Robby said happily. "You want to try it?"

"That's disgusting," Whopper said. "Turn that shit off."

"Hey, try this one," Robby said, loading another game into the player. "It's got this dead guy lying on the ground and you figure no big deal, and you walk over it like it's road pizza and all of a sudden it's alive and starts taking chunks out of your leg, scratching you and stuff, so you stomp down on his skull, and it goes ploosh like a grape, blood flying all over the place."

Whopper reached over and switched the game off.

"Hey, come on, dude, I was gonna let you play."

"That stuff fuck you up in the head," Whopper said. "Like you hit Blue Girl with that pole. Like you think it's okay hit a girl like that?"

"Hey, that's like nothing compared to what you guys do in gangs all the time. And you hit me. You hit me and Baylor and Dad."

"That was different."

"Wasn't."

"Yeah it was."

"How."

"Your sister was wantin to kill me."

"So, your gang is gonna kill us."

"We was just keepin you in line. We weren't gonna hurt nobody."

"Anyway I came back, didn't I? Like she was okay, and this," he said, holding up his controller, "is just a game, shithead."

Whopper faked hitting Robby, and Robby faked a flinch. "Don't be callin me shithead neither, fuckin pea brain. Anyway, we ain't no gang."

Robby put down his fifteen-button controller. "I thought you said you were *Todos*. Like everything."

"That's just some shit Chuleta made up. Like he be always makin shit up. Make us feel good. I was in Crips, but I couldn't take all that loyalty shit. Like every Crip is perfect, and the rest of the world is all assholes. Like they don't vary. What we got goin is we all been kicked out or rejected by Crips and Bloods."

"I thought you were in a gang, you were in it for life. Like the only way out was you have to die."

"Yeah, they say that. But don't believe everything you hear. Silver kicked out of Folks 'cause he was doin one of the brother's sistas without permission. Been the Bloods or Crips, they would of offed the fucker. Folks just beat him to shit, told him stay the fuck away. Like they tell him they see him again, they shoot him. That's how he got into all that actin shit. Like he had to wear a disguise in his own neighborhood 'cause if they see him creepin around, see who he is, they beat the shit out of him again."

Whopper sat down on Robby's bed, facing him, elbows on his knees. "See, Chuleta was a Blood. They beat him in when he was ten 'cause he was so smart. Only he can't keep his mouth shut. Like he always knows some better way to do shit. Chocolato, the homey runnin Bloods, couldn't stand no little thirteen-year-old kid smartmouthin him all the time, so they beat the shit out of Chuleta, kicked his ass. Put him in the hospital six months. He come out, nobody talk to him." Whopper laughed. "Worse, nobody listen to him.

He make me smile all the shit he's gonna get up to, so we hooked up, started to hang out for a while. See, he's with me, nobody mess with him. I hang with him, I don't have to think about every move I make, see what I'm sayin?"

"So how'd you meet Blue Girl?"

"Chuleta met her in the hospital. She was all beat-up, like sick after she lost her baby. Chuleta said she be cryin an' shit at night, and he creep over to her room, crawl into bed with her, hold her, tell her stories an' shit. He said they didn't do nothin cause she was all messed up. But they close, you know, like they was brother and sister."

"So you're not even a gang?"

Whopper checked behind him, the lights from the cop vehicles coming in the window, making mild blue and red flashes on the bedroom wall. "Shit, Robber, my man, we was a real gang, all you fuckers be dead. Gangbangers, they don't fuck around. You pull that shit you pull, they shoot you in the head. You fuckin lucky we here."

"Tell me about it."

"Chuleta gonna think up a way out of here."

Robby put down his controller and swiveled around in his chair to face Whopper. "All you have to do," he said, "is walk out the door."

Whopper smiled at the boy. Just a kid. "Can't do that, Robber. Silver killed a cop. Whole new ball game now. We walk out that door, they don't kill us, we gonna wish they did."

"Well, go out the back. You could go down the dry creek bed, follow that to Adobe Creek, that's dry, too, now. Follow that all the way to San Francisco Bay."

"Yeah, right, Robby. They got those pumped-up teenage hotshots with assault weapons shoulder to shoulder all the way round this house. No way we can walk out of here. Shit."

"Well," Robby said, "I guess you're stuck with us, huh."

"Got to be a way," Whopper said, going back to crouch by the window.

"Hey, what you fuckers doin?" Silver's scratched face was in the door. "Come on down the kitchen."

"What you do to your stash, bro?" Whopper said, staying where he was.

"Shaved it the fuck off. What the fuck you think I did with it. Maybe you should grow one on your ugly lip. For camouflage."

Up in the cul-de-sac, six black-and-white police cruisers, their lights rotating and flashing red, white, and blue, crowded together with two dark blue Sheriff's Emergency Rescue Team vans. Two bright white Hummers were parked down the street, along with the vans and cars of the media, their aerials sticking straight up into the night sky with excitement. There was even a commissary van for the feds, with hot coffee and jelly donuts. Farther down the road, the neighbors and passersby were kept behind a barrier of yellow tape. Last thing they wanted was some civilian asking, "What's going on, Officer," and maybe getting nipped by some stray slug if there was an incident.

Roy finished off his coffee, tossed the paper cup, and went back to the scan van, thinking these federal fuckers are seriously funded. The scan van was in the middle of the cul-de-sac, an unmarked large dark blue and black Chevy one ton with a camper shell, perched high over four-wheel-drive axles, cables snaking off to the wide-angle and telephoto cameras mounted on the perimeter around the house. A black dish on the camper rooftop with a short spear in the middle pointed up to the night sky, feeding the mainframe in Washington via satellite. There was a glow from the open back door facing away from the Messinas' drive, a little pool of cool fluorescent light spilling over the back sill of the open van door. Inside, Kareem, the black kid with the ex-marine skull cut and the dark blue and black urban night-camouflage uniform, was staring into a small screen. Fuzzy red balls glowed on the dark grid of Messina's house. Kareem said, "Aggressor three coming up to window seven."

Roy, staring into the screen over the kid's shoulder, said, "You want me to off that sucker? My guy says he's got him in his scope."

Outside the van, the fed in the suit smiled a patient smile at the thought. The local cops were ranged around the perimeter of the property, longing to use the guns they never got to fire off the shooting range. "Patience, Royboy," he said in that chicken-shit, condescending, tired-assed I've-been-through-this-before way he had. "The rules of engagement are no first fire."

"I know the rules of engagement," Roy said. Roy didn't mind giving up authority to the man. As long as they nailed that sorry prick holed up in his rich house. But the fed in the suit acted like he thought Roy was dumb, like he had to talk slowly to Roy, as if he were explaining everything. If the chief was here, the chief would have taken a bite out of the guy's ass, but this was too serious to give the guy any shit. Even if the fed in the suit was giving him a ton of it.

The fed in the suit went on as if he hadn't heard the local officer. "They shoot at us, we respond. We know where they are. If they fire the first shot, then you can shoot. But not before." It was a nice night, the fed was thinking. No moon; the moon would help.

But it didn't matter. All they had to do was wait. The one thing they were not going to do was fuck this up. Do it absolutely clean. Keep casualties to an absolute zero if at all possible.

Roy was thinking, the fed in the suit was the dumbest asshole he had come across in a long time. Luis was still down, down there on the ground, and it looked like they were going to leave him there until this was over. If the chief was here, the feds probably wouldn't even be here. The chief would have this wrapped up. Jump the suckers instead of sitting on your ass in the dark. But the chief was in Phoenix, humping that sexy little PR lady at the fucking chiefs' convention. "Just wait," the fed in the suit kept saying, "time is on our side." Which was true, Roy had to admit. Those fuckers inside the house were not going anywhere. But he really wouldn't give a shit if they bombed the whole fuckin thing with a couple of Claymores and went home. Except the paperwork would be ten times worse. Okay, that was fantasy. But it was a ball-breaker to just let Luis lie there and not do anything about him.

In the kitchen Silver was talking loud, saying, "I didn't do it, the gun did it. Fuckin gun just went off. I didn't mean to shoot him. Fuck him. Gun just went off. This is Jay-Jay's gun. I bought it off him yesterday. I never even used it before. The fuck I'm supposed to know the sucker got a feather trigger? See, if it was a Glock maybe, like a Smith & Wesson, that shit never happen." He pointed his gun around the room, his face younger-looking because, Page realized, he had shaved his mustache off. Even with the deep scratches down his cheek, he was handsome, almost pretty, with that delicate nose and chin.

"Put the gun down," Chuleta said, "before you

shoot yourself. That fucker go off, and they gonna spray this whole fuckin house."

"I don't need no strap," Silver said, flicking the chrome-plated pistol end over end to Dan.

Dan caught it awkwardly, with both hands. He pointed it at Silver. Dan looked at it for a second, thinking this little machine blew a man's head off.

Silver smiled broadly, saying, "Pull the trigger, man. Go ahead, there ain't nothin in it." Chuleta held his big weapon pointed idly at Page and Baylor.

"See you later," Silver said. Silver slid open the kitchen door and stepped outside. Like that. Out of reach and in the spotlights.

Kareem, sitting in the SERT communications truck, looked up from his screen because some fucker had moved his coffee. The paper cup was supposed to be there on the shelf on the right where he could reach it without looking up, but it wasn't, so he looked up from his screen to look around, see who had his cup in their hand, his eyes taking a moment to adjust to the darkness. So he missed a small red fuzz of light in the kitchen detach from the larger red fuzz of light in the kitchen area on his screen and move outside the perimeter of the house under surveillance.

Not that it made any difference. Three snipers had Silver in their infrared night scopes, three red dots on his chest. Several other officers saw him, white button-down shirt almost luminescent in the spotlights, chinos, loafers. Hands up in the air. The snipers relaxed and looked up from their scopes. Probably one of the guy's kids. Nice-looking kid.

"Don't shoot," Silver called out into the bright lights. "Don't shoot."

In his mind, when he got the idea, Silver guessed he would be scared shitless walking into the lights. But it wasn't too bad. He was gonna have to get used to the lights in your face for studio shots and night locations. Walking across the grass, up the steps, feeling like maybe twenty rifles were pointed at his forehead, feeling the hairs on his arms and back stand up, feeling his mouth go dry, he was thinking this is it. The setup so tricky there was only gonna be one take, so it had to be right. "Keep your hands up," some cop was saying over some fucking speaker. Like he was the director. Like he was a hundred yards away instead of ten. One step at a time. So far so good. Strong hands grabbed him by the arms and pulled him forward.

In the command van, with its blue velvet upholstery and the guy in the suit behind a desk, Silver held his paper cup of coffee with both hands, hunching over it. Like he needed the warmth. The guy in the suit cocked his head to the side, looking at Silver's face. "What happened to your cheek?" the suit said.

"Dad went a little nuts," Silver said into his coffee cup.

CHAPTER

22

Chuleta was thinking the pain was way down now since Baylor gave him a handful of Advil. Like he could almost think about something else. He was still bleeding, like Baylor said he would, holding another paper towel to his nose. But if the dead dude outside the front door was any guide, Chuleta still had around a gallon of blood left. Poor bastard lying out there. The fuck did he do? At least he didn't feel no pain. Just a tic when you wonder what's happening, then black. Like what was gonna happen to him when the slugs got to him. He was better off when all he could think of was his smashed nose. Smashed back into his brain, it felt like. Like what the fuck was Silver up to? Maybe he was doing something for them, but it didn't look that way. Definitely did not. Probably giving up names, saying Chuleta shot the man. Saying Whopper some kind of killer, let me plea-bargain, I'll give you his home phone. Some shit. The phone rang.

Chuleta picked it up and handed it to Dan. Page, Blue Girl right there, watching them. Robby watching from the doorway, flicking his green hair back with his hand. They all knew who was calling. Chuleta picked up his phone so he could listen in.

Roy said, "I thought you'd like to know your son is safe. He's a little shaken up, but I guess we can all understand that."

"He's not my son. They call him Silver. Check his fingerprints, you probably got a record on him."

"We'll do that, Dan. But in the meantime, why don't you come out and join us? Have a cup of coffee, sit down, see how we can straighten out this whole mess."

"I'd be happy to do that, Roy. But right now there's another kid with a gun pointed at my wife's head."

Roy said, "Right. Well, you just stay put for the moment. You've had a hell of a day, haven't you?"

"Listen to me. That kid you got is the one who shot the cop this afternoon. Look out for him. He's dangerous."

"Dad," Silver called out over the link-up to the command van, his voice heavy with pain.

Roy, talking from the dark cave of the scan van said, "Don't worry, we're looking after him. You got a lot on your mind. I talked to your boss at Gopher Graphix a few minutes ago, and he said you lost your job today."

Page looked at Dan, her mouth open, her eyes questioning him, like why hadn't he told her.

Roy was going on. "And Howard Widmer called the Sunnyvale Police himself to report you stole his wallet. From what I hear, he is really pissed off, and the sooner you can talk to him, the better. But hey, Dan, you gonna steal a wallet, I guess that's the one to steal. This has been a crazy day for you, Dan. Come on out, and we can straighten this whole thing out."

"I don't understand why you don't believe me. There's a gun pointed at our heads."

"You got that right, Dan. There's a lot of guns pointed in your direction. We count seven people in there, Dan. Who've you got in there?"

"I told you. There's my wife, Page, and me, and my son and daughter, and this gang. They're *Todos*, like the *Todos* gang."

"*Todos*? I never heard of any *Todos* gang around here, Dan. Who do you have in there really, Dan? You want to make some kind of political statement?"

In the command van, after he called out to his "father," Silver asked the guy in the suit he could go "take a leak." The suit guy and Ralph Leon, his assistant, were in the van with Silver, but primary concern was not the kook's kid. Nice-looking kid, but the wacko in the house was the guy they wanted to hear. See what made him tick, what he was gonna do next.

The suit guy was busy monitoring the phone call, taking meticulous notes. Thinking he could interrupt if he had to, but this local yokel Roy had a nice touch. He looked at the guy's kid, thinking the boy was gonna have some facial scars, but they were probably less than what the kid was going to suffer emotionally. Thinking the kid didn't need to listen to this. Just screw him up to hear his dad getting nailed. "Sure," he said, without looking up. "Keep an eye on him," the suit said.

Ralph started to get up, when the suit, still not looking up, said, "Run a check on this *Todos* gang. See what they got in San Lucas."

Ralph held up his hand to Silver, to signal the kid to wait a second while he got hooked up with their San Lucas computer, checking the number on his laptop. Thinking maybe they should print the kid before he takes a leak. Wondering if the kid looked a lot like his dad.

"I'll be right back," Silver said. "I really gotta go."

Seeing the kid leave the van out of the corner of his eye, Ralph thought give the kid a little privacy. Catch up with him in a minute.

While Ralph stared into his computer screen, trying to find the damn number and today's log-on code, and the suit took notes as he listened to Roy and Dan talk, Silver stepped out of the van and walked between the cop cars and trucks down the road to where a yellow plastic tape held back a small crowd of neighbors. A heavy woman with a ski parka thrown over a yellow T-shirt with a crest that said Mauna Lani Golf and blue jeans asked Silver if they "got him yet."

Silver said, "They're workin on it," and walked past them. When he was far enough away he broke into a run. He figured he had five maybe ten minutes before they came after him, and he needed all the distance he could get. So he stuck to the road, running downhill, only going off it when he heard a car coming.

Robby, standing in the kitchen door, watched his dad hang up the phone. It was crazy they didn't believe his dad. Although, if you were objective about it, what difference did it make? Hey, big difference, dummo. If they knew you were hostages, the zillion cops would be on your side. Instead of against you. Eerie the way they believed Silver was part of the family. Jesus, he wouldn't give that sleazeball an empty bag. But the cops must have just ate it up. Whopper was still up in Robby's room, looking out the window.

Listen, if Silver could do it, he could. If they didn't

shoot Silver, who was practically grown-up, they weren't going to shoot a kid, right? Okay, it was a risk, but no pain no gain, right?

Robby, moving quietly up the stairs, smooth as a cat, pictured himself walking up to the cops, saying something like, "I believe there's some mistake." No, dorkhead, nobody talks like that. More like cool, like just out here for a little walk, hands in the pockets, saying, "Lighten up, assholes. Like, let me lay out for you what's goin down here." Well, something. Didn't matter. A chance to do something right. Get a little credit for a change. Not to mention getting Mom and Dad out. Not to mention Baylor. He could see himself being interviewed on TV. "And what were your thoughts when you rescued your parents?"

The carpet was soft and thick on the stairs and down the hall and in his parents' bedroom. Yeah, he thought, quiet as a cat. He opened the window on Mom's side of the room, next to her dressing table, and stuck his head out. Around the front of the house there was a blaze of lights, but he was in shadow here. Nice clear cool night. Felt good to take a deep breath of fresh air. He could take the gun in Dad's night table. It was right there. Let them know he was serious. No, that was dumb. They'd shoot him. He pulled himself out onto the flat roof, keeping low, on his hands and knees. Around the front of the house the lights were like a white wall in the black night. The generators sounded like a carnival.

Philly was up in the redwood just about nodding off. Not dozing really, but close. Working on keeping an eye open. Freelance stuff was killing him. He liked the word, freelance. Sounds better than moonlighting or second job. Freelancing has a kind of class sound like you have clients. Like a knight on a horse. Whatever they call it, Roy would have his butt in a grinder if he found out he was working off duty running a fork in San Lucas for AmDell. But with Julie having that earache, wouldn't go away, pouring those $168-a-bottle drops down her ear and the ache was still there. That and she was needing new clothes all the time and making the mortgage payments on the house now that he didn't have Sheila to split the payment with him, freelancing wasn't a choice. He had to have the money. Had to. Story of America, working harder to get farther behind.

Philly shifted against the trunk, feet wide apart for good tripod, but the left branch was higher than the right, so he had to take the weight off his right leaning against the trunk. Thinking, the trunk of your redwood is like leaning against an alligator's back, all lumps and knobs.

Tricky thing about shooting from a tree is the tree is always moving. Always. You don't see it on the ground, but trees have this built-in pendulum motion. Way to see it is get up in the tree, thirty feet off the ground. You set up the sight, lock in on the target, and either the world is moving or the tree is. So you have to compensate. Then, too, if there is a breeze, you have to compensate. Five-mile-an-hour wind will cause a .30 mm to drift .3 inches every fifty yards. And you have to compensate for the trajectory. To put that sucker into some perp's pocket at a hundred yards, you got to compensate for all kinds of stuff. Being precise is a process of a hundred compromises. Finding the right mix. Same thing with finding the right spot in the tree. Got to be enough cover so you don't get light glinting off the scope or the barrel although it is all matte, and you are covered in flat black, still you got to have good cover and still be open enough to see out. Got to be high enough off the ground to give you a good overview, but not so high you're shooting down onto like a little circle, like the top of the perp's head. Got to be able to move the barrel through an arc if the target is in motion. Got to find a stable, comfortable spot, and there aren't any stable comfortable spots. Not with cover and visibility, so compensate again, you go for the best you can. It's all trade-offs. So much to keep track of, because the slightest motion out there, you have to be ready for it. You get like a half, maybe three-quarters of a second on average, and that is it. Ninety-nine times out of a hundred you are not going to see the head pass through the window frame again. Never get a live-action rerun. Like the animals do, what you look for out there is movement.

Like he was telling Irvine down at the loading dock after Irv was saying that old what goes around fairy tale. And I told him, yeah, and by the time it comes around to you everybody has taken bites out of it. So you better get your piece of it first chance you get. 'Cause there is not enough to go around, and if you don't take your bite soon as you see your chance, you are going to go hungry in America.

Philly shifted a little more weight against the tree, giving his eyes a rest for a moment. Julie giving him all that lip. Like she is twelve for twenty minutes and she has to dress like she is a nineteen-year-old hooker or the kids are gonna make fun of her at school. Way he thinks of her is she is around nine years old. Still just a kid. He was gonna have to get over that. Like he was thinking that she could pass for like nine, ten maybe last night, after dinner, helped her finish her homework, and they were watching *Seinfeld*. Seinfeld's buddy wants to use the bedroom 'cause he's got this new girlfriend who is Seinfeld's old girlfriend. And Julie, those little green eyes like his looking up at him, telling him she had a boyfriend, and it just blew him away.

Philly's eyes stayed shut just for the slightest second longer, remembering his first girlfriend. How when he was at the tenth grade at Los Palos High thinking with his little stumpy body no girl was ever gonna like him. But Mary Broadwyler did, and wow did he like her. Nothing like that electric jolt when you are a kid. As good as it gets, and you never get it back. Thinking he really better get serious with maybe that Dianne or some damn woman. On the plus side Dianne was an enthusiast, trying all the time to convince him how great she was in bed. On the minus side you can get tired of that. She was not gonna work out. Wouldn't even go to church on Sunday. Philly was thinking what he needed was a serious woman who could be a real mother to Julie, make that a priority, to find a serious woman who could give Julie some guidance on the right way for a young woman to behave in the eyes of God, maybe get her to start reading The Word when, with his eyes half-closed, he saw something move off the roof. Catching the movement in the corner of his eye. Bringing the scope around and, seeing the weirdo, green hair in the floppy gangsta outfit get up off the ground and start running toward him, gun in his hand, Philly, all of a sudden awake, pulled the trigger.

Philly looking through the scope at the freak down on the ground, not seeing the gun. Thought he saw a gun in the freak's hand, but couldn't find it. Moving the scope around, it is a kid, looking for the kid's gun, seeing just a kid down there, guilt rising up his throat like water.

■   ■   ■

Page knew. She was resting her head in her arms on the kitchen table, and when she heard the hollow crack of the rifle and the thump, she stood up, looked around the room, and said, "Robby?" Looking around the room, she asked Dan, "Where is he?" She called out, loudly this time, "Robby?"

"He's with Whopper, Page," Chuleta said. "Whopper's looking after him."

Whopper was in the doorway, filling the frame, saying, "No he ain't."

Page called her son again, "Robbeeee," her voice already filling with longing and sorrow. And they were all quiet, listening for an answer. There was no answer, so they all knew.

Dan stood up, feeling as weightless and invulnerable as a player in a video game. "I'll get him," he said.

"You ain't goin out there, man." Chuleta said, waving his gun at Dan. "They shoot you, too."

"Maybe they will. But you won't." Dan stood there, facing Chuleta and the gun. His stood between the gun and his family. Behind him, Page and Baylor, walking slowly and carefully at first, picking up courage, ran out the door and into the night. So Dan was alone, staring at Chuleta's gun and not fearing it at all. Looking at the gun as if it were a toy, he turned his back on the boy and walked out the kitchen and into the darkness without looking back.

The front of the house was lit up like a stage, the green bushes and the lawn sloping down to the low blue-grey house with the scratched oak door. Robby lay sprawled on his back, close to the house at the edge of the swath of light. Baylor fell on her knees next to him, one side of her bright white in the flood-lights, the other black, saying, "Are you okay?" Robby was not okay. He was shot in the chest. In the distance she could hear yelling behind the wall of lights. Men calling out, "Don't shoot. No fucking shooting. Put your guns down. Here comes another one."

Seeing the blood bubbling out of Robby's chest, Baylor bent over her brother, pulling off her spandex top. Ripping Silver's bloody shirt into strips and stuffing them into the hole in Robby's chest and pulling the stretch spandex over his head and around his chest for a bandage. She screamed, "Help."

Page was alongside her, kneeling by Robby's head, saying, "Come on, Robby, go for it. You can do it. Stay with us, darling. Keep on strokin.'" Robby's eyes fluttered open, and, he thought at least he did that. Got her out of there. At least he did that right. He gave Mom his winner's smile, the one he'd been saving, before his eyes shut again.

Dan ran uphill into the lights.

Behind the lights all hell was breaking loose. Roy was on the bullhorn saying, "No fire, there will be no fire. Stay calm." Thinking Jesus, they'd shot a kid, and feeling sick, like this thing was slipping out of control. It was like they had really stirred up the crazies because they were running out of the house, some girl in pink spandex and a woman in a T-shirt bending over the kid, and it looked like their guy was running. No weapons that he could see, but he made one funny move, they would put that son of a bitch away. He pointed his bullhorn at Dan. "Stop where you are. Freeze."

The guy shifted course, still running uphill, but heading straight for Roy. "Don't shoot the bastard," Roy said to the deputies standing next to him, braced, guns pointing at Dan's chest.

Dan ran through the lights and, slowing down, stopped in front of Roy. "You shot Robby," he shouted. "You shot my son."

"That's not your son," Roy said, thinking he was looking into the face of a homicidal nutcase. "Relax now, Mr. Messina. We got your son back in the trailer. He's okay."

"He's not okay. He's the kid who shot your cop." Dan lunged at the big cop and three men grabbed Dan's arms and neck, twisting his arms behind his back, getting the handcuffs on him. Dan didn't feel it. "ROBBY. ROBBY. YOU SHOT ROBBY, YOU DUMB FUCKING ASSHOLE." Dan had to blink, suck in some air, breathless from running and shouting. He said, "Get him, get him, you get him to the hospital now. He'll die if you don't get him. If he dies, you killed him."

There was a man in a suit standing just behind Roy. Dan nailed him with his eyes, and said, "Do it."

The suit looked at Dan, then at Roy, and said, "Do it."

Inside the house, Blue Girl was saying, "The fuck we do now, Chuleta? You let them walk. Now how we gonna get outta here?"

Chuleta shut his eyes a moment. "I'll go to the front door, make a lotta noise, wave my gun around, you two go out the back. Maybe, all the shit goin down, you can make it out of here." Looking at them as if asking if that would be okay.

"No way." Blue Girl said. "You go out that door, I'm goin with you."

"Don't worry about it," Chuleta said, looking into her eyes. "I'm a juvie. They can't put me away for more than like a few months in some juvie hall. Some shit. I'll catch up with you in a month, two months."

Whopper put his big hand on Chuleta's shoulder, his voice low. "I know you down for us, Chuleta, but it don't make no sense, me goin with Blue Girl. We be fightin before we gone ten minutes." Whopper picked up the envelope with the cash in it and handed it to Blue Girl. "You take this, get this turkey out of here. The fuck they do to me, they ain't gonna do anyway?"

Chuleta put his arms around Whopper. "No way, bro. I started this shit. Let me finish it. 'Sides, Blue Girl need somebody strong like you protect her an' shit."

Blue Girl, looking out the window, said, "I can look after my own ass, but you better do somethin quick 'cause the cops be comin down the hill."

Whopper took the gun by the barrel and pulled it gently out of Chuleta's hands. "Like the lady say, she tough enough, bro. She don't need me, she need somebody got some sense. I don't see nobody with no sense around here, so you gonna have to fake it. Now go. 'Fore I whip your ass." Whopper pointed the gun at them and motioned them through the kitchen door.

In the living room the three of them stopped, the lights from the cops going flash, flash, flash in the front windows. They hugged. "Down for you, bro. Down for you." Chuleta and Blue girl went out the back as Whopper opened the front door with one hand, the gun in the other.

Roy, bullhorn held up to his face in one hand, his .357 Magnum held straight out in the other, was jogging down the hill, leading five deputies and two medics toward the two women bent over the boy, when the front door opened and a big black guy in a warm-up suit, looking like a clown at a children's party, came out the front holding an assault weapon. The police stopped where they were.

Roy raised his bullhorn. "Put down your weapon. No more shooting, you hear?"

Whopper held out the gun he had taken from Chuleta, holding it out away from his body, barrel pointing up into the night sky. "Yo, what's kickin out there, bro? How come you muthafuckers turned on all the lights?" Wanting to drag it out as long as possible. Blinded by the flood of white light.

Roy saw the black guy was shouting something. He heard "motherfuckers," but the roar of the generators behind him drowned whatever else the sonofabitch was saying. Sonofabitch was standing there, waving his gun in a threatening manner, around four feet away from Rubero's body. "Put it down," Roy called out again.

"Hey, this ain't nothin. We be dressin up, playin games. Havin a party. Just a damn toy." Whopper said, shaking the gun high over his head, holding it sideways to show them. His body was covered with shaky little red dots.

Roy looked down at the boy at his feet. The green-haired kid he'd seen in the village. All grey face, the blood leaking out of him, his mother looking up at Roy as if he was supposed to do something. Roy felt himself being sucked into the vacuum of loss. Felt all the feeling draining out of him. How did it get so fucked up? He looked back at the black clown on the front porch, waving his fucking gun. Threatening them. Yelling. Taunting them. Like he was proud of what he did. Looking a little blurry to Roy, so his eyes must be tearing up. Up to Roy now. His call now on the front line. Like how much more of this shit was he going to put up with? Roy raised his Magnum and fired. It missed Whopper, going way over his head and hitting Chuleta's gun, splintering the barrel, knocking it out of Whopper's hand to smash against the house, the wood and plastic that Chuleta had spent so many hours gluing, sanding, and painting, shattering like the toy that it was.

Seventeen deputies shot their rifles and their pistols at Whopper, smashing his rib cage, his pelvis, and his skull with forty-three rounds of fire according to the autopsy.

Blue Girl and Chuleta, moving carefully through the dark shadows down the steps to the pool, heard the shooting and stopped, holding each other. Saying nothing but feeling horror. Breathing hard.

The shooting went on and on, and then it was over. The two teenagers started to jog downhill, starting slowly and picking up speed as the hill got steeper.

Jason, coming up on his third month on the force, pulling all the shit duty like standing on perimeter, complete opposite side of where all the shit was going down, was looking up at the house on the hill all lit up from the other side so the back of the house is a shadow, and trying to figure it out. Suddenly it sounded like every gun in Silicon Valley was going off at once. Then, nothing. Real quiet. Which probably meant it was over, but nobody was saying anything.

Silence for a while. Stars overhead. No moon. Getting cold.

Then he heard crashing above him, like a deer running. Jason stood up, raised his gun, and braced himself. Ready for the guy. If it was a guy, could be a deer. And suddenly the dark sky is full of this black girl all legs and elbows flying down the hill and knocking him flat on his ass. Knocked the wind right out of him, and when he got his breath enough to get up she was gone.

Nick Bartolini, the big prick who was always on his back giving him a hard time, stationed sixty feet to his right, yelled over to him, "What the fuck was that?"

Jason called back, "Nothin. Fuckin deer almost tripped over me." No way was he gonna let on he was knocked over by a girl. Put up with all that shit.

A wild siren screamed over the valley and the ambulance took off, Dan and his wounded son inside, racing for the healing white lights of the hospital in San Lucas. A quarter of a mile down the hill, where the gully forked into the soft and sandy dry Ohlone Creek bed, Blue Girl and Chuleta, Blue Girl carrying the packet of money like a football, Chuleta three steps behind, were running under the arch of trees toward the San Francisco Bay, disappearing into the soft black night.